# This Dark Thing

**Marisa Moffa**
**This Dark Thing**

All rights reserved
Copyright © by **Marisa Moffa**

No part of this publication may be reproduced, distributed, or transmitted in any form or by any means, including photocopying, recording, or other electronic or mechanical methods, without the prior written permission of the publisher, except in the case of brief quotations embodied in critical reviews and certain other noncommercial uses permitted by copyright law.

Published by Spines
ISBN: 979-8-89569-212-7

# This Dark Thing

MARISA MOFFA

# Foreword

"I am terrified by this dark thing that sleeps in me;
All day I feel its feathery turnings, its malignity."

- Sylvia Plath -

*To All My Beautiful Little Monsters*

# Prologue

## 1980

**"Like the brief doomed flare of exploding suns that registers dimly on blind men's eyes, the beginning of the horror passed almost unnoticed; in the shriek of what followed, in fact, was forgotten and perhaps not connected with the horror at all. It was difficult to judge."**

**- William Peter Blatty -**
**THE EXORCIST**

# 1

There's an expression that goes something like: "It's not the end of the world, but you can see it from there." This would accurately describe the tiny seaside hamlet called Pete's Beach, NJ in the summer of 1980. The town was uncompromising in its simplicity. Quite a noteworthy accomplishment for a municipality situated just two miles north of Atlantic City.

Clinging serenely to the jagged Jersey shoreline, Pete's Beach remained a sleepy little burg, virtually untouched by the burgeoning tourism trade of the more popular New

Jersey beaches in the late 1970s. Then the legalization of casino gambling loomed large and ominous over the little town. The huge casino halls brought with them the tourists, pouring into Pete's Beach's neighbor to the south. Still holding onto their old small-town values, the city fathers (now in their eighties and nineties) cast a displeased eye toward the big casino hotels visible in the distance. A thin wisp of watery marsh was all that separated the two towns. One large and sinister in its decadence, the other meek and unassuming with its pristine charms.

Quaint and picturesque, Pete's Beach remained virtually untouched from its earliest days as a fishing village, with its single long fishing pier. That is, untouched except for the incongruent behemoth of a building that was now perched at the entrance to that very same pier. The architectural monstrosity that was Pete's Beach's single tourist attraction: The Haunted Castle.

The Castle was really nothing more than a hastily-constructed plywood structure, embellished with a dismal grayish-green faux stucco edifice. It rose roughly five stories above the teeming arcades and concession stands of the remodeled fishing pier.

Visions of peaceful fishermen and their sons waiting for a tug on their lines at the end of the pier paled before the present-day hustle and bustle. The tourists streaming in and out of its shops created a hum that was not unlike the din that takes place in a beehive. The shadows of the old fishing village tried their best to be seen through the lights, flashing in rhythm with the ringing bells and buzzers in the arcade booths. But their quaint shadows would only fade deeper into the memories of the older citizens of Pete's Beach.

While the town elders scowled and voiced their protests, their sons knew the real value of the Castle and its questionable clientele. They were the city councilmen and other politicians, and as such they couldn't help but realize the great value of the tourism trade to the once-quiet community. And so, the Castle, the pier, and consequently most of the businesses in the small fishing village prospered. Even if it *was* at the cost of their own integrity.

It was only on the coldest, rainiest, most gloom-filled nights that the citizens of Pete's Beach would look up at the sinister silhouette of the Castle on the far north end of their little island and feel the slightest twinge of guilt. Guilt at the thought of their having allowed such an awful and ominous presence to spoil their idyllic home. To cast its shadow across their playgrounds and their beaches. It was on the darker nights in particular that they might have noticed, had they been observing the structure more closely, the dark figure scurrying busily beneath the pier. The load he carried across his hunched shoulders would far surpass the horrors depicted in any of the ghastly scenes within the Castle Proper, for this much was true…the infamous haunted Castle housed one very *real* monster.

# 2

Pam heard the toaster in the kitchen as it signaled that her Pop-Tart was ready. She finished lacing up her sneakers and headed out of the bedroom. Mom had left her the usual short list of chores, which Pam had completed in record time today. She was anxious to meet Becky at the drugstore. Exactly at twelve o'clock, that was what they had decided.

The summer had dragged somewhat for the two friends, but this last week before school started should be a little more exciting. Their time was their own, now that they had quit their jobs at the local Dairy Queen. They would manage to enjoy the last bits of summer vacation together.

With the Pop-Tart poised between her teeth, Pam locked the back door of the little cottage that she and her mother shared. Mom was hard at work as a dealer in one of the new casinos, and Pam had been something of a latchkey child for the past three months. She would complete her daily chores and linger on the beach until it was time to head to work on her bike. The days all looked the same, and the monotony of the little town of Pete's Beach had more than worn on her sixteen-year-old nerves. But this week would be different. She and Becky had discovered the wonderful world inside the Haunted Castle pier, despite their collective parents' warnings to stay away from the place.

She walked her bike out of the little back shed, and hopped onto it, feeling the soft breeze off the ocean as she began to pedal. The little summer houses whooshed by as she made her way north toward the Castle. She smiled as she looked up at its dull green form in the distance ahead. She was wearing her tube top and shortest shorts. Looking down at the big mood ring on her index finger, she felt particularly bohemian. Grown-up.

When Pam arrived in front of the drugstore, Becky was already there waiting. She was holding a double popsicle, the kind with two sticks. Upon Pam's arrival, she popped the sticks apart and handed half to her friend. Cherry, of course. Armed and ready for the rest of their short trek, they made their way to the Castle pier.

As usual, the pier was bustling with activity. It was a direct counterpoint to the quiet sleepiness of Pete's Beach's quaint neighborhoods. As if it knew that it must hurry and thrive through the last weeks of summer. Before the long winter hibernation would come. The girls abandoned their bikes at the foot of the pier and anxiously walked the midway, taking in the sights and sounds. They stopped at the arcade booth that offered record albums as prizes. Pam had recently had the good fortune to win the *Supertramp* album that she kept carefully hid from her mom underneath her bed.

They watched as the Cashier inside the little booth in the Castle's lobby changed the sign in her window from "closed" to "open", and took her seat, awaiting the first patrons. Pam and Becky giggled as they headed toward her for the fourth time that week. They had made their pilgrimage to the Castle daily, once they discovered the amazing world atop the pier. It was like forbidden fruit to them. They had practically memorized the Castle's scenes and all the actors' speeches. They flirted with most of the boys inside. Older, college-age guys that gave the girls the attention that they so craved. They longed to be a part of the mystifying world inside this place. It fairly cried out to them.

Once inside the darkness of the Castle halls, the girls pointed out little nuances that they might have missed on their previous trips and smiled enticingly at whatever actor would look their way. They stared longingly up at Dracula as he gave his welcome speech, and joked with the Jester in the Throne Room, making sexually charged comments about the jingling bells on his costume. It was there, as the Jester performed his silent mime act for the little group of gathered customers, that the girls' gaze was drawn away by the strange man in the top hat.

He stood in the shadows of the next room, the Sick Room, and beckoned them to come to him. At first, they just giggled and nudged one another, as if it were a joke. But wasn't this what they had hoped would happen? They were noticed by one of the people they admired most. They would hardly let such an opportunity pass by, and so they soon found themselves walking through the room with the stranger. He led them to a hidden hallway just before the entrance to the Swamp Area. At the mouth of the hallway stood a long mirror, tilted at an angle that reflected back into the room. Inside the dark narrow passageway, he beckoned them again, and they went closer, closer until his outstretched arms surrounded the two girls. He gently turned them to face away from him, performing for them as a magician would. They were now a willing part of his magic act.

Pam smiled and looked over at Becky beside her. She felt the man's arm around her, barely touching her. Becky giggled audibly. Then, in a quick motion, he covered their faces with chloroform-soaked bits of cheesecloth. As they breathed in the toxic fumes, the light diminished to a pin spot, and everything went black.

As the group that Pam and Becky had once been part of exited the Sick Room, the man in the Top Hat flicked a switch and a light shone on the dark hallway. The group suddenly saw a reflection in the long mirror at the hallway's mouth. Inside lay the two unconscious girls, strewn like rag dolls on the floor. And just like that they were an unwilling part of the cast of the Castle they so loved.

# 3

From somewhere out of the fog that surrounded him his hand appeared, and in it the menacing knife. It glinted in the dim light as if smiling back at him. He held the blade before him, staring longingly at the distorted reflection of his own face in the polished steel.

Ever so slowly, he moved toward the writhing silhouette of the girl. She watched his approach in horror. Her wrists screamed inside the rough tangle of rope, bound tightly, causing her every movement to bring another flash of pain. She squirmed and writhed so violently now that the post she was tied to shuddered. But her weight was no match for the thick wooden beam, planted deep inside the heart of the Castle. The heartbeat of the beast pounded up through the wood and into the frantic girl's head like the beat of so many drums. It vibrated and hummed the sound that would become her death dirge.

Beyond the field of her vision, the poorly fashioned cemetery glinted in its fluorescent-painted splendor. The little group of spectators, witnesses to the crime, huddled together tightly. Somehow it felt safer. All wide eyes were riveted on the girl and her captor. The man held the knife higher as if to both taunt and entice the crowd. This was where he lost all sense of himself and became one with the place that surrounded him. That had possessed him. That had, in fact, *created* him.

Pam's eyes widened as he drew closer. The crunch of gravel beneath his shoes was deafening in her ears. She wrenched her wrists back and forth in their bindings, gradually scraping back the flesh, layer by painful layer. Her stifled attempts at screams all but withered on her cracked dry lips. She just wanted it to stop. To allow her to rest. She shot frantic pleading looks at the group of wide-eyed onlookers assembled not more than ten feet away. Her cries for help were lost on them. Their only reply was an anxious shuffling of feet, gasps at the appropriate times, and some muted snickers.

Now the knife was near her, above her, and she heard her captor's vile peals of laughter. Her ears began to ring with the sound, finally feeling the pain of the blade inching its way deeper and deeper into the flesh of her neck. Suddenly bright flashes of white light joined the tumult in her head, mixing with the drumbeat heart of the Castle beneath her trembling body. It was like an incredible symphony of horror, playing on all her senses. And now it was reaching its crescendo.

Then, just as suddenly, it all stopped. The light diminished, squeezing finally down to a pin spot, then snapping off suddenly. Only the tiniest bits of sound seeped through the fog of her consciousness. She faintly heard the group of onlookers talking, whispering perhaps, then giggling in an awful minor key that resonated through her battered brain, just before it all went silent. Painfully, incomprehensibly silent.

There was blood everywhere. On his hands, his face, his clothes. His shoes seemed to well with the blood inside them. He worked diligently to sever the girl's head from her twitching body. The great weight of it made his shoulder throb as it fought against release from its tether to her spine. His audience watched wide-eyed, amazed at the realistic look of it all. They analyzed his every move.

How could this seem so real? Hidden somewhere within their minds lay the singular thought that they themselves could be in danger. The mere act of witnessing this horror had made them possible victims themselves. This heightened sense of danger was what created the perverse pleasure that was the only logical explanation for their visit to this frightful place.

Finally, the head released itself from the stump of Pam's neck with a crack, and he held it triumphantly aloft. He swung his gruesome trophy high over his head, the blood spilling down on him like rain. He felt the river flowing down his arm, into the open mouth of his rolled-up shirt sleeve. There came a quiet ripple of gasps and groans from the crowd, followed by a muffled wave of meager applause for the bloody pageant they had just witnessed. Then they moved tentatively away from the railing and their eyes wandered from the scene. To the next. To whatever lay ahead.

That was the way of the Castle. It was a funhouse. They were there to be amused. They knew in their minds and their hearts that the acts of murder and torture committed here daily and nightly were just being staged for their collective amusement. They all knew this. All, that is, except for the man who now stood alone with the grisly dangling trophy of his work poised in his bloody clenched fist. The river that had run down his uplifted arm was now congealing into a thick cord that tugged at the tiny hairs of his forearm. The last drops of the girl's young life dripped out onto the gravel-covered floor below. For *this* man, the Castle was where reality *began*. It was his only reality. The killing was his food.

He stared down at his mangled prize. Before this she had been nothing more than a prop, a plaything. She came to him willingly, if not knowingly. Now she was his forever. His latest mate. She had become a very real part of his surreal world.

All the while the shallow frightened breathing of his next bride, Becky, seeped under the crack of the door that opened into the dark closet behind him.

# Part One
# Thursday

"See - one side of my face is gentle and kind, incapable of anything but love of my fellow man. The other side, the other profile, is cruel and predatory and evil, incapable of anything but the lusts and dark passions. It all depends on which side faces the moon at the ebb of the tide."

- Lionel Atwill –

# 1

In the three short years during which the Castle had been open to the public for business, it had gained quite a reputation, and a significant following as well. The thrill was not reserved for the young. Patrons of all ages boasted of their bravery within the Castle's walls. It was a typical seashore funhouse. A form of entertainment that graced many of the amusement spots that dotted the Jersey shore. But this one was something more. Added to the recipe for the usual old-time funhouse fare was the element of live actors, who assumed the personas of all of history and cinema's most notorious monsters. With a few added horrors exclusive to the monsters of Pete's Beach thrown in for good measure.

Many of the actors were local theater students from the state college that was located just inland of Pete's Beach Island. They honed their craft at the Castle. Vampires, werewolves, freaks, geeks, hunchbacks…these were the staples of the Castle's cast. The black shroud of the wraith was their uniform.

At the end of the day, these horrible creatures were just a collection of fresh-faced coeds, seashore drifters, and fun-loving ex-hippies. Some were young, some were older with young hearts. The Castle was their chosen niche for the summer. Their drifting or studying would be put on hold for three months of the year. They had found their vacation home in the damp darkness of the Castle.

The actors' orientation to the Castle cast included quite a long list of do's and don'ts for the rookie monsters. A yellowed piece of note paper posted on the Dressing Room wall since the first season that the Castle had opened outlined the tenets of its behavioral code. Rule number one: NO TOUCHING THE CUSTOMERS. Rule number two: IF YOU TOUCH THE CUSTOMERS, DON'T GET CAUGHT.

Harry, the pier's owner, never bothered to go inside the Castle. The workings within were far too menial for Harry to waste his time with. He had only agreed to the crazy idea of opening the amusement pier after carefully analyzing its feasibility as an investment. It was just an added facet in his already- lucrative slot machine rental empire. He had been persuaded to invest in the pier by his financial advisor, his wife Connie. Connie herself never set foot on the pier. Never set foot on Pete's Beach, as a matter of fact. She happily sat in their spacious North Jersey mansion, making spa and lunch dates with friends, content to dispatch their two teenage daughters to the pier to check on the "quality" of the staff. This kept Harry from having to ever inspect the workings of the Castle himself. He was content to watch the fistfuls of cash pass from the patrons' hands to those of the Cashier inside the admission booth, via closed-circuit camera. Harry had never *once* passed through the entrance. He despised this sort of place. To Harry, it represented nothing more than a colossal waste of time. A very *profitable* colossal waste of time.

And so, Harry had a wax replica of himself placed in the Castle, so he could "keep an eye on things", even if only in spirit. This wax figure was mysteriously moved to a different location at the beginning of each Castle workday. Jokes were often made referring to the figure as "cursed", much like the curses borne by the tombs of the pharaohs. Anyone who dared invoke the wrath of the mighty Amin-Ra-Harry by touching the figure might lose a hand, or foot, or some other vital appendage.

Just behind the Castle itself lay the true heart of the funhouse: the Dressing Room. This was where the greasepaint was applied by the all-too-capable hands of Sandy and Little Mack, the Castle makeup artists.

The level of activity inside the Dressing Room was at its height at the beginning and end of each shift, with actors hurriedly looking through the racks of costumes to find just the right one for their character, then taking their place in line at the makeup table. It was a bright and cheerful place during these times, making it hard to believe that this room's only separation from the murky gloom of the Castle's interior was a single thin plywood door. The brightness and noise provided a distinct contrast to the gloom of the Castle itself. Every time the door opened a tiny wisp of that gloom found its way into the Dressing Room, creeping silently across the floor with sinister stealth. Only to finally be trampled and dissipated by the scurrying feet of the actors.

Sandy was a pretty woman of about thirty years. Her halo of curly chestnut hair framed her face as she leaned in toward the faces of the actors she painted. A clean mixture of peppermint Tic Tacs and patchouli oil hung in the air around her like an aura. She wore a boho mixture of clothing layers. Light airy printed fabrics. Always different. Always the same. She embodied the earth mother so popular in these times. Post hippie. It was, after all, the early 1980's. Even flower children eventually had to grow up. She was thoughtful and good- natured, self-assured and wise. And slightly off-the-wall. Sandy always tried to take as domineering a stance as her diminutive five-foot-two-inch frame would afford her.

She oversaw the task of keeping the Dressing Room in order and running smoothly. Not a small accomplishment amid a sea of arrested adolescence. She could quite often be heard screaming at the actors for even the smallest of infractions, invoking one or more of the rules scrawled on that yellow piece of paper. She reserved the screaming for the minor screw-ups. For the major ones, she muttered obscenities quietly and bit her lip. So often did she employ this practice that a tiny but noticeable white scar eventually graced her bottom lip permanently. In moments of true self-consciousness, Sandy would retire to a quiet corner to dab it with lip color before returning to her station at the makeup table.

Her playfulness shown out from her deep brown eyes, even during her most fervent tirades, and all the actors treated her as nothing more than their equal. This made scheduling work hours a nightmare for Sandy, so finally she just began asking each actor when he or she felt like coming in to work, and which character they wanted to play that day. As luck would have it, her method ran as smoothly as she could ever have hoped it would. It was as if the Castle itself wanted to keep her.

Two actors were seated on stools, facing the long mirror above the Dressing Room's makeup table. They silently admired their newly applied ghoulish visages. The time and experience in Sandy and Little Mack's talented hands made the transformation from mortals to demons happen in ten minutes or less. It had to be done this quickly; time was of the essence at the beginning of each new shift.

From the beach below, the bright noisy doorway of the Dressing Room shone like a tiny colorful block of light against the dark silhouette of the Castle's form as the sunset finally surrendered, giving way to the darkness of night.

**"Listen to them, the children of the night. What music they make!"**

- **Bram Stoker** –
**DRACULA**

# 2

Anyone who knew Atlantic City at all knew that if you planned to be a successful local musician in 1979, you had to land a job playing in a casino lounge, but the choice of vocation was not an easy one at this young stage of the gambling town's development. There were many more of the bright glistening casinos yet to be built than were currently open and in operation. The promise of a bright future did, indeed, lie ahead, but there remained a meager handful of leftover disco lounges and struggling independent watering holes from the pre-casino era that the lesser of the local bands fought to maintain their grasp on. They were the aging musicians who had flourished in polyester pants with flamboyant shirts, twisting in syncopated rhythm as their guitars muttered the droning sound of disco's finest. Some still clung to the security blanket of that polyester. Others, the smarter ones, knew that the casinos were where the money was. The musicians migrated there, as the smaller bars faded into the shadow of a younger Atlantic City, hiding unimposingly on darker back streets. They were the hideouts  of the holdouts. They were still the haunts of the town's  natives. And because of a strange loyalty and limited funds, the locals came by to see what show these little side alley bars could provide. They came without joy, but present, nonetheless.

This was just the sort of establishment that Archie's Lady Luck Bar was. It was a seedy little dive with absolutely no charm. But it was all Archie's. Bought and paid for with a little bit of ambition and just the right amount of good timing. A younger Archie had stood in front of the then-shining facade many years before, posing for the black-and-white photo that still hung in a dirty frame behind the mahogany bar. His enormous smile in the photo spoke volumes of the pride he must have felt that day. The pride that years of struggle had squelched soundly, along with his beaming smile. He now stood sour and sullen at the end of the same bar, an older version of himself, watching with distaste as the latest of a long parade of washed- up bands took the stage. Precisely at nine p.m. Just as it had been every weekend night for these last 28 years. And this was just another night. Or so he thought.

On this night he had the great misfortune to have hired the sordid little group of locals who went by the unappetizing name of the "Festering Wounds". The name itself should have been warning enough, one would think. All Archie knew was that these guys labeled themselves a "heavy metal band", the lead singer and another band member donning the requisite face paint and electric mane of long hair that was all the rage with the kids these days. They managed to blast out the loud roars that were the signature of this kind of "music" through their over-amplified instruments. This was the only requirement for them to secure the privilege of gracing Archie's stage.

The faces that populated his bar were a sad little amalgam of locals, a few lost tourists, and some underage college students seeking a drink without the hassle of being "carded". There was a brisk turnaround of drug dealers meeting their patrons, street people, and even a few ladies of the evening who wandered in nightly to escape the elements. The latter entered the bar briefly, only to be hustled out by Archie's leviathan son-in-law Bruce, prompted by a quick nod of Archie's head.

Still longing for the days of hack piano players pounding out poor renditions of Sinatra or Bennett songs, Archie saw this same unattractive group of people night after night, year after year. As some faded and drifted off, a new sour face would eventually replace them.

Archie's daydream was interrupted by a distinct

tapping sound. It was Bruce, tapping intrusively on the microphone that was situated at center stage. "Uh, Archie? Arch, it's time." Archie strode onto the little stage and nudged the bumbling behemoth out of his way. He grabbed the microphone roughly off its stand, ripping it from Bruce's sausage fingers. Shooting him one last unforgiving glare before turning back toward the audience, he clumsily replaced the microphone in its plastic cradle. He began to reel off a shaky, less-than-sincere introduction of the band. It was a parody of an introduction.

"Ladies and Gentlemen, it is my great pleasure to introduce to you a new band. Certain to take their place among the legends of rock music…"

Upon the mere utterance of the absurd declaration, one of the microphones prophetically leaked a piercing scream of feedback, causing the audience to squirm uncomfortably, thus shifting Archie's already-active sweat glands into overdrive. He cleared his throat again. The microphone calmed, briefly threatening another whine.

"Uh, it's my pleasure, uh, ummm…Oh, what the fuck… Here's the Festering Whatevers!"

He gave Bruce one more leer and a shove with his elbow as he fumbled past him and off the stage. The audience provided a chorus of sparsely distributed hand claps as the amplifiers belched static. Two flash pots onstage sent up waning trickles of smoke. Not an explosion, as intended, but thin, twisting lines that wound their way in twin ribbons toward the ceiling as the smallest shower of sparks made their prescribed appearance. A display so unimpressive that the fire marshal would surely approve of its indoor presentation wholeheartedly.

With exaggerated bravado, bordering on the absurd, the Festering Wounds bounced to their places onstage. Danny Neumann was their frontman, dressed in the most ostentatious costume, complete with silver face. It was an unsuccessful homage to their glitter rock idols. A hybrid of *Las Vegas Elvis* and *Kiss*. A costume rental nightmare in silver pleather.

Gordon Flemming played drums in a similarly bizarre outfit. While Gordon's costume lacked the imagination that obviously had gone into Danny's, it was no less garish. Both managed to look ridiculous against the backdrop of the stage and alongside their three bandmates, who wore street clothes.

The band had known Danny for quite a long time, and they'd accompanied him on his odyssey through a handful of music genres, in search of his "style". Blues, Disco, Country, Pop…and now Heavy Metal. The band's name had changed with every resurrection, and their wardrobe had morphed through a pathetic parade of genres. In spite of Danny's unbridled enthusiasm with every change, the faces of his bandmates grew increasingly more bored and sullen. Finally achieving utter blankness. Yet the band remained perennially loyal to their all- too-ingenious leader. And loyalty was the cornerstone of Danny and Gordon's long friendship.

Danny bounced around the stage maniacally,

screaming nearly unintelligible lyrics and bumping into both his bandmates and the equipment. Gordon's eyes widened as he continued to hammer the drum kit, watching Danny's prancing feet barely miss the open container of powder that fueled their less-than-dazzling pyrotechnic effects.

Danny glanced down at the audience from time to time. The ugly sea of faces (not a sea, really. More of a pond) ran together like spoiled paint in Danny's eyes. Little flashes of whiskey-tinted glass added a bizarre occasional glimmer to the oil painting. Like tiny fireflies. Bizarre, yet apropos.

Now the musical set was reaching its anticipated apex. The moment when Danny planned his disgusting enactment of an *Ozzy Osborne* staple: He would bite the head off a bat, or rat, or in this case, a parakeet. (since bats were in short supply at the local mall pet shop). It was not a moment he looked forward to, but it was all for 'the cause', and Danny was nothing if not a trouper.

Gordon was still more preoccupied with the prospect of Danny knocking over the small powder keg at his feet. His eyes darted nervously from Danny's face to the keg, hoping to catch his attention and direct him away from the volatile powder. Suddenly the lumbering man-mountain Bruce ran up onto the stage to move the mass of tangled wires near the amplifier on stage right. His clumsy feet knocked over the container, raining a trail of powder onto the stage floor. He knelt on one knee, working feverishly to right the keg, scooping at the powder with his thick fingers. A lightning bolt of panic struck Gordon as the song came to a close. This was the designated moment when the explosions were timed to erupt. The moment hung long and stretched further and further. Nothing. In a place somewhere between disappointment and relief, Gordon realized that the intended smoke and flames were not coming.

Danny's gruesome finale took on an even more pathetic tone, as he opened the little box at his feet and extracted the ill-fated parakeet. He held the bird in his fist a moment, then went forward with the plan. It was only when he felt the movement of the live bird's head in his mouth that he was catapulted back to the reality of his insanity. The frantic bird fluttered angrily in his hand, startling Danny properly, thus making its escape. It flew upward, then made a grand swooping pass at the stage, diving down at the musicians while they played. It then lit out toward the tired little audience, swooping at individuals in the crowd and creating a sad version of what should have been panic, as they ducked its angry dives. In the melee, one of the band members, dodging the kamikaze-keet, knocked over a tower of cymbals. The deafening clang was accompanied by a wide plume of smoke, as the anticipated explosions from the flash pots now made their appearance. But not in the controlled way that had been planned, in carefully timed intervals. They arrived at full force and unbridled, wreaking their complete mayhem of flame and smoke on the tiny stage. The audience hesitated briefly, then rose slowly and began to meander through the maze of little tables, some seagulling drinks as they passed. It was a disappointed exodus for this little crowd, with the problem of finding another watering hole for the evening ahead of them.

A haze of white smoke sat in a flat layer at eye level from the stage. The amplifiers gave a few last desperate squeals of feed-back through the fog, and Archie watched in amazement as the cigar fell from his gaping mouth. His eyes followed Bruce, as if in slow motion, when he grabbed a pitcher of water and headed toward the flames. He watched the slow arc of the water crashing against the tiny flash pot, dousing it quite decidedly, then passing above the steam of the squelched fire toward an amplifier. On impact, the water produced a fresh shower of sparks from the amp.

Now the band was forced to abandon the stage, grabbing what they could of their instruments and equipment as they exited. Members of the Atlantic City Fire Department began to trot through the doors, accompanied by a backdrop of flashing red lights that rivaled the pathetic stage lighting. They stood with axes in hand, surveying the lack of emergency in the room.

"What now, Kimosabe?" Gordon voiced the all-too-familiar phrase to Danny, still seated at his drum kit.

Danny glanced at the chaos of the room around them "Now we run."

The Festering Wounds hopped down from the stage, foregoing the little set of stairs at either end. They passed members of their former audience, amid a wave of lame claps and whistles. The parakeet flew past Danny's left ear and out into the night. He felt a weird feeling of satisfaction. They had finally gotten their coveted ovation.

# 3

When Danny and Gordon entered their apartment, they were greeted by a noxious cloud of cheap aftershave lotion. Somewhere hidden in the depths of this cloud stood Jules, smiling emphatically at the mirror above the bathroom's pedestal sink. The scent wafted menacingly from the brightly lit crack of the slightly open bathroom door. Danny and Gordon winced in unison.

Gordon opened the two windows facing Pete's Beach Boulevard and glanced briefly down the street at the lighted facade of the Castle, imposing against the black sky behind it. He plopped heavily into one of the tattered easy chairs of their little living room as he called to his friend, "Jesus, Jules, easy on the Old Spice! The goal is to *attract* women, not stun them into submission!"

Jules stuck his head into the living room, surprised at the sight of his two roommates, "What are you guys doing here? I thought you were playing in AC tonight."

Danny leafed through one of the many magazines strewn across the coffee table (which was nothing more than an upside-down apple crate, with a varnished plank on top. It had been pilfered from a long-ago summer job at a peach farm some twenty-five miles inland. The faded red letters on the side of the crate that read *Donato Bros. Farms, Landisville, NJ* peered into the room accusingly). He stared absently at the weeks-old magazine's pages as he spoke.

"So, Jules, we can only surmise that all of this cologne can't possibly be meant for me and Gordon."

"Actually, *Sandy* asked me out for a drink."

At this, Danny's gaze left the magazine abruptly. He stared at Jules as words found their way to his mouth through the heavy mist of jealousy forming in his head.

"*Sandy?*"

The weird crack in Danny's voice made Gordon look up from the *TV Guide* in his hands. This could get interesting. The thought of Jules seeing Danny's ex in anything more than a strictly work-related environment was more than he could take right now. Tonight. After all that had happened.

Jules emerged from the bathroom, clicked off the light, and took his place on the living room's beaten sofa.

"Yeah. Sandy. Did I stutter or something?"

Danny worked hard to keep his astonished look in check. "No. I just think it's a little odd that you're seeing *her, of all people*. That's all."

"What's that supposed to mean?" Jules' stare challenged Danny.

"Well, all I mean is, the two of you have barely exchanged 'hellos' for the past ten years."

"What are you talking about?" Jules snapped, now fully engaged. His tone changed to a simple statement of fact, "Sandy and I see each other every day at work.

We've always been friends. Besides, before you get yourself all twisted up in knots, let me repeat, *we're just going out for a drink.*"

"It's just a little strange, that's all," Danny muttered like a denied child.

Gordon smirked as he watched the exchange between his roommates. He was quite used to the most innocent of conversations escalating into verbal free-for-alls, with Danny frequently ending up the worse for it. When it came to biting sarcasm, Jules was king. He heard himself saying, "What Danny meant to say was that *he* was going to ask Sandy out for a drink tonight, himself."

Danny's eyes flashed at Gordon, "No I wasn't. I didn't say that."

This had been a running bit since the day that Sandy and Danny broke up. Years ago. Gordon loved to egg him on, and it worked like a charm every time. Danny's face always grew an interesting shade of red, before he finally blew up at his friends. He would sometimes even go so far as to exit through the front door to walk off the head of steam. His feelings were still raw even after all this time. He had been in love with Sandy since they were in high school. That had been several failed relationships ago.

Danny's angry glare flashed again at Gordon, then back at Jules, "Yeah, okay. We had something going, then it ended. I'll admit that I've mentioned asking her out again a couple of times in the past."

His friends glanced at one another again. Jules allowed

a snort to escape him.

"Alright. A *few* times! And she shot me down every time."

Gordon laughed at the ridiculousness of the statement. "*A few times!?* You've done everything short of setting yourself on fire in front of the woman, just to get her attention!"

"Something which *you* would have remedied for me tonight at Archie's. Maybe she should have been there!" Danny added triumphantly. Touché. Chalk one up for the Heartbreak Kid.

Jules stared at the two of them with a wrinkled brow, "Okay. I'm game. What happened at Archie's tonight?" A tiny pause. "Wait…don't tell. Let me guess." He feigned deep thought. "You were…*fired* perhaps?"

Danny rose and walked into the kitchen. He popped open the door of the ancient refrigerator. It was devoid of anything that might resemble food. However, the door shelves were well- stocked with neat rows of beer bottles. A crumpled ball of tin foil, no doubt containing some disgusting sort of science experiment crouched in the far back corner, as if hiding from view. No one had bothered with it for weeks. No one would.

Danny scanned the rows of bottles briefly. He grabbed three of them between the fingers of one hand, and shut the refrigerator door, again hiding the dim glow of its cavernous insides. In three quick sweeps he opened the bottles expertly on the metal opener that was permanently affixed to the underside of the Formica countertop, then rejoined the others in the living room. Extending a beer-laden hand to each of his friends, they nodded their silent thanks as they grabbed the bottles.

A smirk was etched across Jules' face.

"So, uh, what happened Dan?" He chugged one quickly, "Did the nice bar owner ask you politely to leave?"

Danny shrugged and smiled, holding a mouthful of beer behind his pursed lips. His face betrayed a false embarrassment that was close to pride. He was used to this question. They got fired a lot.

"Oh, wait." Gordon placed his beer on the coffee table, just shy of a beat-up cardboard coaster that boasted the word *Schlitz*. He strode across the room and was out the door in an instant. Nobody questioned his hasty exit. Almost as quickly, he returned, a little breathless from his sprint to the car. Jules took the book he had lent to Gordon only the day before from his extended hand. *The Art of Pyrotechnics Made Simple*. Danny's eye caught the bold lettering on the book's charred front cover, also noting the quizzical look from Jules.

The absurdity of the night's events finally caught up with him. He couldn't help but smile at the thought of Archie's Bar. Of Archie's enormous son-in-law trying valiantly to manage the growing flames while Archie screamed his elaborate symphony of curse words at the band. He drew a slow mouthful of beer, noticing how it hurt a little to hold it in his mouth with the smile that had erupted on his face, and swallowed just short of doing a spit take.

"Thanks for the loan of the book, Jules," Danny finally said as he watched Jules turn the ruined pages, surveying the unexplained damage. "But if Gordon ever asks to borrow a book on stunt driving or sword swallowing, think twice before you give it to him."

They laughed, as the beer had a mild relaxing effect on all of them. It had been a long day for everyone, and the night still stretched out ahead of them.

"You know, the way you guys are talking, you'd think you burned down the bar, or something." At this, Danny and Gordon looked at one another, exploding with new laughter. This time the spit take was not held, as a fine spray of beer left Gordon's pursed lips. Jules joined in their laughter, sipping at his half- empty beer. The absurdity of his own words was lost in the haze of beer and the faint smell of leftover smoke from Archie's Bar.

"Hey, Jules," Gordon asked now, "Would I be in the way if I came along with you and Sandy? I could really use a drink."

Jules looked at the beer bottle in Gordon's hand. "What's *that*, a hand grenade?"

"No, I mean a *real* drink. This stuff has become nothing more than glorified soda to me after working in so many dive bars."

Jules didn't have time to answer. There was a gentle and unmistakably feminine knock at the door. Danny was at the door in an instant, opening it before Sandy had finished her stylized "secret knock". She entered the room, looking surprised to see that Danny and Gordon were already home. Even though she had to have just walked past Danny's car.

"Hey, guys. What are you doing here? Jules and I were just on our way out to catch your act."

"I'm afraid there's nothing left of our act to catch," Danny said dryly. With this, he turned and retreated silently toward the hallway and into the bathroom to wash off what was left of his stage makeup. As the sound of the running water made its way to the others, Jules looked at Gordon, as if remembering the point where their earlier conversation had left off.

"We were fired," Gordon offered without provocation, "Let's just say that it had something to do with an explosion."

Sandy's eyes widened and darted to Jules.

The questioning seemed to have come to an end as Danny rejoined them in the living room. The tension eased slightly. Jules simply said, "Danny and Gordon are going to join us for a drink."

Sandy's face lit up. She took Gordon's arm as he held it out chivalrously. The jingle of car keys and some quiet chatter began to fill the cold gap in the air as the four friends left the little apartment. The forgotten reel-to-reel deck continued to blast its eerie Castle soundtrack in the corner of the room as they clicked the light switch off and pulled the front door closed.

The volume continued to gradually increase as the tape neared its end. The icy moaning sounds reached an ear-splitting pitch just before falling off into complete dark silence. As if the silence were a great pit that hungrily swallowed that moaning voice.

# 4

The Sand Bar was small and seedy. Its motif was a bad attempt at nautical, peppered lightly with memorabilia from the owner's past as a Golden Gloves boxer. The framed photos of his glory days hung between the dim neon glow of beer lights. There was no air conditioning, and the ocean breeze blew through the little screen door at the bar's entrance and bounced off the bodies packed into outdated booths and little square tables. This was not one of those establishments that catered to the tourists and day trippers of Pete's Beach. It was comfortable and well-worn. The locals knew the Sand Bar well, and over time it had come to know them too.

The music from the old jukebox, which was planted snugly in a corner of the bar between the Star Wars pinball machine and the cluttered waitresses' station, was overwhelming. Danny and his little party of four struggled to hold their conversation, leaning toward each other at their table when they spoke, to be heard above the noise.

Danny gave the conversation his best shot, "I don't know. I hate to just get a 'regular' job because I know that that would be *it* for me. I wouldn't have any time left in my life for music, and I'd just end up abandoning it."

"Why don't you try taking something *temporary*?" Jules shouted back, "The summer is winding down, and a lot of the college kids are leaving to go back to school. The fact that you will only be at the job for a month or so might be just what you guys need. You know how the shore is at the end of the summer. Everybody is scrambling to find help. In the meantime, you can put another act together."

Sandy had drifted off on her own tangent. She looked around the room at the many faces, both familiar and not-so- familiar to her. She was a native of Pete's Beach, as was Danny. She was raised playing in the dunes just beyond the bar's parking lot. She was the mascot of the Beach Patrol by age ten. There were more familiar faces in the bar than she cared to admit. She absently peeled at the edge of the label on her beer bottle and folded her cocktail napkin in creative ways. It was obvious that the bar atmosphere was not within her comfort zone.

All the while Danny's eyes had never left her. He admired her every movement, savoring the fact that she was so unaware of his gaze. She suddenly looked up from her fidgeting, catching him in mid-stare. At first, she seemed surprised, but then she smiled her familiar smile.

Now the bar's screen door swung open with a crack, drawing all eyes to the rowdy group of young people who entered. Most of them appeared to be anywhere between high school and college age, but there were more than just a few men and women who were well into their twenties or even their thirties. The luster of youthful exuberance still showed on their faces as brightly as it did in their younger companions, sharing a distinct overabundance of enthusiasm that was nothing short of theatrical. Most of them were eccentrically dressed in vintage, mainly thrift shop garb. Women donned men's ties and throwback fifties blouses that buttoned down the back. The occasional military uniform piece dotted the landscape of odd couture.

Danny was the first to note the entrance of the Sand Bar's newest patrons. "Oh, check out *this* group. They look like a walking advertisement for the *joys of homelessness*."

Sandy and Jules now jumped to their feet, offering cheerful greetings to each passing newcomer. Both Danny and Gordon watched in amazement, mouths agape, as Sandy exchanged pleasantries and the occasional peck on the cheek with the strangers. The odd handful earned a laughing bear hug from Jules, slapping each other playfully on the back as random indiscernible comments were made.

Slowly, Danny and Gordon realized there was only one place that could house such a cast of characters. The look of bewilderment washed from Gordon's face, like a wave from the nearby beach. He noted quietly, yet profoundly, "So...*these* are the infamous Castle monsters of Pete's Beach."

Sandy smiled. "That's right. And the two of you can stop staring at them. They're really pretty normal Actually, they're a great bunch." Their gazes were still riveted, taking in the nuances of the cast of the Castle's attire and demeanor. Sandy added, "They're a little more open-minded than the average person," and still there was no reply, "…but so are most musicians, *usually*." Her eyes fixed on Danny, his wide-eyed gaze still unblinking. "You can pull your jaw back up any time now, Dan."

"Everyone likes to descend on the Sand Bar almost every night after work. You can practically set your watch by it. That's why *we're* here." Jules was saying. He went on to explain that the cast had just finished taking their work makeup off and exchanged their gory costumes for street clothes before making their nightly pilgrimage to the south end of the island.

The freshly scrubbed faces of the actors still bore the tell-tale shine of the Albolene cream that they used to remove their greasepaint. A few still sported dark rings of eyeliner as a tribute to its hasty removal, or maybe for some as a bold statement to go with their evening ensemble.

Overall, they appeared to be a happy group, and it didn't take long before each of them was holding a drink of his or her own and their chatter filled the room. Snippets of Castle stories from the day bounced from wall to wall. Their youth was even more obvious in the sound of their voices. They weren't other- worldly at all. They were college kids, retelling the excitement of their day. Boasting of their best "scares". They gradually became more human, less odd. They all had names. They ordered French fries, corned beef specials, and beer and were exactly like real people.

"You know, the two of you," Sandy nodded to Danny and Gordon, "should consider putting some hours in at the Castle." There was a brief pause, enough to make her realize she had caught them off guard.

"Just for a little while, so you can make some quick cash while you're deciding what to do about a *real* job."

Their faces remained stony, unchanged. The words 'real job' produced a dull sting in Danny's ears. Sandy could feel the words rushing through her lips, afraid that even a moment's hesitation might afford them a chance to rebut her suggestion, "What could it hurt? We're only open a couple more days anyway. The summer crowds are already starting to leave Pete's Beach. A lot of our cast has left for school, and there is plenty of room for new employees to finish out the season. Labor Day weekend is the most fun time to work at the Castle, anyway."

It was the suggestion that they all knew Sandy was bound to make. She was constantly trying to share the bubbly enthusiasm she had for her work at the Castle with everyone. She was like a drinker, insisting that her bar companions partake as heavily as she did. They looked at her shining eyes, which seemed to await her friends' answer hungrily.

Not that hers was necessarily such a bad suggestion. In fact, it very well might make all the sense in the world. But for Danny, it meant another wasted week. Another seven days away from his precious musical "career". Away from the climb that would surely bring him to ultimate fame. And for Gordon, Sandy's idea held a particular kind of dread.

"Uh, no thanks, Gordon said weakly. "That place gives me the creeps from the *outside*! I made myself a promise a long time ago, that I would never set foot inside the Castle."

Jules stepped on Gordon's words, "You weren't out of a job before. Besides, it's different when you *work* there; it's only scary to the customers."

Sandy smiled at Jules' words. She knew that the idea of the Castle only being scary to the customers was false. At least it had always been so for her. She dreaded even a short walk through the Castle's scenes unaccompanied. She feared that someone would find it amusing to jump out and scare her, and it wasn't any more reassuring to think that it would be one of her friends. This was why she always passed the duties of checking scenes for trash or a lingering customer at the end of the day to a coworker. To Jules, or Little Mack. It had literally been years since Sandy had wandered the halls of the Castle interior alone.

Now another wave of "Castle Dwellers" poured through the bar's open doorway. This group was not as lively as the last, but equally interesting to look at. Danny's eyes were instantly riveted on a pretty blonde in the middle of the group. She glanced around the room anxiously, anticipating whom she might eventually leave with. Danny watched her, drawn. His contrary tune may just have changed.

"Now let's not be too hasty, Gordon," Danny started. His eyes remained with the girl across the room. "Jules may be right. We weren't out of work like we are now. Maybe we *should* give it a shot." There was a distinct pause as his voice trailed off, "It's only for a few days, anyway."

His gaze had not wavered for even a moment, remaining fixed on the girl across the bar. She looked like a throwback to 1967, complete with a fringed suede jacket and mirrored peace sign earrings. Her paisley dress was the perfect foil for her lace- up combat boots. She was an intricately woven tapestry of a thrift shop nightmare. Yet, Danny thought, it suited her, giving her the ragged edge of a true artist. In an odd way, it actually embellished her beauty.

Sandy, Gordon and Jules couldn't help but follow Danny's hypnotic gaze toward the girl.

"Maybe we should give it a *shot*?" Gordon repeated Danny's words. "It looks more like you're saying maybe you should give *her*", he nodded to the object of Danny's interest, "a shot." He paused, "What part of your anatomy is doing your thinking for you now, Dan?"

Gordon knew that this little infatuation they were witnessing blossom before them could very well determine the path that his own life was about to take. Danny's fascination for this little monsterette could mean that he might just find himself inside that dreaded beast of a building. This was a prospect Gordon did not relish in the least.

No matter what the reason for Danny's change of heart, Sandy was overjoyed. Enough said. They were as good as in, she thought, and began to congratulate them, "I'm so glad you're giving it a try. I think that you guys will make terrific monsters!"

"Wait a minute, here!" Gordon's voice possessed a hint of desperation, "I haven't agreed to any of this yet!" Gordon knew that it was a losing battle. When Danny made up his mind, nobody in heaven or on earth could change it for him. Not even his lifelong best friend.

Danny was immersed in the observation of his captivating subject across the bar. It was as if a perfect spot of light hung over her. He liked the way she looked as she laughed; the practiced way that she tossed her long hair off her shoulder and adjusted the overstuffed Army backpack that hung there. She gave Danny a few quick glances, noting his interest as she remained actively engaged in the conversation with her friends, dedicating her attention to the stories they were telling. Stories, no doubt, about the Castle.

Gordon offered one final argument, "I can't set foot in that place. What about the promise I made to myself?"

"Gordon, you should be *used* to being lied to. You work with Danny, remember?" Jules' smile did not waver as he spoke. It was his own weird form of ventriloquism.

Sandy lifted her huge patchwork handbag from the seat beside her and placed it on the table. Her three friends all grabbed their beer bottles quickly, to avoid the inevitable wipeout that the satchel would produce. Her arm disappeared up to her elbow as she felt her way through the bag's contents.

She looked up at Gordon, "You don't have to agree to take the job right away. You can take a tour of the Castle tomorrow, then just let me know what you think." She fished through the handbag a few seconds more, finally producing two yellow tickets from the bag, which she held happily in Gordon's direction. His eyes met Danny's for an instant, then he snatched them reluctantly from Sandy's fingers.

Printed beside a rough sketch of a medieval-style castle were the words THE HAUNTED CASTLE AMUSEMENT PIER. The Gothic lettering was intended to add to the foreboding image of the Castle's logo. It fell well short of its task.

"Those are free passes. Let the girl in the Admissions Booth know that you're friends of mine. She'll call me to let me know when you're there."

Jules lifted his beer in a toast, "Here's to our two newest ghouls!" They all clinked their bottles and took a long drink. Jules stopped abruptly in mid-swig, "Oh, shit." He chugged the last of his beer. "I have to get going soon, or those soundtrack tapes won't be ready for the morning!"

Somewhere during the toast, Mia passed tantalizingly close to their booth. Danny's interest reignited in a wide-eyed stare as he drank, somewhat taken by surprise at how close by the vision was passing. Heat rose in his throat, creating a quick barrier, and an uncontrollable fit of coughing. His friends took turns slapping him on the back as if to help. Maybe hitting just a little too hard. It all ended in their usual laughter at Danny's expense.

Seated at a small table in one of the bar's darkest corners, an intense-looking bearded man watched Sandy and her little party with great interest. Their laughter assaulted him as he downed the brown contents of the brimming shot glass on the table in front of him. The drink was only a brief respite from his keen observation of the group. He watched as one of them rose and gave his quick goodbyes before exiting the bar. Allowing Jules enough time to get to his car, the man rose with a look of grave distaste for the little group of friends.

The man was Richard, the Castle's Manager, and a few members of the cast greeted him weakly as he nudged his way through the crowd toward the door. The actors' greetings went unacknowledged.

Sandy noticed Richard as he was exiting. She watched through the seaspray-streaked front windows as his dark form moved beneath the streetlights. Finally, he was nothing more than a small black speck, silhouetted by glowing pools of light in the distance.

# 5

Even the twinkling lights of Atlantic City on the horizon seemed too bright for the Watcher's eyes. His intense headache was now on its way to finally subsiding. The headaches didn't *always* arrive before the violence, but somehow, they always managed to reach their peak when his physical strength took over. They pounded his brain, tenderizing it, weakening it, until he could bear it no more. Then, he thought, no one could ever blame him for the actions that followed. This had always been the way. The violence came so easily to the Watcher, and it came with no remorse at all. He had always been clever enough to make it work for him; his will made the pain its slave. The pain was a valve, by which his great tension escaped. No one ever knew. No one ever *would* know. Because he waited patiently. He thought everything through, oh so thoroughly. He bided his time. He watched. He was the Watcher.

# Part Two
# Friday

**"Rivulet of dark wine, moving in a straight line, smudging up the stop signs, running down the lifelines. Terminal eyes at the edge of the night."**

**- Al Stewart –
TERMINAL EYES**

# 1

Danny and Gordon walked amid the games and concession booths of the Castle Pier. There were certain distinct similarities that the faces of the tourists around them all shared. The expression of joy, wonder, and the freedom that vacations brought. After a short time, the faces all began to gel together to make the single definitive face. A race all its own. A Lovecraftian mass of Hawaiian-shirted morphs.

Danny turned to his friend, "This doesn't look so bad."

In a small way, the prospect of entering the infamous Haunted Castle of Pete's Beach had ceased to hold the imposing sense of dread that it had held. It was slowly becoming what it was intended to be. An amusement.

As the two passed by the open doorway that was the exit of the funhouse, a screaming swarm of teenyboppers barreled out and slammed into them. It all happened so quickly that there had been no time to move out of their way. Gordon was knocked backward into a burly clown, who promptly lost his grip on a handful of brightly colored balloons. The balloons escaped to the open sky above. The spray of multicolored dots made its way higher and spread farther and farther apart in the air above them. They weren't balloons anymore. They weren't toys. They were just a flock of oddly colored birds, fluttering over the noisy pier.

The irate clown tore his eyes away from the floating fiasco. Now he would spend another hour preparing a fresh batch of the helium-filled monstrosities before returning to the pier's promenade to finish his shift. He locked his angry gaze on Gordon. His gruff voice was not at all in keeping with the painted-on smile that graced his greasepainted white face.

"Thanks a lot, Asshole."

Danny and Gordon looked at one another sheepishly as they moved out of the clown's earshot, "Uh-oh. Mr. Bozo isn't too happy with us."

Now they passed by a contrived space in the facade of the Castle Lobby. The gap was gaudily painted to resemble a crumbling portion of the wall. It was designed to give patrons outside a brief peek into what would await them within, should they dare to pay the purchase price of a ticket. A group of screaming customers could be seen hurrying up the stairs inside, allowing everyone in the Lobby to witness their unmistakable terror. This was all the advertising that the place would need.

A line of customers wound through the Lobby. A serpentine wait. Danny and Gordon finally arrived at the little ticket booth at the Castle's Entrance. They caught sight of the girl who was seated inside the Cashier's booth, which was a tight niche carved out of the same Styrofoam-coated rocks that lined the Lobby. The eerie green light within gave the girl a haunting glow of her own. Her makeup was not terribly impressive in and of itself. Yet she was effectively a beacon for what would await the Castle patrons within. It was all very ominous.

In reality, the girl was just an average freckled high school student, wearing thick glasses over her ghoulish makeup. The glasses seemed to punch a hole in the intended fantasy that her makeup sought to create. As if that was not enough to break the spell, she snapped a wad of pink bubble gum loudly as Danny and Gordon stood at the barred window, staring in silence at her as if she were an apparition. She stared back at them. Finally, she spoke, jolting them from whatever nightmare they were busy concocting in their collective minds.

"So? How many?"

"Oh, umm, we have free passes," Danny said as he dug deep into his pocket for the elusive yellow tickets. When he couldn't seem to locate them briefly, some of the long line of customers behind them allowed audible groans to escape. Others were simply too busy corralling their broods of impatient children to care about Danny's dalliance. The bespectacled girl behind the bars' eyes passed indifferently from Danny's face to Gordon's, then back again. It was a great relief to Danny when his fingers finally felt the two tickets, clinging to the inside lining of his pocket in a frustrating dance with his hand.

"Okay, here you go," Danny said to the girl with a little too much emphasis. He slapped the tickets triumphantly onto the counter in front of her.

Unimpressed, she swept them into a little tray on her lap. "You and your date can step through the turnstile on your right." They began to move ahead slowly, and Gordon produced the angriest glare he could muster as he passed the girl in the booth.

Suddenly, Danny leaned back, over Gordon, and spoke quickly to the Cashier, "Oh, wait! Sandy said to tell you to give her a call when we got here!"

Now the girl appeared to be losing patience. She wrinkled her makeup-laden brow once quickly, leaving tiny streaks of gray in her otherwise-pallid forehead.

"Okay...well?" It was between those two words that she decided that she would be done with this. Today. Tonight, she would quit. She had had enough of this job and these people.

"Okay...well tell her we're here," Danny shot back.

Her tone grew shorter with each word, "It would be easier to tell her if I knew your *names*."

Gordon peeked timidly into the Cashier's cage. Neither the girl's ridiculous glasses, her thick wad of pink bubble gum, nor her obvious local accent served to assuage the knot of anxiety that was beginning to grow in his chest. To him, the word *fun* had no business being part of the word *funhouse*. There was nothing fun about hearing your own heart pounding inside your ears or about feeling that sick twist in your stomach. He had quit doing drugs for the same reason.

The Cashier's hand was on the button of the little intercom to the left of her. She leaned in toward it as she spoke. Her voice remained unchanged from the monotone of earlier, "Code, uh, ummm…" she faltered for a second, looking up at the booth's ceiling. "Little Mack, are you there…? It's Judy in the Cashier's Booth. I can't remember the friggin' code number for call-back!" After a few crackles of static, a cheerful male voice came through the little box. It was Little Mack; his genuinely amused laughter preceded his words, "Judy, you twit, how many times do I have to go over the codes with you? Now, what's the problem? Why did you need a call-back?"

As Judy began to explain, an obtrusive fumbling sound came through the intercom's speaker from the Dressing Room. It culminated with the sound of a loud slap, and Little Mack's distinctive "OUCH! Cut it out, Sandy! Here…*you talk*!"

It was Sandy's voice that they heard next, "Judy, just tell them to go ahead through the Castle tour. They can come around the pier to the Dressing Room afterward. I'll be here waiting for them."

The Cashier's voice took on a much more pleasant tone as she spoke to Sandy, abandoning the acerbic quality, "You got it, Sandy."

She took her finger from the intercom's button and pointed it toward the turnstile that they had already visited once. Déjà vu. Danny moved along obediently in silence, but Gordon stood frozen. The girl stared back at him for just a fraction of a second, then lunged forward, her eyes wild behind the glasses, "BOO!!"

Gordon stumbled through the turnstile after Danny. The musty odor of the dark passageway hit him hard, serving as smelling salts of sorts. It punched through his senses as he fumbled forward in the semi-darkness. He gripped Danny's shoulder ahead of him as a guide in the dark, and Danny gave a single annoyed shrug, releasing Gordon's hand.

They passed by a Plexiglas-encased scene worthy of the worst wax museum's Chamber of Horrors. It was a tableau of an elaborate Dining Room, the table set impeccably with fine china. The plates held bits of human remains, and the goblets were filled with wine. Or was that blood? The guests at the long dining table were none other than Frankenstein's Monster, the Wolf Man, the Mummy, and at the table's head, of course, Count Dracula himself. All frozen in time; making their toast under the dim flickering orange lights of an ancient chandelier.

The soundtrack of rock music gradually morphed into a sinister speech, welcoming the latest guests to the "Baronial Hall of the Haunted Castle". Gradually the background music was replaced with Bach's Toccata and Fugue in D minor. A haunted house staple.

Having taken in all its grisly details, they moved slowly away from the scene.In the dim light, a distinct dark patch could be detected in the wall up ahead to their left. It was an opening of some sort, and it was creating an uneasiness in the pit of Gordon's stomach. This was to be his first test. It was just the sort of thing he had envisioned and feared. It was exactly what had kept him out of the Castle up until now.

They had not taken more than two steps forward when the dreaded creature that lived within the dark recess emerged. It stretched its grimy arms toward them, and the shackles on each of its wrists clanked noisily against the iron cage at the opening to his lair. He grabbed the bars and shook them now, growling in anger. His growl became a scream, and for a moment the two stared at the monster, dumbstruck. Then they ran.

It was only when they reached a waiting area at the top of the steps that they realized that the little group that had amassed at the window of the Baronial Hall was right behind them. All of them had fallen victim to the startling appearance of the creature in the wall. They continued forward at a brisk pace now, halting only when they were met by a red velvet rope, which blocked any further passage. Gordon barely managed to keep his balance when the rope caught him just below his waist. He looked back at the short stairway they had just climbed in utter terror. In the distance, at the bottom of those stairs, they could see the creature, hanging menacingly from a space between the bars of his prison. He continued to watch them hungrily.

They stood silently in the dimness of the hallway, happy for the chance to catch their breath before moving on. The smell of moldy wood and suntan lotion mixed to make the small space even more dank and cloying. More customers appeared from the passageway behind them, arriving in twos and threes, and each time their entrance was heralded by the familiar crash of thunder and lightning flashes. Then came the screams of their encounter with what the cast of the Castle knew as the First Cage. That was the official name for the hole in the wall, from which the unidentifiable monster had made his appearance.

The waiting seemed to drag on forever. Danny was the first to comment. His tone was exaggerated, like a performance, "Anybody know what we're waiting for?"

He looked toward the regal-looking pair of wooden doors, just beyond the velvet rope. "I guess we're supposed to stand here and wait for god-knows-what to come out of there and get us!" His speech was just a little too theatrical.

Gordon leaned toward his friend, "What are you doing? Just shut up and wait." He paused, "Do you think we could all be missing something? Like a secret passage we're supposed to take?"

Danny spoke in a tone made audible to the entire group, "I don't know, but this is getting a little boring. We didn't pay to stand around waiting." (Someone in the crowd muttered that *he* hadn't paid at all. They had seen him present the Cashier with the free passes.) He now called out to an invisible presence.

"Hey!" Nothing. "Anybody? Hey, there's a bunch of people out here! Can we please come in?"

His impatience became contagious. The little group began to flutter with a growing sense of frustration. A big fellow in a yellow surfer tank with the words *RON JON* across the front and cut-off jeans knocked on the wall to the group's left. He leaned in and spoke to the wall awkwardly, "Hello! Could one of you monsters get off your…" he paused and smiled at his entourage in the group, "*Coffee break,* and let us in?" It appeared that Danny had fueled the fire of bravery among his newest group of brothers-in-arms. Several more challenges to the wall rose up through the little group. They formed a strange bond. It was a bond that would last the thirty-odd minutes it would take to navigate the Castle. They were all in this thing together.

Danny volunteered his observation to them, "There's a doorway up here, just beyond the rope. Maybe I should try the handle?"

That was where the brotherhood ended. The others backed off, breaking back into their various cliques, as they all had been before the little dialogue began.

Pretending to be tough had its place, but nobody wanted to be thrown out for breaking the rules. This place, after all, was what it was.

Undaunted, Danny began to unhook the velvet rope from the brass loop on the wall. Suddenly, and without warning, a booming voice came from the small black alcove just beyond the doors. The sound stopped his hand short, "DON'T TOUCH THAT ROPE!! FOOLISH MORTAL…". Then the voice was again silent.

A hush fell over the group. Everyone was startled momentarily, not least of all Danny.

"Maybe you triggered something when you touched that rope," a voice finally said. Danny looked down, where a boy of twelve or thirteen years was staring at him. The boy's friend, standing beside him, looked annoyed at this theory. He rolled his eyes and nudged the boy's arm roughly, "Shut up, Billy!"

Now Danny called out to the darkness, "Excuse me. Can you let us in soon? It's starting to get hot out here!" And it was. They had all ignored the intense closeness of the hallway until now, but it was becoming increasingly more uncomfortable as time passed. And truly hot. Was this just another facet of the Castle experience? Discomfort?

Danny turned back to the group, trying to assess whether he would be told to knock it off by one of the more upstanding customers. He looked from face to face behind him. Oddly, none met his eyes. They all seemed to be trained on something behind him. He turned forward again, finding himself nose-to-nose with a grim-looking whitewashed little man in a tuxedo. His hair was slicked back with visible grooves left by a thick comb. He smelled oddly like sweat and dryer sheets. The wrinkles around his eyes were expertly painted on in delicate strokes. The gray shading of his temples and eye sockets did little to hide the actor's obvious youth. Probably not yet out of his teens. Upon initial scrutiny, this specter did not appear to be terribly threatening. More sickly than menacing.

As he managed a step backward, Danny couldn't help but notice the immense battle axe that was poised in the Castle Butler's bony hand. The smirk slowly washed from his face. The red-rimmed eyes glared back at him, filling with anger as he spoke. His voice was theatrical, and his intonation was precise and practiced. It held an astoundingly resonant quality, much stronger than the Butler's slight frame belied.

"I said…" he started out quietly, building to an angry growl, "*DON'T TOUCH THAT ROPE!*"

It was then that Danny realized that his hand was still resting on said rope, and he retracted it sharply. The hasty retrieval of his hand drew a subdued round of laughter from his little group of newfound friends.

The Butler cleared his throat and stiffened slightly as he launched into his prepared speech. The words fell effortlessly from his thin black lips without a hint of hesitation. Or thought. With his left hand, the one unencumbered by his axe, he unhooked the red rope from its brass eye on the wall. The huge battle axe lurched forward toward the crowd as he did so, and they all gave a startled jump backward. "Works every time", he thought.

"Please enter my Master's Portrait Room." He beckoned their passage through the set of double doors, as he rested the axe in the alcove and opened the doors with both hands now. "When you have entered the room, step all the way to the front. Do not leave the room until you are told to do so. My Master will be arriving to greet you shortly."

With the last of his little performance behind him, the Butler guided the group into the Portrait Room. It was, just as the name implied, a room lined with hideous, poorly rendered images of ghoulish people from a long time past. There was a gaunt- cheeked old marm, whose stern gaze was intended to evoke a sense of moral guilt. Beside her was the portrait of a young man. Something of a milquetoast in appearance. Perhaps the woman's nephew or other kin. There was a stately older man in a tight suit with a waistcoat. His jacket boasted several unidentifiable medals, either for social valor or military service. Closest to the room's great fireplace and mantel was a portrait of a buxom beauty, her cleavage all but spilling out of the ornate frame. Her lips were a dark crimson, and her eyes seemed to blaze with a hungry fire. This was the "bride" of the Master, whose own portrait held the place of prominence above the mantelpiece itself.

Threatening shadows seemed to protrude from every corner of the moldy little room, and fearsome plaster gargoyles guarded either side of the fireplace. A simulated fire burned within the hearth, its embers glowing orange against the dull grayness of the room itself yet providing no cozy sense of warmth. An iron chandelier hung at the ceiling's center point. The little reflections of its flickering amber flames caught the carved edges of the Count's Portrait frame like so many fireflies. The huge fireplace seemed oddly out of place in the little space, with its carved columns reaching some six feet above the floor. Even the tallest of the visitors in Danny and Gordon's little group would have to stretch to reach its mantel. And above this long narrow slab of marble was the ornate gold frame that surrounded the portrait of the Master, Count Dracula himself.

This Portrait was different from the others in its detail. It immediately commanded the attention of all who entered. As it should. The Portrait itself was eerily lit from the ceiling above, with an intensely hot spot of light on the face of the Count. The very presence of the painting drew a hush from everyone as they entered.

Once the group of visitors had moved forward sufficiently, they quietly took in the sights and strangely enveloping atmosphere of the Portrait Room. The smell of suntan lotion and cotton candy that they had brought inside the room with them as souvenirs of the bustling pier below was their only link with their former reality.

The Butler paused, having completed his task. He waited for silence from the restless shuffling feet of those farthest back from the Portrait. Making sure that the last stragglers were clear of the doors, he grasped them with both hands as he announced loudly (and, indeed, somewhat breaking his staunch character), "SO LONG, SUCKERS!!"

The group wheeled back to face him, just in time to witness his disappearance behind the slamming doors. He was gone.

Now the hush that had fallen over the group upon their entrance had morphed into complete silence. A silence that seemed to pull the very oxygen out of their collective lungs. Just when the tension finally reached its height, the eerie Portrait above the stony mantel came to life.

With a resounding slam of his shoe against the faux marble, Dracula now stood above them. Ominous. Towering. The exaggerated height of his place on the mantel created a sort of dominance all its own. He leered down at them, as though his eyes were drinking in their very essence, passing over each face hungrily. He slowly began to smile. The smile was disquieting in nature. Filled with lust and punctuated by his blood-tinted teeth and gums. Finally, he spoke, "Good Evening. And welcome to my home…"

**"The Opera Ghost really existed…Yes, he existed in flesh and blood, although he assumed the complete appearance of a real Phantom, that is to say of a spectral shade."**

**- Gaston Leroux -**
**THE PHANTOM OF THE OPERA**

# 2

When Danny and Gordon emerged from the Castle's exit some thirty-five minutes later, they were relieved and laughing. They trotted breathlessly through the exit, knowing that the creature that was following close behind could not venture out onto the pier. Castle rules.

They squinted in the blinding sunlight that greeted them. It was true that they had hated the experience, every single  minute of it, but it was over now. They knew that from now on when it came to the business of being scared inside the Castle, they would be on the *delivering* end.

They had paid close attention to every scene, studying them for their own use. They noted the way each actor behaved, held themselves, and changed the tone of their voices to create just the right amount of tension. They kept in mind which frightening gags worked best. They learned. It was a crash course in a very particular sort of acting.

From high above them, Danny and Gordon's antics on the pier were being studied closely by the unfeeling eyes of a predator. On the uppermost peak of the Castle known as the Parapet stood the Watcher. His heavy breath mingled with the humid sea air, giving the sight of him the illusion of a bull about to charge.

The happy noises of the arcades and concessions below were swallowed up by the ocean winds that whistled past. They gave the sensation of constant movement to the creature called the Haunted Castle. From this vantage point, she did not feel like a wooden structure. Not a building at all. If one were to close his eyes and leave behind the memory of the contrived plywood facade, painted gaudily to mimic weathering and age, mundane in its own effort to be interesting, he could imagine himself atop a living, breathing organism. That was exactly the way the Watcher saw the Castle. It moved and groaned beneath him. It was a great dinosaur, caught in the soft beach sand below. Petrified by the elements and now one with the island.

The Watcher did not hear the laughter that floated up from the tourists on the pier below him. He only heard the strangely liquid sound of his own heartbeat, pounding in a syncopated rhythm with the pulse of the dinosaur.

His headache was intense now, as it had been for the last hour, maybe two. He was never sure of how long the headaches lasted. The cool breeze on his face relieved some of the burning that accompanied the kill. He knew that very soon he would be in control of himself again, and only the dimmest of memories would remain. Sometimes no memories at all. That was always the way it worked. It had become his grisly routine. He had worked on the process of remembering one or two key details so that he could take a tiny souvenir back with him when the headaches finally dissipated. The Watcher possessed two very distinct parts. The first part, the dangerous part, would seek out a victim to quell his ravenous desires. And then there was the Other…the one who battled daily to keep the Watcher in check and clung to the single detail or two his addled brain could retain from the time of the kill. It was all too much for him to ponder. Not with the searing pain that still had a home in his head.

The Watcher stared down at his blood-stained hands. He stood swaying in the wind, transfixed for what seemed like a long time. In fact, it had only been a matter of seconds.

Down on the Parapet floor, behind the dentil-topped walls, lay the mutilated form of the girl. Her blood mixed with the dirt of the Parapet walkway. This was a girl he didn't know. A girl he would never know. Just an unfortunate insect who had stumbled into the Watcher's web.

She had been part of an overly large group that had exited the Castle after their tour. She was alone, appearing to be a little high from the joint she had enjoyed alone on the end of the pier as she gazed out over the waves. Once inside, the strange man in the black top hat had beckoned her from the dark doorway in the Human Sacrifice Room. Her curiosity had gotten the best of her, and she had wandered just a little too close to hear the man's whispers. The last thing she would remember was the scene filled with glow paint in the Castle's Swamp. Had she been tied to a post? Was that the same man approaching her with the huge knife?

The Watcher wiped his hands hurriedly on his clothing. Today he was Jack the Ripper. This was one of his favorite costumes; the cape and top hat gave him an imposing dignity as he performed his unspeakable duties. This pleased the Castle. This gave it its food.

He bent down and lifted the girl with what seemed like no effort at all. He positioned her limp body across one of his shoulders. Bending down again he also retrieved her severed head, which lay a scant foot away. He had no fear of being seen. Sights like this one were commonplace here. As he walked toward the door that led off the Parapet, the bloody knife which he thought he had so carefully lodged in his belt loop dropped noisily to the floor. He quickly kicked it away, watching it careen across the walkway until it found a new home under some nearby fake shrubbery. He eyed it from a second angle, satisfied that its discovery would not come too soon for him to return for it later, then he continued his burdened walk to the door. The knife was just another detail. It was the details that unnerved the Watcher the most. Bits of business that weren't in the script of his madness in the first place. He would need to remind his Other Self to take care of the knife, along with other bits of the cleanup that he now had no time for. He would need to remind him. The Other Self was, after all, his servant. He was slower and clumsier than the Watcher. He was his Doppelgänger in negative. The light counterpart to his dark soul.

He thought about the part of his work that still lay ahead of him. He had a lot left to do before he could rest. Just then the dinosaur beneath him heaved a tremendous sigh.

# 3

Jarrett was sure that he had seen the figure of a man in a top hat lift something heavy across his shoulders and walk back toward the Castle's battlements that faced the open sea. Of course, from his distant vantage point on the beach below, he could not be sure. His vision was prone to playing tricks on him, growing foggy and blurred because of his "medication". The mere thought of the pills made Jarrett instinctively feel the outside of his front pants pocket for the shape of the familiar plastic vial. His fingers ran briefly around its edge. It was definitely there. He was able to relax once again.

He looked up at the Parapet a second time. This time he saw no one, so he began to wonder whether there had ever been anyone to begin with. Jarrett's pills, soothing though they may be, sometimes altered his ability to think clearly. They scrambled his thoughts while they provided relief from his pain. They were his family. They had lived with him for so long that he no longer remembered life without them. Now he shrugged off the thought of the man in the top hat and laid back on the soft beach sand.

Atwill Jarrett hadn't always depended upon the

medication to keep his pain at bay, thus keeping him sane. He had been a happy enough child. In spite of having endured his share of ribbing from the other children in the schoolyard. The first reason for their taunting was his tremendous height. Even in grammar school he was easily a foot taller than any of the boys in his  class, rivaling the height of most of his teachers as well. From an early age it singled him out; made him awkward. It turned his thoughts inward and made him grow strange and separate.

Then there was his strange first name. It hadn't been easy growing up in a tough Camden neighborhood with the name Atwill. He played among the children of Italian immigrants. Boys named Tony and Frankie. It embarrassed him to say his name aloud to them. By the age of nine Atwill Jarrett had managed to firmly establish a suitable nickname for himself. One that would help him blend into the group of neighborhood children. He wanted to simply be referred to as A.J.

As time passed, A.J. grew more popular on the playground. His height eventually proved to be a boon in almost every sport, and he became the instant first pick when teams were chosen. This was fortunate, because where A.J. excelled in stature, he failed miserably in mental acumen. He was somewhat slow- witted naturally. Sadly for Atwill Jarrett, his overly-ambitious father had always interpreted his poor grades in school as a sign of rebellion and laziness. The man had had his son at a very late age, and his old-fashioned values did not allow for a child who was special. A child who needed a little extra help. It made this child weak in his eyes. A.J. gave up trying to please the old man long before he dropped out of high school at the age of fifteen.

It hadn't been easy to find a job for the young Jarrett. His stunted ability to learn quickly left few options open to him. He took on several low-paying jobs as a laborer but couldn't seem to hold any position for more than a month or two. He moved from one sad job to another, unable to decide what he was best suited to do. The draft board made that decision for him shortly after his eighteenth birthday. As luck would have it, he was shipped overseas immediately following boot camp. This, Jarrett thought, would finally make his father proud. If only his father had lived long enough to see it.

During his army days, serving in Vietnam, A.J. was simply known as Jarrett. This was perfectly fine with him. There was no longer the need to endure the odd looks and mispronunciations that were sure to come when he mentioned his given name. He even began to sign official documents and what little correspondence he could manage to maintain with his mother with the single name. As time passed, he himself often had to pause and think for a moment when asked if he did, in fact, possess a first name. He was Jarrett. Just Jarrett.

The army gave him more than a new identity. It was during his first tour of duty that Jarrett sustained serious head injuries. He was never quite sure if that fateful blast that rang out beside him, sending a spray of loose dirt and Jarrett himself into the air had come from the enemy or from U.S. howitzer fire. In the hail of bullets and blasts that rained down all around his platoon, the ability to distinguish anything was impossible. Afterward, all of it seemed to swirl and melt into the fog of Jarrett's memory. It made no difference what the source of the blast had been. The outcome was the same. Jarrett found himself in an army hospital. He was given to understand that his injuries had required a number of surgeries before he had regained consciousness, and a steel plate now replaced a large portion of his shattered skull.

This was how Jarrett had come to possess the collection of open prescriptions for painkillers to numb both the haunting memories and searing pain from his injuries. He never even remembered coming home. All courtesy of the U.S. Army. Now his only peace and comfort lay in his precious "medication". He guarded the little vial in his pocket with the same dedication with which he had guarded his country. Both had in one way or another saved him from himself.

Sadly, any adherence to the proper dosage had become a thing of the past. Long, long past. Because of the open nature of his prescription, he had begun to eat the pills freely, sometimes before the need for them arose. The people around him regarded him as a "burn-out". A remnant of the battlefield somewhere in Southeast Asia that had taken his health and the lion's share of his soul with it.

Naturally, Jarrett's friends at the Castle were more than willing to take advantage of the generous supply of pills he would happily dole out to them simply for the asking. They would hover around him as he reached for the little orange vial. Like so many moths to a flame; like so many vampires to a droplet of blood. They would disperse when Sandy saw what was happening and shooed them away.

Sandy liked Jarrett. She saw him as a sweet soul trapped in a damaged body. She had given him one steady role at the Castle. A role that was his alone. Since his acting abilities were rendered extremely limited by his patchy memory, Jarrett could never seem to master even the shortest of scripted monologues. Even the silent menace of the Wolf Man, who skittered through the Swamp Area terrorizing unsuspecting patrons with a growl and a sneer and a flash of pointed teeth required a certain degree of finesse that he simply could not attain. His damaged brain would afford him neither the quickness nor the agility required of such a role. It was for this reason that Sandy and Little Mack had put their heads together to find the perfect place for Atwill Jarrett. Little Mack came up with the ideal way to utilize both his great height and his sympathetic nature to their best advantage. He would be the horror favorite: Frankenstein's Monster. But not the mundane monster from any other funhouse. Jarrett's makeup was well thought out, and Mack was happy to spend the extra time every day crafting the death mask of a face, the scarred neck and temples, and the meticulously applied skull cap. He would always be mindful not to hurt the gentle giant while working around his real scars, and near the sensitive area on his scalp where the metal plate lived.

As it turned out, the role was one that Jarrett seemed to be born to play. He was incredibly frightening while maintaining an empathy that was endearing. It was because he *was* that monster in so many ways. He was inherently sad for the loss of his past life; the life before he relied so heavily on the pills. He was every bit the monster in his own mind that he was now outwardly made to portray. He felt as though he was made up of spare parts, patched and sewn together.

For the first time since those playground days when his height had made him a champion, he was applauded for his performance. For his abilities, limited though they were. Gradually this infusion of confidence grew into a real love for the Castle. He felt a sense of camaraderie and oneness with his fellow actors. Even for those who only seemed to be his friend at the appearance of the little orange vial.

Jarrett looked up at the ramparts towering over the pier again. He squinted against the bright blue of the sky. From between two of the jutting squares that crowned the Parapet, the man in the top hat appeared again. Now he seemed to be staring down at the tourists on the pier beneath him. Or was he looking at Jarrett? The angle of the man's body rendered him little more than a blurred silhouette, especially at his great height and distance from the beach. Jarrett had to shield his eyes to maintain any view of him at all. He struggled repeatedly to hold his focus on the tiny figure, but to no avail. Instead, he glanced down at his wristwatch. His eyes watered as if in thanks for the relief from the brightness as Jarrett began to gather his few belongings from the sand. The time for him to begin the process of getting ready for his workday was fast approaching, and he was due in the Dressing Room for his ritual of makeup application in just over half an hour.

He stood up, struggling a little with his footing on the soft sand, and began to trudge his way up the beach toward the boulevard. He took the little vial out of his pocket carefully, so as not to lose any of its precious contents in the sand, and dry- swallowed two more pills. One more quick glance up at the Parapet reassured him that the man in the top hat was finally gone for good.

# 4

It was evident to Danny and Gordon that all eyes were riveted on them as they walked through the huge faux stone archway and up the ramp toward the Dressing Room as Sandy had instructed them to do. The conversations around them began to wane as the monsters collectively observed the strangers' arrival. It was like a sea of greedy black eyes, taking them in. A hushed ripple of movement coursed through the group of monsters like the schoolyard birds in the Alfred Hitchcock film they all loved so well.

Inside the Dressing Room, Sandy was busy stuffing a tangle of laundry into the ancient washing machine at the corner of the room. Her two friends entered without fanfare. Safely unnoticed, Danny gave her a quick whack on the backside. This startled her properly and she wheeled around to face him. The look on her face was not one of amusement. Realizing it was Danny, she threw her arms around his waiting neck and hugged him tightly. Danny took in the earthy scent of her curly hair, which seemed to engulf him as they hugged.

"Hi, Boss Lady." Danny's voice came through her hair, muffled and cheerful.

Sandy took a step back to look at him, "*Boss Lady*, huh? I like that. Does this mean that you guys are taking the job?"

The two feigned indecision for a moment, then Gordon finally replied, "Yeah We'll take it. There really wasn't anything scarier in there than we've come across in the bars we've played at all these years."

Sandy's look of complete joy was undeniable, "Great! C'mon, I'll introduce you to some of the others." She swung around, her long curls bouncing from side to side, just brushing Danny's chin as she passed. A wonderful patchouli scent always seemed to surround her, like a beacon from years past. The scent reminded Danny briefly of the times he'd kissed her. The patchouli lit the spark again properly. It was downright Pavlovian, and Danny fully realized its effect.

He wanted to kiss her right now. Pushing the urge away, he heard himself blurting out suddenly, "Uh, maybe you can start by introducing me to that cute blonde we saw at the Sand Bar last night." With this, the spell that the patchouli had woven was broken.

Sandy gave him a compulsory frown, then walked over to the piece of paper that was tacked to the central post of the Dressing Room. She ran her finger quickly down the center column, searching through the list of names that were written beside each character.

"Okay. The girl you're looking for is Mia." Obviously, Sandy knew exactly who Danny meant. His interest at the bar had not been lost on anyone. "She's in the Swamp. It says here that she's playing the Rippee today."

There was a short pause, then Gordon went for the obvious question, "What's a Rippee?"

"Simple. The guy who cuts the girl's head off in the scene is the Ripper. As in Jack. And the girl who gets her head cut off…". Her voice trailed off just long enough for them to fill in the blank.

"…Is the *Rippee*!" Danny and Gordon obediently answered in unison.

"Exactly. You catch on quickly."

"Hell, yes. We'll be promoted to Swamp Creatures before you know it," Danny added. To this, Sandy just gave him a sidelong glance as she passed by, noting, "There's no such thing as a Swamp Creature."

She stopped at the little intercom that was mounted on the wall between the door and the long rack of costumes to the right. Both Danny and Gordon recognized the little box from its twin, which they had seen in the Cashier's cage.

"Let me call your Rippee down for her break, that way you can at least meet her. I mean, since you'll be cutting her head off the rest of the night."

"Thanks," Danny said. His heart leapt, and he worked to keep it from showing on his face.

"Then we'll go outside and meet some of the others."

She pressed the intercom's orange button, speaking gently into it in a somewhat more official tone, "Code eight, Butler."

"What's a 'code eight'?" Gordon whispered as her eyes scanned from his to Danny's, while she awaited the Butler's reply.

"That's the 'call back' code. We have different codes for whatever situations might pop up inside. That way we don't have to spend a lot of time explaining ourselves when we call the actors. She paused again, then added, "Or if they have to call us with any kind of emergency."

"Emergency? What do you mean by emergency?"

"Oh, things like security problems, customers getting too familiar or starting fights, somebody getting sick, broken props...". She looked at Gordon for a reaction, and when none came, she continued, "Sometimes a customer will be too scared to continue."

Danny laughed, "You mean a little kid, right?"

"Not necessarily. You'd be surprised. We've had to call a NO SCARE for a lot of adults. Some of them grown men."

Just then a loud voice with a noticeably false British accent came through the little speaker, interrupting her in mid- sentence. The accent was pretentiously elegant and proper. Odd in any setting, but ridiculous in this one.

"Barry, is that you?" Sandy asked.

Barry was part of the little clique of Castle Elite; veterans who had earned their right to act in the most outlandish ways inside the Castle. Although comedy was frowned upon by the management, this little group of friends did their best to make every shift and every scene fun. They did it mostly to amuse themselves, and always to amuse their fellow monsters. Most were students (some were even roommates) from the local college. They all possessed a certain type of wit that was far ahead of their years.

Danny and Gordon smiled and listened as the conversation continued, "Okay. Will you do me a favor, Barry?"

Suddenly the voice in the little box made a drastic change to garden variety South Jerseyan. The stuffy British persona was gone entirely, "Sure. What d'you need, Sandy?"

"Could you run over to the Ripper scene and tell Mia that I'm sending, umm…" She looked around the Dressing Room, her eyes scanning every inch carefully for unsuspecting prey. Finally, she spotted two girls chatting in the corner, behind the open curtain to the Changing Area. "…*Liz* up to break her now."

Barry replied quickly that he would, as Liz quite obviously displayed her displeasure with the role assignment.

Sandy turned back to Danny and Gordon cheerily, "Okay, ready? Let's go."

They followed her obediently outside, through the Dressing Room's open door and into the violent midday sun. Its brightness was a shocking white compared with the cool dimness of the Dressing Room. They found themselves surrounded by the same group of suspicious eyes that had greeted them on their way in. This time the eyes only briefly glanced up at them, noting that they were in the company of Sandy.

Sandy swept the area with her gestures while she spoke, and Danny noticed that she still possessed the ability to move like the dancer she had been in college.

"Okay, this is what we call the Actors' Area. Whenever you're in costume and makeup you *cannot* leave this area. You'll take all your ten-minute breaks out here. And if you're going out for your one-hour dinner break…by 'out' I mean anywhere beyond that gate…", she pointed at the ramp they had walked up earlier, "you *must* remove your makeup and change your clothes. You're only a monster here, in this area, or inside the Castle. No show-boating on the pier, either."

They walked over to the row of picnic tables that lined the Castle's southern face. Seated at the table closest to the Dressing Room door was an athletic-looking young man with unruly black hair and a likable grin. He looked up at Sandy and her entourage as they approached. This was Little Mack. He knew Sandy's "New Monster Tour" speech by heart, enjoying every overstated, self-important word of it. He leaned back against the false stone facade of the Castle's base and continued to smile broadly.

"Mack, I'd like you to meet two of my oldest friends and our newest cast members. This is Danny…And this is Gordon."

Little Mack stood and reached his hand out to shake Danny's. With this, Sandy added, "Little Mack is my assistant at the Makeup Table and in the Dressing Room."

"She'll never admit it, but I run *rings* around her when it comes to makeup." Mack looked at Sandy. He bore the grin of a devilish imp, unsure of what mischief he would get into next. "Right, mom?" he added.

Sandy drew a surprised breath, "Mom? Watch it, Buddy!" She laughed to herself mostly, because Mack truly *looked* like he could be her son, despite their scant ten-year difference in age. He was short for his nineteen years, and his thick black mass of hair added to his childlike air.

Little Mack turned to Danny and Gordon in a more reserved and serious tone, "It's nice to meet you guys."

"It's nice to meet you too. *Little Mack*, is it?" Gordon asked, as if on cue, "That's an odd nickname. Where did it come from, McDonald's?"

Little Mack's smile was automatic. He obediently answered the question that he had obviously endured a million times before.

"Actually, there was another guy on the pier named Mack, if you can believe it. It's not exactly a common name. And, yes, that *is* my real name. It wasn't odd enough that two of us with that weird name found ourselves working in the same place, but what was even more odd was the fact that people started to mix us up. Especially since the other Mack was six-foot-five. Basketball player material. As for myself…well…"

He paused, holding his arms out to afford them a better look at his five-foot-eight form, "As you can see…not so much. Anyway, we just made things easier on ourselves by taking the nicknames Big Mack and Little Mack. Big Mack left a few days ago. I guess his season was over."

"Yeah, too bad he never said goodbye. Never even let us know he was leaving. One day he was just gone. That wasn't cool," Sandy said, wrinkling her nose to emphasize her distaste.

"And even though Big Mack is gone for the year, I'm noticing that everyone is still referring to me as 'Little' Mack. I guess I'm stuck with it for good now."

Overhearing their conversation, the bearded fellow seated across the picnic table looked up from his clipboard, which he had been studying. A jumble of coffee-stained papers rustled beneath its rusty clip.

"Don't listen to any of that crap, guys. He got the nickname Little Mack 'cause that's the size of his pecker. *Little*."

Everyone laughed at this, including Little Mack. He walked around the table and sat beside the man, still smiling broadly. Draping one arm across his shoulders, he pulled him close. The man winced at the closeness. "Oh, Richard," Little Mack whispered jokingly, "You promised not to kiss and tell…"

Richard managed little more than a smirk. His rugged-looking face, with its piercing deep-set eyes, all but cancelled out any trace of amusement in his expression. He was wearing a beat-up baseball cap and a weathered Castle logo tee. As he looked down at the scribbled notes on his clipboard his shadow fell across the words. Richard was the consummate veteran ghoul here. His presence had graced the hallowed halls of the Castle every summer since the amusement pier had opened several years earlier. He had at one time been its premier actor, assuming roles from Dracula to the Wolf Man, to Renfeld the Butler. He had played every role with great enthusiasm. Richard had even been responsible for creating many of the stock speeches that the characters still used. Although he was several years older than most of the other actors even from the start, Richard was embraced as a true professional.

Of late, though, he had hung up his Dracula cape in exchange for the clipboard and overloaded keyring of the Castle Manager. He was the liaison between the cast and Harry, the Castle's owner, who observed Richard's competency through his many random toadies, which he dispensed to the pier daily. Lately, though, the responsibilities of management had begun to wear thin with Richard. He was caught in a frustrating place between the excitement he had once felt inside the Castle, and his disdain for being watched by Harry, who often recited his minions' reports to Richard by phone, from his ivory tower in North Jersey.

Sandy made the necessary introduction to Richard, careful to emphasize his position of authority as Manager to Danny and Gordon. Richard extended his hand to them in an awkwardly formal greeting. "How ya doin'." Not a question, just a greeting. "Sandy told me she had a couple of friends who'd be joining the cast. Just remember not to use the end of the season as an excuse to act too wild in there. It's easy to get carried away at first. Scare 'em. Have fun, but keep it calm. Don't touch any of the customers and don't screw up any props or walls." The speech had a well-rehearsed quality to it.

Sandy laughed, "Yeah, nice to meet you too, Rich!"

Richard's face did something briefly that could almost be interpreted as a smile. Very briefly. Then, he turned his attention back down to his clipboard. The brim of his baseball cap shut out the others and plunged him back into the world of his scribbled pages.

Sandy led Danny and Gordon over to the pier railing. Danny's gaze followed her hand as she pointed to a group of actors who were seated at one of the more distant picnic tables. "The three guys sitting over there are Greg, David, and George. They're some of our most creative actors. Fun to work with." She paused for a second, "When they aren't here, they do drag shows in Atlantic City." Now she called over to the trio, "Greg, guys, these are my friends Gordon and Dan! They're just starting. I'm going to count on you to make them feel at home, okay?"

The three men turned and called back their hellos to Sandy and her friends. Each one of their faces boasted an extra bit of intricacy that the other monsters lacked. Obviously, the products of their own time spent lovingly applying the greasepaint, and not the result of the often-rushed application that might take place at the makeup table. These were true masterpieces.

They no doubt had a different exquisite ghoul reserved for each day of the week. Even their costumes looked fresher, better kept than those that hung inside the Dressing Room on the heavily- picked-over rack.

Danny's smile remained painted across his face. Sandy leaned toward him as she whispered, "You can stop staring now. They don't bite."

Danny seemed to regain his composure, looking a little offended that she would think he was anything less than comfortable.

"The one in the Riff-Raff costume from Rocky Horror Picture Show is Donald. Nice guy, but don't expect him to break character when you talk to him." She leaned away a little and added in a whisper, "I think he really *thinks* he's Riff-Raff." They all laughed as quietly and unnoticeably as possible.

Now a young man in Dracula garb stepped briskly up to them. Both Danny and Gordon recognized him from his stint earlier in Dracula's Portrait. He had heard every word of their conversation and had watched as Sandy introduced his fellow actors to her friends, fully expecting to be included in her next introduction. When that did not seem to be forthcoming, he simply insinuated himself comfortably between Sandy and the two strangers. As he extended his hand toward them, his black fingernail polish glinted in the bright beach sun. The attention he had clearly paid to this disturbing detail was not lost on Dan and Gordon. They shot a fast glance at one another as the new stranger spoke.

"Bobby B here. Nice to have you gentlemen with us. My friends just call me Bob. Or Prince of Darkness…heh, heh. Whatever you're most comfortable with."

Danny could not hold in a snort as he thought to himself "Bob, the Prince of Darkness."

Little Mack sat quietly behind his copy of *Fangoria* magazine, listening to the exchange. He lowered it slightly, exposing his laughing eyes, and called over to them, "His *friends* call him Bob? *What* friends?!"

It was all very good-natured, but a certain dislike for his coworker lurked below the surface of Little Mack's barbs. This dislike, however, was not true for the rest of the cast. Most of them found Bobby's arrogant nature quite charming. He often had groups of the younger girls amassed around him outside the Dressing Room as he regaled them with his infinite wit and wisdom. His haughty attitude only served to reinforce his portrayal of Count Dracula. He strode home every night after his shift ended, to his well-appointed bungalow on the beach block not far from the pier. Bobby's unapologetic wealth when compared with the spartan lifestyle of the other Castle members was a gift from his affluent parents. He gloated at his own talent and flawless portrayal of the Count. Bobby B's house was undoubtedly decorated with an abundance of mirrors.

Gordon exchanged a handshake with Bobby, "Nice to meet you, Bob. I see you're playing Dracula today."

Bobby recited his reply with a grand theatricality that the moment absolutely did not call for, "Today and every day. I *am* the Prince of Darkness here! Others may play the role, but only I am the true embodiment of the Prince. You might say that I've found my niche at the Castle."

This was a comment that was not without humor given the fact that the Prince of Darkness spent most of his day sitting in the dark little 'niche' in the wall above the mantel. It was slightly less glamorous than the grandiose declaration implied.

"Yeah. Be careful guys, the fangs are real." It was Little Mack again. Bobby turned quickly to shoot him a look of disgust, calling over to him, "What are *you* supposed to be, the comic  relief? Don't you have a load of laundry to put in or something?" A slight wind seemed to sense the lapse in conversation, rustling the folds of his massive black satin cape and making the starched collar quiver around his jaw. Now his already-forced tone fairly reeked of insincerity, "It's been a pleasure, gentlemen. I'll see you in the Portrait Room."

He offered Little Mack a final reprimanding glance, and turned sharply, snapping the edge of the cape loudly at him as he headed into the Dressing Room.

Mack produced a big wooden crucifix from inside the canvas bag of props beside him on the bench. He held it in the direction of the door that Bobby had just entered, a la Van Helsing. Everyone in the Break Area who had been watching the exchange enjoyed the laugh at Dracula's expense. Bobby's type was in no way alien to any of them. In fact, they had all run into more than a few Princes of Darkness in their lifetimes.

If it weren't for his staggering size and lumbering affectation, no one would have noticed the approach of Atwill Jarrett at all. His painful hike up the beach had drawn the stares of passersby and beachgoers alike. But once he had made his laborious way up the planking of the pier toward the Actors' Break Area, the sight of the towering figure became familiar, common-place. The actors had stopped paying attention to his daily arrival a few scant days into the season.

Here he was now. All incredible six-feet-seven-inches of him. He moved slowly, almost appearing to glide up the ramp toward the Dressing Room door. At times the remnant of shrapnel that was still lodged in his skull would touch the proper nerve, causing one corner of Jarrett's mouth to drop slightly lower than the other. This happened to be one of those times. His march continued silently past Danny and Gordon, offering them little more than a glance and the slightest nod of acknowledgment. They remained speechless as if waiting for Sandy to tell them that the serene giant was nothing more than a figment of their collective imaginations. Or, better yet, a ghostly apparition that had mistakenly found its way out of the Castle's dreary interior.

Finally, Sandy spoke, breaking the spell that had been so successfully cast upon them. "That's Jarrett. You guys can stop staring any time now…" she said, "He's a really nice guy. A little bit slow," her words trailed off, "and a little burned out. He sustained some pretty bad head injuries in Nam."

Little Mack's hushed voice floated between them from the picnic table, unsolicited, "Yeah. If you want any drugs, like the good stuff, Jarrett's the one to ask." He put one hand to the side of his mouth as if to conceal his words from any prying eyes, "He's got a bottomless bottle of pills."

Gordon leaned back, peeking through the open doorway into the Dressing Room. He spied Jarrett pulling on the tall Frankenstein boots that would add another four inches to his already-tremendous height. Jarrett looked up at the reflection in the mirror above the makeup table just in time to catch Gordon's eyes on him. In the split second before he looked away, Gordon caught a flash of friendliness as it crossed Jarrett's distorted features.

Suddenly the air was shattered by a loud blast of Spanish curse words outside the Dressing Room door. Standing a few yards away was a flamboyant redhead with a round face that was meticulously painted in garish makeup. She was dressed in a nun's habit. Not the modern skirted, comfortably veiled type that became commonplace in the Catholic Church in the late 1960s, but in the heavy full-length drape that had been the staple for centuries before. The veil included a tight square headpiece that evoked unmistakable austerity, with layers of black muslin that flowed beneath. A thick black inverted cross dangled over the vast white wimple on her chest. This was no common nun. She sported tinges of blood at the corners of her mouth, and her eyes glowed an unearthly green with the assistance of contact lenses. It was the character of a possessed nun. Her deep angry voice bellowed through the salt air as she argued with Richard, the bearded Castle Manager. The deepness of her voice matched her strange looks perfectly, adding a particular realism to the contrived possession of her nun character. It was obvious that Richard was not having an easy time holding his own with her. She had a clear advantage over him in both vocal volume and physical stature.

"I don't care, Juanita. If a customer files a complaint with the office upstairs, my hands are tied. They said that your costume is offensive. That means you change it. Period. I get it, you spent a lot of time on it. I can see that. But we're not in the business of making personal statements, and this isn't Broadway! Lose the cross. In fact, lose the whole nun get-up! I didn't approve of the damn thing in the first place! Who gave you the authority to dress that way?"

"I gabe myself de authority, det's who!" The strange deepness of Juanita's voice was not its most notable quality. It was the thick Spanish accent, the butchering of every syllable, that stood out most. The complete ease with which she assaulted every word was downright artistic. It was her own backyard version of Esperanto.

"How was I supposed to know dat sawm fawking

scawmbag would take dees sheet seriously!? Let alone go and complain abow my costume!" She glared at Richard, as though he had been part of the plot to defrock her.

When it came to dealing with Juanita, Richard had always had very little patience. They might as well have come from two different planets. She had arrived with the glittering wave of actors who peopled the drag shows, with an instant affinity for overemphasizing the importance of her role at the Castle.

Richard's scruffy beard, paired with the beat-up Phillies cap he rarely removed from his unkempt hair made him look more like a trucker than a thespian. He had known more than his share of theater practice and its people. He knew the rules, and Juanita clearly had broken them. He wanted this ridiculous confrontation to end as soon as possible. That was obvious. His body language fairly screamed it.

"I really don't need this shit right now, so why don't you just change the costume and get back on the floor? Okay? Your scene has been unmanned since you left it fifteen minutes ago! People are paying to see a show, not to walk through some dark hallway with nothing in it."

Juanita was not accustomed to having her creativity squelched. She had flourished as a headliner on the stage of one of Atlantic City's better drag shows since 1978. The club owner never minded the complete outrageousness of her costume choices. In fact, he had welcomed them. And Juanita did not disappoint. Her characters were the biggest draw for the show. Their ever-changing nature made her a hit, and eventually drag show royalty.

And yet here, at the Castle, at this place where she and a handful of her fellow drag performers took a brief summer stint, she always seemed to run into complaints. This was just a job she had taken for *fun*. Not important, really. But the ultra- conservative patrons complained about Juanita on a regular basis. The outrageousness of her attire was not acceptable to the boring rabble that peopled the lines awaiting entrance in the Castle Lobby. These were families, with plenty of grandmas and little kids who needed protection from the likes of Juanita.

Whenever one of these frequent complaints arose, Juanita would vociferously threaten to "queet". Yet she always seemed to find her way back, sometimes within mere hours. It was due to her great fear of missing out on something. Anything. Juanita was drawn to even the dimmest of spotlights.

She pivoted sharply on one heel of her black lace-up shoes and headed into the Dressing Room. Her voice left its guttural trail of mangled words behind her as she strode away. "Dat jawst feegures, don't it? De meenit sawmbawdy ees a leedle createev een dees place, dey get fawked!"

Danny and Gordon watched all of this, transfixed. Their eyes shot to Sandy, then back again. Gordon finally asked, "What the hell was *that?*"

Sandy smiled, "That's Juanita," she replied coolly.

"When she first came to work here, she used to be Juan." She didn't make any pretense of lowering the volume of her voice. What she was saying was certainly no secret to anyone at the Castle. Juanita herself would gladly apprise anyone who asked about her new gender status.

"She can be a little pushy."

Sandy continued, this time careful to lower the volume of her voice so that no one could hear, "Be careful of her. She likes to start fights." She peeked through the Dressing Room door as she added, "I just think it's her way of flirting with you. You can expect her to cozy up to the two of you as soon as she notices you're here. She'll size you up to see if you're her type."

"I think we can take care of ourselves," Danny replied with just a little too much confidence.

Sandy added, "Anyway, Juanita's not a big threat once she gets used to you. Just don't get too chummy. She's not one of Richard's favorites."

As she introduced them to some other members of the cast, Sandy's thoughts returned again and again to Juanita. While she had no real reason to dislike her, she felt a kind of dull tension whenever she was in her presence. She found herself judging Juanita's costume choices, and even criticizing the makeup that Juanita insisted on applying herself. Sandy secretly took a certain enjoyment in watching her storm off when she didn't get her way. She wondered if she felt this way because there could only be one "Queen" in the Dressing Room. And that was Sandy.

Now Mia appeared from inside the Dressing Room. Her eyes scanned the Actors' Area and finally came to rest on Danny's face. It was obvious that she recognized him from the Sand Bar the night before. As she took a pack of cigarettes from her oversized purse and sat at a nearby table, Danny's attention was riveted on her. It was as though a high-powered magnet in his head would not allow his gaze to be drawn anywhere else.

Mia dabbed at the pasty whitish-green makeup that covered her face. Even with its unnatural glow and thick consistency, it could not mask her undeniable beauty beneath. Danny's interest from the night before was rekindled instantly.

Now he spoke, almost robotically, "Hey, Sand, there she is," adding a weird gesture toward the girl with his chin, as if this odd movement would be less conspicuous than simply pointing.

"Introduce me."

"No way, Casanova. Introduce yourself," Sandy said curtly, unable to hide her mild irritation. "Gordon and I are going to go inside to find him a costume. Don't hang around out here too long; you guys are already late for your shift as it is!"

She scooped up Gordon's hand emphatically and headed toward the Dressing Room. Gordon purposely allowed the slack of his arm to snap taut, performing an exaggerated tripping movement as she yanked him to her side. He sidled up to her, rolling his eyes and smiling sheepishly at Danny. Danny just smiled back at his idiot friend, as he watched them go, frowning through his amusement.

He looked back at Mia, seated at the table with her cigarette poised between her index and middle fingers. Thinking to himself "Here goes nothin'", he headed toward the table gingerly.

Mia took a dainty sip of her Dr. Pepper, then fumbled with a plain white book of matches. She looked up at Danny, drawing closer as she tried to light her cigarette in the whipping winds of the ocean breeze. She struck several matches with the same sad result. Each time they appeared to extinguish themselves as if for spite.

The cigarette. This would be Danny's icebreaker, he thought. A chance to rescue a damsel in distress. A call to chivalry.

Danny reached out his hand, "Here, let me help you with that." He took the cigarette from her hand as if he were the most seasoned of smokers. Holding the end tight in his pursed lips, he set about the task of lighting it for her. Ultimately, he would prove to have more trouble than Mia had had, practically using up every match in the little book.

After a few more fruitless attempts, Danny's eyes caught sight of Mia's hand covering his own, pulling it gently toward her. She practically cupped her hand around the tiny flicker of the match, thus preventing the wind from extinguishing the flame again. Lifting the light to the tip of the cigarette she held between her teeth, the tobacco caught hold and began to glow a bright orange. Success. Danny watched her face as it was illuminated briefly by the little flame, then as it moved up and away from his hand. Everything seemed to move in slow motion for him. It suddenly sped up, bouncing him back into the reality of the moment as the flame reached the bottom of the match and began to burn his fingertips. He released his grip with a yelp, and the match extinguished itself in the wind as it dropped down through a gap in the boards at their feet. Chivalry was *not* dead, as it turned out, only wounded.

Mia looked up at Danny, who instinctively sucked on his burnt finger. He stopped abruptly and stared back at her. The clear blue of her eyes was nothing short of devastating.

"Thanks," she was saying, "Do you work here too, or do you just have a thing for monsters?"

"Actually, both." Danny said, "I'm just starting here today, and I like what I've seen of the monsters so far."

It was then that Danny's comment reached the ears of Greg, one of the drag show performers Sandy had pointed out. He leaned uncomfortably close to Danny's face as he and his friends walked past, and whispered, "The feeling is mutual, I'm sure." Danny looked up quickly to meet Greg's smiling face, stunned, as the three men disappeared into the Dressing Room.

He glanced back at Mia now, the air of his previous confidence leaking from every pore, like a pierced balloon. Any bravado that he had managed to muster was now trampled soundly. Yet Mia remained nonplussed. If only Danny had realized that his goddess was beyond the art of blushing.

She extended her manicured hand to Danny, completely ignoring Greg's remark. She didn't like Greg anyway.

"My name is Mia."

"I know. I mean, I'm Dan. Nice to meet you, Mia."

She now puffed on the last of her cigarette. There was a pause that was palpable. "So why are you joining this nut house so late in the season? I mean, all the good summer crowds are practically gone. God knows that the rest of us have had about all we can stand of this place."

He wanted to blurt out that *she* was the reason that he had taken the job but then thought better of it. After all, when it came to matters of the heart, Danny was an expert. Not in a good way. He was an expert at being 'shot down'. He'd been snubbed by lesser women than this.

"Oh, uh, Sandy. We've been friends for a long time, and she told me she was shorthanded with all the college crowd leaving early. She thought I might want to kill some time here until I find another j—," he bit down hard on the word, squelching it long enough to shift gears, "...another music gig."

"Music gig? You're a musician?"

"Yeah, I am," Danny said, feigning modesty. He was hoping that she wouldn't ask too many questions regarding his less- than-illustrious musical career. He looked down at his hands, absently twisting the spider ring he still wore from the final performance of the

*Festering Wounds.*

"Wow, I'm impressed," Mia was now saying, "I love musicians. What instrument do you play?" The word 'impressed' mingled with the word 'love' and hovered briefly in front of his lovestruck eyes for a few seconds, then dissipated.

"I play guitar," he replied. "A little. Badly." Ugh, shut up, Danny, shut up, his inside voice pleaded. He watched the smile begin to flicker on her lips, but managed to make a quick recovery, "But mostly I sing. I'm the lead singer."

Did that sound impressive? Danny wasn't quite sure. She looked so young to him now, sitting there wearing the glow makeup, unwrapping her umpteenth piece of chewing gum to mask the smell of the cigarettes. Yet she behaved in a very worldly-wise manner. Danny was unable to distinguish which of these qualities attracted him to her more.

"What's the name of your band? Do you play around here? Maybe I've heard of you."

"Oh, we're kind of in a transitional period right now. Working on a new name. You probably wouldn't have heard of us anyway. We've been working outside of this area for a while. California, actually." Not a total lie. He'd been to California once. That line always worked. It was clean, it was succinct, and most importantly it was untraceable.

"Oh. Well, what kind of music do you play?"

That was a good question. What kind of music, indeed. What was it this week? Or last?

"We're trying out some reggae stuff," he paused, "What do you think of the name *Danny and the Dreads*?"

Oh my God. He paused now with the utter inanity of the name ringing sourly in his ears, adding quickly, "I didn't come up with the name myself. One of the other guys in the band did. It was kind of a joke at first, then it started to stick." He laughed uncomfortably, "I don't know."

Danny had to turn away to keep from laughing out loud. It didn't matter to Mia, though. She stared back at him blankly, choosing to skip over his story completely, "Oh, you're right. I *haven't* heard of you."

Danny quickly changed the subject, "How long a break do you get," he asked now, "I mean do *we* get?"

"We just get ten minutes. Then Richard starts to give you the hairy eyeball." She paused. "Now that you mention it, I'd better get back up there." She inspected the long smear of glow makeup that wound its way up the length of her sleeve, "I really hate playing the Rippee, but I always seem to get stuck in that scene because I can scream so loud."

Danny heard himself ask the obvious, "...*Can* you scream loudly?"

Before he had time to brace himself, Mia unleashed a blood- curdling scream. Its volume nearly knocked Danny over. This girl could scream with the best of Hollywood's horror heroines; Janet Leigh had nothing on her. Momentarily stunned, Danny stared wide-eyed at the diminutive girl by his side. She smiled back proudly as she popped yet another stick of gum into her mouth.

"Yup, you're right. You *can* scream loud. I bet that's a real plus when your head's being cut off."

"Yeah, but it's sort of a curse. I get stuck wearing this glow-in-the-dark itchy shit for double shifts at a time. Plus, I've come down with Castle Throat twice this season already."

*"Castle Throat?"*

"That's what they call the laryngitis that goes along with all the screaming. You get it most often at the beginning of the summer. Before you learn to regulate your voice so that your throat isn't raw every day. It plays havoc with the vocal cords."

Danny and Mia hadn't noticed the tall figure, clad in a Gorilla suit, who had emerged from the Dressing Room and was standing silently beside them. His presence gradually eased its way into their consciousness, and as they looked up simultaneously at the grimacing mask, Gordon's muffled voice made a welcome appearance.

"I had a feeling she wouldn't be crazy about you, Dan, but I never imagined that your ugly face would make her *scream.*"

Their eyes remained fixed on the mask. A lit cigarette stood poised between the Gorilla's thick plastic teeth, placed there carefully for the maximum comic effect, no doubt. Gordon gingerly lifted off the mask and the cigarette never wavered, its smoke winding oddly out one of the mask's eye slits. They all began to laugh. Gordon had a very natural way of being funny. It was effortless and genuine. His quick wit had stolen more than one new girlfriend away from Danny in the past.

# 5

Juanita derived great pleasure from playing the role of the Rat Professor. It was the one role in the Castle that seemed to bring out the best assets of both genders. The role had traditionally been that of a male, but she creatively twisted and morphed the character to accommodate a touch of the feminine. No one else in the cast of the Castle could claim to play the part of the gay male better than Juanita. It was a role she had played in real life for some thirty-two years.

She was still disgruntled with having been forced to change out of her Nun costume because some old bitch had complained to the management. She had been proud of the attention to detail that she had given the nun's habit, considering it one of her best creations to date. It even rivaled her recent Nazi Dominatrix outfit, which had so reviled one customer that he had threatened to sue the Castle for emotional assault. She just grumbled quietly as she concentrated on the task at hand. She knew that there were plenty more brilliant ideas where those two had come from.

The few battered props that were normally stashed inside the podium in the Rat Professor's Area were conspicuously missing now. She checked the top and bottom shelves, but nothing was there. She looked anxiously around the dark alcove, hoping to find something to accentuate her carefully practiced speech. A pointer, or even a rubber rat. Anything.

She felt a growing anger. For all Juanita knew, someone had thrown the props over the jagged wall of the Parapet to the beach below. Or, in an equally stupid move, had brought them down to the Dressing Room with them when their shift had ended. She recognized the revulsion she always felt in the face of complete incompetence.

There was only one place left to check. She tried unsuccessfully to squeeze behind the corpulent wax figure seated in the little alcove to the left of the podium. It was the infamous likeness of Harry, the Castle's owner. Today it had managed to find its way to the Rat Professor's Area, serenely watching over Juanita and those who would be her reluctant guests. Even Harry chose to judge her performance.

In the semi-darkness behind Harry, Juanita could make out the neatly-stacked little pile of props. She breathed a sigh of relief as she reached into the darkness of the alcove. The first prop that she was able to grab and drag toward herself was the thick copy of *Gray's Anatomy* that would customarily grace the top of the podium for all to see. A testament to the validity of the Rat Professor's academic credentials, evoking a sense of the great knowledge that the Rat Professor undoubtedly possessed. Next, she grabbed the makeshift pointer that she liked to use in the scene to highlight the key areas of the massive diagram painted on the wall behind the podium, labeled *The Anatomical Parts of the Rat: Genus Rattus*. Finally, her hand fell upon the Rat Professor's square spectacles. "Ah," she whispered, "*there* they are."

She pulled each prop out of the darkness toward her, quickly, as though there might be something terrible lurking beside them, waiting to grab her unknowing fingers. She squinted into the alcove again. There *was* something else lying inside. She could see its shadowy form. Juanita paused to remember what other props from the scene might be missing. She couldn't recall but knew that she would not rest until that item, too, had been retrieved.

Hiking up one sleeve, and leaning against Harry's bulky form, she balanced herself on his shoulder to lengthen her arm's reach. Her hand stiffened, grabbing at the item within. Suddenly she felt a horrible sensation and retracted her hand abruptly. A wet, sticky mass clung to her fingertips. Holding her hand into the daylight, Juanita could see that it was covered in a gooey brownish-red substance. The substance had the strange rusty tint that stage blood was never quite able to duplicate. Her stomach leapt. Her head swam with the horrid sight, as it mingled with the putrid air of the Rat Professor's Area. Juanita scrambled blindly toward the bright daylight from the open doorway. She halted just short of the light, grabbing wildly for the intercom on the wall behind the podium. She pressed the little button repeatedly with her clean hand, holding the red fingers as far away from her face as her arm would allow as she screamed into the intercom in Spanish- studded bursts.

Down in the Dressing Room everyone looked up from their various tasks, shooting questioning looks toward Sandy as the strange sounds exploded from the intercom. Juanita's guttural rantings were punctuated with breathy shrieks, making the entire scenario both frightening and comical at the same time. Jules looked up from his battered copy of *Famous Monsters of Filmland* magazine, "What the hell *is* that?"

For a moment Sandy dismissed it as another one of the cast's pranks. One of the hundred jokes that she endured throughout the course of the season. She remained her usual calm self, working diligently at teasing a zombie's hair.

"It sounds like the usual suspects are messing with the intercom. Jules, hold that button for me, will you? I've got a handful of styling gel here."

Jules walked over to the intercom, convinced that this was just another joke as well. He pressed the little button, and Sandy spoke loudly across the room to it from her post at the makeup table.

"Barry? Is that you?" She waited for the inevitable laughter to emanate from the little squawk box. Nothing came.

"Hey! Rollie? If this is your idea of a joke, it's not funny. Now stop screwing around and get back to work! Don't make me come up there!"

She looked at Jules, indicating that he could release the intercom's little square button. "Those guys never get tired of getting fired."

No sooner had she said this when the intercom screamed out to them again, even louder than before. This time they all could recognize the unmistakable Spanish accent. It came through more clearly, with a deafening accompaniment of static, "Thees ees Juanita!" She growled the J sound, pronouncing it with the crispness that its Latino roots demanded.

*"Send sawmbawdy up to de Ret Professor Area right away!!"*

Jules was out the door first, grabbing the enormous black flashlight that he reserved for run-ins with visiting troublemakers and had nicknamed *The Peacemaker*. The flashlight sat poised on the shelves closest to the door that led into the Castle. It was strictly off-limits to anyone except Jules and Richard.

Little Mack followed closely behind Jules, always at the ready for action. There was nothing that these two friends liked better than a good fight with rowdy Castle patrons, often members of motorcycle gangs that ventured down the Jersey coast from New York. As they disappeared through the squealing door, Sandy called after Mack, "Hey! She only needs *one* of you guys to help her! Mack, get back here and finish Jarrett's makeup!" The sounds of the Castle's various soundtracks seeping into the Dressing Room from the crack beneath the door as it closed behind them were her only reply. Mack was long gone, taking the spiral stairs of the Belltower two and three at a time toward the top.

Sandy turned her gaze away from the door, looking forlornly at Jarrett's intricate Frankenstein Monster makeup, and at the single remaining neck bolt lying on the makeup table. Jarrett stared back at her in an unintentionally comical way, his looks made even more ridiculous by the unglued corner of his square rubber cap, which flapped with the slightest movement of his head. The lone bolt that protruded from one side of his neck fairly cried out for its companion on the table. Sandy shook her head as she walked toward the incomplete monster. She set to work silently on righting his makeup's many wrongs.

When Jules and Little Mack reached the Rat Professor's Area, they were both breathless. They had spanned the Castle's four hundred-odd stairs in record time, racing against each other at many points. Now they looked around the little space for signs of Juanita. Finally, they spotted her, huddled in a crumpled pile at the foot of the podium. She sat cross-legged, wiping her tainted hand vigorously on the dirty carpet.

Jules' eyes scoured the area for the offending group of customers that surely must still be lurking nearby. He was anxious to find the trouble that he had raced to break up. His gaze trailed out to the Parapet. Had they fled into the Rat Room? Where were they? His heart sank with the realization that there would be no fight. Not here. Not today. He looked questioningly at Juanita, who sat in a near-catatonic state on the floor. Little Mack's eyes darted from Jules to Juanita. His look of anticipation melted as well. They both circled the little area restlessly, stepping out into the sunlight of the Parapet more than once.

Finally, Little Mack found the words, *"Well...?"* He gestured with his own smaller version of *The Peacemaker*, "Where's the trouble, Juanita? You called like you were being murdered up here!"

Juanita stared back at him, incredulous, "I deed have sawm trawble! Look et my hend!" She held her large, meticulously manicured fingers closer to their faces. The rusty stains that were fresh blood minutes before had become streaky lines that could have been almost anything. Juanita waited, expecting the horror of the sight to wash over Jules and Mack with the same impact it had had on her. They just stood staring in silence, glancing blankly at one another, then back at her hand, trying to put together the pieces of the nonexistent puzzle.

"What did you do? Cut yourself?" Jules finally asked.

Juanita could feel her anger inch up a notch, *"No!!* I just stuck my hand een dat freegin' hole een de wall because sawm asshole heed de props on me!" Jules and Mack stared at her as they navigated through each unintelligible syllable she uttered. "And *DEES,"* she waved the rust-colored digits in the air before them, *"DEES* ees what I got back!"

Jules looked questioningly at Mack, "Stage blood?"

"Nah. Looks too brown for stage blood. That shit's made to stay red for a long time."

"Well, then," Jules began to move toward the alcove,

stepping past Juanita while giving her still-extended hand a wide berth. "...Then let's have a look *'Een de freegin' hole...'*"

Juanita did not appreciate his mocking her thick accent. She scowled as he looked back at her, "Where was it, exactly?"

She pointed in the general direction of the alcove, past the wax figure of Harry, now tipped to one side by her hasty retreat. Jules unhooked *The Peacemaker* from the D-ring on the back of his belt. He held the flashlight tight against his stomach and clicked it on. The bright beam of light pierced the blackness of the little alcove and came to rest, as if by instinct, on exactly the right spot.

All three saw the startling sight at the same moment: the ghastly eviscerated body of an all-too-real rat. It was huge in size, pinned to the plywood back wall of the alcove with an ancient wooden-handled ice pick. It hung there, glistening in the flashlight beam, creating a particularly haunting tableau beneath the words:

YOU'RE NEXT, FREAK

The words were scrawled on the wall in the rodent's own blood.

The dead silence held them for what seemed like a very long time. They took in every inch of the grisly scene with their wide eyes. Finally, Jules let out a barely audible "...Jesus Christ."

He snapped off the flashlight's beam abruptly. The negative of the rat and the words above it hung in the air of the alcove as their eyes struggled to readjust to the light. The grim scene would remain permanently etched in their minds, as it sat now just within the alcove, behind Harry and a thin veil of near darkness.

Little Mack turned to Juanita, unable to erase the stunned look on his face that had found what felt like a permanent home there. Juanita returned a look that was only slightly less shocked, but equally shaken. There had been absolutely no doubt from the first sight of the bloody message that it was intended for her.

This was not the first time she had been targeted because of her nonconformity.

"Juanita, I'm sorry…" Mack finally blurted out. Then added quickly, "Listen, don't let this shit upset you. This is just some asshole's idea of a joke."

Her eyes traveled slowly back to the dark alcove. It was obvious that they were beginning to fill with tears. "Thenk you, Leedle Meck," she said in a quiet tone that was disturbingly uncharacteristic of her. She moved slowly away from the podium toward the stairs, "I jawst want to go downstairs end wash my hends. Okay?"

Little Mack was caught off guard by her quiet strength. For the first time he felt something toward Juanita that he had never felt for her before. Something akin to admiration. "Oh. Uh, sure. Go ahead. I'll clean this up."

"Yeah, go ahead," Jules was saying, "We'll take care of this, and we'll cover the scene for you until you get back."

She started down the stairs and Mack called to her, "Tell Sandy to send up a Rat Ranger to work with you. You shouldn't have been scheduled up here alone in the first place."

"Thenk you." In another second she was gone, and Jules and Mack were left with the gory task and a heavy silence between them. Their eyes met several times as they set to work, but neither one could come up with a single word to say. They didn't have to say anything. The bloody writing on the wall inside the alcove had said it all.

# 6

Danny and Gordon had started their shift watching Bobby's practiced vampire technique in the Portrait Room. When Bobby finally made his resounding entrance onto the mantel, the crowd shrieked as if on cue. He had waited just past the moment when they began to relax the slightest bit, slamming his foot loudly against the marble slab as he jumped toward them from the Portrait frame. For all his arrogance and conceit, Danny had to admit that Bobby *did* make a fine Dracula. His intonation was impeccable, and his timing had been honed to razor-sharp precision. His jabs were keen and clever and quick. He was actually very talented. The unfortunate thing was that he knew this.

Danny was dressed for his stint as *Jack the Ripper*, with top hat and cape, just as any English gentleman in London of 1888 would be. He rehearsed the few lines that the character spoke over and over in his head as the crowd exited the Portrait Room into the Jester Scene.

He would move silently past the group and take his place in the Swamp, alongside Mia. They could practice the act briefly once or twice before this same group caught up with them at the Ripper Scene.

Gordon's role, however, was not so comfortable. Playing the Gorilla, he sweated the shift away in the heavy rubber full body suit that the role demanded. The suit itself was sickening by virtue of the number of sweaty bodies that had occupied it during the course of its lengthy life. The Castle only had two of these suits, so they were constantly in use. The inadequate practice of turning them inside out and spraying them heavily with Lysol at the end of the night did not help to make donning them any more appetizing. Gordon hadn't realized the weight of his decision when he had happily agreed to take on the role for the entire night. The only thing he remembered Sandy mentioning to him was that he would have no lines to memorize. Public speaking was yet another thing that Gordon was not fond of.

The entire premise of the Gorilla Scene was based upon the "creature" (as Gordon's partner for the evening, Shelby, repeatedly referred to him) being securely shackled to a brick wall. Shelby carried a whip and was quite provocatively dressed, to keep the attention of the less faint-of-heart gentlemen in the audience. Horror with a hint of porn.

Her speech was brief because she would almost immediately be interrupted by the monster breaking his shackles and running amok toward the crowd of spectators. If all went as planned, any Gorilla worth his weight in salt could drive a screaming group down the short hallway to the exit in mere seconds.

The premise was all good in theory. Unfortunately, the patrons weren't always willing to be scared by the hokey circumstances described in Shelby's speech. They knew from the daylight streaming in below the red exit sign just ahead this was the end of the line. In their minds, they were already outside.

Routinely, the poor Gorilla ended up growling, screaming and running himself into an exhausted heap to no avail. This had been the sad case for Gordon during the first three hours of his shift. But that was all about to change.

At about five o'clock a large group made up almost entirely of young women came cautiously down the Belltower stairs toward his scene. As Shelby dutifully began to deliver her speech, Gordon peered out through the sweaty eye slits of the Gorilla mask. His eyes passed back and forth over the faces in the group, to "size them up". He moved his head inside the rubber dome of the mask and cursed his limited field of vision under his breath. Finally, he was able to make out the many pretty faces watching Shelby as she spoke. Good crowd, he thought. Then, as if by magic, one girl's face emerged from the rest.

She was taller than the others, slim and pretty, but her most striking attribute was her air of confidence. Gordon instantly sensed her unattainability. If there was such a thing as being out of one's league, Gordon was about to test it. He knew that in mere moments this girl would walk down the hallway and out of his life. He would take his chances and leave his natural nervousness behind; the urgency resonated in his head with every peal of the blaring church bells that was the soundtrack of the Belltower above.

Gordon could hear Shelby reaching the part of her speech that described in excruciating detail the jungle expedition that had yielded the discovery of The Creature. The Missing Link. Gordon. *The Island of Dr. Moreau* had nothing on this jungle. Her words seemed to drag, and Gordon had grown intensely bored with the speech, having heard it repeated an infinitesimal number of times. He couldn't even bear to wait through the few lines that would lead up to his designated cue.

Instead, he broke the chains that held his wrists well before the moment that Shelby had so carefully planned. He could repress the urge to jump no more. And so, jump he did. More accurately, Gordon *flew* over the railing toward the group.

Just as would be expected, most of the tightly huddled group of girls screamed and scattered nicely. All of them found safe haven behind other customers, watching Gordon with huge, frightened eyes. All but one. Gordon's true intended target remained in place, watching silently as if waiting for something more. A playful smirk appeared and disappeared simultaneously on her perfect lips.

He lunged directly at her, coming dangerously close to knocking over several of the other customers. Then, suddenly and without warning, Gordon grabbed the girl. Actually *grabbed* her. Before he could stop himself, he was lifting her off her feet, scooping her up by the waist, facing him. Her smile turned to a wide-eyed look of disbelief as he carried her down the short hallway toward the exit, dodging the daylight and ducking behind a huge Styrofoam rock. The rest of the group, still shrieking and laughing at the girl's predicament, passed by the rock and through the exit, blissfully unaware of the dim alcove in which the couple now stood.

Breathless inside the Gorilla mask, Gordon smiled at his own brazen accomplishment as he watched the group disappear. Then his gaze turned back to the girl's face. He waited for the inevitable retribution that must be forthcoming. He studied her eyes. Nothing. No scream. No anger. Nothing. He leaned back against the faux stone wall and lifted off the heavy Gorilla mask. He was visibly winded and sweating. The girl stood watching silently, leaning against the same dark patch of wall. She didn't appear to be angry, or in a hurry to leave their dark hiding place. She took in Gordon's face, all at once, since it had been hidden by the mask until now.

Gordon was certain that the look of amusement on her face would melt into what would eventually become an impending lawsuit. It was *Rule Number One*: NEVER TOUCH THE CUSTOMERS. Sandy wasn't the only one who had warned him. Virtually everyone repeated the same line, verbatim. He was clearly in violation of *the* cardinal Castle rule. The *Big No-No*. Yet here he stood, staring at his catch while his breath finally began to arrive in less labored gasps.

Finally, she spoke, "What now, Tarzan?"

With the words came a cool sense of relief. No lawsuit. No problem.

"Actually, the name isn't Tarzan," he replied between breaths, "It's Gordon."

"That's a terrible name for a gorilla."

Unimpressed, if not unamused, the girl methodically dusted the streaks of Castle dirt from her beige linen shorts. She stole one last smiling glance and began to head toward the exit. The realization of what was happening suddenly became clear to Gordon. Their brief encounter was reaching its end, and he struggled to find words, desperately aware of his self-made opportunity slipping away.

"Wait!" He finally managed to blurt out, "Have dinner with me. I'm due for my break any minute now."

She turned to face him, "How do I know that you're not a maniac or something?" Her eyes scanned quickly up and down his sweaty face and dirty costume, "I mean, look at you. I don't know who you are or…*what* you are." She paused, hoping he would offer some sort of rebuttal, "It's not like we were formally introduced or anything. What was your name again? Gregory?"

"Gordon."

"Oh, right. As in Flash." She just stared at him now, silently.

Suddenly, Gordon's signature grin appeared across his makeup-smeared face. The black circles that Sandy had carefully drawn around his eyes where they met the black eyeholes of the mask now dripped down both his cheeks in an Alice Cooper-like manner. He took slow, small steps toward the girl. The slow carefulness of his approach made him seem even creepier, and Gordon realized this in midstep. He stopped, removing the glove from one hand and extending it for her to take. Her palm was cool and dry compared to his, and he gently led her back toward the Gorilla Scene. She was a perfect vision, and he was a ridiculous parody of a morphed jungle animal.

They stopped at the railing where Shelby was standing. She tapped the riding crop she had used in their scene to tame the beast against one post as they approached her tentatively. It was obvious that she was highly aggravated. The words that she had been rehearsing in her head for the past five minutes burst forth like water behind a crumbling dam. Gordon stood quietly and allowed the flood to wash over him. When her tirade seemed to reach its end, Gordon interrupted the finish of her sentence with a curt "Sorry."

The immediacy of his apology caught Shelby off guard. The anger drained from her face instantly, and she looked blankly back at him. Sorry. That was it. Surprisingly she felt suffciently appeased by his answer.

"Okay, then. Don't let it happen again."

Her eyes now darted from her recently tamed gorilla to his 'catch", who stood calmly beside him, just taking in all she could. Gordon gently pulled the girl closer to Shelby, as if presenting his prize.

"Shelby," he gestured as he spoke, "This is…uh, umm,

I'm sorry. I don't think you told me your name."

"Susan."

His eyes never left hers as he continued with the introduction, "Shelby, this is Susan. Susan this is Shelby."

The formality of the introduction was made even more comical by the wave of his giant gorilla hand glove. Susan looked at the floor to stifle a laugh as the two girls exchanged pleasant hellos.

Gordon heard himself speaking again, "Shelby, it was called to my attention several moments ago, behind yonder rock, that the fair Susan and I have not been properly introduced. Would you be so kind as to do us the honor…since you now know both of us fairly well?"

Shelby's smile broadened. She cleared her throat in an overly theatrical manner and assumed her best haughty affectation, "I would be happy to, sir."

She turned her gaze to Susan, "Susan, I'd like you to meet a very close personal friend of mine. We go back, oh, absolutely *hours*. He's a gentleman, a scholar, and one hell of a great guy." She paused, "This is Gordon."

Susan extended her hand and Gordon grasped it.

Pivoting curtly on one heel, Shelby now faced Gordon. "Gordon, I'd like to present my newest old friend, Susan." Gordon, still holding Susan's proffered hand, brought it to his lips and kissed it gently. His eyes remained caught by the green of her own.

Her task completed, Shelby now bowed to Gordon, genuflected to Susan, and wheeled crisply on the same heel before striding to the back of the scene. She laughed quietly at the ridiculous playlet that she had just taken part in.

Alone again, Gordon stood smiling at Susan.

"There. Now we've been properly introduced. I'm not a maniac or an axe-murderer, as my good friend *what's-*

*her-name* over there will attest. Now will you agree to have dinner with me?"

"Well, I guess that after all that I couldn't possibly refuse, could I?"

Gordon shook his head in a silent no. There was no shyness in the girl's voice, only an arrogant confidence that made Gordon's heart pound.

"Do you have to eat dinner here on the pier, or can we go somewhere?"

The question seemed completely foreign to Gordon's ears.

He thought for a moment.

"Oh, I think we're supposed to stay on the pier. Maybe we could meet at the pizza stand out front in about half an hour."

"The pizza stand, huh? You *are* a romantic fool, aren't you?"

Now Susan turned and headed for the light shining through the open exit.

Gordon called out, "Half an hour!"

She did not turn back to look at him. Instead, she waved her farewell with her back to him and Shelby. He watched her long legs carry her silently to and through the doorway, and her silhouette was finally swallowed up by the stream of daylight from the Lobby beyond.

Gordon slid down the wall to a sitting position in the darkness of the Gorilla Scene. He sat briefly, smiling, immersed in thoughts of the coming hour. He was snapped from his daydream by the sound of Shelby's laughter nearby.

"I've gotta hand it to you, Romeo, you're smooth," she said as she approached him from the darkness beneath the Belltower stairs. "Now all you have to do is figure out how  you're gonna keep that date. These people aren't too quick when it comes to handing out dinner breaks. They need somebody ready to go when it's time to fill your spot. Unless that person is already sitting at the makeup table this very minute, you're shit outta luck." Gordon's eyes widened a little. "And besides, you came on late. I'm not even sure that you *get* a break tonight."

He looked worried for a moment. Then something suddenly dawned on him.

He looked Shelby in the eye and wagged his finger at her as if to say "No". She watched his hulking ape silhouette hurry down the short hallway and out of sight as he ducked through the doorway to the Dressing Room. She could faintly hear his voice below the clamor of the Castle soundtracks and the chatter of the crowds in the arcades outside. He was calling for Sandy.

Shelby turned back toward the empty scene, muttering to herself, "Sandy. That figures. Fucking favoritism."

No sooner had she spoken the words, than the sound of another group could be heard making its way down the Belltower toward her. She prepared herself to man the scene alone, nestling into the shackles that had adorned the Gorilla's wrists not long before. She stood very still, waiting for the group to assemble before her as she silently eyed them with a maniacal look. When all stood staring curiously at her, waiting for the inevitable lunge, she obliged them. She screamed her most asylum-worthy scream and vaulted onto the railing that stood between the patrons and the Gorilla Scene. As if on cue, they shrieked and scattered toward the exit, disappearing out onto the pier and out of her life. Easy Peasy.

# 7

Danny was roving happily through the Castle in a Hunchback costume. His short stint with Mia in the Ripper Scene had been a pleasant start to his Castle tenure. They had exchanged bits of conversation between groups of customers, and it had come to an end with their dinner break in the Actors' Area. Now, as was customary, Danny changed character for the evening shift.

Sandy had assigned him the role of "Rover" so that he could observe as many scenes as possible. He was enjoying the freedom that roving the Castle gave him, watching the veterans in their appointed scenes, and learning a few tricks of his own.

In the Throne Room, he exchanged quick hellos with the jovial little fellow who was playing the part of the Jester. He sat on one of the plaster pedestals that flanked a large stained-glass window. Across from him was a wall that was covered with medieval-looking weapons, including lances, crossbows, and swords. All just a little too realistic and impressive. The Jester fiddled with one of the jingling bells on his prop Marotte, which was actually just a thinly veiled repurposed cat-o-nine-tails.

Danny moved toward the door of the Portrait Room beyond, making sure that there was no group of customers waiting silently within. This had been another one of Sandy's particularly important points: NEVER WALK INTO THE PORTRAIT ROOM DURING DRACULA'S SPEECH. Bobby derived great pleasure from embarrassing his fellow actors by dressing them down in front of the customers. More than one actor had quit after one of these encounters.

Danny listened for a second, then popped his head unobtrusively into the room. No customers, he noted. At that same moment, the Jester came to life, echoing, "No shoobies."

Danny looked back at the Jester and smiled at his reference to the tourists with the local epithet. Then he proceeded into the Portrait Room quietly. He looked anxiously up at the Portrait frame above his left shoulder. Bobby was there, seated in the oval hole of the Portrait. He sat deep in the alcove, tossing darts lazily at one of the Portrait's inner walls. Danny spoke a quiet hello. At this, Bobby turned toward him and pretended to lob a dart at him in a rapid motion. He laughed loudly when Danny instinctively ducked. Real funny, Bob. Danny was not amused in the least but managed to pretend that he was for Bobby's sake.

"You look very busy," Danny joked as he looked up at the vampire.

"I hate these slow times," Bobby replied as he nestled back into the Portrait alcove, "I have to make up new amusements for myself to keep from going crazy."

"What are you throwing darts at?" Danny laughed, "I mean, besides me."

"I have one of the walls lined with corkboard, and every day I put up a different photo to throw darts at, Bobby said proudly."

"Whose picture is up there today?"

Bobby obligingly pulled a poor photo of Richard, the manager, off the wall in front of him and held it out for Danny to see.

"Ah, I see. Aren't you worried that he might get mad if he sees that?"

Bobby laughed, "Of course. He'd probably throw a fit if he saw this," he said glibly as he rummaged through a pile of papers on the floor beside him. Finally holding up a photo of Sandy that was riddled with dart punctures he said, laughing, "That's why I keep *this* handy in case he comes in."

Now they both laughed as the Butler appeared, squeezing awkwardly between the barely open double doors.

"We've got a bunch of live ones," the little man in the dusty tuxedo announced. With this, Bobby straightened quickly in his seat and adjusted his cape. He transformed into the vampire, positioning himself so that the little pin spot hit one eye, creating a glint that added to the illusion that he was in fact only a portrait, and not flesh and blood.

Danny continued his rove from the Portrait Room to

the Butler's Area. As he reached for the doors Danny glanced back at the figure in the Portrait with the intention of saying goodbye. He stopped short, stunned by Bobby's complete stillness within the frame. The shading of his cheekbones and the long line of his nose were enhanced by the amber light of the pin spot. He honestly could be mistaken for a painting. His look was intent and frightening. It was the sinister look of the Master awaiting his guests.

The group now filled up the Portrait Room, their noisy entrance shattering the quiet tableau and filling the room with life. The vampire remained motionless, silent, waiting. As their chatter died down, Danny slipped through the big Portrait Room doors. He managed a final fast glimpse of the man in the Portrait, and a shiver coursed down his spine as he noticed the tiniest hint of a tear playing in the corner of the vampire's eye. The odd movement of the tear seemed out of place in the Portrait's complete stillness.

In another instant, the vampire was in motion. The loud bang of his shoe against the mantel broke the thick silence that had befallen the room. And now he was standing above them. They all screamed loudly and jumped back in unison at his sudden appearance. Danny closed the doors, squelching the sound. He stood outside the room, with Bobby's practiced speech coming through the thick wood of the doors in a softened form. He passed inconspicuously through the Butler's Area, where the Butler was already busy corralling another growing group. As he struggled awkwardly with the odd latch on the gate that separated the Butler's Area from the Belltower stairs, a soft voice came from behind him, "Can I help you with that?"

Danny turned around sharply, finding himself face-to-face with Mia. The look on his face was something between surprise and complete horror. Of all the people to witness his clumsy attempts, it had to be her.

Mia laughed quietly, "Sorry, I didn't mean to scare you." Danny bristled at the word 'scare'.

"That's okay. You didn't scare me…much." Danny watched with mild disgust as she easily opened the latch. He rolled his eyes at her, and she smiled back her reply. She started to head up the stairs, and before she disappeared around the stairs' wide curve, Danny called to her quietly, "Hey! Where are you going?"

"Upstairs to the Plaza Area. Why don't you take a rove up there and visit me later?"

Danny didn't really need to answer her. His broad smile had already done that for him.

"Okay, maybe I will…". No maybe about it.

As suddenly as she had appeared she was again out of sight. Danny lingered at the gate, which now stood ajar for his exit. He decided to rove back down the Belltower stairs. He passed by the large Styrofoam rock at the exit and slipped through the hidden doorway into the Dressing Room, where he looked around to see if anyone had witnessed his entrance. No one was there.

He walked through the room toward the doorway to the

Actors' Area outside, and instantly felt the air change. The breeze off the ocean created a sharp contrast with the stale heat of the Castle interior. Danny looked around, spying Gordon and a pretty girl in street clothes that he didn't recognize at one of the farthest picnic tables. They were deeply engrossed in their conversation, and Danny sensed that he wouldn't be able to draw their attention if he tried. He looked from their table to another one closer to the door.

Atwill Jarrett sat there silently eating a slice of pizza. His Frankenstein makeup was smeared and lacking the pristine quality it had had earlier in the day. He didn't look up from his little dinner; he simply sat eating, lost in his own thoughts.

There was no one else. Danny turned back to the Dressing Room and passed straight through it hesitantly. Back into the Castle.

Outside, Gordon turned around just in time to notice as Danny stepped back into the Dressing Room. He wouldn't bother taking the time to wonder what his friend was doing. He had more important things on his mind right now. He looked back into the cool green eyes of the girl sitting across the picnic table from him.

Someone else had also been aware of Danny's movements. He had passed by the dark shrouded figure seated in the corner of the Dressing Room without taking note of him at all.

The Watcher had been crouched there, near a pile of recently worn costumes. He sat on the floor with his knees drawn up close to his face. Only the smallest slit allowed him to peer out of the shroud's deep hood.

As he watched Danny leave the Dressing Room, the Watcher smiled a raw, knowing smile. Then he nodded his head at the stranger.

# 8

The Plaza was an open area with twin passageways leading away from it. One passageway led into a dark mineshaft, and the other one wound past the scene known as the Headless Woman. Danny was seated on the steps that led to the Mineshaft.

This passageway was almost never utilized, since the big bucks had been spent on the Headless Woman Scene. He sat quietly, staring out at the Plaza Area, where Mia was working.

She was dressed as a ghoulishly green dead prom queen. Sandy had spent extra time applying the latex gashes on her face and neck, painting streaks of stage blood down from the appliances. She had finished by liberally dripping more blood on the dirty, tattered pink prom dress. And yet Danny sat there, openly admiring her beauty, which he thought could never be completely hidden.

Mia's movements were less than polished. She was not an actor in training, as so many of the other monsters here were. She had no doubt led a rebellious lifestyle that her parents (probably upper middle class) abhorred. Her chain-smoking and manner of speech gave that aspect of her life away in spades. Mia loved to come off as the "bad girl".

She looked up, feeling Danny's eyes on her. His scrutiny made her slightly defensive for a moment. Just a moment. Then the defensive thoughts drained into a smile, "What? Do I really look that bad?"

His expression remained the same. He held his chin in one hand, the elbow braced by his knee as he sat on the hard wooden steps. Then he shook his head, as though awakened from a catatonic state, "No. Was I staring?" He laughed, "I was off in outer space."

"Oh."

There was a long pause, with both acutely aware of one another's presence, and of the thick silence. She spoke first, "I see that you have some pull with the management. Nobody ever gets to rove around the Castle on their first day. Rookies usually get stuck in the First Cage or the Gorilla Scene."

Danny smiled as he couldn't help thinking of Gordon being "stuck" (as she had so aptly put it) in the Gorilla costume for the entire shift.

"Yeah, I've got a real gift when it comes to persuasion." He laughed at his own comment.

"Actually, I think your girlfriend Sandy would just fall over backward to make you happy."

His laughter was cut short. Jealousy. This was something that Danny hadn't expected to hear in her voice.

"Naaah. We're just friends. *Old* friends."

It was the truth. They really were just friends. Although Danny had wished otherwise in the past. The fairly recent past. But now, for his current purposes, his failed past relationship with Sandy proved to be a plus. Mia moved closer to him with wide enticing eyes. Danny could feel the blood begin to rise to his face. The pallid greasepaint did little to mask his excitement. He felt his heart begin to pound a little. Was it getting hotter in here?

Now Mia became more persistent. She took hold of his shoulders firmly and leaned closer to him, fairly straddling his legs on the stairs. The soft folds of the prom dress seemed to envelop them both. Her face was scant inches from his.

"Am I making you nervous?" She asked from an incredibly close distance.

This couldn't be real, Danny thought. He closed his eyes and upon reopening them was surprised to see her face still so close to his. Then her lips were on his lips, and Danny's hand slipped around her waist, pulling her close against him.

Danny could feel the beating of his own heart. Or was that hers? They remained locked in a long and passionate kiss, and Danny became acutely aware of the mingling of the greasepaint on their faces, and the warm wet sensation of the theatrical blood as it touched his cheek . Slowly, she moved back from him, and the prom gown's fabric rustled as they parted. As he sat on the steps staring back at this strange and mystifying girl, he wondered whether it had all actually happened, or if it was just another daydream that he would be disappointedly roused  from. Would he find himself back in the moment just a short while before, staring at the girl's undeniable beauty through her makeup?

Slowly the reality of the entire incident settled on him. The smeared remnants of stage blood on his face were evidence of that. Mia laughed as she wiped the blood from his face with the hem of her gown, taking a good bit of his greasepaint with it. Now his pink flesh peeked through the grayish white of the makeup in a streak.

He feigned nonchalance as he cleared his throat awkwardly, "Wow. Nice."

Suddenly, the familiar scuffle of feet on the stairs that led up to the Plaza Area broke the spell. The recognition of the sound registered across Mia's face first, and she instinctively began to hunt for a hiding place.

"Here comes a group! Quick, get into position!" With this, she pressed a tiny piece of torn cardboard into Danny's hand, then ran and crouched behind the huge wooden barrels stacked at the entrance to the mineshaft.

Danny possessed neither the hiding instinct nor the reflexes for such a move as hers. The fact was that he was still a little stunned by what had just happened. He looked down at the piece of cardboard in his palm. It was a torn piece of the matchbook cover he had struggled with. On it were the words, *"Meet me after work"*, written in Mia's delicate hand. The date he struggled to make in his mind had made itself.

Realizing he couldn't possibly move quickly enough to avoid being seen by the group, Danny simply pulled the hood of his shroud forward, hiding his face entirely. He remained poised on the steps, ready to pounce. It had seemed like a good plan until the group was upon them and he attempted a surprise lunge. Not realizing that his shroud was caught beneath his sneakered feet, his forward motion produced nothing more than a ridiculous tumble into the middle of the group as they approached him.

A shriek from the opposite corner of the Plaza drew their gaze away from the inept hunchback who was now lying on the floor. The shriek had come from Mia. The grisly vision of the mutilated prom queen shown eerily in the green light emanating from the passageway to the Headless Woman Scene. The sight was oddly reminiscent of the prom scene in the movie *Carrie*. She dominated the Plaza Area now, corralling the group masterfully around her and into the passageway. Danny was taken aback at how good she was. This was a pleasant surprise. Something he had not expected from her.

When the last of the group had finally disappeared around the corner, Mia turned her gaze to him. The frightening wide- eyed visage she had worn for the sake of the customers melted back into her familiar smile.

Danny looked up at her from the spot where he had landed on the Plaza floor and laughed, "Well, that went pretty well, didn't it?"

# 9

Gordon was standing outside the Dressing Room in the Actors' Area. Sandy had been very cooperative, letting him take his dinner break early when he had asked her. As payment he was forced to finish the shift in the Gorilla Scene, where he had started. And now he was working with a much angrier version of Shelby. She had been forced to man the scene alone for the entire time that Gordon was gone for his impromptu dinner break.

Relishing the final moments of his break, Gordon lit a fresh cigarette and moved to the picnic table where Jules was seated, happily thumbing through a magazine whose cover sported photos of various electronic gadgets. Gordon couldn't help but wonder how anyone could find such a magazine interesting. Now Jules looked up from the pages, smiling, as Gordon sat beside him.

"Well, Buddy, what do you think of 'monstering'?"

Gordon smiled at the silliness of the word. To Monster: (verb). I monster, you monster, we monster, they monster. It was all completely absurd in his mind.

"I guess it's okay. There's a lot of wasted time in between groups. That wasn't something I had pictured in my mind."

Jules went back to the magazine, "The waiting around can really get to you after a while. Imagine how the people who have been in there all season feel by now. They tend to get stir crazy by the time it's a couple of hours into the shift."

"Yeah," Gordon said, "I've seen some of them get pretty bonkers in there."

Jules exhaled in a laugh, adding a croupy cough at the end of it for emphasis. This cough had become something of Jules' trademark laugh. Gordon was used to it, barely noticing the  odd tic.

"Well, some of them *are* a little bonkers, but a lot are just bored. After you've been doing this long enough you begin to take your boredom and exhaustion out on the customers," Jules looked up at Gordon, as an impish smile played at the corner of his lips, "You make up little games that you play with them. Harmless but funny little games that just border on breaking the rules. All strictly for your own amusement. I should say…for your own amusement and the amusement of the other actors. It's all in fun. To help you cope with the heat and the boredom throughout the day."

"You said games. What kind of games?"

It was obvious to Gordon that Jules had told and retold these stories countless times, to countless people, probably never straying from the same wording every time. In watching him, Gordon thought, the excitement became contagious.

"Well, for one, we would separate one or two unwitting victims from the end of a group. Always making sure it was a particularly large group, so they weren't immediately noticed. It's common for one or two a-holes to lag behind the others, so this isn't so hard to do. Once you have them under your control you make them bark."

His voice trailed off for emphasis. The look of delight on his face was unmistakable now, "…Or make them crawl around on the floor before they're allowed to leave the scene. We would keep a running total of how many we each got, and at the end of the night the winner would be announced." He made it all sound very official. "Of course, you had to have another actor present to confirm each one. Each 'kill'."

There was a brief pause, then he added quickly, "My favorites were always the fetal position contests."

"What's a fetal position contest?"

"Oh, it's simple. You just count how many times you can scare people to the point where they sit on the floor, curled up in what's basically a fetal position. Eventually they beg you to stop. Some even start to cry."

The thought appalled Gordon, but he managed not to say so. "Rollie and I are tied for the record in fetal positions. We're at forty-one in a single day." He paused as he watched Gordon's reaction. "You'll like Rollie. He's a maniac. He doesn't speak often in the Castle, but he's probably one of the scariest monsters we've got. It comes naturally to him."

"How do you scare people if you don't even say anything?

"It's not the words, Gordon. It's in the *look*. Rollie's got that look, and he knows when to use it. That's what makes him so good at the fetal position thing. I've seen him reduce customers to tears lots of times. And not once did he say a word to them."

Gordon laughed, then thought better of it, "God, that's horrible."

It was as if a switch was flipped off suddenly in Jules. He sat down, carefully taking up his magazine where he had left off moments before. He spoke now with much less excitement and zeal, "Yeah, I suppose it is, but after three months of twelve- hour shifts, six days a week, it becomes a question of the customers' sanity versus your own."

"I can understand that," Gordon said flatly. He really could understand it. After just a few hours of dealing with smug customers, some of them looking for a fist fight more than a scare, Gordon's own level of animosity toward the human race had escalated just the slightest bit.

Remembering another story, the light returned to Jules' eyes. "One night Barry and I decided to see how many customers we could stuff into the Mummy case in the Plaza at one time. We could hear them complaining about the heat and how tight it was once we shut the door on them. And that door was *heavy*."

He paused, remembering, "We had to stop at eighteen."

"Eighteen!" Gordon was genuinely amazed. He had seen the Mummy case that Jules was talking about in its new home outside the Tilted Room. It was large enough for three or four actors to hide inside comfortably To fit eighteen adults into a space that size was commendable mischief indeed.

"Wait." Gordon said, suddenly recalling Jules' words, "Why did you say that you *had* to stop at eighteen?"

Jules laughed. He had been waiting for the realization. "Because Richard was at the back of the group!"

"No shit," Gordon laughed now too, "What did he do to you?"

"He fired us both on the spot. No big deal. We'd been fired plenty of times before. Unfortunately, in all the excitement, when we went downstairs to punch out and gather our stuff, we forgot to let all those people out of the Mummy case. They stayed in there a good fifteen minutes until our replacements found them."

Now they both laughed. Out of the corner of his eye, Gordon noticed Richard staring at him. He glanced quickly at his watch to check how long he had gone over his allotted break time. By his calculations, his ten-minute break had turned into a twenty-five-minute break, and Richard looked properly pissed. Gripped with a mild panic, Gordon gasped and rushed through the Dressing Room door. He poked his head out again once as an afterthought, "See you later, Jules! I'm late!"

"See you later, man." And with this, Jules was engrossed once again in his magazine.

Richard looked down at his clipboard, scratching out his latest scribble. He stood now, giving Jules a final glare before walking heavily into the Dressing Room, crumpling his aborted attempt at a work schedule as he passed by.

Jules simply shook his head and muttered to himself, smiling, "Our Leader…"

# 10

Inside the Dressing Room, Little Mack lounged atop the washer/dryer pair that was situated against the far wall. He balanced a silver dollar coin expertly on his knuckles, flipping it playfully from one finger to the next. Suddenly the interior door to the Castle burst open with a loud crack. The sudden noise left Little Mack unscathed. His silver dollar never missed a beat. An irate young man dressed in Dracula attire entered and scanned the room with his eyes, seething. Little Mack looked up lazily from his little game, "What's the matter, Seth?"

"What's the matter? Do you really have to ask?" He shot angry looks all around, "I'll tell you what's the matter…Fucking Bobby!" He paused for emphasis. "He just walked into the Portrait Room in the middle of my speech. Didn't wait for the group to leave. In fact, I had barely started talking when *Bam!!* He just leisurely strides in from his break."

"So…?"

Seth rolled his eyes at this, "So, now there are two of us standing in the room, facing one another, dressed as Dracula!" The volume of his voice attracted the attention of several actors who had been taking their breaks outside.

"And you're getting all bent out of shape over *that?*" Little Mack had barely looked up from his hand. This was typical "Bobby".

"Mack, it's not just that, and you know it. Everybody here has had all that they can take of that guy. He pushes buttons. God forbid anybody should walk in on *his* act. Let alone dressed like his clone!"

Now one of the girls seated at the makeup table wheeled her chair around to face him, "What did you do when he came in?"

Seth's angry scowl eased, as he smiled broadly, "First I told the group that he was my vampire lover. Then I jumped off the mantel and kissed him on the lips."

His words hung in the air for a tick. Mack looked up at Seth before breaking into an uncontrolled fit of laughter that sent the silver dollar careening across the room and under a pile of dirty laundry. Seth laughed too as he worked at the laces that held his long cape together at the neck.

He stopped at the cork bulletin board that was tacked onto the wall behind the washer and dryer, where Little Mack was seated. The same clippings and photos had graced this board since the day that Sandy had hung it up in late May. Today there was something different tacked there. It was a blurry Polaroid photo of one of the familiar props used in the Castle: a fluffy, unassuming bunny rabbit hand puppet. How it had even made it into the prop bin was the real mystery. Nonetheless, the little bunny had become the actors' favorite. The workday didn't go by when it wasn't employed in one scene or another. And one of the Castle's more creative cast members had nicknamed it "The Beast".

Well, here in the grainy photograph was the beloved Beast, tied with what appeared to be a bungee cord and gagged. Scrawled beneath the photo was what was intended to be a ransom note. Seth pointed to the photo and laughed. Little Mack turned his neck painfully to follow Seth's gaze. Seeing the bizarre image of the kidnapped bunny brought him to another fit of laughter, with him finally falling backward on the washer. His head banged loudly onto its hollow surface.

The Dressing Room began to slowly fill up with other actors finishing their shifts. It was nighttime at the Castle. Prime Time. As they filed in one by one, the actors smiled and pointed out the plight of The Beast to one another. The notoriety of his kidnapping had quickly made the photo the featured item of the corkboard, overshadowing all others. Including one, hidden almost entirely by the now-famous Polaroid. It was a torn piece of matchbook cover, speckled with traces of human blood. Across it was scrawled *"Meet me after work"*.

**"...this life we think we're living isn't real. It's just a shadow play, and I for one will be glad when the lights go out on it. In the dark, all the shadows disappear."**

**— Stephen King –
THE INSTITUTE**

# 11

Every time the headaches came, they were a little more severe. The first ones had never incited the Watcher to violence. This, however, was no longer the case.

Each time the pain started he found he was less likely to cope with it. The Watcher was losing patience. That was why his relief had required a bit more creativity of late. He had forced himself to come closer to being caught in the act. The sense of danger made his adrenalin flow more freely.

As he sat crouched in the darkness, he could hear his own heart pounding. One by one the soundtracks in each of the Castle's scenes came to their abrupt end. In their place were left dark pockets of silence. The beating of his heart had taken the place of all other noise. He struggled to see, since his vision was nearly completely clouded by spinning circles of light that swirled in front of him. These "stars" came from the Watcher's brain, released miraculously into the air before him as the pain in his head reached an unbearable level.

Where was she? He struggled to stand now. Finally, he

was on his feet, moving. He went swiftly, too swiftly for a blind man, from scene to scene. She should have passed by him by now. Had she passed by unnoticed? Did the brainstars conceal her from him? At this thought, the Watcher grew angrier, and with the arrival of the anger his throbbing head sent another electrical surge of white pain down his spine. It spread and reached into his clenching and unclenching fists as he moved. He continued to glide swiftly, methodically, with a blind knowledge of every step he took. The Watcher did not need to see his surroundings to know exactly where he was. The Castle was his home. His mother. His heart. The Watcher felt comfort here. His home. The Castle. It was his. It was *him*. An extension of the Watcher's angry self.

# 12

Mia was sneaking one last cigarette in the Plaza Area even though she knew that the actors were strictly forbidden to smoke inside the Castle. One properly placed fire could easily turn the entire building into a five-story chimney, ignited before anyone inside would have the time to think, much less move. But Mia never cared for rules. It was part of her charm, or so she thought. Rules like that were made for idiots who were careless. And if there was one thing that Mia *wasn't*, it was careless.

The whole place felt deserted, except for her, and she savored the silence of the usually chaotic room. She had discovered this quiet, serene side of the Castle quite by accident when she had been working in the Tilted Room alone on a particularly slow weeknight. As closing time had grown near and the groups of customers were few and far between, Mia had lain down on the tilted floor and dozed. No customers had come through to wake her, and the other actors had left at closing time without bothering to check for Mia. When she awoke, she found herself in total darkness. As she made her way downstairs, she could hear the chatter of the other actors while they changed their clothes. Mia had only missed closing time that night by about half an hour. She had paused at the doorway to the Mortuary as she lit her cigarette, listening to them.

So now she knew that the perfect time for a quiet cigarette in the solitude of the Castle was at closing time when the rest of her colleagues were downstairs comparing anecdotes from their most recent shift. The fact that she was breaking one of Richard's precious Castle rules made her after-hours smokes that much more enjoyable to Mia. No one had found out about her nightly cigarette ritual yet. She felt it was another little rebellion that was all her own. Chalk one up for Mia.

She took one final moment to savor the silence of the usually noisy room, then she hurriedly squelched the glowing tip of her cigarette on the little tin ashtray she had concealed in the pocket of the shorts she wore under her costume.

Suddenly she was hit with a cold realization. "Oh, shit, Danny! I almost forgot about you!"

Mia rushed toward the Headless Woman Scene, when her passage was abruptly blocked by a dark figure in a shroud. The faint green light from the scene gave the hooded form an otherworldly glow. Her anger at being discovered began to mix with an uneasy sense of dread. The figure now made a quick lunge toward her, and Mia gasped.

"Jesus! Stop it! You scared the hell out of me. I thought everybody else was downstairs changing."

She moved to one side, but the dark figure anticipated the move and blocked her again. Now she tried the other side with the same result. She grew increasingly angrier with each seemingly choreographed move the shrouded wraith made.

"What's with the games, here? Let me out!"

Suddenly she stopped short, stunned by a realization. This was just some stupid prank. It was one of those assholes who got their kicks from making others look foolish. Those fetal position contest jerkoffs that she couldn't stand.

Maybe, Mia thought, her late-night cigarette breaks weren't so secret after all, and this was someone letting her know that he was onto her. Maybe it was someone who didn't like the idea of her breaks. Maybe this was Richard. Or maybe Danny's little girlfriend was jealous of their rendezvous set for later that evening. This could be Sandy. Or, what if this was Danny? After all, she didn't know if he was some kind of weirdo. They had just met, after all. Maybe he was playing a sick practical joke on her; letting her know that he had the upper hand.

Well, whoever this was, Mia was growing impatient and didn't feel like playing games.

"Who are you?" She took a step backward. "Danny, is that you?"

A disembodied cackle seemed to rise from within the shroud's deep hood and float into the silence of the suddenly ominous Plaza Area. The dark figure continued to inch toward her, moving stealthily, eerily, spectral in the green glow. He took his time. He tasted the fear growing in her.

Now he spoke to her, in a voice so utterly alien to her ears that it made her skin crawl. Its strangeness made her feel cold and vulnerable. The voice was thick and raspy, yet the words it spoke were intelligible enough.

"Miiiiaaaa…". The creature almost seemed to chant the words, "Miiiiaaa, Danny can't come out to play today."

The ridiculousness of the trite line made Mia exhale in a laugh. This was straight out of a hokey horror movie. Not one of her favorite things.

"Won't you play with me, instead?" it was now saying. By now they were at the farthest end of the Plaza, and her eyes darted toward the flight of stairs that led down to the Swamp. The Watcher's eyes followed, noting her intended escape. He now blocked her way with one shrouded arm. This was no joke.

Suddenly panic gripped Mia as the figure quickly gave her shoulder a powerful shove. She struggled to keep her footing as he seemed to anticipate her every move, her every dodge. She realized that making a run for it would be out of the question. If that shove was any indication of this person's strength, Mia knew she had no chance of fighting it.

In a desperate effort, she tried to slip under his extended arm, but the Watcher was too quick. He held out his other hand, and Mia could now see what it held. In a quick motion, the Watcher plunged the long knife into her stomach, just below the ribs. She swayed on her legs, which were turning into liquid beneath her. Her eyes bulged unnaturally as she fell. The Watcher caught her with an ease that was inhuman, as his raspy laugh punctuated the scene. This was no joke. And it was certainly not funny.

# 13

Danny was waiting for Mia at the midpoint of the ramp that led to the street from the Actors' Area. He looked anxiously at each passing face, finally growing weary as the last of the actors walked by.

Sandy locked the Dressing Room door with the single color- coded key on Richard's keyring. She had given Richard this key herself at the beginning of the summer, taking the time to paint the top of it with purple nail polish to identify it among the others on just such an occasion as this. Its bright coloration stood out against the sea of dull metal keys it swam amid on the big ring. She wondered briefly what all those keys could possibly be for. The Castle's few locks had all been keyed alike, so the many other random keys must be strictly for show.

With the Dressing Room secured, she headed down the pier's ramp toward Danny. Careful not to make eye contact with him, she looked out toward the lights that lined the long thoroughfare that wound down Pete's Beach like a glowing ribbon alongside the moonlit shoreline. Just as she was about to pass by him, she looped her arm emphatically through his and pulled Danny into stride beside her. Down the ramp they went, arm in arm, with Danny battling her mildly.

"Uh, what are you doing? I'm waiting for somebody."

Sandy stopped abruptly in her tracks, forcing Danny's feet to skid on the down-sloping boards of the ramp. She looked him in the eye. Her gaze was markedly surprised.

"Who? Mia?" The look on his face was answer enough for her. "Wow, you really *do* work fast!"

She paused, looking back at the Dressing Room door she had just locked.

"Didn't she already leave? Maybe you missed her when she walked past you."

"No," Danny said with all certainty, "I would've seen her go by."

"Then I'm afraid you've been stood up."

"What are you talking about?"

Sandy looked just a little too jovial to be the bearer of such bad news, but she fairly chirped her words. "Everybody's already out of the Castle. I just locked the place up for the night."

"Can't be," Danny fumbled with the words, "I left the Plaza before her, and I'm pretty sure I watched everybody walk out of here. Maybe she's still inside!"

He started to walk back up the pier ramp, but Sandy managed to catch his shirt sleeve as he passed.

"Dan, she's not in there. Richard did a 'crawl through' of the place and he told me himself that everyone was out."

Danny stared at her as the words sunk in. Then he looked briefly up the ramp toward the Dressing Room door one last time.

"There are lots of other ways out of this place if you're trying to avoid somebody," Sandy said. Her words were beginning to sink in. "Believe me, it isn't the first time that one of these 'monsterettes' has stood a guy up."

Danny mumbled quietly to himself. He couldn't believe that Mia had just been toying with him. The way they had left things in the Plaza just didn't add up to her ditching him. He shook his head, looking down at his feet, then back up at Sandy.

"I don't know, Sandy. *She* was the one who came on to *me*. It doesn't make any sense." His hand fumbled with the contents of his pocket for a moment, searching for the little piece of matchbook, but finally gave up. He must have dropped it, he thought.

Sandy gave him a few seconds to listen to himself. After all, he didn't know the way things worked here. He didn't know this girl with whom he had formed an instant infatuation. He didn't know actors and their whims, much less funhouse actors.

"Do you want to stand here all night waiting for this girl who just doesn't give a damn?" She knew this hurt, but it was the truth. "Or do you want to come out with the rest of us and have some fun? You know the nights left to party at the Sand Bar are limited now. Summer's almost over."

This was funny. She was bribing him, like a child. Danny smiled at her and the spell that had overtaken him was broken. Worrying about something so silly was unlike him. This was, after all, *Sandy* asking him to have a drink with her. Would he like to go? Of course he would.

He pretended to weigh his options briefly.

"Let's go," he said. He took her hand, and they resumed the descent toward the road. Sandy smiled at him, but her voice took on a serious tone now, "Are you going to worry about Mia all night? 'Cause if you are…"

Danny halted her words in mid-sentence, "…Mia who?"

They headed toward Sandy's little yellow Volkswagen Cabriolet, which was parked along the Boulevard. The rag top had been down all day, and the seats were still slightly warm from the heat of the summer sun, even though sunset had been hours before. The salt in the air had washed over them, making everything tacky. Tacky but not unpleasant.

As the familiar whir of the Volkswagen engine filled the air, Danny couldn't help but wonder if he would see Mia at the bar. Would she simply ignore him, as though their encounter in the Plaza had never taken place? The screech of the car's tires as Sandy gunned the engine erased those thoughts nicely.

# 14

The sound of laughter from the passing yellow car was barely audible above the din of the crashing waves on the beach. It was lost to the couple inside the wooden shelter of the empty lifeguard stand, who were drinking in the beauty of the beach at night. Gordon and Susan looked out at the dancing bits of moonlight that were scattered along the ocean's surface, from the beach all the way to the horizon. Since the moment they had met in the Gorilla Scene earlier that day, they had spent every possible moment they could together. There wasn't much conversation to their conversation now, but Gordon felt comfortable with the silence. He wasn't one for wordy relationships. If pressed he might argue that he had always had trouble speaking to women, that he rarely had found anything in common to talk about with them. This was not the case, however, with Susan. She seemed to know a lot of things that Gordon found interesting. He may have met his match. And he was thoroughly enjoying it. They sat inside the sandy recess of the lifeguard stand, listening to the murmur of the ocean. Feeling the cool breeze as it kissed the top of the waves. Right now, their biggest concern would be to not bring too much beach sand into the house with them.

# 15

This time it was not only Jarrett but the entire pier that was on fire. The familiar electrical storm was raging, but the driving rain didn't even begin to quench the flames. The howl of the wind was tremendous, creating what seemed like a great vacuum amid the torrent. Its ferocity made it difficult to breathe. Jarrett could feel the flames beginning to consume first his left arm, then his right. They began to move slowly across the width of his chest and up toward his head. The sensation tore through him and lingered afterward. His body had become a great weight, and through it all he could clearly hear that horrible laughter. He repeatedly caught glimpses of the hideously familiar face in the black hooded shroud. It was the face of the Watcher, and Jarrett could not find the strength to utter his name through the pain. He felt his consciousness slipping away as the blazing pier beneath his feet began to slowly crumble. This time the Watcher had taken everything down with him; not only Jarrett but the entire cast of the Castle in a final grand sweep of murderous destruction.

Jarrett hoped and prayed that this would be the last of it. As he had hoped all the other times he had endured the terrible dream. The dream that always seemed to arrive immediately upon his falling asleep, never after any restful length of time. The dream was always incredibly vivid and horrifying, and in it Jarrett always met his end. Without fail. Another unflagging similarity was the presence of fire, sometimes in huge raging amounts and other times just as a flame flickering in a corner. But it was always there. And, of course, there was that face. In his dream Jarrett could identify it readily, but upon the instant of his waking the face and any memory of it always vanished. He tried time and time again to make himself remember the identity of that terrible shrouded figure, but always to no avail. Consciousness always wiped that memory clean.

So here he was again, his heart fairly leaping from his chest and his body covered with a thin glaze of sweat. He reached for his medication. This time relief had no feeling of guilt attached to it. Jarrett knew that he only felt guilt taking the pills when he was with his Castle friends. The pills made him popular. Often, he would end up dispensing his entire supply to actors who wouldn't think twice about begging him for one or two. Even on those occasions, Jarret knew that he need only pop another pill himself to make the guilt go away.

Now he felt his nerves begin to relax a little. He breathed in deeply, enjoying the purity of the air in the real world. His lungs still felt full of the clouds of smoke from his dream. The burning sensation of the fire engulfing his chest had penetrated them, setting his veins ablaze like so many twigs in a wildfire.

He looked down at his wristwatch, always in its place on his left wrist. Wearing his watch while he slept was a habit left over from his days in the military. Often the old habit of checking his wrist for it with his right hand would occur even in his sleep. This was especially true if he happened to be dreaming about the hellish days he had spent in combat. On particularly horrible occasions his dreams of war would mix with his dreams of the Watcher, and it might take three or four pills to calm him down afterward.

It was now one-fifteen. He had only been asleep for half an hour. Jarrett sat up in his bed. He couldn't possibly go back to sleep now. If he did, he was sure that the horrible dream would revisit him, picking up at the exact moment he had woken from it. The pain was still fresh in him, and he would not put himself through it again. Not now.

The Sand Bar. That was where all the others would be at this late hour. They would only have just arrived after the late shift and Jarrett could join them there.

He stood and began to dress, cursing himself for not having gone there right after work, as the other actors were always sure to do. A crowded bar seemed just the place for him to forget the visions of the burning pier and the search for his tormentor's elusive face.

The walk to the bar was uneventful enough. The hum of the waves on the sand seemed to keep him company. At one abrupt point, Jarrett stopped to look back over his shoulder at the lurking silhouette of the Castle in the distance. He lit another cigarette with the butt end of the one he was finishing. He thought for a fleeting moment that he saw the shrouded figure from his dream hobbling across the back of the pier. He knew that he was not prepared to confront the mysterious Castle phantom tonight, so he dismissed the sight of him as just another hallucination. One brought on by his utter fatigue or as an after-effect of the medication. His hand automatically went to the outside of his pants pocket to make sure that the vial of pills was in its proper place. It was.

The jukebox in the corner of the Sand Bar blared at its usual intolerably loud level. The noise and the crowdedness of the room felt welcoming to Jarrett. He scanned the bar and located an empty barstool with relatively little effort. Taking his place beside the familiar faces from the Castle gave him an even warmer feeling. The addled state that his dream had plunged him into was finally slipping away. He caught the eye of the pretty blonde barmaid (Jarrett thought that he recalled her name as being Kendall) and ordered a mug of draft beer. No one had made a fuss over his entrance. In fact, had anyone been asked, they probably would say that Jarrett had been sitting there all along. He sat and sipped his beer silently, his eyes still passing over the many faces in the bar. He couldn't help but wonder if any of the others had experienced the same horrific nightmares that had tortured him of late. He wondered if anyone else took home a frightening little bit of the Castle every night, as he did. And if they kept it locked up tight inside their subconscious mind, freeing it upon their unsuspecting sensibilities when they were asleep. Suddenly Jarrett became keenly aware of his complete vulnerability while he slept. He understood that in sleep the soft underbelly of his psyche was exposed. And with this Jarrett decided that he would keep his place in the noisy safety of the Sand Bar until closing time.

# 16

A drunken Danny with Sandy in tow stumbled into the apartment and snapped on the light switch just inside the front door. The little lamp beside the worn sofa came to life with a meager amber glow. It appeared that Jules was not at home, yet the tape machine he most often tinkered with was playing one of the many Castle soundtrack tapes, as it always did. A sudden loud crack of thunder in the tape jolted Danny and Sandy as they entered, sending them into drunken peals of laughter.

Outside the window of Danny's little beach apartment, unnoticed by the two friends now sitting drunk and contented on the couch, there was activity on the pier. A dark shrouded shape labored to carry Mia's limp body. He worked diligently at the task of moving her under the pier. The Watcher's breath was labored and heavy now. The headache that had overtaken him in the Plaza was almost completely gone, and with it his strength, too, had all but vanished.

This girl had gone quietly. She had gone easily. Much more easily than the last one had. A struggle could be quite a nuisance, the Watcher thought, and he so hated any unanticipated details.

Her added weight in death and the softness of the beach sand served to make the Watcher's labors even more difficult. As he struggled the Watcher could feel the Castle laughing down at him. The whole huge structure shuddered with evil omnipotent laughter, directed at him, such a small and insignificant being in comparison with the massive gray form that hovered over him. It mocked him now. It was as if the Castle only approved of him when the violence and the anger and inhuman strength were upon him. It enjoyed his anger. It *fed on* the anger. The Castle seemed to ignite beneath his feet when the anger came. The heat was its approval of what he did. He loved and hated and feared it all at once. The Castle was his mother, and the Watcher was always an obedient child. That was why he continued to work so diligently at the task at hand. He would continue to struggle until he could take no more.

# 17

At first, the moonlight that came through the opening of the lifeguard stand had startled Gordon. He sat up, jostling Susan who was still sleeping against his arm. She slowly woke, at first unsure of where she was. What time was it? The entire night had gotten away from the two of them. They pulled themselves up onto the little bench inside the wooden stand, smiling with the remembrance of the events of the day.

"My back feels like I slept on a bed of nails," Gordon said.

Susan just smiled. She leaned forward a little to assess the location of the lifeguard stand on the deserted beach. The tide had drawn closer, but the edge of the water remained a safe distance away. Without a word, she slipped down and out of the stand. The coolness of the sand on her bare feet was both refreshing and halting. In another moment Gordon was beside her. He took her hand as they surveyed the beach and the waves, and the dark silhouette of the Castle scant yards down the beach from them. It was as if it followed you on the island, its form visible from so many areas at once. One with the topography of Pete's Beach.

Gordon spied something odd now. A dark silhouette emerged from beneath the pier and, unaware of their presence, headed back up the beach toward the Castle's parking lot. Gordon silently drew Susan closer by her elbow, until they were again concealed behind the empty stand. He indicated to her to remain silent, holding his finger up to his lips as he would to a child. Her eyes grew wide as they watched the man walk away. Once he was safely out of sight she asked, "What do you think he was doing? It looked like he was wearing a costume."

"Yeah, I know, he was wearing a shroud." Gordon peered out toward the parking lot again. There was no sign of the man.

"This may be a stupid question, working where you do, but are sights like *that* commonplace here?"

Gordon was a little reluctant to offer any sort of reply. "Well, I haven't been working here long enough to know for sure but judging from most of the people I've met at the Castle…that's not all that odd."

"Oh." Her smile had returned.

Gordon slipped his arm around the small of her back and pulled her close to him. She stared into his eyes, and she knew that the subject was closed. For now. She continued to watch his eyes for what felt like a long time, with just a trace of a smile on her lips. Then the smile was soundly erased by a kiss.

They weren't about to find out what was going on underneath the pier. They really didn't care that much anyway. The only thing that might make them move from their sandy bed was the rising sun, and that wouldn't appear for a few more hours.

# 18

By three a.m., the moon had changed its position in the sky and was casting shadows in quite a different direction than it had when the Watcher had labored his way under the pier with his grisly burden. He'd sat in the shadows of the parking lot for well over an hour, sick to his stomach and drained of all energy. Finally, he gathered enough strength to move up the ramp, silently, stealthily, and entered through the Dressing Room door, which he had been so careful to leave unlocked when he had exited with Mia in his arms.

Inside the Dressing Room, he carefully removed the traces of his evening's work. This was the other side of the Watcher. The part of him who meticulously wiped away all evidence left behind by his sinister half. His Thinking Self, who erased the blood from the floors and the walls of the funhouse. The Thinking Self knew that he must be careful.

The Watcher looked down at his latex surgeon's gloves, covered now with thick blots of very real blood. He looked up at his reflection in the mirror. His look was wide-eyed and hungry. Slowly lifting his blood-covered index finger to his lips, he carefully traced his smile with a thick crimson layer. He continued to stare at his macabre reflection as he removed the gloves and laid them gently on the makeup table. Oddly they did not look out of place amid the array of tinted props and facial appliances on the table. The Watcher laughed quietly, that terrible raspy laugh, as he reached out to remove the gloves from the table, then quickly thought better of it. No one would notice them in the Dressing Room bustle of the coming morning. They would just be tossed away like any other dirty piece of stage makeup without a second thought. He would leave them where they were, as a sort of calling card from the building's one true monster.

Next, he hurriedly threw his worn shroud onto a pile of dirty costumes on the floor. It would be laundered along with the other clothes when Sandy came in the next morning. The brownish-red stains of Mia's blood would mix with the stage blood and the sweat of the actors' previous shift. A sense of urgency began to grow within the Watcher. He was feeling more and more tired. The pain and the violence brought with them an inhuman strength, and when that strength was gone it seemed to take all his essence, his being. He felt as if he might be melting. He laughed to himself at the thought, a contrived witch's voice from a childhood movie favorite bubbled to his lips. Staring into his ruby red lips he whispered, "What a world, what a world…who would think that a good little girl like you could destroy my beautiful wickedness…"

# Part Three
# Saturday

**"I think playing villains is lovely! After all, we spend most of our lives trying to be good, trying to do what is right, don't we? We try not to hurt other people, or to give in to our wicked impulses. But at heart, we are primitive, like children. Often we'd secretly like to do the very things we discipline ourselves against. Isn't that true?"**

**- Claude Rains —**

# 1

The midday sun on the sand of Pete's Beach had created a heat so intense and intolerable that the greater number of beachgoers chose to loll in the waves or at the water's edge. The sand itself sported a smattering of colorful umbrellas, with less aquatic sunbathers taking their refuge beneath.

It was the sort of heat that the actors of the Castle dreaded. While it seemed just a little bit easier to take in the earlier days of the summer, it had become a great nuisance in the waning days of August. They gathered in the Actors' Area, a scant thirty feet above the burning sand of the beach. Many voiced their frustration at the prospect of being subjected to the plywood oven of the Castle Proper. On such sweltering days, the temperature in the Dressing Room could easily reach 110 degrees, and the interior of the Castle could be as much as 5 degrees hotter. The security staff made rounds constantly, doling out water, salt tablets, and the occasional smelling salts to the cast. Tom, the resident EMT, carried his heavy medical bag from one scene to the next in case of emergencies. He muttered to himself as he did so, cursing the overzealous actors and their complete disregard for safety. They would run and jump themselves into sweaty heaps, often to the brink of fainting.

Inside the Dressing Room, Little Mack was applying makeup to the face of a girl in a witch costume. Not the standard Halloween witch, though. This was to be one of Little Mack's more grisly concoctions. He had worked on the costume and makeup diligently. This witch was beyond frightening, made of the stuff that could scare MacBeth's own weird sisters, complete with vines that appeared to grow from thick scars on her face and arms. Latex eruptions peppered her neck, with little colonies of plastic spiders popping out from within.

Little Mack continued to converse with the witch in a completely normal and mundane way. Between bits of his makeup application, the girl tilted her head from side to side, admiring his work.

The conversation mingled with the drone of voices as the actors in the Dressing Room dressed and selected their props for the day. Little Mack's obvious flirtations with the girl in the makeup chair were a sight so commonplace that it went completely unnoticed by the others.

At the opposite end of the room, Danny was rifling through the metal rack of timecards on the wall beside the doorway. He looked carefully up and down the rows of cards, scanning each name at the top, all written in Sandy's perfect Catholic School penmanship. His eyes reached the bottom cards of the rack, and as if in distrust of them he started at the top again. This time he scanned more slowly, fighting with his brain to pay closer attention. Again, he reached the bottom of the rack not having found what he was looking for. He turned away abruptly and found himself face to face with Richard, who had been observing him for some time. Danny stepped back, startled.

"Lose something?" Richard asked.

Danny stumbled over his words, taken completely off guard by Richard's sudden appearance. As he spoke, his brain raced. This was his first personal encounter with the Castle Manager. Admittedly, Richard had intimidated him from the time they had met. His quiet, brooding demeanor and piercing dark eyes added to the mystique of the strange, bearded man.

"N-No. I, uh, I was just checking to see if Mia had punched in yet."

"Mia?" Richard said this as if her name was foreign to him, although it couldn't possibly have been since she had been under his management since the beginning of the season.

"I have to talk to her," Danny heard himself say. The nervousness in his voice was evident. "I can't seem to find her card though."

There was a long pause while Richard stared into Danny's eyes as if looking for a deeper meaning than his words were imparting.

"Oh."

With this, Richard turned and walked through the exit. Danny watched him go in weird puzzlement, feeling the depth of the jolt that Richard's appearance had given him. He worked to squelch the fluttering of butterflies in his stomach. They flew randomly between the uneasiness of his strange encounter with Richard, and with the disappearance of Mia and her timecard. He began to feel as if her presence in the Castle was being erased. Finally, Danny exhaled the big breath that he had unconsciously been holding in his lungs since they spoke, making room for more butterflies.

Richard grumbled as he walked out into the oppressive heat. He hated it when anyone poked into Castle business of any sort, even if it was something as minor as rifling through his timecards. Working inside the Castle had made him callous. He was finding it increasingly more difficult to relate to anyone outside his circle of friends.

Danny left the card rack and stepped out into the sunlight. He would table his search for now. He didn't want to provoke Richard any further. He spotted Sandy at the railing a few yards away. Watching her for a few seconds, he enjoyed the fact that she was completely unaware of his eyes on her. Her long curls danced with the sea air, and her layered peasant top and skirt were silhouetted by the white sands below and behind her. It all made for a very surreal picture.

Now Sandy noticed him as well. Walking to her, he couldn't help but marvel at her fresh face, smiling back at him. Sandy's ability to avoid the ravages of a hangover was nothing short of miraculous. He had awoken this morning to the customary pain and guilt he always felt after a night of heavy drinking. It was only with the help of Tylenol (and barbecue-flavored potato chips…Danny's secret hangover remedy) that he could function at all. Yet here stood Sandy without the slightest trace of morning-after remorse.

"Mia's timecard is gone," he said flatly.

Sandy didn't reply. She just continued to watch him. "I haven't seen her yet this morning," Danny added.

"So maybe she quit." He detected a new dryness in her tone.

"Without saying a word to anyone?"

She looked at him and Danny felt a more sarcastic vibe

from her. "She didn't exactly hold an executive position here, Dan. People come and go all the time. They quit pretty suddenly in this place, especially at the end of the season."

"Alright, maybe she *did* quit. But why would her timecard be missing?"

"Because when you're leaving in a hurry you grab your timecard, punch out, show it to the boss, collect your pay, and get the hell out." Sandy's eyes flashed for an instant. Perhaps she had some jealousy of her own. "She probably brought the card up to Harry's office last night before she left. That would explain why you didn't see her leave."

There was no real reason that Danny should have felt the anger he was feeling well up in himself at this.

"You've got an explanation for everything. Maybe you just can't accept that something might have happened to her last night. In *there*!" Danny said this a little too loudly. A few pairs of eyes came to rest on him, and then the murmurs of the other actors mingled with the sound of the ocean again. He saw the anger beginning to well up in Sandy; this was one department in which Sandy would not be outdone. In fact, she reserved a special twang in her voice for just such occasions. She would later refer to it as her Jersey Girl twang.

"And maybe *you* can't accept that she *stood you up*! Listen, Dan, your friend Mia is a common type around this place. Whatever line she fed you had nothing to do with the truth. Now why can't you just drop it?"

They stood facing one another in a heavy silence. If

tension truly could be cut with a knife, a hacksaw might suffice in this instance. Sandy was the first to regain her composure, or maybe she was just the first of the two to pretend she had regained it.

"I'm sorry, Danny. I don't mean to sound unfeeling, but you might need a reality check here. This is not some mysterious haunted house with a monster lurking inside. The kids that work here are basically transients. When the season is over, they find another job…or go back to school. She paused briefly, possibly for emphasis. "Or just live off Mommy and Daddy again for a while. Judging from what I know of Mia, this was probably the case with her."

Danny had to admit that she made more sense than he would have liked her to.

"My advice to you is just drop it. It'll only get you more aggravation."

Danny turned and stared out at the ocean for a while. The sense that there was something very wrong would not release its grip on him, but he knew he must resolve to simply do nothing. He would just watch and wait to see if anything out of the ordinary actually did materialize. The hardest part would be the fight with the feeling in his gut. The facts weren't much to go on, but his intuitive feelings had always been quite reliable to Danny.

He turned back to face Sandy, "I know you're right. God, I must sound pretty stupid to you."

"A little."

"Don't help…"

Sandy just smiled. Danny felt her unusually cool hand slide over his own hand on the pier railing. Sandy *did* understand. That was why he had confided in her in the first place.

Inside the Dressing Room, the witch's makeup was almost complete now. With each new addition, Little Mack worked even harder at the real task at hand. He asked the girl his question for the umpteenth time, already anticipating her answer.

"I don't know, Mack. I've heard about you on dates," Penny said resolutely.

Little Mack skipped over the remark as if he had never heard it. He was aware of his reputation for womanizing at the Castle. It was legendary. In fact, many times he himself had worked hard to perpetuate that reputation. He never thought twice about using his position in lower management to influence the occasional monsterette. Now he assumed his most innocent tone and looked Penny straight in the eye, "All I'm saying is we could get some beers and sit on the beach. We can talk for a while, with nobody there to bother us."

"Talk? So, you're saying we're going to sit on the beach all by ourselves and just *talk*?"

He spun her chair toward him and looked deeply into her eyes (which were all but buried in the hideous mass of green-gray makeup surrounding them), doing his best to feign surprise, "Absolutely. Yes. Talk."

Mack was a pretty good actor, too.

Penny smirked now. The expression on her face was

barely discernible through the rubber appliances covering her cheeks and nose, along with the long false witch's chin.

"Well, then maybe all the stuff I've heard about you *isn't* true."

Little Mack laughed a little nervous laugh. He thought of telling her that his escapades were all exaggerated. How the girls he had dated before hadn't been unwilling to begin with. He dismissed these thoughts quickly, deciding to stick with the innocent act he had already initiated.

"Why don't we meet at the bottom of the ramp, after closing? Say twelve-thirty? I'll run out for the beer beforehand."

Penny shook her head and smiled. She looked around the Dressing Room at the other smiling faces who had been privy to their conversation. She tossed the scenario around in her head one last time. How bad could it be? After all, she was a big girl. She could handle the likes of Little Mack with no problem.

"Twelve-thirty sounds good."

Jubilantly adding some final touches to Penny's makeup, he planted a ragged pointed hat atop her mass of purposely matted and tangled hair. As cliche as the character was, Little Mack's innovative work had transformed it into something that would be sure to get real scares.

As Penny stood up from her seat and walked to the shelf where her handbag lay, Mack began to straighten the mess atop the long makeup table. He absently put the pencils and jars of greasepaint back in their rightful places, grabbing randomly as he went along the tabletop. Suddenly he grabbed something sticky and still wet in certain folds. It was a crumpled rubber glove that had been tossed into the fray of the other makeup tools. Its odd feel gave Mack a start.

"Whoa! Geez, what the —? Who left *this* here?" Lifting the glove up before his face, he drew a few snickers from the others in the Dressing Room.

"I don't know what kind of perverted shit you guys are up to in your scenes, but I think we can draw a line where good taste ends!"

There were a few more giggles as Little Mack emphatically tossed the glove into a nearby trashcan. The rusty hue of the wetness in its folds glistened in the bright lights of the Makeup Area.

# 2

Mia's sense of reason was clouded behind a veil of pain and periods of complete unconsciousness. She didn't know where she was, or what had happened. She knew one thing for sure. She was dying.

There was no light in this place. Or perhaps there was, but Mia could not focus her eyes enough to truly comprehend this. There was an overwhelming smell of something she recognized. It pinched her nostrils and burned the inside of her lungs with each shallow breath she labored to take. What was that? Was it tar? She couldn't think. She struggled against the encroaching darkness. Was she dead already?

Muffled sounds made their way through her death veil. She didn't know if they were the sounds of the pier, but they certainly could have been. They were joyful sounds. Transposed to the least joyful place she had ever been or *ever would* be. Laughter echoed through her tired brain, suddenly bringing back a horrible remembrance. The terrible raspy laughter of the creature with the knife. The memory roused her, and she struggled to scream but could not make a sound. Because now, finally, Mia *was* dead.

# 3

After having spent a somewhat uneventful morning, Danny was seated at a table in the Actors' Area, sipping the last of a soda from a tall paper cup. He winced at the watery concoction that the noonday sun had made of it and mopped the thick layer of condensation from the cup's mushy wax coating. Just then Juanita appeared from the Dressing Room and plopped down on the bench beside him. Practically on top of him. Danny squirmed away from beneath the folds of her costume and managed awkwardly to put a few inches of distance between the two of them. He didn't have to look at Juanita's face twice to recognize who she was. He had been strategically avoiding her since Sandy had described her from afar when he first came to the pier.

Danny's eyes remained locked downward, staring at his wet glistening hands from the moisture on the soda cup. He glanced inconspicuously at her from time to time as they sat in silence.

He noticed the way she had affected the various feminine traits that she must have studied for years in women, while herself being trapped in the body of a man. Mostly he could not help noticing the heaviness of her hands, and how even the most careful manicure could not hide their inherent masculinity.

Now she was speaking to him. Her acid Spanish intonations were less forceful than they had been when she was arguing with Richard, but no less difficult to translate. She turned to face him, and Danny moved his eyes reluctantly up to her face as she spoke, "Hallo, Baby. Jou gonna be de Bawtler today?"

Forgetting the costume he was wearing, Danny's brain struggled to figure out how she could know this. Thankfully his mouth was working on autopilot, and he heard himself reply, "Yes, uh, I am. I'm the Butler."

There came a long pause. Then his voice found more random words to say.

"And what are *you* playing?"

Juanita proudly puffed out her fledgling breasts, displaying the risqué black leather corset that she donned beneath a modest robe. She produced a long, braided leather whip from inside the canvas satchel that sat on the bench beside her. She had obviously been waiting for the question, baiting Danny until he bit. The costume was her own, as were all of Juanita's costumes. And she had said to the management at the beginning of her tenure at the Castle that she must always do her own makeup, explaining that her skin was hypersensitive, and adding that she could only use certain cosmetic products or otherwise risk an outbreak. The real reason that she applied her own makeup, of course, went unmentioned. But everyone knew that Juanita always bore the slightest of five o'clock shadows.

"I'm de sadeestic animal tamer een de Meesing Leenk scene. I jawst lawve being de Sadie Lady" She laughed emphatically at this, adding to what had already become an uncomfortable conversation for Danny. He smiled and heard himself say, "Yeah, I'll bet you do." Thankfully she let the comment pass unnoticed.

"What's jour name, Baby?"

"Danny Neumann." There was a pause. "…And yours?"

"My name ees Juanita." She grated the "J" sound in the back of her throat roughly, like catching a piece of popcorn there, "*Jost* Juanita."

"Oh. One name. Like *Sting*."

"Like *Cher*." (This came out "chair")

"Of course," Danny replied.

"Eet's bery nice to meet jou, Denny Neumann."

"Thanks."

Just 'thanks'. Not 'It's very nice to meet you too'. Juanita very rarely heard that reply. It was a reaction she commonly received from others, and in truth it had never bothered her in the least. The tolerant climate that would be created by the LGBTQ movement was still decades away, so anything short of animosity toward her and her friends was a gift.

Danny felt them slipping into another awkward silence, and Juanita sat watching him, wearing her incredible painted-on smile. Suddenly he was speaking again, "Have you been working here at the Castle since the beginning of the season?"

"No, no. I started here abow a mawnth ago. I was een Las Vegas before."

Somehow, she seemed to struggle with every word of the sentence, except for the words *Las Vegas*, which she gave the perfect Latin pronunciation. There was the slightest pause, then she added, "I jost love dees place, don' jou?"

Danny smiled. "It's definitely different."

He relaxed just the slightest bit as he said it. Finally, his words didn't lack sincerity. The fact that the job was 'different' was a point that no one could argue. Not even Juanita. While the rest of the world looked at her in a strange and suspicious light, she was accepted here. She was not odd. Within these walls she could be herself, and that made her as acceptable as anyone else. Perhaps her eccentricity even made her a little bit *more* acceptable.

"I like all de cute leedle American Wow-wows rawning aroun here. I could jost eat jou all up!"

The comment cemented Danny's nervousness thoroughly. He instinctively edged away from her on the bench, moving as inconspicuously as possible, a scant inch at a time. Juanita continued, blissfully unaware of his movement. Or maybe she did notice, but simply didn't care.

"What deed jou do before jou came here?" She asked.

"Huh? What?"

Now she looked straight at him, her eyes locked on his. He was forced to halt his careful retreat from her for the moment.

"Whatsa metter, Denny Neumann? Do I make jou nervous?"

"No. No, of course you don't," Danny answered instantly, "I was a — I mean, I *am* a musician. A singer."

His words filled Juanita with utter elation. She fairly had to hold herself back from embracing him, and the look on her face did nothing for Danny's wracked nerves.

"Dat's wawnderful! I *lawve* seengers!"

With this, her hand came down hard on Danny's knee. He automatically jumped to his feet with her heavy touch. It was purely a reflex action; Danny couldn't have prevented it if he tried. Juanita looked up at him, surprised.

"What's de metter, Denny? Deed I scare jou?"

"No."

But Danny backed away as he spoke to her, looking over his shoulder at the open Dressing Room door. His sanctuary. He couldn't help thinking that the door seemed to be miles away.

"No. I just remembered that I have to get up to the

Butler's Area right away. I'm already late."

He backed toward the door as he spoke, "My replacement must be wondering why I'm taking such a long break."

With the words barely through his lips, he now made a mad dash into the Dressing Room, bumping into a small group of break-bound monsters on the way in. Juanita continued their conversation, as though he were still sitting beside her. She was used to this sort of reaction from men. Straight men.

"Okay, I'll talk to jou later, Baby."

Now finding herself alone in the Actors' Area, Juanita scanned the other tables with her eyes, in search of another unsuspecting 'victim' to talk to. Upon realizing she was alone, she took a small compact from her purse and painstakingly applied more makeup to her already-overdone face.

**"...there was a formidable air of strength, agility, and courage, constituting a singular exception to the eternal rule which ordains that force, as well as beauty, shall result from harmony. He looked like a giant who had been broken in pieces and ill soldered together."**

**— Victor Hugo —**
**THE HUNCHBACK OF NOTRE DAME**

# 4

It had truly been a long and arduous night for Atwill Jarrett, and the coming day promised to be even longer. He had left the Sand Bar at four a.m. and had moved on to a twenty-four-hour bar down the street after that. He found it hard to force himself to make his way home, knowing that his horrible nightmares would be waiting for him there.

The drinking and the pills had made his limbs shaky, and his lack of sleep made each step he took difficult. He felt as though someone or some*thing* had knocked the wind out of him. Someone had. It was someone in a black hooded shroud who visited him nightly, stealing the very breath from his aching lungs. This shrouded figure was fast becoming his master. His evil boss, from whom he sought refuge in the noisy company of others. Whose raspy laugh could only be drowned out in his head by a hefty dose of self-medication.

With great difficulty, Jarrett began the slow process

of readying himself for work. He tied the tall platform boots, which added another four inches to his already-abnormal height. The boots were heavy, forcing Jarrett to wonder whether he could make it through the entire shift while wearing them. He realized that he must. It was crucial to the role he had played so many times before. He finished lacing up the shoes, then made the short lumbering journey to the makeup table, where he took a seat.

When Little Mack started to apply the base makeup to Jarrett's face, its coolness felt wonderful on his burning skin. He drank in the moment of absolute relief, and his fingers slowly began to let go of the tight hold that they instinctively had on the little bottle of pills in his pocket.

# 5

The Watcher's vision was almost completely obscured by the brainstars now, as he crouched behind the railing in the tiny back loft of the Portrait Room. He had already watched two groups pass through the room, and he sat contented with his invisibility to everyone inside. That was until the familiar pin spot of pain in his head began to grow. It swelled little by little. It pulsed like a tiny heartbeat in his head. It beat and it grew. Now it was reaching unbearable proportions, and his ability to stave it off was being swallowed up. The Watcher knew that it would only be a matter of minutes before he would have to leave his comfortable hiding place to seek the horrible relief that was his only escape from the heartbeat in his head.

He was blind from the thick layer of brainstars that covered his eyes, and deafened by the overwhelming noise that was the pounding of his own heart. The pounding that covered up the sound of his victim's screams. His own dime-store version of Poe's *The Telltale Heart.* The Watcher's fingers began to nervously scratch in time to the rhythm of his heartbeat on the dusty wooden floor of the loft. His scratches grew louder and stronger with every beat. He was oblivious to the sound of his fingers on the wood, just as he was oblivious to the growing pain in his right hand as his fingers began to bleed. It was just another bit of blood that his Thinking Self would have to clean up later. And there would be so much more blood than this. Pools of blood that would take real time to soak up. Beautiful glistening strands of red against white flesh and soaked into the folds of clothing. The thought of the blood was quieting in an awful way and made the Watcher anxious for the horrible relief from the throbbing ache in his head. His strumming intensified.

Now he found himself humming softly as he scratched. A steady tone, constant and unwavering. The hum of white noise. His hum blended with the drone of the soundtracks from the other areas of the Castle, and the sounds bled together like the murders in his mind. Surely someone out there must have heard him. Now he added a slight, almost imperceptible rocking motion to his strange symphony. The loft's floorboards creaked faintly beneath him as he rocked back and forth.

Another unknowing group of customers had been led into the Portrait Room. Their shuffling and whispering were quelled when Count Dracula made his appearance, and they seemed enthralled by his every word. Once his speech had ended, they stood quietly as he motioned with his heavy cape toward the door to the Jester's Area. They heard the odd rhythmic scratching and the hum that was like a musical accompaniment to the Count's words. It drifted down into the crowd from above and seemed to grow louder as they began to file out of the room.

It was then that the heavy shrouded figure with one profusely-bleeding hand leaped to the floor behind them. The floor shook as his solid weight came down at full force. Some patrons at the front of the group hurried through the door into the next room, but most stood dumbstruck at the sight. This was quite an elaborate special effect for a funhouse, and several of the screaming customers couldn't help but be impressed. Even Dracula looked a bit stunned.

The Watcher stood before them now, smiling eerily. It would only be a matter of moments before he would select and isolate his next victim, separating them from the others in the group. He would probably do it in the dim forgiving light of the Swamp, just scant steps away. Soon the pain and the noise would be gone. The brainstars would clear from his eyes, no longer clouding them with their brilliant flood. Relief for the Watcher was in sight.

# 6

Danny bolted up the Belltower stairs to the safety of his position in the Butler Area. He swung the iron gate closed behind him with a bang. Thankfully he had no trouble with the gate's latch today. In his haste, Danny would have gladly crashed through the gate if he had to. He looked back anxiously through the bars at the empty staircase, as if Juanita might be in pursuit. She would no doubt still be carrying on the inane conversation from the Actors' Area, throwing odd sexual innuendos in for good measure.

But the stairs were silent. She had not followed him.

Danny turned slowly, still panting from his frantic flight, and realized that the Butler Area was filled with customers. The gathering of anxious faces stood staring at him wide-eyed. Their surprised gazes were mirrored in the face of his Butler replacement, who had been anxiously awaiting Danny's return. Handing over the huge battle axe, he beat a hasty retreat through the gate and down the stairs, mumbling complaints about Danny. The word "asshole" was integrated into the tirade in several key spots.

Danny felt a sting of panic as he looked at the large group of customers amassed behind the velvet rope. This was an especially large group; larger than any he had seen in the Portrait Room at one time. He didn't want to break them into two parts, so he took hold of the rope and unhooked it from the wall. He began his practiced Butler speech, still gasping for breath from his run up the stairs.

"Please enter my Master's Portrait Room," Another gasp, "Please step all the way to the front of the room." He gasped again, unable to continue with his speech. All air had left his lungs with his last word. He ushered the huge group inside, making sure that they filled every spot in the room that was available. Finally, he gave the last of them a good shove to get them out of the way of the swinging doors. One girl wheeled around to face Danny with an irate look, "Hey! I thought the monsters weren't allowed to touch you in here!"

Danny gave her a deadpan look and simply replied, "We're not."

He slammed the big doors closed before she could offer a reply, leaving the distinct image of the girl standing in open- mouthed wonderment etched in Danny's mind. He leaned against the back wall of the Butler Area's dark alcove. He was almost breathing normally now.

The darkness in this little area was nearly complete. He kicked at the small pile of trash at his feet and muttered to himself softly, moving the pile of discarded items around with his toe. He could clearly make out the shape of a small square foil packet with one end torn off in a rough diagonal. No doubt torn in haste. He shook his head at the empty condom packet, muttering again.

"Really? Here?" He laughed, "You bastards are even sicker than I gave you credit for."

Danny kicked gently at the little packet and heard it make a tiny clicking sound as the jagged foil edge of the torn end caught on the carpet. He decided not to investigate any further, lest he find its spent contents also living amongst the trash pile.

Inside the Portrait Room, Bobby was finishing his stock Dracula speech. Danny noted the familiar scuffle of feet as the group prepared to exit the room. In a few seconds he would open the doors. He wasn't in much of a hurry to do so, as this would necessitate his engaging in conversation with Bobby. The Count would be sure to complain to him about the huge size of the group, lecturing in his most superior tone of voice. Maybe Danny would just let the doors stay closed for a few extra minutes this time.

From within the room, he suddenly heard a loud thud, like a great weight had hit the floor. Danny looked up from the debris at his feet, wondering if there might be trouble inside. He moved to the big doors and pressed his ear against one. All he could hear were the shrieks and laughter of the startled group, who were mostly walking through the Throne Room, where the Jester was surely beginning his act by now. The noise, he thought, must have been Bobby, jumping down from the mantel to produce one last scare. This was something that Bobby would do if the group was taking too long to leave the room. It was a classic Bobby move; he was never satisfied.

From behind the doors, Danny could make out Bobby's voice talking with someone. Satisfied that he was sufficiently occupied, Danny retreated into his dark hiding place. He moved the pile of litter further into the alcove once and for all. In doing so his foot met something soft, bigger than the rest, hiding deep in the back corner. He bent to pick the object up. It was a dirty dress. No doubt the accompaniment to the condom he had discovered previously.

He held it up in the light now and noticed that it had huge tears in it, along with an undeniable blood stain in the stomach area. A chill ran through him as he recognized the dress. It was the pink prom gown that Mia had been wearing in the Plaza the night before. Danny gasped quietly at the recognition of it. He held it up for what seemed like a long time, studying the stains that were not there when he last saw Mia wearing it. He whispered hoarsely, "Mia…?"

Suddenly a sound came from the Portrait Room, just inside the big double doors. There was the scuffle of feet, and then a deep raspy voice. It was the voice of the Watcher, whispering through the crack between the doors. He was talking to Danny.

"Your little friend won't be able to play with you anymore, Danny. It appears that she had a little…accident."

Danny turned toward the voice, as the dress slid soundlessly from his open hand. It fell back into place amid the pile of rubbish at his feet.

"Who is that?" He put his palm flat against one of the doors, trying to give it a shove. It wouldn't budge. "What are you talking about?"

The only reply was the Watcher's quiet, scratchy cackle. The sound was somewhere between laughter and the scraping of fingernails on a chalkboard. Or the sound of scratching fingers on the floor of the Portrait Room's loft. Danny remained frozen now, stunned by the words that this mysterious creature behind the doors had spoken to him. He had said 'friend'. Did he mean Mia? He had said something about an accident.

Now Danny's confusion began to mingle with a sick fear. He looked at his own hand, still poised against one of the Portrait Room doors. The door's cool feel was something of a surprise to Danny. He had expected it to burn his fingertips, with the fire of the beast that spoke to him from the other side. He braced one shoulder against the door on the right and waited, hoping to catch his tormentor off guard. He waited a beat, then shoved with all he had. The doors still did not open. They were wedged shut by a great weight on the other side. Or a great *strength*. The strength of the Watcher's Angry Self.

Danny battered the doors once again with his shoulder, then leaned in to peer through the crack between them, where the awful sound of that voice had come from, calling in to it now, "Where's Mia?"

He shifted his weight and gave the door on the left a try. This too produced no more than the slightest quiver. The

Watcher's otherworldly laughter trickled out toward Danny once again. He took a small step back as the raspy voice was speaking to him.

"C'mon, Asshole, you can do better than that. Even your little girlfriend was tougher than that."

Danny took a few steps backward and looked hard at the doors. He lunged at them suddenly, thinking foolishly that he might take the Watcher by surprise. The doors gave way just the slightest bit this time, but not enough to make a difference. The disembodied voice wasted no time in answering, "Oh, now *that* was better."

A long silence followed. Danny began to wonder if the strange being had left, or if he still hovered behind the doors. And why wasn't there a new group of customers amassing here in the Butler's Area? Surely there should have been a few people by now. Danny wondered why he was all alone. Where was Bobby? Was he a party to this strange exchange? Was this him? Or was it just a terrible joke being played on Danny by the other Castle pranksters? All these questions swirled through the muddle inside Danny's head. Then, suddenly the rasp of the voice broke the silence.

"Am I making you angry, Danny?" A little laugh that was nothing more than a growl rumbled up through the Watcher's throat, "I made Mia angry too. Then we got a little better acquainted. You might say we became close."

Danny looked down at the torn dress at his feet. The empty cackle filled another long pause.

"Then I killed her."

Danny stood stunned for a moment, having anticipated the horrible words before they were spoken. This was straight out of any one of the slasher films that he and his friends had watched on countless occasions. His brain registered it all as nothing more than a bad joke, surreal words in a make-believe scenario.

The tiny hysterical smile that had found its way to his lips slowly began to dissolve. He felt his anger boiling up to the surface, as he leaned in against the doors and muttered under his breath to the horrible presence on the other side, "You son of a bitch."

He stepped back and attempted another lunge. This time the doors swung open on impact and Danny crashed into the room, halting his own momentum once he was inside. He looked frantically from one side of the room to the other, but it appeared to be completely deserted, including the gaping frame of the Portrait. It stared down at him ominously from above the mantel. And Bobby was nowhere to be found. Add cowardice to his list of unsavory attributes, Danny thought.

Still angry, but wary of his lingering presence, Danny called out to the Watcher. He spoke quietly at first, then a bit louder, then even louder until finally he was shouting the words, "Where are you? Where are you, you bastard?! Show yourself!"

The only reply was the hollow echo of Danny's voice in the empty room. He walked forward cautiously, turning from side to side in anticipation of the attack that seemed imminent. He eyed the gaping mouth of the Portrait again.

The pin spot that normally shone on Bobby's face dissipated into an amber haze at the back of the recess in the wall. Approaching the doorway to the Throne Room, Danny peered carefully around the corner. That room, too, was deserted. He continued his cautious advance into the next room, The Sick Room. The two girls currently manning the scene looked up at him from their gossipy chatter. Danny considered whether it was worth it to ask if they had seen anything. He thought better of it and moved on. The girls just shrugged their shoulders and rolled their eyes, then resumed their conversation, uninterrupted. They glanced back at Danny's form, illuminated in the doorway by the red glow of the Swamp, and then he was gone.

# 7

All eyes in the Lobby were fixed on the opening in the wall beside the First Cage Monster, which was now filled with what seemed to be a long queue of customers. They were not running, not moving at all. They were just standing, waiting.

Judy had seen the crowds watching the wall behind her little booth, but she reacted with the complete lack of interest that was her norm. Finally, the rotary phone on the wall beside her began to ring. She reached over and picked up the receiver. She knew who it was. It was Management upstairs, complaining about something or other that she couldn't care less about.

"Judy, is there anybody from security hanging around the Lobby right now?" It was Richard, and he sounded particularly agitated.

"Oh, hi Richard."

"Whoever is there, tell them to get their ass to the First Cage! We've got a bunch of customers who can't get through the hallway."

Judy stood up from the little stool in the booth and opened the barred gate into the Lobby. Her emergence predictably caused a little wave of panic from the customers standing nearby, and they cleared a path for her obediently. She looked around and finally spied one of the several ancillary employees who sported a blue polo shirt with the word SECURITY printed on the back in neat white letters. She motioned for him to come to her.

"What's up? What's happening inside? Looks like we've got a traffic jam", she said, pointing to the growing line of customers visible through the wall's opening. "Richard wants you to go see what's happening with the First Cage. And hurry up, he sounded pissed."

The young man, Jimmy by name, hastily made his way through the growing throng. He disappeared amid the sea of bodies at the entrance to the jammed Castle.

Judy shook her head as she grudgingly pushed past the same group of people who had just made way for Jimmy to pass. She opened the booth's gate and reclaimed her seat at the window. Reaching below the shelf in front of her she now produced a black painted sign with big white letters that read: SORRY, WE ARE TEMPORARILY

NOT ADMITTING VISITORS. She couldn't help but smile a little as she opened the little paperback that sat concealed on her lap. This day was shaping up nicely, she thought.

Jimmy had finally managed to squeeze past the greater part of the stalled crowd at the entrance and made his way to the First Cage. Inside the dark cage, the actor who had been charging repeatedly at customers until the crowd on the stairs grew too large and all movement had halted, sat in silence. Jimmy simply nodded to the young man as he passed by. Finally, he reached the narrow passageway before the stairs to the Butler's Area. He saw what was stopping the customers from passing through.

It was the wax figure of Harry. His massive form lay stretched across the foot of the stairs. The shroud he wore was shredded in several places, and smeared with thick, messy globs of stage blood. Or so Jimmy thought. A massive knife protruded from the place where Harry's heart would beat, that is if he were indeed a living breathing human being. Impaled on the knife was an incredibly realistic-looking human heart. A trail of gore led up to the figure on the floor, and the patrons had avoided getting near it for fear of treading on the bloody stream. The red path wound about ten feet beyond the figure and up three of the stairs. That was where Harry's severed head sat, gazing at the crowd. His glasses were askew, and the fixed smirk on his lips gave him an even more macabre air.

The sight of it knocked the wind out of Jimmy's lungs. He stared at it all for a minute and wondered what the hell he was going to do now. His hand instinctively went to the walkie- talkie on his belt.

# 8

The Watcher began to stir again, safely hidden within the deep recess of the Portrait frame. Danny was gone, somewhere in the Swamp, and the Watcher's Thinking Self had quite a task ahead of him now. He stood up in the frame, and the spotlight that usually gave Dracula's makeup its eerie glow flashed across the Watcher's own bizarre costume. He wore a detailed Grim Reaper mask and a tattered shroud. As the light's beam touched his eyes through the mask's slits, a sharp bolt of pain found its way into his brain.

Reaching down, he pulled the body from the floor. Fortunately, Bobby was thin and quite light, otherwise the job would have been impossible for his tired Thinking Self to manage. The killing was over for now, and all he could think about was rest. But first he had to do away with the traces of his other Self's handiwork.

He dragged the body out of the deep recess, down the ladder steps that led up to the Portrait, and across the floor of the Portrait Room, leaving in its wake a dark, glistening trail. He paused at the double doors, peering anxiously down the hall for witnesses. There were none. His roadblock at the bottom of the stairs was doing its job nicely. Thanks, Harry, ole pal.

He pulled the limp form through the open doors and into the waiting prop closet across the hall from the Butler's Area. Once safely inside the closet, the Watcher slammed the narrow wooden door shut with a quick thrust of his foot, and he was once again alone with the former Prince of Darkness. Bobby truly was the vampire now. His smeared white makeup and the very real wooden stake that protruded from his blood-stained white shirt were a testament to that. The profusion of blood that soaked the fabric put Little Mack's tiny trickles of stage blood to shame.

For a moment the triumphant violent part of the Watcher emerged, and he laughed down at his latest victim. He lightly placed two fingers on Bobby's eyelids, closing them in a way that was unfittingly tender. Not unlike a caress.

He put his face close to Bobby's, and with eyes fixed on the vampire's dead lips he whispered, "Good night, sweet Prince…"

He punctuated his own words with an explosive burst of raspy laughter as his hand reached up and extinguished the closet's single hanging light bulb with a quick pull of its chain.

# 9

The Human Sacrifice Room was an inherently dismal little room at the heart of the Castle Proper. It was cut off from the other scenes by winding passages and stairs, thus making it an entity unto itself. The very nature of its isolation gave it a particularly creepy aspect. Add to that a fiery cauldron, zombie-like dwarf figures, and a soundtrack of primitive chanting, and you had the makings of a truly frightening experience.

The room was never a favorite among the actors, either. Many felt nervous there, especially when working alone. This was not only due to its creepy surroundings but also because of countless stories of incidents that had supposedly taken place there. Most popular was the tale of some five real-life Satan worshippers who used to work at the Castle, and who had performed authentic rituals of devil worship inside that very room. Since that time, the storytellers would say, the room itself had proven unlucky for several actors. One had suffered a broken leg while running at a group of customers and slipping (mysteriously) at the top of the stairs. Another had "accidentally" plunged a sharp prop knife into the soft flesh between his thumb and index finger, thus impaling himself on a nearby Styrofoam wall. Yet another had suffered a concussion when one of the heavy branches of the plaster-of-Paris tree in the corner of the room fell on him during his speech. The customers had laughed at the poor fellow's misfortune, thinking it was part of the act, and had walked away from the scene, leaving the boy alone and unconscious. It was a full quarter of an hour before he was discovered.

So, cursed or not, the Human Sacrifice Room had its share of unsettling lore. It was the most haunted place in a haunted place.

Still hungrily stalking his unseen tormentor, Danny's heart pounded a Latin tempo in his ears. His eyes darted from corner to corner of every scene as he passed through them, inching his way cautiously through the building. Now he silently entered the Human Sacrifice Room and could sense the presence of another person, although the dim lighting made it impossible for him to be sure. He tried to force his eyes to adjust, but to no avail. His heart's Latin tempo became a pulsating jungle rhythm.

From the darkest corner to his left, Danny heard a cracking sound, like footfalls on dried branches. He could just barely make out the form of the brown-robed man in the corner, who was turning eerily to face him. The man's face was hidden deep in the shadow of the hooded monk's robe he wore. The sight forced a low gasp that started in Danny's chest and worked its way up to his lips. A beam of light from one of the tiny pin spots caught the face in the depths of the hood.

There was a thick moment of apprehension, and then Danny let out a long sigh.

This was no shrouded demon. It was Gordon. The recognition brought some of the blood that had drained from his face back again. He stepped toward his friend and was speaking before Gordon could offer so much as a "hello".

"Gordon, thank God. I think I'm losing my mind, man."

A look of concern began to replace the smile on Gordon's face, "What is it, Dan?" He looked a bit closer, "Geez, you really look like shit."

"It's Mia," Danny continued, completely disregarding Gordon's remark, "Gordon, I think she's dead. Somebody in this place killed her.

The words seemed to come toward Gordon from a deep pit. He couldn't be serious, he thought. This was a joke, right?

"I'm telling you she's dead. I know it."

Now Gordon began to laugh. His eyes remained fixed on Danny's, waiting for him to break down and admit he was kidding. Danny was always making this sort of joke. Sick ones. But now he just stared back at him in silence, and Gordon's laughter abruptly stopped. He looked at Danny hard, searching his friend's panic-filled eyes for a clue.

"Wait a minute. I think you're serious about this."

"I am serious! Mia was murdered by someone here. She was killed in this place!"

"Killed." Gordon had trouble saying the word out loud. After a moment he added, "You were right when you said you're losing your mind."

Danny seemed deaf to Gordon's comment, "Okay, now get *this*," he said, "The guy who killed her just spoke to me in the Portrait Room. He *told* me that he killed her."

Gordon stood frozen, his eyes locked on Danny's. There were no words now. No clever retorts, no argument or agreement. Nothing. He had never spoken to a lunatic before, he thought.

"Alright," he began hesitantly, "I know that you're a rational person. If you say that someone told you that, well, I believe you."

"You do?"

"Yes. I believe that someone told you that. Whether they truly did what they said is another story. Maybe that explains it. Somebody could just be screwin' with you."

"Why would someone go so far to do that?"

Gordon laughed. "Are you serious? In this place? These people *live* for that kind of stuff." He thought briefly of the fetal position contests, "They love to play with other people's heads. It's how they make their living for Christ's sake!"

Another figure in a brown robe stepped up silently beside them. This person had surely been hidden in the shadows of the room during Danny and Gordon's whole exchange. With their sudden approach, Danny jumped back slightly. He had reached his limit for sudden scares. A soft woman's voice finally came from within the dark recess of the robe's hood, "Hi Danny. What's up?"

Susan pulled the robe's hood down. She adjusted it neatly around her shoulders. Monster chic.

"Oh." Gordon was saying, "Danny, you remember Susan?" "Sure. Hi, Susan."

"She's our newest cast member."

Things between Gordon and this girl were apparently heating up, Danny thought.

Susan could see that Danny was in an agitated state, and his extreme reaction to her appearance evidenced that something must really be wrong. She was immediately apologetic, "I'm sorry, did I scare you?"

Deep down Danny felt the need to explain his fears to her as he had with Gordon, but he thought better of it. Why should he risk having *two* people know that he was losing his mind?

"No, it's not you. I'm just a little jumpy today, that's all."

"Then I think you're working in the wrong place," she laughed.

"Yeah, I'm beginning to think that myself." But he wasn't laughing. He was absolutely serious about that.

Susan moved silently away, toward the orange-painted surface that served as a grill for the Human Sacrifice Room's bubbling black cauldron. She took a seat and reached behind the pot to the container of dry ice hidden in the shadows.

Shooting a quick nervous glance at the little army of troll- like dummies that peopled the shadowy forest behind her, she replenished the cauldron's supply. Fresh billows of "smoke" poured down the pot's outer surface in ample waves.

With Susan out of earshot, Danny spoke to Gordon in a whisper, "I don't know what's going on around here, but I'm beginning to get the horrible feeling that it's real. And now I'm involved." Gordon could see the growing panic in Danny's eyes with the realization. "He knows my name! Oh shit. He knows my name."

Gordon put one hand on Danny's shoulder, "You know

you're my friend, and I care about you man, but you have got to sit back and listen to yourself. You sound a little crazy." He paused. "It's this place. It's working here, where everything is designed to scare you; nothing is real. Your whole problem is just somebody's idea of a joke. You've seen how these people are."

"Yeah, well all your explanations may sound good, but I know what I saw. And I know what I heard. Nobody is that thorough when they're kidding around."

The angry tone growing in Danny's voice made Gordon fear that the conversation could lead to a fight between them if he didn't choose his words carefully. Danny was obviously irate and confused, and any more talk of calming down might send him in a bad direction. Gordon made his next suggestion carefully, "Why don't you ask Sandy if you can leave early today? Go home and just hang out. You look like you could use the rest."

There was no denying that. Though the anger was slowly ebbing away now, it was leaving in its place an overwhelming sense of helplessness and fatigue. Gordon was right. He *did* need a rest. More so, he needed a break from the Castle and its dark winding passageways. And its secrets. He nodded in silent agreement with his friend.

Seizing the moment, Gordon gently led Danny toward the doorway. "Let's go up to the Rat Professor's Area. There's an intercom there. I'll call the Dressing Room for you." He paused to look at his haggard friend, "Where were you working? The Butler Area? I'm sure they've noticed you're missing by now."

Danny nodded and they began to head toward the

stairway. Gordon called back over his shoulder to Susan, "Cover the room for a few minutes, Sue. I'll be right back."

Susan was at the doorway in a shot, watching them ascend the stairs. Her pleading eyes belied the calmness of her reply, "Okay, but make it quick."

Despite the short time she had been at the Castle, Susan had caught wind of the tales involving the Human Sacrifice Room's lurid past. In truth, it wasn't the creepy stories that bothered her. It wasn't even the dismal air of the room itself. What frightened her, *truly* frightened her, was the tiny doorway that was situated at the far end of the room. It was in a dark corner that was almost never utilized by the actors. Even the patrons of the Castle seemed to avoid congregating near it as the room filled up. It was almost instinctive.

The open doorway led to a small storage area. It would have been an ideal hiding place for braver souls who wanted to avoid work for a while without being caught. The small space was crammed with old parts of the Castle's many scenes. Retired relics from years past. There was nothing mysterious at all about this hole in the wall. And yet the thought of being alone in the room with the doorway so close by filled Susan with dread. She could only imagine something horrible living within the dark space. Something waiting to pounce when she least expected it.

She called to them as they disappeared up the stairs, "Okay. See ya, Dan! Hope you feel better!" This was obviously for the benefit of whomever, or whatever, was listening from within the dark little doorway. She glanced back toward it again. Maybe she had managed to fool whatever creature lay in wait for her within for now. But what would she do five minutes from now?

Up above the Human Sacrifice Room was the Rat Professor's Area. The light from the doorway to the outdoor parapet gave the little area a cheerier glow, and the distinctly fresher air it provided was a welcome respite from the Castle's interior murk. Barry was playing the role of the Rat Professor today. He wore the white lab coat and spectacles that were customary for the character. From underneath the lab coat peeked a very nineteenth-century style waistcoat and tie. As the shift progressed, Barry's costume routinely became more disheveled, and somehow it even seemed to grow more ill-fitting. It was common knowledge that Barry's performance was at its best when his costume looked its worst.

He was just finishing his speech to a group of customers, so Gordon held Danny's sleeve at the midway point on the staircase, so as not to interrupt the Rat Professor's act.

Barry spoke with a heavy affectation, in an old man's voice, "…And if you should feel the little rats nipping at your ankles as you walk through our Rat Room, simply reach down deep into your pockets and gather up all your loose change. If you throw lots of money at the rats, they won't bother you anymore!"

At this, a big stupid-looking guy in the group (who

could only be described as a 'big stupid-looking guy in the group') broke into Barry's monologue, halting his words.

"Yeah, right man, then *you'll* go in and pick up all the money."

Barry smiled back at the others in the group, as though they were in on his private joke. He looked at the large man, with an expression somewhere between revulsion and disbelief showing through the pallid makeup on his face. He broke character now, losing the thick accent he possessed moments before, and breaking into his native West-Jerseyan. "Brilliant. You figured me out."

The big stupid-looking guy just nodded his head proudly as the rest of the group laughed at his expense.

Barry assumed his Old Englishman persona once again and continued, "Alright, now you can all follow me and I'll force you— er, I mean, I'll *show* you into the Rat Room." He gathered his little wooden pointer, wielding it as a conductor would his baton, and began to hobble toward the doorway, "Come along now…"

He led the group across the Parapet, between the wall of the Rat Room and the battlements that were at the top of the Castle. He mimicked an aging pied piper leading the throng of rats in Hamlin.

The bright light of the Parapet served to make the guests' eyes more vulnerable to the complete darkness that they were about to encounter inside the Rat Room. The less they were able to see in there, the better. You see, the "rats" were just varying lengths of rubber hose, attached to the walls of the narrow passageway at roughly ankle height. The complete darkness, however, transformed these innocent objects into very real, very ominous rodents to any nervous customer. The hoses gave way just enough upon impact to give the illusion of a horde of rats brushing against their legs in the narrow hallway.

The customers streamed past Barry, who held the door open for them to enter. They bumped into one another repeatedly upon entering, laughing as they did so. Once they were inside the dark passage-way, Barry gave a wicked laugh and closed the door, but not fully. He left a meager crack so that a single sliver of light trickled through. He paused, leaning with one ear against the door, "How is it in there, kids? A little dark?"

Voices chimed out of the passageway back to him, with various comments, "Yeah, turn on some lights!", or "I can't see! What's touching my legs?!" Every sentence seemed to be punctuated with a scream or two. Barry just smiled and winked back at Danny and Gordon, who remained at his podium.

"Well, then, let me see if I can do anything about the light.

Oh, here, is this better…?"

He swung the door wide open for the briefest moment, letting in a flood of sunlight, then slammed it properly, sending them back into complete blackness. A universal scream rose from within.

The door moved several times under his weight as

Barry leaned into it, ensuring no escape. Finally, it calmed, and the group must surely have moved on.

Barry redirected his attention to his guests in the Rat Professor Area. He smiled at them, leaning his head back to view them through the tiny square spectacles that were perched on the end of his nose.

"Hey, guys. What's up? You need something?"

Gordon took a step toward the little alcove to Barry's left. "Can we use the intercom? Danny here is sick."

Barry sidestepped the two.

"Sure, use anything you want if he's sick. Just don't puke here or anything, okay? Somebody already did that once to me today."

Danny looked at Barry apologetically, "I'm not *that* kind of sick. Just dizzy."

Barry brushed past the two toward the little squawk box on the wall. He skirted Danny nervously as though he might be ill on him at any moment.

"Here, I'll call for you." He pressed the intercom's orange button, "Code Eight, Rat."

Little Mack responded to this almost immediately, "Yes, Ratsy, what can I do for you, your imperial wretchedness?"

"I have a guy here that's sick, and he wants to come down."

"A customer?" Little Mack's voice asked now.

Barry eyed Danny from head to foot and smiled, "Well, let's just say that if he's a customer, he has a very interesting way of dressing."

Danny leaned in beside Barry and spoke softly to him.

"My name is Dan. I was playing the Butler."

"It's Dan, the Butler," Barry repeated in a louder tone.

Now Little Mack's voice came through the box much louder and crackling with static.

"*The Butler*! That's miles away from your scene! What the hell did he leave and come up there for? He could've called from the intercom in the Butler Area!!"

Mack waited, but no explanation appeared to be forthcoming. Nor did he really want to hear one. After a few moments, the intercom awakened again with Mack's voice, "Never mind. Just tell him to come down to the Dressing Room and punch out for the day."

Barry gave the little box on the wall a quick "okay", then stepped back. After a beat, he pressed the button again, "Say goodbye, Mack."

"Goodbye, Mack." Came through the speaker obediently.

They decided that it would be much quicker if they just walked down through the Rat Room, instead of retracing their winding steps backward through the Castle. As they passed by Barry, Gordon turned back and waved, "Thanks a lot, man."

"Hey, no problem," Barry called to them, "Just remember, any loose change you find in there on your way through is *mine*. And don't think you won't find any!"

# 10

Inside the Dressing Room, the sound of fumbling noises came through the intercom a second time. These crackles and thumps were followed by the sound of a girl's voice. Her words were rendered nearly inaudible by the girl pressing her lips against the squawk box as she spoke. Hearing the staticky sounds, Little Mack walked to the intercom and pressed the button.

"You got Little Mack, here. Say it again, but this time don't stand so close to the box!"

Now the girl's words were somewhat more coherent, "I said, umm, code eight Butler."

It was Joanie, jokingly known to Mack and his friends as one of the "Castle Nitwits". Her finger was pressed firmly against the button of the intercom, and she felt that she held the fate of the Castle in her hand. Her friend Carol, another Castle Nitwit, stood beside her, chewing gum loudly and looking back over her shoulder repeatedly at the gathering group of customers behind the red velvet rope.

Little Mack rolled his eyes and pressed the button again, "Yeah, you got Mack. Who's this?"

"Oh, it's Joan." She paused a little longer than was called for. A low soughing sound came through the speaker, as Mack stood silently listening to her breathe into the intercom. "Listen, Mack. I don't know who's supposed to be the Butler today, but there's nobody here, and the customers have just been walking through the scene without seeing any show." Another pause. More soughing.

"Bobby's not in the Portrait, either."

Mack shifted his weight from one foot to the other uncomfortably and thought for a moment, muttering to himself.

"Okay, I'll get somebody in the Portrait right away," he said quickly, "You cover the Butler Area, and just walk people through the Portrait Room 'til a replacement gets there."

"Okay, but it's going to be pretty hard to scare any of them…". Joanie rolled her eyes and walked into the Portrait Room. Carol remained in the Butler Area a moment longer. As she turned to follow Joanie, a customer who was standing behind the rope called to her, "Hey, Blondie, you gonna let us in, or what?"

Carol gave him the most deadpan look she could muster, cracked her gum, and offered a curt "Shut up" before she disappeared through the double doors.

Little Mack muttered again quietly as he walked away from the intercom.

"Why don't you just breathe heavy at them and snap your chewing gum? That should be scary enough," he grumbled, "— And where the fuck is Bobby!? He's another pain in the ass Primadonna…"

He walked to the big rack of costumes adjacent to the makeup table and rifled through them roughly. Finally, he found what he needed. Standing now with one of the many Dracula capes in hand, his muttering continued as he walked out into the Actors' Area, searching for a likely Dracula. For once the area was entirely deserted. He quietly cursed to himself as he walked back inside. He threw the cape onto a nearby stool in front of the makeup table and began to apply the white vampire pancake makeup to his own face.

# 11

Up in the Plaza, Jarrett, Seth, and Rollie were trying to control the stream of customers who had been flowing past them for the last twenty minutes. It was strange. Why was nobody regulating the groups like they were supposed to? The thought occurred to Jarrett that all the other actors in the Castle had gone home without notice, leaving the disconnected crew of the Plaza alone to handle the crowds. To satisfy his curiosity, he followed the current group in the Plaza through the passageway past the Headless Woman Scene and the Butcher Shop (thankfully he saw that there were indeed actors manning those areas), and then up the stairs to the Tilted Room.

Inside the Mortuary the tone was serene and peaceful. Greg sat quietly behind one of the room's two caskets, awaiting the arrival of the next group. Jarrett stepped gingerly over the wrought iron railing that separated him from the path through the Mortuary. He passed by the stained-glass window that flashed a synthetic streak of lightning at intermittent intervals for visual effect. Greg made no movement, staring down at a comic book that was nestled in his lap.

Now Jarrett was standing before him, staring blankly at him for a few silent seconds, wondering whether Greg's eyes were open or closed. Suddenly Greg looked up at him.

"Hey, Jarrett! Got any 'little red ones' for me?"

At first, his words made no sense to Jarrett. His brain wrestled with the riddle as his hand instinctively went for the vial in his pocket. This was how it was for Jarrett. The logic always seemed to lag a few seconds behind the action. Now the pills were in his hand moving toward Greg.

"Thanks." Greg looked back up at Jarrett, "What's going on in this place, anyway? We haven't seen a legitimate group come through in an hour."

Jarrett just smiled at Greg. He was relieved to hear that the Plaza wasn't the only area that was struggling with the flow of unguided guests. This day had been trying enough for Jarrett, what with his hungover head and virtually no sleep the night before because of the haunting nightmares. The fire, the shrouded man laughing at Jarrett, the silhouetted man in the  top hat who stood high atop the Castle, mocking him from far far away. He was shaken from his daydream by the electric buzzing of the lightning flashes behind the room's big stained-glass window.

With this, he hurriedly started on his way back to the noisy Plaza, where he had left Seth and Rollie. The noise seemed safer to him now. In the noise it would be harder for the visions to find him.

As he lumbered out of the serenity that was the

Mortuary, Greg called after Jarrett dryly, "Thanks for the stuff, Jarrett!"

It was pointless, though. Jarrett was already gone.

# 12

The Watcher was standing on a tiny balcony at the side of the Castle, high above the beach. The bright sunlight stung his eyes, which were still accustomed to the darkness inside the Castle. He looked down grudgingly at the tourists and vacationers who played happily on the beach and in the waves, soaking in the last bit of summer that was left before heading back to their workaday lives at the season's rapidly approaching end.

Mostly the Watcher looked angrily at the women, laughing unabashedly as they sunbathed in their tiny bikinis and applied copious amounts of sunscreen to their already-too-brown skin. The Watcher had always had trouble where women were concerned. As a young boy, the very thought of speaking with a girl could send him into a full-blown state of panic. He had grown more reclusive and angrier as he had gotten older, but the fear and intimidation he had felt in his younger years remained buried within his aching breast. This was where the spark that ignited the violence lived. Anger seemed to express itself much more easily for him than any other single emotion could. He enjoyed the feeling of power the anger gave him, and in the beginning, he had felt little or no remorse at all for his actions. There was no consequence to the violence. And then the headaches began. The Watcher felt as though the headaches were his payment for the pleasure of feeling such power, and they grew to be a sign as well. He knew that when he began to feel the slightest twinge that would germinate and grow into the exquisite pain in his head, he must begin his deadly work. Pay before you play.

He killed women most often, but it was not beyond him to take an occasional male. This was the Watcher's special brand of sexual ambiguity. It was as close to a sexual act as he had ever come. And his mother, the Castle, approved wholeheartedly of each one of his lovers. He would bring them to her to show her his handiwork.

He looked at his aching fingers, now beginning to show meager signs of healing here and there. The Watcher had no recollection of the bizarre symphony that his fingers had played on the floorboards of the Portrait Room's loft. The headache had been much too intense at the time to recall so trivial a detail. But the throbbing ache in his hand now was making him weak and vulnerable, and he was glad for the cool breeze on his face, and the brief chance to rest.

Below the Watcher's lofty perch, walking down the pier's ramp toward the beach, was Danny. He was just another brightly colored dot on the vast miniature beachscape. The Watcher saw him. He recognized him and smiled. A single brainstar floated past his eyes and dissipated in the air in front of him.

# 13

Danny walked down the beach, as the odd events of the day swirled in his head. Reaching a short stone jetty made up of black rocks a few hundred yards from the pier, he sat down heavily. He felt an odd sense of dread.

It wasn't long before Danny recognized a familiar face approaching him from the direction of the pier. It was Sandy, and she was carrying a Styrofoam cup, carefully side-stepping holes in the sand in an effort not to spill its contents. An occasional gust of wind tousled her curly mane, and she looked more like a feathery impressionistic painting than a human being.

When she was finally within earshot she smiled broadly and called out to him, "Hey, Stranger! Can I buy you a cup of coffee?"

A tiny spark of relief touched Danny as she drew nearer. She sat down lightly on the sand beside the jetty, and Danny began to reach for the cup in her hand. He stopped short, asking, "Did you make this yourself?"

She gave him a sidelong look, still smiling, "Of course I didn't."

"Then I'll take it. Thanks." He took the cup from her hand and sipped it, spilling a little bit on his shirt. "Guess they were out of lids, huh?"

"Shut up." Sandy said, still smiling.

"I remember what your coffee tastes like," he said, and Sandy kept right on smiling at him.

A look of concern gradually crept across Sandy's face, "How ya doin'? I heard that you felt a little, uh...*dizzy*?"

Danny felt a slight pang of embarrassment at the word. He knew that Sandy saw through his lame excuses.

"Who told you? Gordon?"

"Yeah, Gordon said something about it. But look, he only told me because he's worried about you." She waited a moment, giving Danny the time to steel himself for what came next.

"He said you heard voices in there. He also said you were hunting for dead bodies."

Danny shook his head and looked down between his knees at the sand and rocks of the jetty. "Boy, he didn't leave anything out, did he?" He looked up, and his eyes locked on Sandy's, taking her by surprise.

"I wasn't hearing voices. Somebody spoke to me in the Portrait Room. He was *there*. He knew my name!" Danny held Sandy's eyes with his, "I asked Gordon for help. He shouldn't have told you. Now you *both* think I'm crazy."

Sandy stood up slowly, hooking her thumbs in the front pockets of her patched jeans. The wind appeared to dance with her hair. From his seat on the jetty rocks below her, it reminded Danny of an auburn halo. The sunlight behind her seemed to fill every moving strand. Her voice was soft, "Nobody thinks you're crazy. We're just concerned. We want to help." She paused briefly, then added, "*I* want to help."

The word 'help' held an absurdly condescending ring in Danny's ears. He began to feel the anger and helplessness he had felt earlier well up again in the hollow notch at the base of his throat. He struggled past the lump that was rapidly forming there, and leaning forward, feigned a laugh.

"Ha. Good one." He looked away from Sandy, training his gaze on the group of teenagers playing volleyball down the beach from them. His eyes never left the group, but there was no doubt that he was still very much a part of the conversation, "I know that there's something very wrong in there. And whoever it is that's been doing these horrible things *wants* me to know."

"…And that's the person you say spoke to you?"

"Yes. But he knows I can't prove anything." He paused to think about his own words, then his eyes returned to Sandy. Suddenly the ridiculousness of it all dawned on him.

"He's right! I *can't* prove anything. Shit, listen to me! Do you hear how stupid I sound?"

He looked up at her for a long time, the confusion remaining fixed on his face, "Sandy, do you honestly believe anything I've told you? Don't you think I sound crazy?"

Even with the sun at her back, Danny could make out the smile on Sandy's lips. "Of course you sound crazy! You're talking about murder and monsters here. I'd be lying to you if I said that all of this sounded perfectly normal. Or even *possible*!" The volume of her voice had grown to the point that it drew stares from a couple of beachgoers nearby. She quieted down as she continued, "But I *do* believe that someone might be trying to make you *think* that these things really happened."

Danny tried to smile, but the closest thing his lips could achieve was a straight line. "Did that bit of wisdom come from Gordon too?"

Sandy didn't answer. She just stared out at the ocean. The smile on her lips withered and dissipated, and Danny felt sorry instantly for being the cause of its disappearance. He apologized quickly, hoping to catch the last traces of it before it had vanished completely.

"I'm sorry. I'm just so out of it. I can't even think straight. I'm sure I'd be saying the same things if I was in your place."

A pair of bikini-clad young girls passed close by the jetty now, and Danny's gaze seemed to latch onto them as he spoke. His eyes followed them absently for several yards and Sandy laughed, taking her comforting hand from his shoulder and giving him a playful slap on the arm.

"Geez! And I'm standing here worrying that you're not feeling well!"

"Well, I may be crazy, but I ain't blind."

He leaned forward to give the girls one last look as they passed by. He leaned back again, rolling his eyes and shaking his head. He looked up at Sandy. Just the sight of her laughing had made Danny feel better.

"I came out here to cheer you up, but obviously I wasn't carrying the right ammunition!" She said, still giggling.

"Oh, I don't know...have you got a bikini on under those jeans?"

"No."

Danny smiled as the last bit of laughter slipped away. He took Sandy's hand and pulled her down to the jetty with him. Looking deep into her eyes he could feel the familiar spark that Sandy had always known how to ignite in him. This time he felt that maybe she was feeling it too.

"Thank you. You really *have* made me feel better."

Her tone grew quieter now as well. More playful. "Thank God! I thought I'd have to bring out my pasties and G-string to get you to hear a word I was saying!"

Uncharacteristically, Danny let this pass. He took her hand and squeezed it.

Sandy stood up, and he stood too, holding her eyes with his. Danny had seen this before in a dream. He was certain of it. They moved slowly; every move felt choreographed. There was one difference, though. In the dream, they kissed. In the dream.

As Danny moved forward to kiss her, Sandy expertly dodged his lips, planting a lovingly platonic peck on his cheek. She stepped back from him clumsily, wiping the sand from the back of her jeans and laughing awkwardly.

"Thanks, Mom". Danny said, enjoying her uncomfortable giggle.

She had heard his words, but Sandy asked anyway, "What?" Danny's smile was answer enough. He added, "Nothing. Thanks, Sandy."

"Okay. See you later."

She gave him a quick smile and turned to head back toward the Castle. Danny watched her effortless lilt as she crossed the beach sand. She was no more than twenty feet away from him when Danny called out to her.

"Hey! Sandy!"

She turned back to look at him. The wind danced with her hair again.

"What?"

"Do you really own pasties and a G-string?"

Sandy's smile broadened and she wheeled around toward the Castle, shaking her head as she made her way down the beach.

# 14

The Watcher felt his way along the outside wall of the Castle. The pain was just beginning to fill his head, but his vision seemed to be diminishing even more rapidly than it usually did when the attacks began. He moved carefully along the jagged outside facade of the building. His fingers gripped each well-known crag and dimple in the faux stonework as they had so many times before.

Finally, his hand came to rest on the frame of the stained- glass window. It had been through this same window that the Watcher had managed to make his way out onto the balcony earlier. As he gently pushed the window inward, it gave way easily on its creaky hinges. He stepped carefully over its thick sill, and in another moment, he was standing in the dark passageway just outside the Human Sacrifice Room. He could not know whether anyone had observed his strange arrival through the window because his vision was a swirling blur of brainstars. He closed his eyes briefly, hoping for a momentary respite from their harsh light, but it seemed as though even more of them lived inside his eyelids. He began to move like a blind man up the passageway in what he surmised was the direction of the Rat Room, guided only by his keen familiarity with the place, and following the sound of the Castle's beating heart.

He had only one thing on his mind right now. Relief. One of these poor pathetic creatures must be his relief, his next mate. Mother would show him which one. Mother always did.

# 15

Susan was new to the job, so the sight of a man stealing silently through a window into the darkness of the Castle's passageway didn't really present an immediate cause for alarm. She watched him from her place on the cauldron's grill inside the Human Sacrifice Room.

Gordon had taken a little too much time returning from his trip upstairs with Danny. But he was back now, and she was calm once again.

Sitting safely atop the grill, the man in the hallway posed no threat to her. Besides, once he had entered through the window and closed it behind himself, he had headed up the stairs toward the Rat Professor Area. Away.

Out of sight, out of mind. He had acted strangely, she thought. As if he was blind.

Gordon startled Susan, moving silently behind her and abruptly planting a kiss on the top of her hooded head. She mused at the thought of how much she was enjoying this silly job, and more so, how much she liked working with Gordon. He was incredibly funny, and she liked showing him the finer points of her own sense of humor as well. It would be a fun way to pass the time for the next couple of days.

And then her mind began to travel forward in time to what she would be doing in the next few weeks. The decision as to whether she would be returning to law school the next semester had not yet been made. Her time was growing short now. Her father had been counting on her joining his practice since the day she had jokingly said she would, years before. Now it had become a foregone conclusion, and she was feeling more than a little trapped.

But that decision seemed to fade beside the suddenly more pivotal question of whether Gordon would be included in her future plans, whatever they would turn out to be. Deep down she had no doubt that he would. Her mind wandered far beyond the role she was now playing. Far beyond the Castle walls. Far beyond the recollection of the man who climbed through the stained-glass window just moments before and was now stealing his way blindly toward the Rat Room.

# 16

The Styrofoam cup in his hand was now empty, and Sandy had disappeared into the Dressing Room door on the distant pier once again. Danny had watched her every step of the way, noting the familiar way that she walked along the sand, with the wind in her clothes and the crashing waves as her backdrop. He knew one thing. That he wanted her as much as he had ever wanted her. He looked down sullenly at the empty cup in his hand and couldn't help but turn it into the obvious metaphor for his life that it was. He began to gather up the little pile of belongings he had thrown onto the sand beside him: a backpack, cigarettes, and a disposable lighter. He stood up, dusted the sand from his jeans, and began to head down the beach. His brain was aching from the day's events, and even though the sun was barely touching the horizon Danny was ready to call it a day.

Sandy watched Danny make his way toward Beach Boulevard and further and further away from the pier. Her eyes stayed with him all the way to the front door of his little beachfront apartment. She felt a strong bond with him. She saw Danny as just as much a child as he was a man right now. A frightened child in a strange place. She felt a great desire to be closer to him.

Now her gaze turned from the street toward the few actors who were seated at the picnic tables in the Actors' Area. She transformed immediately from concerned friend to Castle Matron, shooing the malingerers from their seats and back to their respective posts inside. She was in charge once again, sweeping the floor, checking the laundry, putting the tubes of makeup back in their proper place. On duty. But still, the vision of Danny's tiny silhouette disappearing into the distance was foremost in her mind, clinging tenuously to her every thought. Hiding there.

Sandy scooped up the sweepings in a metal dustpan and secured them with a folded piece of cardboard that she had retrieved from the trash. Wheeling around quickly, she tossed the dirt out of the Dressing Room door…and directly onto Juanita, who was about to enter. Sandy stood dumbfounded and wide-eyed as Juanita began to swipe at the dirt on the front of her costume. She was not laughing, but then again Juanita rarely laughed when Sandy was present.

"Dat was a good one, Sendy. Next time aim a leedle higher, my face ees awp here!"

Sandy tried to stifle a laugh as she gingerly began to brush the dirt off Juanita's chest. Suddenly she realized what she was doing and backed off embarrassedly.

"God, Juanita, I'm sorry. I guess I didn't see you coming!"

"I guess jou deedn't *look*!" Juanita snapped, "Never mine. I'm jawst gonna get my seegarettes and have my deener break out here tonight, anyway." Juanita bustled past Sandy, who stood frozen. The back of her hand, still holding the dustpan, was pressed tightly against her lips to stifle the laugh that seemed determined to escape.

She tried very hard to look busy while Juanita retrieved the pack of cigarettes that was tucked into the front pouch of her enormous handbag. Locating them, Juanita was quick to exit the Dressing Room, giving Sandy one last glare on her way by.

It was only when Juanita was safely outside, and out of earshot that Sandy sat on one of the makeup table's row of stools and leaned on both her elbows in front of the long mirror. She covered her face with both of her cupped hands and the laugh that had been stifled finally escaped her.

# 17

The Watcher was lying in the hot darkness of the Rat Room, laboring to catch his breath after the terrible struggle. His latest conquest lay on top of him. The air in the tiny passageway was stagnant and the weight of the murdered girl seemed to increase as the Watcher's meager store of strength drained. He knew the task that lay ahead of him. He must remove her from this place without being seen.

Everyone in the group had witnessed the shrouded figure chasing the screaming customer from the Plaza Area and up toward the Rat Room just minutes before. Some of them even recognized her. She was one of the local girls who had been a permanent fixture on the pier since the beginning of summer. She and her friends had spent endless hours and countless dollars at the Castle and its surrounding concessions. Money well-spent in their parents' eyes. After all, it had kept them out of their hair all season.

He looked up at the dimly lit display case at the far end of the passageway. It featured the figure of a scantily dressed woman being eaten alive by a plague of bloodthirsty rats. The display was set inside the wall itself, covered by a sheet of thick Plexiglas. The Watcher knew that there was a narrow space between the back wall of the display and the actual wall behind it. He knew all the Castle's gaps and spaces. He would put the girl inside that tiny opening until he had more time to better hide her, later tonight. No one would think to look there. After all, no one else knew the Castle half so well as the Watcher did.

He dragged the girl's limp body as silently as he could down the corridor. Her dead weight thumped across each rubber hose noisily. He must work quickly, he thought, because he knew that another group of customers could come through the room at any moment.

Now he struggled to lift the girl up into the narrow gap beside the display case. He folded her failing arms over her chest and shoved her body deeper into the crevice. Her haunting visage continued to peer unabashedly out at him, as he leaned toward her slowly and caressed her pallid cheek. His fingers ran lightly over the dark bruises on her throat and gently touched the deep red slash just above them. In the darkness, he couldn't quite see the blood. It only appeared as a dark patch on his fingertips and its warm wetness told him that the fatal wounds had indeed been inflicted. He leaned in toward the girl's face and kissed her taut graying lips tenderly. As tenderly as *any* man would kiss his lover.

A sudden noise in the dark hallway startled the Watcher, rousing him from his erotic death dream. He had not heard the group of customers entering the room moments before, and he was not aware of their steady approach around the bend in the passageway toward him. He had been much too busy with the girl.

He now gave her body a final push to reassure himself that she would remain safely out of sight. It was in this instant that he felt a light nudging at his elbow. The group was much closer than he had assumed they were, and the silent forerunners of this pack were literally at his heels.

Embracing the complete blackness of the Rat Room, the Watcher scrambled quickly away. His eyes were accustomed to the darkness, no doubt unlike the eyes of the throng of customers behind him. It was the Watcher's singular advantage over them now.

He ran ahead and crouched on the floor of the far corner of the passageway. The corner was deep and accommodating. He would curl up here, covered by his own shroud, and wait for the group to pass by. He would not run ahead of them, taking the risk of being seen. The chase that he had made earlier to catch his latest prey had been risky enough. When this group was safely through the room, he would steal back across the Parapet to safety.

The group was now noisily making its way past him, brushing unknowingly against his knees as they passed by, assuming that he was just more rubber hoses attached to the wall for effect. They were almost all past him when he looked up. Their faces hovered above him like spectral apparitions, illuminated for the briefest time by the dim glow of the display case down the hall. Some of them appeared to bear the same grimace as the girl in the cubby.

In the semidarkness, he saw the face of a pretty teenage girl just above him. She paused, waiting for the slow train of people she was caught up in to begin moving again. He saw the deeply tanned face of her boyfriend not far behind. The girl's delicate features and smooth white complexion sparked the Watcher's unquenchable desire, and he impulsively reached up toward her. He was powerless to stop his involuntary need to touch the beautiful apparition that passed so close above him now.

His hand went up and jabbed clumsily at her elbow. The girl began to shriek uncontrollably at the first sign of his touch. Blinded by the darkness, she lunged into the wall of the passageway ahead of her. Her boyfriend fought back his laughter as he tried to steer her back in the right direction, but the girl was far too terrified to be controlled. She suddenly stopped and began taking smaller steps, afraid of what she might meet next. The Watcher could hear their voices above those of the others in the group.

"Stacy, what's the matter with you?" It was the husky

voice of the boyfriend.

"Something touched me!!!"

"It was probably just one of the fake rats or something…"

"No, this was *alive*! It reached out to me. It grabbed my arm!"

"Well just keep going. We'll be in the light soon."

The volume of their voices began to diminish as they moved slowly away from the Watcher's hiding place.

"I hate this place. You *made* me come in…I didn't want to come in here in the first place!"

And in another moment, they were on their way down the short flight of stairs to the Tilted Room. The Watcher remained seated in the safety of his dark corner, laughing low at the little scene that had just played out before him. The ache in his stomach that had been the longing he felt for the girl just moments before began to fade.

He slowly stood up, taking a last look at the narrow opening beside the display case. The girl was safely out of sight. He would return later, and his Thinking Self would finish the job. He made his way silently back through the darkness to the door that would lead him to the Parapet. Back to safety.

As he opened the door a thin shot of sunlight flashed through the Rat Room and lit up the tiny rivulet of blood that was inching its way out of the crevice near the Plexiglas case.

# 18

Down in the Plaza, Jarrett was about to leave for his dinner break. He had taken a few more pills today than even *he* was accustomed to. His brain swam in a euphoric stew, somewhere between pleasure and pain.

His legs ached from the weight of the cumbersome platform shoes. He desperately needed a break. And now he would have an hour's rest. Most likely he would not even eat. His stomach was quite full of the various candy-colored pills, and the vial in his pocket was lighter than he normally allowed it to become.

As he stumbled his way down to the Dressing Room his mind wandered back to the strange sight he had witnessed earlier. He pictured the shrouded man he had seen chasing the frantic girl across the Parapet and into the Rat Room. Jarrett had recognized the shrouded man from his own nightmares. It was *him*. Jarrett was certain of that. The very sight of him had driven a cold spike through his drug-befuddled brain and rendered him helpless as he watched his cloaked nemesis pass by him. The closeness left him speechless.

The shrouded demon had managed to slip through the thin veil that separated Jarrett's dreams from reality. He passed by without a word from Jarrett, without an action. Now the moment was gone, and so was the man. Jarrett felt a twinge of anger at himself for having been unable to chase the shrouded man, to tear back the hood and reveal his face. To play out the scene he had watched so many times in his frightful dreams.

He passed quietly through the Swamp, greeting the young man and glow-painted girl in the Ripper Scene. He decided that he must simply blunder through the remainder of his work shift, hoping he could make it through until closing time. After that, he would deal with the true horror of returning to his bedroom and seeking sleep. He knew that tonight he *must* sleep. Even his miraculous pills wouldn't keep his body moving through another day without rest.

Passing through the empty Butler Area, he opened the latch on the gate, and in another moment was standing in the Belltower. Maneuvering down the steep spiral stairway in the tall shoes was always challenging, and he took his time, thankful that there was no one pushing their way through behind him.

At the bottom of the stairs stood a group of customers. They were all intently watching the antics of the actors in the Gorilla Scene. A blonde girl at the back of this group was the first to notice the hulking Frankenstein Monster making his way down the stairs toward them. She let out several shrill screams, and the expression on her boyfriend's face told Jarrett that this guy had had about all he would stand of the girl's antics. The girl had been hysterical since her experience up in the Rat Room, and her boyfriend had lost all patience with her overactive imagination. They both felt a great sense of relief as they finally emerged from the Castle into the bright sunlight of the Lobby.

It would not be until later that day, in the safety of his

pickup truck on their way back to some nameless burg in Pennsylvania, that the girl would notice the thick streak of red across her forearm. A grim souvenir of her brief encounter in the Rat Room with the Castle's very real monster. At this point, the fear would have long left her, and she would become angry that "someone" had smeared fake blood on her in the horrible funhouse.

At that same moment, up in the darkness of the Rat Room, the rivulet had become a pool, and it continued to grow.

# 19

Juanita was walking back from her dinner break to her position in the Gorilla Scene. It was a short walk, but Juanita took her time. She arrived with her own props, which she was careful not to leave for the actor who provided her dinner break to use. Her props, like the rest of her costume, were sacred to her. They were not just for Castle use. She had many uses for every one of them onstage in her nightclub act.

As she climbed over the railing into the scene, Juanita spotted the young girl who had been her replacement during her break. She was talking jovially with the young man in the gorilla costume, who held the Gorilla mask under one arm as he chatted. As Juanita approached, the girl climbed over the railing and said her goodbyes. She headed up the stairs and disappeared around the curve.

Now the Gorilla turned to Juanita, "Juanita, did you

notice anyone coming out here to give *me* a break? I've been in this suit for four hours straight, and it's really *hot!*"

"No, I saw a lot of people stending beck dere, but no goreellas." She rolled the "r" emphatically, but otherwise seemed uninterested in the young man's problem.

Suddenly the sound of customers' footsteps on the stairs above them jolted them both into action. The boy plopped the gorilla mask onto his head as they took their positions. They waited silently through the group's final descent toward the scene.

When the first members of the rather large group had reached the bottom of the stairs, Juanita emerged from behind a stack of crates with a flourish of her cape. This produced a few short, stifled screams, and a smile of satisfaction found its way onto Juanita's face.

She walked slowly toward the railing, keenly aware of all eyes on her.

"Hallo. Det's right, step down here and take a look et wan of de world's gret meesteries," Juanita said as she eyed the group carefully, feeling them out for their most vulnerable members. "I haf cawncealed behine thees curtain a creature of eencredeeble strength end power. A creature so frightening end so rare thet we would venture to call heem," she paused, "DE MEESING LEENK!"

She pulled back the heavy velvet curtain with great emphasis to reveal the Gorilla, his back against a brick wall and heavily manacled. There was a general groan of disappointment at the Gorilla's meager appearance after so grand an introduction. The Gorilla strained against his binds, snarling as menacingly as possible. The little group just looked on, unimpressed, at the railing.

"Thees fearsawm creature was captured een de darkest jawngles awf de Amazon!"

The growling persisted, and Juanita now turned on one spiked heel and cracked the whip she had been concealing behind her back. The thwack that the braided leather made caused more than one member of the group to jump.

She strode purposefully to the back of the curtained wall, pulling the curtain with her to conceal the beast once again. Suddenly there was a loud scuffle from behind the thick maroon velvet. Several screams and growls ensued, then silence. The group waited while the silence continued. They stirred anxiously, looking at one another, unsure whether the show had ended.

Suddenly, with a tremendous growl, the Gorilla came into view, pulling the curtain open as he lunged toward the group. Juanita stood in the Gorilla's former place, manacled to the brick wall.

The Gorilla hurdled the railing effortlessly and the group let out a universal scream. In another instant, he was halfway down the path to the exit, in pursuit of what appeared to be most of the group. There was pandemonium for a few minutes as customers scrambled here and there to avoid the crazed Gorilla's attack. Throughout the melee, Juanita continued to call to them, "Whatever jou do, don' scream! He assolutely hates det!

Down, Baby! Down! Oh no, I theenk jou really got heem med dees time! Jou better rawn away…I'd feel bed eef he keeled jou!"

With the last of the group dispensed to the exit, Juanita and the Gorilla breathed a sigh of relief. She pushed through the false back of the brick wall she was chained to, and the panel swung back and forth on its hinges noisily.

Now the Gorilla removed the heavy rubber mask, wincing as though the effort was immense. The black circles around his eyes were practically invisible now, mixed with his sweat and rubbed into the rubber inside the mask. He breathed in the fresh air deeply.

"Whew! It gets harder and harder to keep up the pace in this suit!" Turning his face now in the direction of the door that led into the Dressing Room, he shouted even louder, "When is the Gorilla getting his break? I'm dying here!!!"

Little Mack's voice was muffled by the door, and by the many sounds from the Lobby just beyond, "Shut up, I'm working on it!"

Almost instantly, an actor in another Gorilla suit appeared through the door. He climbed over the railing and entered the scene silently. At the sight of his replacement, the Gorilla tipped his sweaty brow with a fur-covered sleeve and heaved a sigh. "Thank God! I really thought you guys had forgotten me!"

He scaled the railing and was down the hall in a shot, calling back to them, "I'll see you later. It's so late now that I'm sure they'll just let me punch out after my break!" And with that, he was gone.

Juanita looked at her new partner, who stood silently watching her. She felt something foreign begin to grow inside her. This new Gorilla had given her an uneasy feeling. She covered her anxiety in the best and only way she knew how. She covered it with words.

"Eet's a good theeng jou came out wane jou deed. Dat guy cawmplained so much I was going to strangle heem weeth my wheep!"

Now another group of customers could be heard coming down the stairs toward them. The cylindrical shape of the Belltower carried their voices down to Juanita the same way a megaphone would. She scurried quickly to her post behind the crates as the new Gorilla ducked behind the curtain until the group was finally close enough for Juanita to begin her act.

"Hallo. Det's right, step down and…"

Suddenly the Gorilla's hands reached out from behind the curtain, grabbing Juanita's face roughly and stopping her in mid-sentence. He pulled her back until her body was tight against his, separated only by the velvet curtain. She tried frantically to let out a scream, but all sound was stifled by his strong hands in the thick rubber gloves.

The whole scene was quite comical to the group of customers watching intently at the railing. A few giggles and random sarcastic remarks escaped them as Juanita continued to struggle against the unearthly strength of the man behind the curtain.

Finally, the disembodied hands released her, pushing

her forward with the same force they had used to subdue her. She smashed into the hard wooden railing in front of her and fell to the floor, struggling to catch her breath. She looked up helplessly at a Hawaiian shirt-clad man in the group who was now standing above her. Her labored attempt to speak was stifled between huge gasps of breath. Her words were barely intelligible to the face hovering over her.

"H-Help me!"

The man smiled down at Juanita with his thick dry lips, "Honey, you're a pretty good actress, but you're not all that scary."

Juanita's eyes widened at the man's words. He didn't realize that she was really in trouble. None of them did. And why should they? They had been presented with every atrocity known to man from the moment they had entered the Castle. That was why they were here. That was what they had paid for. This strange woman, feigning an attack by some unknown creature was not about to intimidate any of them now. The man stared at the scene a moment longer, and then he began to walk toward the exit, followed by most of the group. Those who did remain stood watching Juanita, waiting. They watched her struggle to her knees. No one made the slightest attempt to help her; it was all just part of the show.

Now the Gorilla appeared from behind the curtain. He was panting heavily, and his eyes darted sightlessly from side to side. Although the cheap mask with its frozen snarl could scarcely be considered ominous, this wild man standing in a ghastly  tableau for the group managed to produce more than a few chills.

It all ended abruptly with the Gorilla's tremendous growl. Juanita's eyes widened with sheer terror. She screamed out to him, her accent becoming even thicker with her mounting fear.

"No, no please!" She turned frantically toward the group, using all her remaining strength to pull herself up and over the railing toward them. "Help me! Sawmbawdy! Thees ees *real*! Please!"

The Gorilla turned his gaze slowly away from his victim to the group of staring faces at the railing. The sound he emitted now was more a scream than it was a growl. The scream of something in terrible pain. The scream of a wild animal in a trap.

Inside the mask, the Watcher knew only one thing. He knew only that he must kill her. Now. Here, with these nameless people watching. Mother wanted it that way.

There was something keen and perverse about killing Juanita with so many witnesses. It was like performing a sex act in public. The very nature of Juanita's ambiguous sexuality made her a perfect mate for him. But there was no love with this one. There was only a burning need for the violence that fed him. Only the cold mechanical actions of a predator feeding. It was empty.

A few customers remained at the railing. One girl looked to the young man at her side, her voice reeking with disinterest, "I think we're supposed to leave now.

C'mon Doug."

Now the Gorilla landed a heavy blow to Juanita's face. The loud crack that accompanied this could only have been some sort of stage trick. There came a gush of blood from Juanita's broken nose as the last shreds of her consciousness drained away. In another moment everything in her world turned a bright white, and she slipped into unconsciousness. The Watcher looked down at her with a growing sense of satisfaction. They were alone now. As lovers should be. He watched as a single brainstar escaped silently through one of the mask's eye slits.

He was triumphant.

He muttered repeatedly as he hoisted Juanita up by her limp arms. It was the same word, over and over again. "Bitch, bitch, bitch…". And with each utterance came a rasping breath from the cavernous depths of his chest. Then the words were punctuated by a sharp cracking of bones as his arms encircled her rib cage.

The Watcher moved slowly up through the shadows of the Belltower with his latest conquest. Performing a death waltz of sorts up the spiral staircase with his new bride. Juanita's body leaned forward limply in his arms, and the stiletto heels of her leather boots caught each successive step in a slow cadence.

The anticipated calm after the kill was not upon him yet. He was still hungry, and of late the hunger had been growing. Even with the increased number of kills. He was insatiable. He licked his lips lazily as his eyes traced the thin trail of blood that flowed from Juanita's nose and mouth and wound its way down the stairs behind them. He waited patiently for the stars to go away, as they certainly would. Soon. After all, his Angry Self must make way for the Thinking Self to tidy up after him.

But, instead, the brainstars appeared to be gradually increasing in number again. They blurred his vision more with every step he took, and he knew that this was not over yet.

# 20

The Belltower looked the same as it had when the Watcher had disappeared up its stairs, carrying his special burden. The only difference was that now the shadows had lengthened, and the night air was beginning to add its own chill to the Castle. A flashlight beam bounced energetically against the walls of the stairwell from above, only a fraction of a second ahead of its bearer. It was Little Mack. He called out to the actors in the various scenes as he passed through, signally the end of the workday.

"Okay, Ghoulies, that's it! We are officially closed for the evening!"

Reaching the bottom of the stairs, he peered into the Missing Link scene and saw that it had already been vacated. Possibly for some time. Trying to recall who had been assigned the roles there, he mumbled to himself,

"—But I guess some of you know that already."

Little Mack was in an even greater hurry than usual. His planned date on the beach had spurned him on with a vengeance throughout the entire evening. The hours had dragged for him, but it was midnight at last. He leaped across the last short set of steps and landed at the bottom with a dancer's agility worthy of Baryshnikov himself. He took the last passageway to the Dressing Room door with a spring in his step as he thought, "Ha-ha. Okay, Penny, I'm all yours!"

The Dressing Room was positively alive with the mad rush to remove makeup and to finish dressing before everyone else. Little Mack walked among them like a diminutive Headmaster, chiding his pupils delicately.

"That's right, Kiddies, gather your little belongings. It's time to get the hell out of here!"

He turned a sharp corner at the costume rack and found himself face-to-face with Sandy. She gave him a knowing look, trying to hide her smile quite unsuccessfully.

"What is it, Mack? Are you horny tonight, or what? I haven't seen you in this much of a rush since you and the other morons discovered the peephole in the Ladies' Room at the Sand Bar."

Mack continued past her, trying to look busy with some costumes that were hanging in the corner. He fiddled with the rack, keeping his back to Sandy all the while.

"For your information, Sandra, Penny and I have planned a quiet rendezvous this evening. During which we will discuss," he paused, "Astrophysics and the meaning of life…"

He turned and his eyes met Sandy's for an instant. His serious look suddenly erupted into a grin. Both he and Sandy knew that this phrase was a sort of code among their little group of friends. It connoted what was already painfully obvious.

"And then we plan to screw our brains out."

Sandy shook her head and turned back to the makeup table. She absently placed liner pencils and brushes into their proper places.

"Judging from *your* brain, that should take all of five minutes."

She paused, the smirk still playing at her lips, "Well, get the hell out of here, then, Romeo. I'll make sure that everything gets put away."

Mack's face lit up, and he tabled the items he was holding quickly lest she change her mind. He grabbed Sandy roughly as he hurried by her, giving her a tight hug and kissing the thick mane of hair at the back of her head. She put a hand up quickly to steady the bandanna that she wore as a hairband as she pulled gently away from him.

"Go on, get out of here!"

He ran to the row of lockers along the Dressing Room's entrance and began to gather his few things in a hurry. The entire process took less than ten seconds.

"See you later, Sandy!" He called as he exited, "See you, everybody!"

A chorus of voices chimed out, "Bye, Mack", "See you

later", "Take it easy", etc. Little Mack trotted down the pier's ramp and disappeared into the night.

Out on the midway of the pier, the concession stands were bustling with activity. Not with patrons, but with employees, cleaning and shutting down for the night. Like everyone else on the pier, the teenagers who manned these stands were anxious to be done with the day and to begin their Saturday night activities. They worked harder during this half-hour of closing than they had during the entire day.

Gordon and Susan were seated at one of the scant high-top tables at the back of the pier, munching contently on thin slices of pizza. The two rookie monsters barely took the time to speak to one another, concentrating on their slices until every morsel was gone. Susan dabbed delicately at her face with a napkin. Gordon watched her for a long time, marveling at her ability to look so beautiful despite the distinct shine of Albolene on her skin and traces of dark makeup that remained around her eyes. She caught him staring at her, and they both smiled.

One by one, the young workers left the area, and the couple soon found that they were in the sole company of the Balloon Clown who normally stood outside the Castle. He too was having a last bite to eat before returning home for the night. Wherever that might be.

For an instant his and Gordon's eyes met, and what Gordon saw there was terrifically unpleasant. A chill ran through him, which he instantly attributed to the cold ocean air. Yet in his mind, Gordon gave the clown full credit for his goosebumps. This was a deeply unhappy person. Maybe even an angry person, waiting to vent that anger on the first unsuspecting little kid who complained about his balloon.

"I wanted a red one."

"Drop dead, kid."

The clown stood up and silently gathered his trash. In a single quick motion, he scooped everything into a nearby trashcan and walked past them. Gordon could feel his austere presence above him as he passed, and his eyes were drawn up to the brightly painted face. The clown was grinning broadly, looking down at Gordon like a sinister overgrown doll. The smile was huge and meaningless. And despite the grin, the undercurrent of anger and hatred was stronger than ever. A sickened feeling flowed into Gordon, like ice water. The grin had a certain unsettling familiarity, though the latex clown mask that extended from the upper lip to the scalp disguised the man's face completely.

And then, in the blink of an eye, the clown was gone. Not miraculously vanished but striding hurriedly down the pier ramp. It was as if he had been uplifted by the moment of fear that he had been able to instill in Gordon. Even Susan's playful chatter had ceased. She looked from Gordon to the clown, then back again.

"Do you know that guy?"

Gordon swallowed hard and strained to catch the last glimpse of the bright polka-dotted suit as it passed under a streetlamp in the distance.

"I kinda feel like I know him *now,*" he said with his eyes still fixed on the dissipating form. He took her hand and pulled her to her feet beside him.

"C'mon. Let's get the hell out of here."

As they moved quickly off the pier, a sudden gust of wind caught their napkins, which were still lying on the table. It played with the corners teasingly for a few moments, then swept them and carried them in a tiny cyclone up the center of the pier as the final workers reached the end of the ramp, pulling a thick chain through the massive gate. Fastening the padlock for the night.

# 21

The Watcher's next two victims had fallen like dominoes after he had killed Juanita. These were nameless, faceless strangers. Customers who had unwittingly found themselves in a real-life house of horrors. Their deaths might well be traced back to the Castle, but the Watcher couldn't be bothered with this minor detail. Even his Thinking Self had become much less meticulous of late, almost complacent. And the whole business of killing had taken on a more frantic bent.

He had killed them quickly. Not with the usual attention and style that was his trademark. And they, in turn, had provided him with little satisfaction.

He pulled off the sweaty Gorilla mask and stared down at the bodies that littered the tiny area behind the Rat

Room. The cool breeze here at the Castle's highest point rustled their hair and ballooned their blouses. His eyes moved from the twisted dead faces of the strangers to Juanita's oddly contorted form. He walked toward her, with the gaze of a curious onlooker. He kicked lazily at her midsection, and oddly tears began to mingle with the beads of sweat on his face. These were not tears of remorse or sadness, but of frustration. Again, the Watcher muttered resolutely at Juanita. He reached down and grabbed her by her thick red hair, pulling her face up toward his own. His mumblings suddenly became screams that echoed over the Parapet and were swallowed up in a whirlwind that made its way across the beach like a waterspout. The word echoed out and over the ocean, crashing with the waves that scooped it up.

"BITCH."

# 22

The red digital numbers of the clock on the living room bookcase were just changing from 12:45 to 12:46 when Gordon walked through the front door of the apartment. He started to put the key into the doorknob when he realized that the door was unlocked anyway.

Gordon entered, trying to be as quiet as he possibly could. He was careful not to wake Jules, who was asleep on the couch with a half-empty bottle of whiskey in his hand. It was an off- brand, whose label closely mimicked the style of an authentic bottle of Jack Daniels. In his other hand, Jules clutched a bulky remote control, whose black cord led to a huge top-loading video cassette machine on the floor. *Saturday Night Live* was on the television, and the volume was set to a painfully high level. Gordon walked to the TV set and lowered the volume. He noticed that the telephone answering machine was blinking frantically.

He stared at the big beige machine, trying to remember exactly how to use it.

Finally, he turned the PLAYBACK toggle switch, and the machine gave a muted beep, then Sandy's voice came through the little speaker.

"Hey, Danny. It's Sandy. I was just checking to see how you're feeling. Well, since you're not answering I guess you're either sleeping, or you're well enough to be out somewhere partying. I kind of hope it's not the latter, 'cause I'd really be hurt if you didn't ask me to join you! Oh well, call me if you want. Bye."

The message was followed by another beep, then Susan's voice, "Hi Gordon. It's Sue. I know you just brought me home, but my roommate just called to say she'll be out for the whole night." There was a brief hesitation, while Susan formulated the right words, "Do you think I could persuade you to come back? I have a bottle of wine that I was hoping you'd help me drink." Another brief pause. "And, who knows, maybe you'll be too drunk to drive home, and you'll have to spend the night here. Let me know, Or just come over. I'm here. Bye-

bye."

Gordon smiled at the message. He liked that she sounded so uncomfortable with the words. But then again, he liked everything about her.

There was another beep, and an unfamiliar voice blared out of the little machine, dissolving the feeling of serene calm that Susan's message had given him. The smile on his face faded as he heard the new voice pour loudly from the speaker.

"Hello? Is this thing on?" There was a bit of fumbling, and then the voice returned, "I'm looking for Daniel Neumann. This is Detective Hartnett of the Pete's Beach Police Department returning your call regarding disturbances at the Haunted Castle Amusement Pier. I'll have time to stop by the pier tomorrow. I'll ask for you. We can talk then."

Hartnett's voice was condescending and businesslike. Gordon shook his head and mumbled quietly as he hit the button on the machine that said SAVE. "God, Danny. Now you've really done it. Calling the cops. Maybe you *are* going nuts."

Gordon thought that that was the end of the messages. But he was wrong. After another beep, the Watcher's gravelly voice blasted forth at an alarmingly loud level. Much louder than the last message had been.

Jules was roused from his sleep, the bottle dropping from his fingers as he sat up. Gordon was forced to lower the volume to make the words of the message intelligible. The Watcher's voice was steady and baiting.

"Hello, Danny." There was a long pause, with the Watcher's labored breathing counting out a weird and eerie rhythm.

"You know who *this* is, don't you Danny." It was more a statement than a question. "How are you feeling now? Better, I hope." A raspy laugh came from the slits that served as a speaker at the top of the machine, mixing with more static. "I'm very disappointed in you, Danny. You told some of the others our little secret about Mia."

Jules looked from Gordon to the machine, the sleep all but gone from his face. Gordon stood there, stunned.

"That made me mad," the Watcher continued, "And I'd hate to be mad at you, Danny. I thought we were friends. You know, sometimes when I get mad, I can't be responsible for my actions."

Again, a long pause followed, and this time Gordon felt unsure whether the Watcher had hung up the phone. Then, suddenly, the voice was back.

"Mia made me mad, Danny."

Now there came a sharp click. This time he *had* hung up. Gordon looked slowly up from the machine; his smile changed to a look of utter shock. He looked at Jules, who was sitting bolt upright, staring back at Gordon with wide eyes. Danny was standing in the bedroom doorway. He approached his roommates, wide awake from the sound of the strange voice. Having been awakened by that voice might well have taken years off his life, he thought.

Jules looked down at the bottle on the floor. Paying no mind to the puddle of spillage on the carpet, he placed the bottle on the coffee table in from of him, then he looked up at the pale shocked faces of his two friends.

"What the fuck was *that*?"

Danny spoke quietly, his gaze flxed on the answering machine. He was like a man in a deep hypnotic state.

"That's him. That's the one who spoke to me in the Butler Area." He found the nearest chair and sat, the look of worry beginning to fill his eyes, "Oh, God, it's real. I had almost convinced myself that I'd imagined the whole thing, but it's real." He looked at Gordon, "Now do you believe it's real?"

Gordon shook his head, "Dan, hold on. Anyone could make a call like that. This doesn't prove that your monster is real."

Jules looked from one to the other, puzzled. "What monster? What are you guys talking about?"

Gordon walked slowly to another chair and sat. He leaned toward Jules, resting his elbows on his thighs, "Okay, I can't believe I'm even repeating this...Danny said that somebody spoke to him in the Portrait Room today. This guy claimed to have killed Mia."

Jules sat back against the sofa's thin cushions. He didn't know whether to laugh or not. He could only manage to repeat the most ridiculous word he had just heard. "Killed." Now a short laugh escaped him. He waited for the inevitable breakdown where one of them would shout "Gotcha!!" It didn't come. "Danny, somebody's just playing with you here. You don't know these people at the Castle. They get their rocks off in weird ways."

Gordon forced a smile and felt some relief at Jules' words. "See? That's what *I* said! One of these assholes is just having fun with you!"

Danny stood up, too nervous to remain seated. He crossed his arms tightly over his chest, hugging himself.

"Jules, you don't understand. I can tell the difference between reality and a sick joke. I found Mia's costume! It was all torn and bloodstained!"

Now it was obvious Jules had to struggle to hold back his laughter. He was unsuccessful, and a few explosive bursts found their way through his grin.

"It was bloodstained. You mean like ninety-nine percent of the costumes in that building? I'll let you in on a little secret: Little Mack goes through those costumes every couple of days, and if they're not bloodied up enough, he takes them out and bloodies them up himself!"

He reached for the mostly empty bottle on the table, "I'm telling you it's all just a joke. A bad joke. And your taking everything so seriously is only giving this asshole a bigger laugh at you!" With that, he took a drink. He wiped his mouth with his bare arm, winced, and looked up into Danny's eyes again. The worried look was still very much there, but he was clearly fighting to hide it.

Danny shook his head and conceded, "Well, I hope you're both right. And if it *is* a joke, I wish he'd get to the punch line and get it over with!"

Jules smiled and held the bottle with its meager contents toward Danny, "Here you go, man. Dr. Jules' prescription for whatever ails ya." Danny took the bottle and helped himself to a swig. He looked down, shook his head, and emitted a painful bark afterward.

"That's smooth stuff, Jules. Really broke the bank on that bottle."

"Hey, whatever gets the job done." Jules laughed. He took the bottle from Danny's hand and extended it toward Gordon now.

"No thanks. I've got somebody waiting with a bottle of wine. And I don't mind saying she's a hell of a lot easier to look at than the two of you. No offense."

Jules sat back again. "Oh, none taken." He paused, "What time is it, anyway?" He looked at the clock on the bookcase, "Shit, it's early. We can still catch the others at the bar if we leave soon."

Danny polished off the last big gulp of whiskey in the bottle as he sat down again. No wincing or bark this time, but he held his breath for a few seconds afterward, afraid the whiskey might find its way out again.

Meanwhile, Jules produced another bottle from the depths of the couch's cushions, like a bizarre alcoholic magician. He unscrewed the cap and held the new bottle up as if in a toast.

"Nothing wrong with getting a head start," he said and took another enormous gulp.

# 23

The Sand Bar was even more packed than usual on

this final Saturday night of the summer season. The room was smoky from the thousand cigarettes that clung to the edges of tiny tin disposable ashtrays. The owner of the bar was busy propping a chair against the front door to keep it open, in the hopes that a breath of fresh air might find its way inside. It wouldn't. It never did. The heat and the smoke that hung in the air above the bar seemed to fight it off like dark sentinels.

As expected, the cast of the Castle populated an entire section of the bar, as well as most of the long booths that lined one wall. The actors had been drinking steadily since Castle closing time just after midnight, and many of them were even louder and more obnoxious than usual. They seemed to give no thought to the way their heads would surely feel in the morning, or to the fact that they would be expected to work their usual shifts without complaint. For most of them, the weekend hadn't passed that summer when they hadn't been hungover at work. It was just another small facet of Castle life.

As Jules and Danny entered the bar, Richard stood up at his place in one of the booths and waved them over. He swayed somewhat as he stood, and it wouldn't have taken a genius to figure out that he had been drinking. Heavily.

Jules nudged Danny with his elbow and pointed to the bearded manager, "Hey, Richard wants us to sit over there with him. C'mon."

Danny felt a bit of apprehension at the thought as he followed Jules to the booth. On the way, he asked his friend, "What makes him so sociable tonight? He usually seems to keep to himself."

"Probably booze," Jules replied, smiling. He stopped in mid- step and turned to face Danny.

"Richard's okay. He just takes his job seriously, that's why he comes off as such a grouch. He was an actor before, like all the rest of these a-holes. When he took the job as the manager, the pressure kinda changed him. Made him more serious." There was a pause as Jules smiled more reassuringly, "Besides, he's been drinking, so he'll be in a good mood. Maybe he'll even buy us a couple of beers if we play our cards right.

Danny smiled back, "Not *too* mercenary, are we Jules?"

Jules shrugged and resumed the arduous trek through the crowd, nudging his way closer and closer to where Richard stood. "Mercenary? Fuck no."

Reaching their destination, Danny realized that Richard was not alone. Seated in the booth with him were the cream of the Castle's bad boy crop. All the most well-known pranksters. These were the guys that Richard loved to hate and to fire frequently. By name: Barry, Rollie, Jay…and now Jules. The only face that was conspicuously missing was that of Little Mack, and they all knew that he was excused tonight on account of sex.

Danny and Jules squeezed into the booth with the others and almost immediately a waitress arrived with beers that Richard had ordered for them as they were crossing the room. Danny nodded his thanks to Richard and took a long drink from the frosted mug. The beer felt good going down, and it seemed right at home atop the cheap whiskey that was already in his stomach.

"Where the hell have you guys been?" Richard's words came out a little more slowly than usual, but no less businesslike. He was an odd sort of drunk.

Jules' grin had a forgivable quality to it, coming off as the innocent child, "Oh, we figured there was no way we could keep up with you guys in the drinking department, so we decided not to even try."

"Bullshit," Richard replied as he finished off his own beer and motioned to the waitress for more.

Rollie leaned forward, as though he hadn't been listening to a word that had been spoken. Which he probably hadn't.

"Listen, Jules, we were just talking about the games."

Jules knew immediately what Rollie was referring to. Danny had caught wind of the many pranks used to pass the time in the Castle. The cruel tricks played on the patrons that his now- friends referred to as 'games'. He listened as Rollie went on.

"You thought up most of the stupid stuff we've pulled inside the Castle. But listen to this. Richard has thought up the *ultimate game...*"

Jules grinned broadly and took a drink, obviously intrigued by Rollie's words.

"Okay. You have my attention. What do you mean, 'ultimate'?"

Rollie looked deep into Jules' grinning face, as though he were imparting the most serious of matters. He was unaware that during his speech Jay had switched his own empty beer for Rollie's full one and was drinking happily.

"I mean like *Twilight Zone* stuff. Customers versus actors. The ultimate scare. A funhouse to the death!"

"That's sick," Danny added without realizing he had said it. Richard's sharp brown eyes darted toward him, and Danny instantly felt embarrassed.

Jules was leaning back in the booth, obviously enjoying himself greatly.

"Okay, go ahead. The 'ultimate scare'."

Barry lit a cigarette, "Go ahead, Richard. This one's yours; *you* tell him."

"Okay," Richard needed no more cue than that. A look of utter joy began to creep over his gruff features, "You give the customer a gun, with only one real bullet in it, the rest are blanks. And all the monsters inside have guns, but only one monster's gun has one real bullet in it. All the other have blanks. And you send this guy into the Castle. No soundtracks playing, and only a couple of crucial lights turned on."

Danny looked from one face to the other, "Why no soundtracks?"

Jules' eyes never left Richard. He smiled knowingly as he answered Danny's question.

"Because with all the soundtracks off, you can hear the actors walking around you, toward you, above you," he paused, "Behind you…". He waited to formulate a final thought before he continued, "That poor customer would have a heart attack before the monster with the real bullet could even get near him!"

Richard returned Jules' stare and half-smile and added, "Everybody would have to be real conservative with their shots, too. They'd have to try to save the real bullet for just the right moment. Particularly the customer, right?" He smiled as he downed the little glass of brown liquor that had been waiting patiently in front of him. The idea was a strange, twisted one, and he knew it. He was proud of it. He called the waitress to the table as he pointed to the empty glass in front of him and motioned to her to bring another round for the entire table.

Danny had just finished his first beer, and shook his head at Richard, indicating that he wouldn't be having another. The alcohol had made him full and dizzy, and he was beginning to wish that he had stayed at home. Amid the noise and smoke of the bar, he was starting to feel that familiar nervousness growing in the pit of his stomach.

As he stood to leave, he spotted a familiar face across the room. He smiled and Sandy's eyes met his, as if by some sort of weird telepathy.

# 24

Sandy's apartment was as neat and eccentric as she was. Everything inside was obviously a thrift shop special but couldn't be better coordinated if it were brand new. The place was utterly Sandy.

It had been a real stroke of luck for Danny to have found her at the bar. Sandy had always acted as a sort of sedative to his frayed nerves. He had made no mention of the day's bizarre occurrences, nor had she pressed him for his thoughts. It was almost as if the horrid events had never taken place. Almost.

Danny looked at her, seated in an austere straight-backed chair. Before he could realize that he had moved at all, he was standing above her with her chin held lightly in his hand. She gazed up at him. It was a pure, innocent gaze, and the tiniest of smiles was just hinted at by her thin lips. He bent toward her, gently kissing those lips, catching the little smile. And her. And the topic of conversation wouldn't be a question for the rest of the night.

# 25

Little Mack was on the beach, not far from the Castle pier, seated close to the dunes, on a wrinkled blanket. He was waiting for his date. He had all but given up on her, waiting for well over an hour, finishing most of the beers he had brought with him to share with Penny. He looked impatiently at the time, then around himself. The beach was deserted, and the breeze was a little chilly. He was well beyond the point of cursing at her for standing him up, but he figured he might as well wait here as show up at the Sand Bar to receive razzes from the others. The thought occurred to him that Penny might be *with* the others now, and they were all having a good laugh at his expense.

Mack took another warm bottle of beer from the six-pack that rested beside him on the blanket. He opened it with the  bat-shaped bottle opener that hung on a little chain around his neck and swiveled quickly, making another scan of the beach and dunes with his eyes. Although Mack had spent enough time on this beach to know better, the dunes seemed particularly ominous to him tonight. He mumbled to himself, drinking from the wet bottle. The condensation ran down his arm to the elbow and dripped onto the blanket.

"Okay, Penny. Where the hell are you? You're a friggin' hour late, and I'm sitting here like an asshole, talking to myself."

He quickly finished the beer and tossed the bottle onto the sand to his right. It clinked as it hit the other empties whose contents he had already consumed. As he reached toward the six-pack again, he heard a rustling sound in the marsh grass behind him. He wheeled around before the rustling had  stopped.

"Penny?" He waited a moment, "Penny, is that you?"

All was silent. Little Mack slowly turned his body to face forward. He looked out at the dark plane that was the ocean in front of him. He was unsure whether the noises had been real, or a figment concocted by his alcohol-soaked brain. He used the bat bottle opener on the last beer and gulped some of it, then dug the bottle halfway down into the sand next to him, murmuring softly, "Another exciting Saturday night."

He was startled by a strange sound coming from the tall grass behind him. This time it was the clinking of metal. He pivoted back to see a sinister-looking opponent standing about ten feet away, near the dunes. He sat stunned for a moment, then managed to scramble to his feet, unable to speak. He faced the ghoulish metal monster, his feet planted in the soft beach sand. He was frozen, unable to move, unable to run. He could only stand and stare at the strange apparition. Slowly he began to recognize his foe. It was the suit of armor from the Castle's Throne Room. The muscles in his neck ever-so-slowly began to relax. The realization that this was just another Castle prank began to bring relief to his unwarranted nervousness. Finally, words came to him, punctuated with spurts of nervous laughter. "What is this? Very funny!" He worked to see the person who must surely be standing behind the suit but saw nothing. "Barry? Barry, this is good! You've outdone yourself this time. Now come out from wherever you're hiding and help me get this thing back to the Throne Room!"

But there was only silence, with an eerie gentle ringing sound that the metal suit made as grains of beach sand pelted it in the wind. Little Mack watched, waiting, and strained to see beyond the metal figure.

"What did you do? Did you set this up with Penny, so you could get me?

Good one." Still silence.

"C'mon guys! Rollie? I can't carry this thing back by myself! Richard will have a fit if it's missing tomorrow!" Still silence.

"Jay?" Mack took a small tentative step forward, still

searching for a sign of anyone in the dune grasses. There was nothing. Then he wondered if his eyes were playing tricks on him as the suit itself began to move. One arm raised up in a ghostly motion, and it began to come ever so slowly toward him. He stepped back in shock, unbelieving of his own eyes. His lips moved, but no sound came out. He felt as if the wind had been knocked out of him. The alcohol made him unsure of his footing, and his mind raced.

The suit continued to take slow, calculated steps toward Little Mack as he stood staring at it. He was still sure that one of his friends would soon lift the heavy helmet off and shout something stupid, like "surprise" or "boo". In Little Mack's confused drunken mind, the scene played over and over, as if it were on a loop, as he waited for it to become reality.

The sound that finally roused him from the daydream was none other than the Watcher's raspy laugh, coming from inside the now more quickly advancing suit of armor. Rolling out of the depths of its metallic throat.

It was close now, almost within arm's reach, when Little Mack began to feel a stab of *real* dread. But he was only alive long enough to feel an instant's worth.

In a single motion, the Watcher thrust the armor's five-foot lance deep into Little Mack's chest. Mack fell to the ground slowly, the Watcher holding him on the lance as he made it down as far as his knees and remained planted in the sand. The two stood frozen against the silhouette of the dunes as Little Mack's life ran out in a stream of red onto the beach.

The Watcher dropped the lance onto the sand, and Mack fell with it. He lay motionless with the lance now a part of him forever. His blood mixed with the beach sand, which seemed to drink it up. The Watcher retreated slowly back behind the dunes, his laborious walk in the armor more than apparent as the fatigue grew in him. His Thinking Self was already taking over. He had work to do.

**"Of what a strange nature is knowledge! It clings to the mind, when it has once seized on it, like a lichen on the rock. I wished sometimes to shake off all thought and feeling; but I learned that there was but one means to overcome the sensation of pain, and that was death"**

**- Mary Shelley—**
**FRANKENSTEIN**

# 26

This time Jarrett had managed to stay with the terrible dream beyond the part where he had been ripped from it time after time. It was the part where the Castle had caught fire and was crashing into the ocean. He felt the floor drop from beneath his feet and the painful lick of the flames that would consume him. The shrouded man plummeted toward the water with him, but he did not seem to burn, as Jarrett did. In fact, the shrouded demon appeared to be immune to the fire. The only part of his face that made itself visible to Jarret was the gaping hole of his laughing mouth, deep inside the hood.

They continued to fall for what felt like hours, as he thrashed and screamed in his sleep. Finally, Jarrett reached out and was able to grab the hood. He pulled it back with all the strength he had left in his aching fingers. And there he was.

Jarrett could clearly see the man's face. It was not the ghostliness of the face that made him cry out, but its painful familiarity. He screamed at the sight, and he awakened, sitting up suddenly in his bed. The bedclothes were soaked with his perspiration and twisted from his thrashing. He was still holding two great folds in his tightly clenched fists. He lay back against his pillow and breathed deeply for a few moments. He had seen the face. In the dream, he had recognized it. He knew the man, but the memory of that face would be kept secret within the confines of his sleep. Upon waking it was as if his memory had been wiped clean again. The knowledge of the identity of the shrouded man vanished.

For a sudden icy instant, Jarrett thought that the shrouded figure might have possessed his *own* face. Was this insanity? Had his abuse of the pills finally put him over the edge? He tried to shake off the thought. It was preposterous, all of it. Even Jarrett's slow and tired brain could deduce that.

Although the thought was horrifying to him, Jarrett knew that sleep had to come again. His body was not equipped to handle another all-nighter. He simply *had* to rest. He felt like a weird crusader, going back into an enchanted netherworld in search of his deadly mythical adversary. Armed only with his wits and a pocketful of multicolored pills, he fortified himself before departing again for that evil world. Two pills this time. At least if he *had* to burn, he might as well dull the pain.

# 27

It was the Watcher's Thinking Self who was busy dragging Little Mack's limp form up the beach toward the marsh grass. His legs bumped clumsily into Mack's contorted shoulder as he pulled him along the sand.

He looked toward the Castle in the distance for reassurance. Its hazy silhouette hovered over the beach like a mirage. He looked to his mother for consolation. There she stood, backlit by an eerie light, majestically watching her son. He had done well. She approved. He was a good boy.

He finally managed to pull Mack all the way up the beach, past the dunes, and he laid him gently beside the other body. He wiped his bloodstained hands across the front of his black tee shirt, leaving a thick scarlet smear over the words HAUNTED CASTLE CAST.

Now the Watcher looked down at the faces of his two latest "lovers". He could almost imagine that they were asleep together on the sand. Little Mack, with his eyes frozen in a wide look of surprise and his chest nothing more than a dark space with his blood trying frantically to fill the obscene hole at its center. And then there was Penny, still wearing the black witch's dress, without the hat. Her expertly applied makeup was all but gone from the Watcher's touch. The slashes across her throat, however, were vivid, fresh, and new.

The Watcher whispered tenderly as he looked down at them. "Now you two kids have fun."

And then there was that horrible rasping laugh.

# 28

With all that had happened that night, Danny couldn't believe that the clock still only read 3:45. He looked over at Sandy, facing away from him in the bed, asleep. He put his arm around her and kissed the back of her neck gently. Her only reaction was a smile and a quiet sigh.

He couldn't sleep and he knew that there was no point in even trying. His mind was racing, and every time it finally slowed down, it was always at the terrible point in his memory where he stood outside the Portrait Room, holding Mia's torn and bloodied dress in his hands. He heard the Watcher's voice tumbling out at him from between the doors.

Danny rolled over now, facing away from Sandy in case she should turn and see the look that must surely be on his face. He slowly stood up and scanned the room for his clothes. A little smile crossed his lips as he remembered removing them and leaving them in a heap on Sandy's living room floor. He moved soundlessly out of the bedroom, careful not to wake her.

As he sat down on the sofa and slowly began to pull on his pants, Danny caught a glimpse of the huge early-September moon outside the window. Its luminescence lit the entire sky, and its reflections on the waves below were as bright as the moon itself. He sat watching and was suddenly startled as Sandy's voice came from behind him.

"Beautiful, isn't it?"

He turned to her. She wore a short pink satin robe, and was cinching its belt around her waist as she moved closer behind him. Her voice was soft and whispery from sleep. He stared at her for a moment.

"*You're* beautiful."

Her perfect smile appeared and seemed to glow with the added luster of the moonlight. She looked down at Danny's jeans, then at his other clothes, which lay in a little pile beside him, "Are you leaving?"

Danny felt a sudden awkwardness. He fumbled over his words, "I, uh, I think I should go home now. I'm still not feeling great," he said, resuming the task of dressing.

Now Sandy moved to a nearby armchair and sat down, taking the neatly folded quilt from the back of the chair and draping it over her bare legs. She pulled her knees up close to her chest and sat hugging them to herself. Danny couldn't help but steal a glance at her graceful movements as he dressed. Her soft voice cut through the calm and silence like a precision knife.

"Are you still worried about the guy in the Portrait Room? Is that the problem?"

"Yeah," he answered quite simply as he worked on the last of his shirt buttons. Danny stood and moved toward the chair where Sandy was seated. He sat on one of the rolled arms and looked down at her pensively.

"I've got to go. I need to be alone now. I need to think. Okay?"

She looked up at him with wide eyes. He was surprised to see no hurt there. She wasn't taking this personally. She understood.

A few moments later Danny was on his way out the door. He left Sandy in that same chair, draped in the quilt. He closed the door behind himself quietly and found himself alone with the night. The incredible giant moon was smiling over his shoulder all the way home. And off in the distance, the black form of the Castle stood mocking him.

# 29

Richard fumbled with the huge keyring as he tried to remove it from his back belt loop. Finally, it was free, and the new ordeal of inserting the key into the lock began. It seemed as if he had been standing there struggling for an hour, but it had only been a scant five minutes. At last, the key found its way into the lock, and he turned it, laughing quietly to himself.

Once he was inside the Dressing Room, his hand found the hanging light fixture instinctively and pulled the string. The naked hanging bulb came to life, and even its meager illumination was painful to Richard's weary eyes. He staggered to the row of lockers against the far wall and strained to see the numbers through the haze in his head. He ran his finger beneath each number as he said it aloud. It was a twisted version of an elementary school arithmetic lesson.

"Eighteen, nineteen, twenty. Okay, here we go, twenty-one…"

The job of opening the locker, too, seemed to take a much longer amount of time than it should have. Finally, the little door popped open, and Richard reached one arm elbow-deep into the rectangular recess. His eye caught the little collection of Polaroids featuring The Beast, which he had taped to the inside of the locker's metal door. From inside the locker's depths, he scooped a handful of shining gold objects. He held them like precious cargo in his cupped hand as he crossed the room carefully. His other hand now fumbled inside the pocket of his black HAUNTED CASTLE windbreaker.

Once he had maneuvered his way safely across the room, he dumped the handful of gold-colored bullets onto the makeup table. His hand appeared from inside his jacket, revealing its treasure. It was an antique Colt .45-caliber six-shot revolver. And it was Richard's prized possession. This had been a gift from a good friend of his who had since passed, many years before, when Richard had first come to Pete's Beach. It had been this gun that he had had in mind when he had concocted his idea for the "ultimate scare".

He laughed and murmured to himself as he picked through the pile of gold shells strewn across the tabletop. He would only need one. That was the rule. He would walk through the dark and silent Castle with the single bullet for protection against whatever lay inside.

Richard closed his eyes and listened intently for any sounds above his head, from inside the Castle Proper. He heard nothing, and opened his eyes quickly as a moment of dizziness swept him up. The alcohol had made his brain slow and his legs shaky. Now the room was spinning, and before he knew it, he was crashing loudly onto the hard surface as the floor came up to meet him.

He lay unconscious, the gun still tightly gripped in his clenched fist. The game's single necessary bullet rolled lazily along the edge of the makeup table, until it lost its meager purchase and fell to the floor beside him. The gun's chamber remained open and ready, but there would be no game tonight. No ultimate scare. Only a tired drunken manager, with an empty gun, in a terrible place.

Richard awoke just one hour later and was briefly startled by the unfamiliarity of his surroundings. He was able to make out the plywood of the ceiling, and the hanging lights. It was the Dressing Room. Propped up on his elbows, he looked down at the heavy object still poised in his right hand. It was his Colt. He scrambled to his feet, barely able to remember how he had come to be in the Castle tonight. Or was it morning? He glanced at the gun again, then at the little pile of bullets on the makeup table. In a single sweeping motion, he was able to snatch them all up in his free hand and make his way to the locker where they had been safely tucked away just an hour before. He threw them inside noisily and slammed the door.

At the makeup table, he stared at his grizzled reflection in the long mirror, and the swaying from earlier began anew. He was still feeling the effects of the whiskey quite keenly, as he plopped onto one of the nearby stools. The room was completely silent except for the uneven ticking of the dusty clock above the door. Four twenty-two. It was still night, but Richard could already feel tomorrow's hangover sneaking up on him.

"Well," he slammed his fist on the table, making every brush and bottle jump in unison. "I know how to keep you away, you bastard," he told the invisible embodiment of his hangover. "… For a while, anyway."

He stood shakily and headed for the door. Fortunately, he had the presence of mind to check for his keyring. It lay on the ledge beside the lockers. He hooked it to the distended belt loop that it called home with uncharacteristic ease, and exited, pulling the door closed behind him. The lights remained on, the single shell remained on the floor where it had rolled, and two new bodies were stored neatly with the rest of the Watcher's prizes in secret hiding places within the Castle.

# Part Four
# Sunday

**"MOTHER KILLED THEM, that's what he said, but it was a lie. How could she kill them when she was only watching —"**

**- Robert Bloch —
PSYCHO**

# 1

Detective Christopher Hartnett was never too busy for a good mystery, but he had had few opportunities for real investigative work since he took the job with the Pete's Beach Police Department. Originally, the job had seemed like it might be the perfect way for him to escape the violence on the streets of Newark, where he had been a cop for the last twelve years. The peace and solitude of the seaside community seemed to be the antidote to his city ulcers. Of late, however, that same peace and solitude had been wearing thin and the words monotony and boredom became synonymous with them. It had all become paperwork describing petty crimes that Hartnett wouldn't have wasted his time with in the city. He found himself growing impatient and annoyed with the whole business.

He shuffled the pile of papers on his desk and heaved a sigh as he looked around the cluttered little office. The metal Venetian blind that shielded the window into the outer receiving area of the police station had a single bent vane that mocked him from across the room. He winced as he took a sip of cold coffee.

"God. I hate decaf. Even the goddam doctors have to take away the only pleasures left in life."

He was talking to no one in particular. As a matter of fact, the police station was nearly deserted on this quiet Sunday morning at seven a.m. Only someone as dedicated (or as devoid of social life) as Hartnett would be here two hours early to work on such meaningless cases.

He picked up the sheet of paper that he had looked at nine times in the past half hour. He had studied it, then let it go repeatedly, dismissing it as nonsense. Probably just a prank call placed by one of the local rowdy teenagers. Yet, for some unknown reason, the whole scenario had intrigued Hartnett, and he felt a nagging compulsion to find out what this was really about. Trouble at the Castle Pier. Something about a murder. Murder? Hartnett smiled at the word. It seemed so out of place here. A murder in a funhouse. This was mystery novel material, and Hartnett *did* love a good mystery.

He had done his job, putting in the requisite phone call to the guy who had reported his crazy suspicions. One Daniel Neumann. But he had received no reply to the message he had left on the guy's stupid phone machine. If the damn thing even worked. Hartnett had little faith in ridiculous gadgets like that one.

That was yesterday. He had decided to give the case a low priority until the next morning, when he would go and check things out.

Well, it was morning now, and he had grown more anxious about the call during the night. Anxious and excited. Somehow it almost felt like real police work again. And if it *did* only turn out to be a joke played by some bored kid, he would make that kid wish he'd never been born. Either way, Chris Hartnett was going to have a more interesting day than he had had in a long time.

He looked down at the Pulsar watch his sister had given him for his last birthday. She had said she was relieved that he was off the mean streets and into a safer job. The watch bore the inscription: STAY SAFE, WE LOVE YOU on the back. That was his sister. All capital letters. Unfortunately, it would be another five hours before the Castle was open for business, and Hartnett would just have to sit on his anxiousness until then.

He leaned back in the wooden chair, propping his feet on the edge of his desk. Reaching for the center drawer he kicked at a few stray papers that inched toward him. He milled through the tangle of rubber bands, broken pens, and paper clips, feeling behind them with his thick fingers. From deep inside the  drawer, he finally retrieved an ancient pack of Camel Filters. This was another no-no according to his doctor, but Hartnett would conveniently forget to mention the cigarette by the time his next appointment rolled around. Just like he'd forget the booze he'd been warned to lay off. He tried to block out the all-too-present memory of himself sitting at a bar just the night before, downing several shots of brown liquor as he chatted with one of the locals. He could easily dismiss both infractions. He would smoke his first cigarette in eight months, and he would hate it. It was his right.

# 2

At about the same time that Hartnett was taking his first vile puff of the stale cigarette, Richard was emerging from the all- night bar where he had staved off his impending hangover by drinking through it. His knees were still an amalgam of Jell-o and bone as he walked out into the rude morning sunlight, and there was a fresh bump on the back of his head from the drunken spill he had taken in the Dressing Room. He would manage to get two or three solid hours of sleep before he had to be at the pier. That had always sufficed for Richard in the past; the lack of sleep would present no great problem to him.

He felt the weight of the revolver in his jacket pocket,

and he laughed quietly to himself as he recalled the off-duty police officer who had spent time talking to him at the bar the night before. The cop had been unaware of the gun, and the thought gave Richard a little thrill. He liked the idea of carrying the weapon. He decided that he might just keep it on him for the rest of the day. He massaged the gun in his pocket. The cool steel felt good on his tired hand as he ran the tips of his fingers across the handle repeatedly. Then his fingers felt something else. It was something small and foreign to his touch. Its shape was not familiar to him, and he fumbled for a few more seconds with it as it eluded his grasp. Finally, he succeeded in snagging it, and he examined it as he continued to walk. It was the brass bat- shaped bottle opener that always hung on a chain around Little Mack's neck. Richard recognized it immediately, yet he couldn't recall Mack giving it to him the night before. Nor could he remember spending any length of time with Little Mack at all during the drunken haze of the previous night.

He placed the opener back into his pocket beside the Colt. Obviously, he thought, he had run into Mack during that dark void between two and four a.m., when the alcohol had chosen to erase the events arbitrarily from his memory. Whatever the case, Richard remained unconcerned. Memory lapses were nothing new to him, especially after a night such as last night. He would simply give Little Mack the bottle opener when he saw him later that day. And maybe Mack could fill him in on the parts of the previous evening that were still so hazy to

Richard now.

The heat was already becoming oppressive as he walked, although the sun was just barely clear of the horizon over the ocean. Richard made a sudden sharp turn to his right as he decided impulsively to continue his walk on the cool beach sand rather than along the street. A light breeze touched his weathered face, bringing him a small measure of relief. He breathed in deeply, filling his lungs with the first breath of fresh air they'd had since the long night began.

He caressed the gun in his pocket once more, holding the bottle opener away from it with two fingers, for fear of its scratching his most precious of possessions. Richard smiled as he thought of the panic that Little Mack must have felt when he realized that his all-important lucky opener was missing. Mack was always making a fuss over how many beers it had opened in just the short time he had had it hanging on the little chain around his neck. It was just another of Little Mack's pointless legacies. But he wouldn't need that legacy now. Or ever again. Because somewhere in the still-dark funhouse there stood an oversized suit of armor with pieces of what used to be the person of Little Mack stuffed neatly inside, awaiting proper disposal.

**3**

The Watcher had not been quite as careful that night as he usually was. His brain had been muddled by drinking, and he had been too tired to properly finish the job. His mother had been angry with him for his laziness, but the fatigue had finally grown unbearable. He had spent what was left of the night trying to drink away the tiredness and the growing feeling of dread.

But it was, after all, a new day. And this would be the day that he would redeem himself in his mother's eyes. This would *have to* be the day, because after today they would close his precious Castle for another winter season, and the Watcher could not feed again until next Spring.

# 4

When Danny finally managed to drag himself out of his bed it was already eleven o'clock. The round face of the alarm clock on his bedside table seemed to frown at him for his indiscretion. He had wandered home late from Sandy's house and had struggled for some time thereafter to get to sleep. Thoughts of the Castle, and the haunting voice of the Watcher had taken over his frazzled psyche.

He rushed to get dressed so that he wouldn't be late for work, though the prospect of going to that dreaded place was stifling to him. He found Jules in the living room, eating a huge bowl of cereal and drinking orange juice directly from its half- gallon container. He was reading the back of the cereal box as intently as one might read *War and Peace.* He looked up at Danny as he emerged from the bedroom.

"Morning, Dan. You look like shit."

Danny said nothing, proceeding past him into the little kitchen. He blindly poured a scant cup of coffee from the bottom of the stained coffee pot. It had been quietly cooking on the heating pad of the coffeemaker for a couple of hours now, and it tasted like it. On his way back into the living room, he grabbed a desiccated slice of pizza from the open box on the counter. The perfect complement to his lousy cup of coffee.

Jules smiled at Danny's breakfast selections, "Geez, you even *eat* like a monster." And Danny could only agree as he took a bite of pizza. He looked around the room dreamily, "Hey, where's Gordon?"

Jules smiled and turned his attention back to the cereal box. He chirped as if he were a schoolboy telling on one of his classmates.

"He didn't come home last night."

For a moment Danny felt a twinge of panic begin to creep through him. The words 'didn't come home' held an ominous ring, with all that had occurred in the past few days. *Supposedly* occurred.

The front window of the apartment afforded a clear view of the side of the Castle pier where the Dressing Room door and the Actors' Area were located. Danny and Jules watched as their fellow monsters trickled into work by twos and threes. They knew that they could take their time getting ready; waiting until the moment they saw Richard walking up the pier ramp, clipboard in hand. That was their sign to get moving. But Richard had not shown up yet, and the Actors' Area was slowly filling up with costumed actors, complete with their full makeup. Sandy and Little Mack must already be hard at work, Danny thought. He suddenly felt a rush of pleasant recall course through him. The night before had not all been harrowing, he remembered.

Danny smiled as he thought about Sandy. He suddenly found himself in a hurry to get to the pier. To see her. He gathered his meager belongings, holding the ever-diminishing slice of pizza between his teeth as he used his hands for other tasks. Jules was watching him with extreme interest.

"Is Richard at the pier yet? Can you see?"

"No," Danny responded, not bothering to look at Jules, "I haven't seen him yet."

There was a brief pause, as Jules waited for Danny to continue speaking. He didn't.

"Then why are you leaving in such a hurry?" Jules asked.

"I don't know. I just thought I'd get there a little early today."

"Oh."

But Jules knew the reason for Danny's rushed exit. He had known it all along. He just wanted to hear Danny say it. He felt that he had to torture his roommates a little each day. That was his job.

As Danny opened the front door, he spotted the tiny form of Richard walking up the beach toward the Castle. It turned out that his hurried exit was not making him early after all. He turned to Jules to report his sighting, reaching behind himself to pull the door closed.

"Here's Richard now. See you at work, Jules." And he was gone.

Jules stood and methodically gathered up as much trash and dirty dishes from the little coffee table as he could carry. Arms full, he made his way toward the kitchen, where he dumped everything into the already full sink and returned to the living room. He picked up his backpack from where it lay on the floor beside the couch, and the two new soundtrack tapes he had just completed that morning from the tall stack of tapes on the end table. He scanned the room in case he had forgotten anything. Heading for the door he smiled and announced good-naturedly, "It's show time, folks," to the empty room.

**5**

When Sandy saw Danny come through the door she remained as passive as she would be to anyone on any workday. An instant flash of her eyes, caught accidentally in the mirror acknowledged his arrival. She indicated that he should sit on the empty stool beside her with a single nod of her head. He did so without hesitation. A sheepish grin now appeared to be a permanent fixture on Danny's face.

Sandy worked diligently through all the other actors' makeup before turning her attention to Danny. Now it was his turn, and he enjoyed the light touch of her fingers as she applied the greasepaint to his face. He felt no need to talk as she worked, although the question of Little Mack's conspicuous absence came to mind several times.

At last, his makeup was completed, and she moved aside for him to admire his utter grotesqueness. Danny smiled at the mirror, producing a few extra wrinkles in the paint for good measure. Then he turned to face Sandy, drinking in everything about her wonderful face. Before he could stop himself, he heard the whispered words "I love you" coming from his smiling painted lips. He felt a twang of instant horror at having said it, though they were alone in the Dressing Room by then.

It wasn't that he hadn't meant what he had said. Danny had been in love with her for years before even setting foot in the Castle. He knew in his heart that Sandy's face was the image that the very word *love* conjured in his mind. No, it wasn't that he didn't mean it. He just suddenly wished that he hadn't said it so soon. So soon after last night.

Sandy immediately sensed his anxiety and decided to let his words pass. She decided to spare them both the awkward moment. Because she loved him too.

"You can take a cigarette break before you go inside, if you want," she told him, "I have you scheduled to just 'rove' today, anyway."

Relieved, and doubly glad to only have the job of roving the Castle, Danny grabbed his battered pack of Marlboros and headed for the door. Walking into the bright midday sunlight, the thick layer of makeup on his face seemed to heat up instantly. He looked around the little Actors' Area and spotted Richard at one of the picnic tables, shuffling through a pile of timecards.

Danny sat down beside him. Not close, but close enough. Richard pretended not to notice him as Danny managed to light his cigarette more easily than usual in the ocean breeze. He flicked the match with two fingers and watched it sail out onto the beach below.

"Hi, Richard. How are you?"

Richard didn't look up from his work. His answer came dryly, and with little emotion, "I'm okay. What do you care?"

"I don't know. I was just making conversation."

"Well make conversation with somebody else. I'm busy."

Danny looked around at the other tables. They were all deserted. He puffed uncomfortably on his cigarette.

"What are you doing?"

An impatient frown settled over Richard's face. He looked up from the cards, staring baldly at Danny, "Checking timecards."

"Oh, yeah, right," Danny fumbled stupidly. Another exaggerated drag on the tiny nub of the cigarette. "Did you ever find Mia's?"

Now Richard answered gruffly, having had enough of the line of questioning, "No. She must've quit."

"Uh-huh. She must have." Danny had to turn away for a moment, afraid that Richard's smoldering stare might burn a hole in him.

"I guess you have a frequent turnover rate in a place like this. I mean, I've only been here a few days, and I've noticed a few faces missing."

Richard turned his entire body toward Danny at these

words. His stance was defensive, as was his tone now.

"What are you getting at?"

"Nothing. I wasn't getting at anything. I just happened to notice…"

Now it was Richard's turn to interrupt Danny. "Listen, it's the end of the fuckin' season here. If you've noticed a lot of people leaving it's probably because they've got new jobs that will last them through the winter!"

"Hey, I didn't mean anything by it, Richard," Danny said apologetically. Unfortunately, Richard did not accept this very gracefully, spitting back a quick retort.

"Good. Just pay more attention to what you were hired to do here, and less attention to who you're doing it with!"

With this, Richard quickly collected his belongings and disappeared into the Dressing Room. Danny watched him go, waiting until Richard was out of earshot before uttering his quiet reply.

"Whom. It's *whom* I'm doing it with, asshole." He laughed to himself.

Then he noticed the single timecard lying on the ground at his feet. He reached down and picked it up, reading the name that was written across the top of it in blue ink: PENNY HELLER. The name meant nothing to Danny now, but had he been on a deserted beach not too far from where he sat at one a.m. that morning, the name would have held a particularly frightening meaning.

# 6

The Dressing Room was quiet when Sandy entered. She had taken advantage of the lull to run home to get her dog, Ceto. The aging Golden Retriever was a common fixture in the Dressing Room. Sandy normally brought him with her when she came to work every morning, but this morning she had been in a bit of a rush. She hadn't had time to take Ceto out for his walk, so she just let him out in her little enclosed backyard. She promised she would return for him as soon as she could, and Ceto had watched her go with understanding eyes.

The dog walked lazily through the door and directly to his customary sleeping spot beneath the makeup table. He knew the routine well. He would snooze while Sandy worked on the makeup and costumes, occasionally munching on whatever snack any dog-loving actor would sneak into his mouth. He liked the Castle, and he loved the cast. They were a big family, and he was their family pet.

As Ceto lay on the floor, his outstretched paw touched a tiny metal object. The object did not go unnoticed by his old-but- keen canine eyes. Ceto had special places for treasures such as this one. He toyed with the little object for a few moments, rolling it gently with his snout. Then he bent forward and picked it up carefully in his mouth. Turning, he dropped it behind himself, shoving it underneath the rack of black shrouds on the wall closest to him. It would be safe here. In his little treasure trove. Where he had concealed three Dressing Room door keys, five earrings lost by various cast members, eleven hairpins, $2.16 in assorted coins, and now one gold-colored .45-caliber bullet.

# 7

Danny looked down as he passed over the Plexiglas-encased mineshaft effect that gave the odd illusion of a bottomless well, when actually the floor was only some ten inches below. He knew the mechanics of this effect from Jules, but he remained wary of crossing it, nonetheless. He had heard the story of an actor who had stamped too heavily on the pane and managed to put his leg through it up to his knee. The entire incident had cost Harry, the owner, quite a bit of money in damages, and had cost the actor almost a hundred stitches, as well as a good deal of blood.

The rest of the Mine Shaft was nothing more than a dark hallway, followed by a sharp curve to the right, where it rejoined the passageway that led past the Headless Woman Scene. Danny soon found himself standing in the red light of the Butcher Shop. Everything appeared still and quiet in this scene. Maybe a little too quiet.

As Danny approached with caution, he noticed the odd absence of actors. It was out of the ordinary for Richard to have overlooked assigning the role of the Butcher, since it was one of his favorites. Richard liked it particularly for its use of gelatin blood capsules. The actor playing the Butcher would bite down on these during his act, producing a vile stream of thick stage blood from the corners of his mouth. This inevitably would produce screams of disgust from the customers. It was one of the more effective scares in the Castle. One could always tell who had been playing the Butcher by the end of the shift, because he would bear the telltale red stains down his chin.

Danny moved slowly toward the huge window of the Meat Locker, to his left. He looked in timidly, fearing the worst. This time he would not be disappointed.

The human torso hanging in the window had been severed at the waist. Its gore hung down from the torn pieces of flesh at the bottom; eviscerated organs reached toward the floor of the window's bay as a pool of thick red blood collected beneath it. Sickening in its utter realism. But it was the face that struck real terror into Danny's heart. He forced himself to move closer to the glass for a better look, realizing that the face that stared back at him in mute horror was none other than that of Juanita. Her eyes were wide and unseeing, and the corners of her full lips were turned up ever-so-slightly, giving the maniacal illusion of a smile. Danny stood stunned, unable to breathe. His feet felt like they had been encased in cement, but he managed to pull them free as he stumbled back from the horrific sight and bumped into the wall behind him. He ran toward the next stairway but was stopped again.

This time it was a sound that caused his blood to freeze in his veins. It was not just any sound, but the familiar raspy laugh of the Watcher. He heard it echoing down the stairs as the Watcher waited for him in the next stairwell. He stood frozen, muted. But wasn't this the confrontation he had been waiting for? He must know who this was. He forced himself to take two small steps in the direction of the horrible laugh.

"Denny…Denny…" the Watcher called to him in a gruesome parody of Juanita's thick Spanish accent, "Do jou like my new costume? Don' jou theenk eet would look wahnderful een my Las Vegas show?" The Watcher's rasp made Juanita's accent harsher and uglier than she ever could. It took every bit of strength and willpower in Danny's being to force himself to take another step closer to the voice.

He must know who his tormentor was. He must end this now, he thought. He moved toward the corner that concealed the stairwell, carefully, as he might have moved across a thin sheet of ice. His knees shook uncontrollably with every impossible movement he made. He had almost made his way around the imposing corner when he was suddenly stopped by a rush of air near his head. He felt a spray of Styrofoam bits hit his face and heard a deafening crunch as the huge Executioner's axe dug into the wall closest to Danny. In another second the Watcher stood before him in full Executioner's regalia. The laugh came through the black leather hood on his head, breaking apart in raspy peals as he grabbed the collar on Danny's shroud and pulled him closer, just inches from the madman's concealed face.

"Take my advice, Dan, listen to your friends. It's all just a joke. None of it is real." He pulled the axe from the wall and held its thick blade against Danny's throat. "Just a joke. Funny, isn't it? Laugh it up!"

The Watcher dragged Danny along the short corridor back to the window where Juanita hung, using the blade of the battle axe as his guide, its long handle dragging along the dusty floor.

"Juanita and I were just laughing about it earlier," he said low, "It's just a joke."

Now he laughed louder, longer, its sound ringing with the insane. Danny felt the grip release from his neck, and the all-too-real blade of the axe left his throat as the Watcher bolted toward the stairs. In seconds he was gone, and the echo of his raspy laugh resounded in Danny's ears. Danny bent over and gagged repeatedly. He tasted the bile as it welled up from his angry stomach. He leaned back against the wall and looked around, breathing unevenly, trying not to allow his eyes to linger for too long on the haunting death smile of Juanita, peering back at him. Through him. He was oddly unsure if the Watcher was really gone or merely waiting for him at the top of the stairs.

Gradually his breath began to come more regularly, and his head began to clear enough for Danny to see the approaching group of customers behind him. They were inching warily toward him, fresh from their scare in the Plaza Area. They held back and stared at him at first, trying to decide whether he would pounce on them or not. They took in the awful sight inside the Meat Locker window, and then moved on toward him, eventually surrounding him, engulfing him. It was a huge group by the usual Castle standards. Possibly one group had lingered too long in the Plaza, and was overtaken by a second mass of people, swelling them to an obscenely large number. Danny became caught up in the momentum of the group's flow. The force of their pushing was now uncontrollable to him. They moved en masse toward the same stairwell that the Watcher had just scaled so lithely. Danny's feet stumbled with each step. He was pulled unwittingly, like a piece of driftwood in a strong current.

Finally, they were in the Human Sacrifice Room, where Danny freed himself of them and slipped into the tiny utility space at the back of the room. He would wait there in the safety of its darkness until the crowd filed out.

He thought about Juanita's face, staring out at him from behind the dirty window. She appeared to be staring out of death back into the living world, as though she could steal one last peek. There was no doubt in Danny's mind as to the authenticity of the mutilated torso, ripped raggedly at the waist. He shuddered at the thought of the posthumously imposed smile on her pallid face. He thought how the same grisly sight had not produced the slightest suspicion in the group of customers who had just passed by it. It was the sort of thing they expected to see in the Castle. It was what they were *supposed* to see. And that was where the perfect murderous world of the Watcher met the real world. That was where this maniacal creature was in his glory. No one suspected. No one would ever suspect.

Danny crouched behind the doorjamb of the little

alcove, waiting for the group to finally find their way up the stairs to the Rat Professor's Area. He was in no real hurry to venture out of his cozy hiding place, back into the dangerous environs that were home to the Watcher. Danny felt as though the very air inside the Castle hung heavy with the demon's presence. Suddenly this forgotten little closet that inspired fear and nervousness in so many of the other actors felt safe to him. It was possibly the only truly safe spot in the entire building now. Danny could at least be certain that he was alone here. The space was much too tiny for anyone else to be hiding beside him. Old prop pieces claimed much of the little area within the closet, along with a few ancient and dusty containers of cleaning products, whose very existence was nothing more than an appeasement to Management. The floor was littered with the evidence of other actors who had been brave enough to sneak a snack in the little closet during work hours.

Danny listened for the sound of any remaining customers in the room. He could make out only the bored chatter of the two brown-robed girls who were working there. Feeling it was now safe to venture out, he took a careful step forward. His foot skidded across the plywood floor on something smooth and flat. This was not just another crumpled wrapper; it was a card of some sort. Bending to inspect his find in the near complete darkness, Danny could just manage to see that it was a timecard. He reached down to retrieve it and felt several more of them at his feet. In fact, there was a small pile of the cards, tucked neatly against the inside jamb of the doorway. Danny held the cards into the meager orange light cast by the cauldron outside. He shuffled through them, struggling to focus his eyes in the dim light. He was finally able to make out the names at the top of each card.

The first one was none other than Mia's. It was the very card that he had searched for in vain the day before. Her last day had no punch-out time listed, as Danny had suspected all along. He rifled through the rest quickly, making note only of the names written on the top lines. They belonged to Juanita, Little Mack, and Bobby. And there was one final card...Danny's.

All the cards were smeared with blood and possessed cryptic comments scribbled on them in the same rust-red. Danny went through them again, more slowly this time, taking in the chilling commentary written on each.

The notation on Mia's card was simple and straightforward. It said just one word: SLUT. Juanita's comment, too, was short and to the point: FREAK. Little Mack's card contained what seemed to be a cruelly tongue-in-cheek epitaph: DIED FOR LOVE. Bobby's stated plainly: DEAD DRAC (A fact that Danny had not been aware of until this moment). Danny hesitated before he looked at the card that bore his own name. The words were scrawled beneath the last time punch from earlier that morning. They read: KNEW TOO MUCH.

Well, if this was a joke, it had certainly gone too far now. Danny couldn't stop staring at the card, with his not-quite- three-days' work times punched onto it in purple ink beneath the drops and slashes of red. He tried hard to swallow, but his throat felt as though it had been lined with sandpaper, and he gagged at the attempt. The idea of remaining inside the little closet for safety vanished as he realized he was standing inside one of the Watcher's own hiding places. A place that he might decide to come back to at any time.

Danny quickly hid the timecards under his shroud and ventured out into the room. The two girls who had been chatting jumped at his sudden appearance beside them. Their conversation only seemed to be interrupted marginally, and Mary Ann, the one with the blue face, resumed where she had just left off.

"Yeah, and neither Penny *or* Mack made it in to work on time today! See, I had to do my own makeup. Pretty good, right?"

The other girl giggled, "You're kidding! Are they here now?"

Danny had grown impatient with the conversation and interrupted, "No, I don't think they'll be in."

The girls both stopped and looked at him.

"Hi Danny," the girl that he now recognized as Rose said, "Where'd you come from?"

Danny ignored the question, unwilling to explain what he still found thoroughly unexplainable. His hand fumbled with the timecards beneath his shroud as he spoke. The odd movement drew the stares and giggles of the girls immediately. He spoke nervously; his eyes moving quickly from Mary Ann to Rose.

"Listen, did either of you notice anybody in the back area of this room at all today?"

The girls glanced at each other, then back at Danny. Mary Ann offered a reply that was patently worthless, "Lots of people hide out back there when a group's coming through. I can't remember all of them. I'm not even sure I knew who all of them were."

Now Danny very clearly directed all his energy toward her. He was intense and stern, "Think. Try to remember some of them."

His intensity was strange and interesting to the two, who thrived on Castle gossip and stories. It was fodder for their rumor mill. Rose perked up and asked,

"Why? Did you find drugs or something back there?" This was getting juicy, she thought.

"No," Danny replied quickly. "I just need to know for personal reasons."

"Joanie and Chris went back there to fool around," Mary Ann offered. You couldn't get much more 'personal' than that. After a few thoughtful seconds she added, "And I saw Richard go in there for a broom or something."

Now Danny's back straightened. "Richard? Are you sure it was Richard?"

Mary Ann laughed. "Yeah, I'm sure. What do you think he was wearing a disguise or something?"

Somehow the idea didn't strike Danny as funny. A disguise, he thought. Like maybe an Executioner's hood?

Now Rose added, "Yeah, Danny. I saw Richard go in there too."

He didn't need them to elaborate any further. Danny headed quickly for the stairway. He couldn't waste any time now. The fear that had consumed him was changing into a kind of strength. He only wanted to push forward and find the truth. He had to find out what exactly was going on, even if it killed him. And it might.

Taking the stairs hurriedly, he called back to Mary Ann and Rose, "Thanks a lot. I'll talk to you later!" He hoped.

Mary Ann called out to him as he disappeared, "Any time, Danny. Bye!" But he was already gone. She turned to Rose and added, "God, he's so *weird*!"

Rose waited a few moments, then added, "Yeah, but you'd probably jump his bones if you had the chance." She turned to Mary Ann with a wide grin.

Mary Ann did her best to look offended, her mouth agape as though she might protest. "Geez, Rose, *crude*." Her upspeak was worthy of any seasoned Valley Girl. Then she smiled as she contemplated the idea. Her eyes wandered back to the empty staircase that Danny had just scaled.

"But you're probably right." They both laughed at this.

# 8

Sandy had come across the brass bottle opener while she was straightening the objects on the makeup table. She had picked it up and held it before her like a gem of sorts, wondering how it had ever become detached from the chain around Little Mack's neck. More importantly, how had Little Mack managed to get through the night without his special bottle opener? It was like a religious relic to him. His pride and his security blanket, all rolled up into one little brass artifact.

Did this mean that he was here now? Had he finally come in to work while Sandy had gone home to get Ceto? She looked around the Dressing Room but saw no other signs of Mack's presence. Her motherly instincts told her that she should start to worry about him, but those instincts had never been right in the past where Mack was concerned.

She laid the little bottle opener gently on top of a tin of pancake makeup and looked around the room for her next task. Something interesting for her to work on. An idea came to her, and she quickly pulled her mass of curly chestnut hair back, securing it with a red bandanna. She began to apply a layer of "mud" to her face from a jar that appeared ancient and unused. She would rove the Castle herself today for a little while. It was the sort of thing that made the last day special. Everyone did things that they wouldn't have the chance to do again. Until next year, anyway.

# 9

Danny ran toward the Rat Professor's Area, and as luck would have it, the only person there was the Professor himself. This actor was not one of Danny's closer acquaintances. The young man's cheerful voice was a stark contrast to his grim appearance, "Hey, are you Danny?"

Taken slightly aback by the instant question, Danny replied cautiously, "Why do you want to know?"

"Because somebody just called up on the intercom for you."

"Did they say what for?"

The Rat Professor began to look like he was losing patience. This was not a game of Twenty Questions. His annoyance was obvious from the change in his tone of voice.

"He said that someone's down there asking for you. Are you just roving now?"

"Yes," Danny said.

"Well," the Rat Professor was saying, "You better get down there and see what's going on. Whoever it was didn't seem too happy about you having visitors here."

"Okay thanks," Danny said as he and the Rat Professor chap noticed that the door leading into the Rat Room began to open shakily, and three eight-year-old boys emerged. They headed directly toward the Rat Professor, with the leader of the three complaining loudly, "Hey, Mister, we can't go in there. Them rats on the floor make us too nervous!"

The expression on the Rat Professor's face melted into one of great compassion for the boys. He spoke softly to them. His words were completely unthreatening. For a moment Danny thought he might call a "no scare" code down to the Dressing Room, that way they would be escorted through the remainder of their trip by a security person. Sadly for the boys, this was not the case.

"Oh, that's terrible," the Rat Professor told them, "Too

bad that's the only way out of here. Would you feel better if I came with you?"

The first boy's face broke into a smile that seemed to spread to the faces of his two friends. "Yeah, that would be better."

Now the Professor (who insisted the boys call him "Ratsy" in a gesture of friendship) escorted the boys back across the Parapet to the Rat Room and ushered them through the door ahead of him. It wouldn't take a genius or a Castle veteran to figure out what was to follow.

After the Rat Professor had watched each boy enter the dark passageway, he pretended to start into the Rat Room himself. The boys looked back at him, feeling reassured that he was still with them. Then, at just the right moment, he hopped back out into the sunlight of the Parapet and slammed the door loudly behind them. They screamed in unison and Danny could hear their muffled cries from the podium area where he was still standing.

"Wait, Mister! You tricked us!"

The door to the Rat Room shook beneath the weight of the Rat Professor, now leaning against it to hold it shut. The frightened boys continued to pound for all they were worth, shouting at the Professor, "You *lied* to us!"

The Rat Professor looked back and smiled sardonically at Danny. His teeth appeared oddly long and jagged, and for a moment Danny was unsure whether the teeth were part of the actor's makeup or a sad feature of his real face. He spoke into the door with the frantic children behind it, as he morphed back from their kindly friend Ratsy to his original demented self.

"That'll teach you to never trust a *rat*!"

In that instant, the whole scene lost its humor to Danny. It inspired a feeling of anger in him. He felt real pity for the poor frightened little boys, trapped in a dark unfamiliar place. He felt a weird kinship with them. He knew exactly how they felt right now, because he was trapped in that same darkness. The only difference was that Danny knew that the monster in his unfamiliar place was real.

Walking determinedly to the Rat Room door, Danny pushed the grinning Professor aside roughly. He opened the door and entered the Rat Room. The little boys let out a terrified scream at the sight of him, thinking that their worst fears were about to be realized. In the flash of sunlight that caught the boys' faces for a split second, Danny could see their red eyes and moist cheeks streaked with tears. The cloying stench inside the Rat Room was suffocating, and Danny gagged a little as he swallowed a gulp of the air inside. It had an odor of sweat and dirt, and oddly the smell of rotting flesh.

Danny couldn't help but think what a good thing it was that the boys could not see his own frightened face as he guided them through the maze of rubber hoses that brushed their legs. He explained calmly that he would stay with them to the end of the room. And that was exactly what he did, finally leaving them to walk on once they reached the dimly lit Tilted Room. There, an actress lay prone on the tilted floor, reaching out toward their passing ankles. This produced another round of screams, and the boys darted out the door toward the Mortuary and out of sight.

# 10

Sandy's elaborate makeup job was really beginning to take shape. She applied a thick coating of the mud to her entire face and waited patiently for it to dry completely before continuing. Once it was dry, she made several exaggerated facial expressions at herself in the mirror. This had caused the mud to crack nicely, leaving deep veins of white flesh peeking through the grayness. Then she painstakingly filled each crack with stage blood, covering the whiteness of her skin, and giving the frightening illusion that her face had been burnt to a crisp and was now bleeding through the charred remains.

She untied the bandanna that held back her hair, bent forward, and shook her head vigorously to produce even greater volume in the already full mane. Each curl seemed to expand on itself, and when she finally stood upright, her long curly tresses appeared to stand on end. The result was truly frightening and other-worldly. She gave her hair a quick and thorough spraying and headed over to the costume rack. There she shuffled through the costumes, searching for a suitable dress to complete her ensemble.

She settled on a sort of Anne Boleyn-meets-Scarlett O'Hara gown with a little cap that would sit in the middle of her unruly mane like the veritable cherry-on-top. The dress slipped on easily, being a size or two too big for her, and several inches too long. No matter. Having to hold the dragging hem up from the floor with her hands would give her walk a more ghostly look. She would appear to float.

She eyed herself once more in the horizontal mirror, smiling, then whisked through the door into the Castle and up the Belltower stairs.

# 11

The heat of the afternoon sun was intense, and the beach crowd was enjoying every ray of it. It was unofficially the last weekend of the summer season, and the true beach bums and "tanorexics" were unwilling to let it go without a real fight. The beach was still teeming with the bikinied girls of summer and the sparsely scattered umbrellas of older, more cautious sun worshippers.

Despite the oppressive heat, Hartnett was still wearing his characteristic jacket. Not a suit jacket, but the light nylon weatherproof type. He looked extremely out of place in the Actors' Area.

He stood at the pier railing some twenty feet from the Dressing Room door, trying in vain to light a cigarette in the wind. That first vile cigarette that he had indulged in at his office that morning had set him back on the road to self- destruction with a vengeance.

He continued with several more attempts at lighting

the cigarette, taking it from his lips once to check that he was not lighting the filter end. He now held it tightly between his teeth in the wind and neared the point  where he would give up. Reaching up with one hand to remove the cigarette from his mouth, he saw a match being struck in a cupped hand, held expertly against the wind. He followed the match with the tip of his cigarette and took a deep drag.

Turning his head slowly toward his benefactor, Hartnett's blue eyes met Richard's deeply set dark eyes, staring knowingly at the detective from not a foot away. Hartnett took the cigarette from his mouth with two fingers and exhaled an unending stream of smoke through his nostrils.

"Thank you very much," he said. Tiny puffs of smoke still accompanied each of his words. He looked up at the man a second time, recognizing his face from the bar the night before. Richard offered no handshake, noting Hartnett's extended hand. He simply held the man's eyes as he spoke, "I'm Richard. The manager here. Can I help you?" It was obvious that he had no recollection of their previous meeting, or if he did, he wasn't about to let on.

Trying to remain nonchalant, the image of the classic gumshoe from so many old movies, Hartnett looked out over the beach as he spoke, "Actually, I'm looking for someone who works here."

"Who would that be?"

Hartnett turned to face Richard again. The cold steel blue of his eyes seemed to challenge the darkness of

Richard's quiet stare.

"Is it important that you know?" The detective asked matter-of-factly.

"I told you I'm the manager here."

"Yes, you're right, you did," Hartnett replied with an irritating half-smile on his lips. He waited a beat before he continued, "I'm waiting to speak to Daniel Neumann."

Richard seemed unfazed by the name. He just continued to stare, "What's this about?"

"It's a personal matter."

Not good enough. "There's no such thing as a personal matter here. He's on my time. He can talk to you when he's not disrupting my show." A few heavy seconds of silence passed, then Richard asked, "Is he in some kind of trouble?"

"No. What makes you ask that?"

A hint of anger crept into his voice, "Because I can smell a cop a mile away. And you're a cop." He looked Hartnett up and down and added, "A very poorly dressed cop."

The smirk on Hartnett's face grew now. He failed to be impressed with Richard's self-proclaimed prowess at identifying a police officer. Any punk on the street could tell that somebody like Hartnett wouldn't be caught dead in a place like this unless it was his job. The smile remained painted on his face like a badge, "Well, I guess you smelled me coming, then."

This seemed to further agitate Richard. The ire in his voice increased exponentially with every word he spoke.

He kept his tone quiet and threatening.

"I may not be able to keep you from snoopin' around here, but I'll tell you this much. I don't like this, and I don't like *you*... cop." Richard walked slowly away, leaving Hartnett neither intimidated nor surprised. They eyed one another coldly from a distance now. Hartnett remained at the railing, and Richard sat at one of the picnic tables nearby.

Turning back toward the beach, Hartnett shook his head and muttered to himself in a low voice, taking a final drag on the waning butt of his cigarette.

"What a charming fellow."

# 12

At least Jarrett had managed to get a couple of hours' worth of sleep last night. Not good, substantial, restful sleep. It was good simply for sleep's sake; drug-induced and dreamless. When he awoke that morning, Jarrett wished he had never slept at all. Now, standing in the Plaza among his friends he felt at peace. The coolness of the air that rushed in the open stained-glass window between groups was enough to invigorate him. And, best of all, in the light of day he needn't fear the Watcher. He needn't fear the fire. In the real world, there were fire extinguishers and friends to help douse the flames and the fear.

Jarrett was truly happy here, and he worked to push the horrid thought of this being the Castle's last day out of his tired head. After today he would be thrust back out into the frightening reality of a "real" job, with people who would see him for the oddity he was. His friends here at the Castle accepted his strangeness and embraced the freak that he had always felt himself to be. He pushed the thoughts away vehemently. Yet somewhere in the back of his worried mind was the terrible feeling that he would never have to deal with any of it anyway. Not after what might happen today. He thought that maybe the Watcher and the fire would solve that problem for him.

# 13

On his way down the Belltower stairs, Danny encountered the bizarre woman with the charred face, wearing the Anne Boleyn gown. It looked as though she might be smiling at him as she passed by, but he was unsure. The look might merely have been a by-product of the gruesomely intricate makeup on her face.

His mind swam with the horrible events that he had just witnessed and made him wary of what might be yet to come. First, there had been Juanita, appearing horrifically in the Meat Locker window. Then the horror of his meeting with the Watcher. And now, this last clue. The timecards he had found in the Sacrifice Room's tiny storage space. Danny felt that he was rapidly losing whatever nerve had been driving him on to find the identity of his shrouded tormentor. But if it was true that there was a murderer among them, he must do what he could to stop him.

The fact remained that this demented person obviously knew who Danny was and possibly even where he lived. Or at the very least his telephone number; the terrible message left on the answering machine was proof of that.

He continued through the door into the Dressing Room, then out into the Actors' Area. He looked around slowly at the faces of the actors seated at the tables and standing along the  railing. All of them looked familiar, except one. The unkempt man in the windbreaker, with the reddish-brown hair. Hartnett. Danny walked to the railing where the man stood and extended his hand in greeting. "Hi. I'm Danny Neumann. Are you the gentleman who wanted to see me?"

Hartnett smiled and shook Danny's hand roughly. "Yeah, I wanted to see you, but I'm no gentleman." His response from Danny was silence and a wide-eyed stare. He cleared his throat gruffly and continued, "My name is Detective Christopher Hartnett. I understand you called the department regarding some disturbances here at the Castle."

At this, several of the actors standing within earshot looked toward them. Danny felt their stares, so he took Hartnett gently by the elbow and led him further away from the Actors' Area.

"You're the detective who phoned my house yesterday."

"That's right."

Danny shot a quick glance toward Richard, who was

still seated at one of the closest tables, and tried to lower his voice even more. He spoke in what was essentially a whisper now.

"I called because I have reason to suspect someone here of… well, that is, I *think*…" Danny hesitated to say the words. They rang of the insane inside his own head. "I think somebody murdered one of our cast members. Maybe two. Maybe more, I don't know."

Hartnett stood staring at Danny for a long time. He was waiting for the young man to break out of his act and announce that it was all a joke. He waited, but those words never came. Finally, Hartnett just repeated, "…Murdered." He waited another heavy moment, then he inhaled deeply. "What exactly led you to believe that they were murdered, Mr. Neumann?"

"Well, the first one, a girl named Mia, was supposed to meet me after work on Friday night, and she never showed up." Hartnett appeared to hang on Danny's every word. He was either summing up the facts to pursue the case, or he was sizing Danny up for a straitjacket. The look could go either way.

Danny continued, undaunted, slipping out of the whisper from time to time because of his excited state.

"The next day I found the costume she had been wearing the last time anyone saw her alive. It was all torn and bloody."

Hartnett waited a few seconds, as though Danny might add another touch to the story. When nothing more was forthcoming, he asked, "And where is that costume now?"

"I don't know," Danny said.

The detective was trying to stay with him, "You don't know," he repeated without emotion.

"No. I dropped the costume when the murderer spoke to me."

"The murderer *spoke* to you?" Hartnett asked, now truly showing interest in Danny's elaborate yarn. "What exactly did he say?"

Danny's tried to lower the volume of his voice again. He leaned closer, and Hartnett accommodated him. The detective felt like he might be humoring a mental patient.

"He said he killed Mia because she made him mad," Danny whispered.

Hartnett straightened his back, taking in Danny's full face again in search of a hint of the joke he was playing.

"A-ha," he said, "And what did the murderer look like? Can you describe him?"

"Well, at the time I didn't actually *see* him, but today he was dressed in an Executioner's costume."

"Wait," he backed up a step, "Are you saying that you saw him again today?"

"Yes, I did," Danny said. He felt a little more confident now, though his story sounded more absurd with every word he spoke. "I saw him right after I found the second body. Juanita's body…or what was left of it."

Now the detective pulled a small notepad from the pocket of his jacket, along with a scuffed ballpoint pen. He scribbled something illegible as he said, "Juanita. That was the second victim. So are you telling me that there are *two* bodies now?"

"At least two. Actually, I have reason to believe there are five bodies. Maybe more."

Now Hartnett just breathed deeply, in and out, three or four times. Just as he thought the story had reached its end, Danny began again, "Oh. And I found a stack of the victims' timecards that were covered with blood."

"Where are these timecards now?"

Danny felt Richard's stare intensify as he began to walk slowly up the pier toward the ocean, with the policeman in tow. He was whispering again, catching Hartnett a little off guard. He strained to hear the words, tilting his head closer to Danny.

"I have them, but I can't show them to you this minute."

"Why not?" Hartnett whispered back.

Again, Danny shot a glance in Richard's direction. The action was not missed by Hartnett, who continued to speak but lost all traces of the whisper, "Oh, you mean your boss, Boris Karloff over there, might object."

"Exactly."

Putting the little notepad back into his pocket, Hartnett took a few moments to collect his thoughts. Then he looked up at Danny's eyes again. This time he had a more business-like manner. He was back to being the hard-bitten cop he portrayed best.

"Well, Mr. Neumann. It seems obvious to me that we have a murder that has no concrete proof to speak of, no evidence that you can show me, *not even a suspect or a motive*! All I have is your increasing paranoia, which was most likely brought on by working in this goddamned haunted house! What I'm getting from all of this is that I'm either dealing with a card-carrying whacko here or a bad practical joker!"

Now he was getting somewhere. Danny perked up, smiling. "Yes! That's exactly what I was thinking," he began.

"No, Mr. Neumann," Hartnett stopped in mid-sentence, "You misunderstand me. I wasn't talking about your murderer. I was talking about *you.* You do realize that falsely reporting a crime to the police is a misdemeanor, don't you?" There was a pause. "Now I would appreciate it if you wouldn't waste any more of the Police Department's time with horror stories or bad jokes!"

Hartnett turned and began to make his way through the clutter of actors spilling out of the Dressing Room door. He headed for the ramp that led to the street below. Seeing his last hope for help disappearing down the wooden boardwalk, Danny called out to him in desperation, "Wait! If...If you don't believe me, go in there and see for yourself! Go see the window in the Butcher Shop! There's a body hanging in there. Go now, and you'll see it!"

Danny wheeled around to look at Richard as he was saying it. Richard was standing now, having obviously heard Danny's words. In fact, every face in the Actors' Area was turned toward him, waiting for more.

Hartnett looked around at the others, then back at Danny. He could tell that this young man was serious, otherwise he would never have risked making such a bizarre statement in front of his coworkers. And his boss. He deduced that not only would Danny have to have been serious, but quite desperate as well. Slowly and laboriously, he made his way back up the ramp toward the shrouded young man again. When he finally was standing beside him, he spoke. His tone was more serious and direct this time. No games.

"Are you telling me that there's a dead body hanging in this place, where everyone can see it?" There was a long silence. Danny didn't answer his question, yet Hartnett knew that his silence was affirmation enough. "Okay, Mr. Neumann, take me there."

Feeling a measure of relief, Danny led Hartnett toward the Dressing Room door, but now Richard stood in front of them, blocking their entry.

"Wait a minute," Richard snarled, "You can't just walk through there with a cop hangin' on your ass, looking for make- believe clues. I've got a business to run here." He looked from Danny's face to Hartnett's now, "You guys and your two-bit detective work will chase away all my customers. Not to mention you'll scare the hell out of the other actors! We only have a few hours left to make the last bit of money we'll see this summer. Don't fuck me up."

There was silence, and Danny's expression waffled from angry, to tired, to sheepish all at once. But Hartnett had other ideas. His glare met Richard's, and his eyes never moved as he spoke to Danny, standing beside him.

"Okay, Danny. I'll go in through the front door with all

the other customers."

Now his tone grew more caustic, "You can't keep me from going in the place on my own, as a paying customer, can you, Mr. Manager? I just *love* a good scare." He finished the sentence with a broad smile.

"No," Richard said hesitantly, "Unfortunately I can't." He quickly added an afterthought, "But just try to make any trouble in there. I'd *love* to throw you out!"

Hartnett wheeled around and strode triumphantly down the ramp now. Once he had arrived at the sidewalk flanking the street, he shook a cigarette from his crumpled pack and pulled it out with his pursed lips. This time he was able to light it without incident. In another moment he had disappeared around the corner, looking for the entrance to the funhouse.

Danny headed for the Dressing Room but was again stopped abruptly as Richard grabbed him roughly by the shoulder.

"Maybe I can't do anything about it right now, but I'm telling you I don't like this shit. You and your half-baked suspicions are getting on my last nerve. If someone here really *is* fucking with your head…Well, I would try to figure it out, too. But you're letting it get out of control. And I won't just stand by and watch you do it!"

Danny looked from one of Richard's dark eyes to the other. His voice was completely devoid of emotion now. "Are you through?"

"Yes."

"Then let me get back to work, please." Danny shrugged off Richard's grip.

He moved straight through the Dressing Room and into the Castle. Richard remained standing in the same spot for a few seconds. He looked around at the other gawking faces, meeting their eyes with an icy stare until they each finally looked away.

# 14

The line of customers wound through the intricate network of twists and turns in the Castle Lobby on this, the last day of the summer season. Tourists and locals alike knew about the antics that might occur inside during the last hours. They clamored for a last look at their beloved monsters and hoped to catch a special performance or two.

Hartnett stood in the line, growing more impatient with each tiny step forward that the crawling queue required him to take. Two little boys in line behind him were pushing and shoving each other roughly. After their third collision with the back of his legs, the detective decided that he had had enough of their games. Coming toward him once more, he bent down and met them with a low growl. They looked up at Hartnett's face as he scowled down at them, and were instantly quieted.

He finally reached the Cashier's cage. He peered inside, where a petite black girl with huge white circles painted around her eyes peered back at him.

Hartnett gawked at her dumbly for a few seconds, "Just one," he said as he peeled a five-dollar bill off the small wad of cash he kept in his heavy Liberty Dollar money clip. The girl handed him his change methodically, in silence. He looked at her as he pocketed the change, "You know you're one heck of a conversationalist."

She looked at him soberly, "I'm not paid to make conversation. You want witty repartee? Talk to the monsters inside."

He shook his head as he walked away from the window and made his way through the dark portal that was the Castle's entrance. Just inside, Hartnett had some trouble negotiating the dark curve in the passageway. With every step he took, he bumped into another wall. He cursed impatiently to himself repeatedly.

"This is getting ridiculous," he grumbled as he struggled to remove a small object from his pocket. "Wait a minute, here," he said.

In another instant the darkness ahead of him was pierced by his tiny keyring flashlight beam, allowing him to move on effortlessly, "Now *that's* more like it."

From inside the crowded Lobby, the police detective's movements were being carefully noted by the pair of eyes peering at him as he climbed the stairs that followed the First Cage. The eyes followed him with a twisted sort of longing. Lust.

The Watcher stood amid the brightness and chattering crowd. He watched the opening in the wall that revealed a slice of the dark interior, waiting for the startled cry that was inevitable at the First Cage Monster's appearance. When no cry had come, and the slouching detective had walked past the opening, clearly smiling, the Watcher became further angered. Further incited. The sounds of the tourists standing all around him began to fade in the way he recognized all too well, only to be replaced by the pounding of his own heart. It grew louder and louder, assaulting him from the inside. He headed back toward the door that led into the Castle, for relief. The kind of relief he was most capable of taking. The bloody kind.

A small group had gathered in the Butler Area, waiting to be let in, when Hartnett joined them. They stared at the out-of-place visitor with the conspicuous jacket as he walked toward them. Hartnett smiled as he greeted them, "Okay, gang, what are we waiting for?"

At this, he received a general look of distaste from the others. Most of them simply turned to face forward again, thinking that they had snubbed him properly. They didn't know that it was impossible to snub someone like Hartnett.

Now the Butler appeared. It was a tall girl in a tattered dress and long black cape. Her makeup was distinctly that of the classic vampire. The shadowing of the makeup below her cheeks and along her nose served to enhance her better features, and the noble dress, though tattered, gave her an air of elegance. She stood eyeing the group for a few moments. Then she seemed to float through the open doors of the Portrait Room and was out of sight, only to return moments later to unhook the red velvet rope. Her haunting gaze remained trained on them as the group began to timidly file past her into the room.

Hartnett was proudly the last to enter. He lingered in the Butler Area for a few seconds after the rest had gone, taking in every detail he could about the strange funhouse. When in Rome. He lingered over the dusty paintings of witches and vampires, and the huge head of an elk, mounted for no good reason over the little area, as though guarding it. He studied it hungrily, as one might study Michelangelo's Pieta. Finally, the Butler could bear waiting no longer. She made an exaggerated sound akin to clearing her throat, which instantly drew Hartnett's attention. He walked to her slowly, then past her, into the room. No sooner had Hartnett cleared the big doors when the Butler slammed them closed.

# 15

The Swamp had always been Sandy's favorite place in the Castle. The rocks and scattered trees afforded excellent hiding places, guaranteeing a good scare or two with every group that passed through. She took her place against the wall of the farthest curve, awaiting her first victims.

She waited patiently, watching the Sick Room doorway for the emergence of customers. Within a few minutes she could feel the slight vibration of footsteps coming toward the Swamp. She stood upright silently and pressed her back firmly against the simulated rock wall behind her. Invisible and ready to pounce, she held her breath in anticipation.

The dark form that emerged from the Sick Room was familiar to her. Sandy exhaled the huge breath of air she had been holding in her lungs as she watched him draw closer. It was Richard. There was no real trick in deducing his identity; his jingling keyring heralded his approach unmistakably.

She watched as he walked through the graveyard area of the Swamp, knowing its twists and turns as well as anyone would know the layout of their own living room. His walk was relaxed and effortless, and he was obviously deep in his own thoughts. Sandy smiled devilishly under the layer of dried mud on her face, deciding to give the Master of Horror himself a good scare. She froze against the wall, lying in wait.

Richard continued to move toward her, then past her, missing her, huddled so inconspicuously in the corner. The darkness had done its job. When he was safely a step or two past, Sandy pounced, locking her arms around Richard's midsection. He let out little more than the slightest of gasps, but it was Sandy who was truly frightened.

Under his light jacket, she felt an unmistakably metal form. It wouldn't have taken an expert to deduce that Richard was carrying a gun. She jumped back at the feel of it and stood staring at Richard as he turned to face her. Even in the minimal light, she could make out his smile.

"That was good. You really got me. I never saw you coming!" They stood facing one another for a few silent moments, like gunfighters on a deserted Tombstone

Street. Then Richard spoke again, "Who are you, anyway? Do I know you?"

Sandy heard the words as if from a deep pit. Her hand flew up to touch her mud-caked face, vaguely remembering the hour that she had spent applying her makeup. Richard hadn't recognized her. He hadn't been in the Dressing Room when she was applying it. A warm wave of relief came over her, and she could feel herself beginning to move. She walked, slowly at first, then faster, faster, away from Richard. Then she was running through the Swamp. She passed through the Sick Room, her Anne Boleyn gown whooshing as she held it above her ankles to keep from tripping. Slowing slightly as she passed through the Throne Room, she listened for the jingle of his keyring, for his footsteps behind her. Nothing. Richard obviously had not followed her out of the Swamp. Now Sandy stood at the doorway to the Portrait Room, where a group of customers was assembling.

She pushed her way through the waiting crowd toward the open double doors at the back of the room, breaking Rule Number Three: NEVER UPSTAGE THE ROOM. There were scattered complaints as she bumped into various customers without apology. Many of them thought better of voicing their displeasure after they caught a glimpse of her charred face. She had made her way through the room and toward the Belltower gate as the Butler was letting the last person into the Portrait Room. He was an oddly jovial man with reddish hair, wearing a wrinkled windbreaker jacket. He smiled at her as she hurried past.

Once inside the Belltower, Sandy made her way carefully down the spiral staircase. She struggled to hold the folds of her long dress, which had grown much heavier in her sweating hands. She dared not hesitate, however, until she was safely past the Missing Link scene and through the Dressing Room door.

As she entered the room, Sandy's eyes were wide, and her breath was coming in erratic gasps. She proceeded to the coolness of the Actor's Area outside and sat down at the picnic table farthest from the door. She sat alone, feeling her pounding heart begin to ease as the ocean breeze touched her face. Her thoughts wandered from Richard's concealed secret to Danny's suspicions of the last few days, connecting the two chillingly in her mind. Could someone indeed have been threatening Danny? And more surprisingly yet, could that someone have been Richard? She didn't know what to think. She started working here at the Castle the same year that Richard had started. She had always trusted him as she would have trusted a brother.

Sandy worked to shake off the disturbing thoughts. So what if she had felt a gun in Richard's pocket? Maybe he always carried it. Lots of harmless people carried guns. Yeah, right Sandy, she thought, tell us another one.

Suddenly panic gripped her. She rushed into the Dressing Room, where she wasted no time in removing the makeup from her face, using two and three tissues at a time. Harmless or not, Richard would never know that the muddy-faced girl in the Swamp had been Sandy. And Sandy would just as soon forget that the man with the revolver in his pocket had been her friend Richard.

# 16

Inside the Portrait Room, the group shuffled nervously in their places, keeping a constant watchful eye on the actor in the Portrait frame above them. At precisely the right moment, Dracula sprung forward from his place inside the wall. A soft rush of air rustled the hair of a girl at the front of the group. She squeaked a surprised cry as the group answered the slam with an equally resounding scream. They all jumped back involuntarily in unison.

Now Dracula stood smiling down at them from the mantel. A wave of nervous laughter rolled through the group.

"Good evening, and welcome to my Castle. I hope you will enjoy your visit here. I know that all my children who dwell inside these walls will enjoy *you*." He paused now for emphasis, leering at the group to further intimidate them. His efforts proved to be successful with everyone except Hartnett, whose lopsided grin would become a challenge to the vampire. Dracula's well-rehearsed speech flowed undaunted from his lips.

"Proceed with caution through these halls. For here you will be greeted by the living, the dead, and the *undead*. Enjoy their company. BUT REMEMBER: those who get carried away, *get CARRIED away...*". He gave the trite tagline a little too much time to sink in.

"Now go!" And with that he pointed a black-tipped finger in the direction of the Throne Room, giving each member of the group a farewell hiss as they passed by him. The group all responded obediently to all the standard scares. All, that was, except the red-haired man at the very back of the line. Dracula did his best to ignore the man as he locked eyes with him. He knew this type all too well. This was one of those guys who loved to challenge the actors, and often ended up becoming a security problem. It was always best to ignore them until they went away. And that was exactly what Drac did.

# 17

Rummaging through the backpack was no easy task, since it was buried deep in the pile of sweatshirts and handbags at the back wall of the Dressing Room. Danny quickly pulled the little silver flask from the pack and hid it under his shroud. He looked around himself guiltily in case anyone had been watching. No one had. That is unless you counted Sandy's dog, Ceto.

He smiled a friendly smile at the dog and whispered confidentially, "This is just between you and me, right Buddy?" As if in reply, Ceto's tail wagged as he yawned and emitted a high-pitched whine. Danny smiled at him again.

"Right."

Standing quickly, he made another room check with his eyes and was off again. He opened the door to the Castle silently and hurried toward the Belltower, still clutching the flask beneath his costume. Once safely at the top of the stairs, Danny checked the Mortuary. All appeared to be still and quiet there. The two actors lying in their coffins might well be fast asleep. He walked by them without a word and proceeded up the stairs that led to the Tilted Room. At about the midway point there was a bend in the stairway. A perfect spot for him, Danny thought, and he nestled down into the corner with his knees pulled tightly against his chest. He reached for the little flask inside his shroud and took a quick drink, which burned its way down his throat and sizzled in the pool of his stomach. The warmth spread toward his fingertips. His nerves slowly began to untangle, and his head swam.

Hartnett must still be inside, he thought wearily. There had been no word of a disruption, so the detective must not have seen anything that he regarded as particularly odd. Yet. Had he made it up to the Butcher Shop window? Had he even gone inside at all? The feelings of doubt were creeping back into Danny's head. The panic stung him. And another sip from the little silver flask would not make the nervousness go away. He thought of Hartnett, and again he was alone.

The distant sound of a group approaching pulled Danny back into the present. He stood quickly, fumbling with the screw cap to the flask. When the group finally arrived at the bend in  the stairway Danny was gone. Whisking his way through the still-silent Mortuary and into the Belltower again.

# 18

From his vantage point at the end of the Swamp, the Watcher could see the group of customers beginning to trickle in. He could see that it was not a large group, and this was reassuring to him. He had an important job to do, and the fewer people there were to get in his way, the better.

Finally, he saw Hartnett's dark form emerge through the doorway. The strategically placed footlights reflected up at him at intermittent intervals, giving his face a particularly sinister glow. The Watcher smiled. He liked the idea of his adversary appearing somewhat sinister.

He began to walk slowly ahead of the group, passing soundlessly by the Ripper Scene. The actors in the scene, deep in their own conversation, only looked up for a split second as he passed by them. He continued up the stairs leading to the Plaza, the brainstars coming into view like a beacon for what would come later. They clustered around the periphery of his vision, forming a tunnel. He was propelled forward as if possessed.

When they had successfully negotiated the first two twists  of the winding path through the Swamp, the group stopped at the Ripper Scene. They congregated against the little wooden railing, taking in the dayglow paint effects of the makeshift forest (completely neglecting the fact that the *real* Jack the Ripper terrorized the White Chapel district of London, and not a patch of South Jersey woods). A short fellow in a bowler hat and sleeve garters appeared suddenly. He delivered his speech with an amusing cockney accent.

"…And I searched 'igh and low for me Mary Clarke. Just when I fought I'd never see 'er again… *'ere* she is, big as loife, roight 'ere in Pete's Beach! Roight under me very nose!"

The Rippee's glowing face could be seen hovering above her black light-enhanced body, which was tied to a nearby post. Her makeup gave her head an ethereal quality, poised above the white dress that was securely held to the post by ropes. She moaned and cried out her protests, peppering the Ripper's little speech with her pleas for help.

"But I'm *not* Mary Clarke! He's crazy! He kidnapped me from a group of visitors, just like you! Help me, please!"

The Ripper wheeled on the girl now, and his demeanor began to undergo an obvious change. He grew more enraged and violent with every word he spoke, "Shut up, Mary! Don't make me do somefin we'll bofe regret," he snarled between clenched teeth. He turned sharply back to look at the group, and they could see quite plainly that he was no longer the pleasant, mild-mannered little man that he had been just moments  before. His eyes were wild and possessed an insane look now.

He pulled a huge carving knife from beneath the

railing, and at the sight of it, the Rippee screamed loudly, prompting several involuntary sympathetic screams from some of the less steely members of the audience. The Ripper looked over his shoulder angrily, as though he were being challenged. He grabbed the top of the Rippee's head, where her hair had been pulled back in a knot, yanking it back roughly to expose her white throat. He slashed the knife across her pallid neck, leaving a gushing trail of fluorescent red. Her screams melted into a hoarse gurgle, then gradually vanished into silence. There was an empty pause as the Ripper stood with his back to the group, studying his work. Now slowly he turned to face them, a maniacal grin emblazoned across his boyish features.

"'Ere, now. 'At's better."

The group held at the railing, transfixed, as he reached over to his victim and took hold of the knot of hair atop her head again. This time he lifted the severed head from its body, and carried it to a nearby spiked post, where he impaled it with a flourish and an unappetizing squish. Taking two long steps backward, and keeping his back to the group of onlookers, his voice transformed miraculously back to that of the sweet cockney fellow. He studied the face of his victim's disembodied head, then mused, "But, you know, in this loight she don't look much like Mary Clarke. No, she don't look loike 'er atall."

He spun around in a fury, his face scant inches from that of a young girl at the front of the group.

"*YOU* look loike me Mary! Yes. I'm sure *you're* Mary

Clarke!"

The girl giggled at first, but realizing that the Ripper was fast approaching her, the giggles turned to screams as she pushed her way back from the railing toward the open doorway and up the stairs that led to the Plaza Area.

The Ripper hopped the railing easily, using one hand to steady his leap. In an instant he was up the stairs behind her. The others in the group all took the cue and began to slowly move toward the same stairs. All of them, that is, except Detective Hartnett, who remained alone at the railing.

He studied the impaled head of the Rippee, waiting for any sign of movement. Finally, the girl released the tremendous breath of air she had been holding and shouted to him from the post, "Well, what are *you* waiting for? That's it! Show's over. I don't do anything else!"

"Actually," Hartnett said in a calm voice that was rife with amusement, "I just thought I'd stand here and annoy you because I know you aren't supposed to move until I'm gone."

"Oh, is that how you get your thrills?" the girl snapped, showing a bright pink wad of bubble gum that she had concealed inside one cheek throughout the act.

"Well, here you go. Knock your socks off!"

With this, she stood up and her head appeared to miraculously float in the air above the spike it had been impaled on, the black lights not registering her black leotard. She spun around once, making her floating head spin as well.

"Look! Linda Blair!" She shouted. "How's that," she asked him, "exciting enough?"

Hartnett stood smiling at the strange sight, a ring of sarcastic satisfaction in his voice, "Great. Just great. Better than a peep show". He slowly started to move along in the direction that the others had taken, "See you later." Then he was out of sight and up the stairs.

"Not if I see you first, Jerk-off," the Rippee mumbled under her breath as she walked toward a stool that was hidden against the back wall.

Hartnett climbed the stairs to the Plaza Area by himself now. His group had traveled well ahead of him, but he was not worried. He preferred traveling alone anyway.

The cast members who were standing in the Plaza were not paying attention as the detective walked past them. They were far too engrossed in their idle talk and laughter when he passed by and oh-so-casually nodded his head good-naturedly, "How ya doin'? Hello."

The actors stood with their mouths agape, watching him stride to the bend in the passageway, then finally out of sight. They looked at one another, wondering where he had come from. The young man who had been playing the Ripper in the previous scene turned to his friends and asked, "Who was that guy? Did you know him?"

"Never seen him before. How about you, Jay?" Gordon asked the big hunchback who was standing beside him, fidgeting with the loose pack on his back that served as a hump.

"I don't know him, and I don't care *who* the fuck he

is," Jay replied.

Gordon gave him a deadpan look, "Eloquently put, Jay," he said and everyone laughed. And just like that the topic of the redheaded stranger in the nylon jacket who had mysteriously walked by was closed.

# 19

The passageway leading past the Headless Woman scene was completely dark, lit only by the dim green light of the scene itself. In the nearly complete darkness, Hartnett had struggled a bit to find his way, but somehow he had managed. He now stood looking through the dirty Meat Locker window, rubbing his stubbly chin. This had been where Danny Neumann had said that he had seen the body of one of the victims. There was no nude woman's torso hanging there, as Danny had said there would be. The figure that hung there now was fully clothed, the body not severed at the waist at all, and it hung facing the other way, toward the Meat Locker's interior. It was dressed in a shroud that was identical to the one that Danny had been wearing when he and Hartnett had met, some forty-five minutes earlier. As he stood observing the hanging figure in silence, it began to turn toward him. The turn was slow and calculated. All part of the suspense of the show. Hartnett was a little surprised that this actor would waste an entire performance on a single patron, but he continued to watch intently. He could feel his neck muscles beginning to tighten instinctively, and his heart did a nervous little dance in his chest as the ever-so-slow rotation of the man in the window progressed. He was almost completely facing full forward now.

Hartnett took a small step forward to afford himself a closer look. He half expected to see Danny Neumann's smiling face peering out at him from inside the deep hood. As the figure completed his slow turn, Hartnett leaned in closer to it, hoping for a better look at its face.

Suddenly a gloved fist crashed through the glass and grabbed the unwitting policeman's throat. The grip was like a vice, strong and immoveable. Hartnett struggled frantically; he clawed at the gloved hand, feeling his airway tighten. A second gloved hand covered his mouth and nose with a heavily chloroformed bit of towel, and the walls of the scene appeared to draw closer. The lights flickered and waned.

It took mere seconds for the Watcher to kick away the hanging shards around the edges of the gaping hole in the glass. He hopped through and pulled the stunned man into the Butcher Shop window. There was still some fight left in Hartnett, but the talons of steel on his throat remained unwavering, and the detective felt consciousness slipping away as his breath grew shallow. He fought to stave off the blackness that began to envelope him. It was all to no avail. The shrouded figure lived in the darkness of that same semiconscious state. He knew it. It made him strong.

# 20

The chatter of the actors in the Plaza was interrupted by the distant sound of breaking glass. Those who were seated on the steps of the Mine Shaft scrambled to their feet after a few questioning glances passed between them. Jay was the first to speak, "What do you think *that* was?"

A girl in a leopard print caftan perked up, "Oh, good, you heard it too? I was thinking that it was just part of the soundtrack tape."

Gordon started to move toward the left passageway, "It sounded like it could have come from the Mortuary or the Butcher Shop." His guess was as good as any. The Castle was made up of an intricate maze of passageways that turned and doubled back on each other. It was almost impossible to pinpoint the origin of any sound at any given time.

They scattered in various directions, in search of the source. The girl in the caftan remained where she was, hollering to them as they disappeared around their respective corners, "Wait a minute! Let's not get crazy here! It was probably just some asshole breaking a beer bottle that he brought in here with him!"

When it became clear to her that none of the others were paying any attention to her protests, the girl finally stood up and followed them. They all knew that the sound they had heard was no beer bottle.

They walked past the Headless Woman scene, calling to the girl in the chair as they passed by. She responded from behind the set of mirrors that concealed her face, her voice muffled and strange.

A loud shuffling suddenly came from behind the little group, who were busy negotiating the dark turns of the passageway. They turned to see Jarrett coming toward them, unsteady on the tall Frankenstein shoes, but trying to move at a good clip to catch up with them.

"Nothing in the Mine Shaft," Jay said as he charged up to them. The hump on his back bobbled from side to side as he moved, a la Marty Feldman. Now the little group of actors looked toward the passageway that led to the Butcher Shop. They exchanged no words, but all knew that it was the direction that they had suspected from the start. As they began to move reluctantly in the direction of the big Meat Locker window, they all felt a faint shudder run through their bodies.

Moving closer to the scene, Gordon could see Jules standing at the end of the hall. He was staring down at the scattering of broken glass that covered the floor. The two girls from the Human Sacrifice scene were standing near him at the corner  that led to their stairway. He looked up as Gordon and the others approached.

"What the hell is going on up here?" Jules asked. He looked back into the Meat Locker window, empty now except for the huge dangling meat hook that the Watcher had been hanging from moments before. He passed the beam of his flashlight over the floor of the passageway, then up to the gouged pieces of wall that would have to be repaired in the off-season. His characteristic grin was replaced with a look of disgust.

The caftaned actress had lagged behind at the Headless Woman Scene, chatting with the girl behind the mirrors. She arrived beside Gordon and the others now, stopping just short of the scattered glass on the floor, gasping, "Oh. Somebody broke the window," she said under her breath.

Jules looked up at her briefly with a frown, "Thanks. I would never have guessed that." He looked at the rest of the group now, "Who was supposed to be playing the Butcher, anyway?"

"I don't know," the girl in the caftan answered for all of them, "I think I saw Greg walking up here in the Butcher's apron earlier today."

Now Jules' face took on a stern look as he realized the seriousness of the mess that he was looking at. "Well, see if you can find him anywhere. Richard's gonna chew out *somebody* for this, and I'd just as soon not have it be me!"

The girl took off to find Greg. You didn't have to tell her twice.

There would be customers coming through any minute, and this glass had to be cleaned up pronto. Gordon and Jay watched Jules as he got down on all fours to start picking up the larger pieces. He stopped for a second and looked up at the two of them, "Don't just stand there, somebody get to the Rat Professor Area and call the Dressing Room for clean up!"

Jay headed toward the stairs in a hurry, the hump now midway between his shoulder blades as he ran. Gordon got down on the floor beside his roommate and began to pick up the remnants of the broken window. Jules looked over at him, and Gordon noticed how his mass of curly hair and dimpled cheeks conjured the image of a little boy cleaning up the mess caused by his baseball crashing through the neighbor's window. He smiled at the thought.

"That's okay, man. Don't get cut," Jules was saying. He paused and then spoke again, not looking up from the task at hand, "I kind of expected something like this to happen on the last day. It just happened a little earlier than I had anticipated." He looked at all the shining pieces of glass that were still scattered along the narrow passageway. The beam of his flashlight, which lay on the floor beside him, caught every fragment, mimicking the night sky from below.

"Wait till I get my hands on Greg, though. I'll wring his neck! If he had been at his position, where he was supposed to be, this would never have happened!"

Gordon had a minor revelation, "It had to be somebody from the last group. Hey, come to think of it, there was a weird guy, walking all by himself, behind that group. We heard the glass break a few minutes after he walked by."

"Well, that guy and that group are long gone by now. Besides, nobody actually saw him do anything. Nope, the ones who are in deep shit here are Greg and me." He looked up at Gordon, who was standing now, "Speaking of leaving one's position, you'd better get back to your spot, before Richard catches you and puts you on the shit list with the rest of us." Gordon smiled, and Jules added, "I need you to stall any groups that come up in the next ten minutes; hold 'em in the Plaza if you can. Cleanup should get here anytime now."

"Okay, I'm on my way. Just call me if you need any help."

Jules smiled again, "You've got a deal."

# 21

The interior of the Prop Closet was narrow but surprisingly long. Hartnett was lying on the floor at the center of the room. He was tied and gagged, and he groaned as he struggled to reach full consciousness. He leaned his head to one side, realizing that his hands were tightly bound behind him with zip ties. The pain in his throat was searing. Bruises and thick red welts encircled the part of his neck above his shirt collar, and Hartnett was certain that he could not speak, although the desire to try escaped him.

Slumped in the far corner was the body of Greg, contorted at an uncomfortable angle, and still wearing the bloody Butcher's apron. He grasped the prop cleaver from the scene in one of his stiffening hands. There was a rusty line of blood that ran across his throat from ear to ear.

Greg was one of the young performers from the drag shows in Atlantic City. Like the others from the shows, he arrived at the Castle every day with his makeup already applied. But now the picture-perfect makeup job was a shambles, smeared across his frozen features. The vivacity that was so familiar in him was stilled forever.

Detective Hartnett's eyelids fluttered briefly, then his eyes opened wide, taking in as much as he could without turning his pain-riddled head. He tried to sit up, but a new flood of pain stopped the movement short. He winced at his foolish attempt. Now he tried to make out the face of the clock on the wall above Greg, but that too was a blur to him. How long had he been here? How long ago had the awful apparition in the shroud crashed through the Butcher Shop window at him? Was it hours, or even days? There was no time here. The little room appeared to be cut off entirely from daylight, and the crashing sounds of Castle soundtracks blared all around him.

The sound of a low raspy voice assaulted him from behind, and Hartnett froze. His heart began to beat more arrhythmically with the Watcher's every word.

"Hello, Detective. You've been asleep for quite a while now. It's very rude to fall asleep on one's host like that." A brief silence followed, and Hartnett strained to hear, lest he should miss a single word.

"Have you met Greg?"

He looked again toward the crumpled heap that had once been the young man called Greg, lying across the room from him, cleaver at the ready.

"Greg was the Butcher today," the Watcher went on, "He wasn't really well-suited to the role, though." He paused as his mocking voice became a whisper, "Too nice."

The Watcher's legs came into Hartnett's hazy field of

vision. Hartnett struggled with every bit of strength he could muster to force his head upward. To see the face of this demon. But all his efforts were to no avail. The pain in his head and neck had affected his vision too greatly. All he could make out was a bright blur where the Watcher's face should have been. And his real fight was about to begin. It was the bout with the unconsciousness that seemed to be creeping up on him. He fought to keep his eyes open. The pain was so intense that he wanted to scream, but he could make no sound. It was as if the screams stopped at the bruises on his throat, and the last of the sound was held back by the gag in his mouth. He began to slowly choke on what could either be saliva or blood. Or both.

He saw the legs begin to move across the room toward Greg. He strained to follow the movements, to move his eyes higher, to catch even the smallest glimpse of a face.

The raspy voice sliced through Hartnett's confused brain like a razor.

"I think that Greg would be better suited to play the role of the Rippee, don't you?"

Hartnett's confusion was compounded by the strange word that the Watcher had used. What was a Rippee? That, too, would not matter. Because now the Watcher's gloved hand came into view, grabbing a tuft of Greg's hair, lifting his head by it. The head separated cleanly from the body at the red line across Greg's neck. It had already been severed neatly.

The dimness of the room gave the scenario a dreamlike

quality, and Hartnett prayed desperately that he would wake from this nightmare. But that moment would not come. He was jolted once more into the present by the scraping laugh, louder still, which reawakened the throbbing vein of agony that ran along his spine and wound neatly into a cord that encircled his throat.

Hartnett shut his eyes tight against the horrible sights and was unhappily surprised when he was able to reopen them.

"Shhhh. We mustn't make so much noise," the rasping serpent's voice said to him, "The others might hear us."

Hartnett tried to rally all his strength to call out but was stifled by the gag. Blood filled his throat, and he felt he would certainly choke this time. He felt cold wetness around his collar, and knew that he had already been chosen as the next…what was it that the monster had said? Rippee?

The Watcher's voice suddenly grew more human, feigning concern, "Now, now, detective — Hartnett, is it? There's really no point in wearing yourself out trying to scream. Nobody would even notice in a place like this."

The false tenderness in the Watcher's voice was sickening to Hartnett's ears. But that was the Watcher's intention. He *wanted* the detective to feel contempt for him. Hartnett must hate him. It would make killing him that much easier. The Watcher most enjoyed putting out the fire behind the smoldering eyes of an enemy. He would never regret killing a foe. It was the tears that he had shed over the innocent ones' deaths that had begun to make the Watcher weak. That had slowly begun to kill him. It was Mother's way of punishing his weakness.

Hartnett's now-sunken blue eyes followed the Watcher's bloody hand above him. It reached toward the volume control knob on the sound system. The voice grew softer, slowly swallowed up by the sound.

"Besides, I can turn up the volume of the bells in the Belltower, and no one will hear you." He turned the knob ever so slowly. The gong of the Belltower's tape grew increasingly louder, more painful. Now the Watcher's hand retreated with a jerk.

"No. No, I wouldn't want to make it *too loud*, and have some stupid Castle toady come running to check the tape!"

He reached across the low table and retrieved a set of headphones, which he carefully placed on the struggling head of one detective Christopher Hartnett. Then he plugged the headphones' metal jack into one of the room's many electronic components. His voice grew louder and more commanding now. "There. Now you can enjoy the full impact of the bells, Detective Hartnett!" Hartnett struggled with the last of his strength as the Watcher adjusted the levels on the big equalizer box, then turned his attention back to the volume control. His hand slowly turned the knob, sending the volume level higher and higher in Hartnett's captive head. And then the knob would go no further. Hartnett's frantic struggles also reached their peak, the blood in his throat choking out the last bit of air he could manage to take in.

The final drops of his life spilled out through the bleeding slit in his throat, and he froze in the ghastly pose that he would maintain in the afterlife. He sat, convulsing and gasping for air, with his steel blue eyes bulging as the sound pierced his eardrums.

And then it was over. The Watcher saw the trickle of blood forming in the corner of Hartnett's left eye. He watched it release and wind a slow and careful tracing down the man's cheek, and finally drop onto his dark jacket. He should never have been wearing that jacket, the Watcher thought. It was too hot outside for a jacket.

# 22

Danny was on the move again, roving through the Castle. He stopped at a bend in the Swamp's curving path, looked around quickly, then retrieved the flask from the folds of his clothing. He shook it to assess its contents. It was quite empty, but Danny took a swig from it as though it were still full. He shook it again to be sure that he hadn't missed a drop. He hadn't.

As he began to replace the little silver cap, a heavy hand landed on his shoulder, jolting him soundly. He stood frozen with fear for a second, then finally mustered the drunken courage to turn around to face whomever (or whatever) was hovering behind him. Expecting the worst, he was relieved to meet with none other than the smiling face of Jules.

"Hey, Buddy, who are you hiding from?"

Jules looked down at the empty flask in Danny's hand and frowned as he grabbed it.

"What have we here?" He unscrewed the little cap before Danny could protest, and held the flask up to his nose, "Now, you *know* you're not supposed to have this kind of thing here." He smiled and brought the flask to his own lips, tilting it for any last drop that might find its way out. He smiled at his friend again.

"Just making sure it's empty." He replaced the cap and concealed the flask behind a nearby Styrofoam rock. "There, that's better." He put his arm around Danny's shoulders and guided him along the Swamp's winding path as they talked.

"You know, Dan, you're a hard man to track down. I've been combing this dump for you for an hour now."

"I've been keeping a low profile," Danny muttered softly. His speech was slightly slurred, and Jules moved a bit further back from the smell of alcohol that surrounded him.

"Wow! I should have known to follow the fumes! I would have found you right away!"

Danny fought back the sudden urge to be sick, watching Jules' silhouette fade in and out of focus. He cleared his throat and spoke with as much dignity as his intoxicated mouth would allow, "I needed something to keep me calm for the rest of the day."

"Well, you succeeded in that department," Jules laughed, "You're calm alright. In fact, you're practically *liquid*! Now, you're going to come with me. We're going to get changed and then we'll get some dinner. Before that little bottle of whiskey eats right through your stomach lining."

"Great. Are you asking me out on a date?"

Jules grabbed a fistful of Danny's shroud, guiding his friend's unsteady steps as they walked, "Absolutely."

"Well, I'll go to dinner with you," Danny said as he clumsily draped one arm around Jules' neck, "But if you think you're getting lucky afterward, you're dead wrong!"

They both laughed now, as the queasy feeling in Danny's stomach threatened to return. Passing through the various scenes, Danny's feet moved mechanically, with the feeling that he might throw up at any moment. He closed his eyes as they passed through the Portrait Room, letting Jules be his guide. By the time he felt he could safely reopen them, they were halfway down the Belltower stairs.

"I squared it with Richard for the five of us: you, me, Sandy, Gordon, and Susan, to all have our dinner breaks together tonight," Jules was saying, "Kind of a last day celebration."

There was silence for a second, then Danny looked at his friend, working hard to maintain his focus on his very close profile.

"Great. Who's Susan?"

Jules laughed and looked back at Danny, half-expecting the question to have been a joke. When he saw the serious look on Danny's drunken face he replied,

"Gordon's new girl."

"Ohhh," Danny said knowingly, "You mean *Susan*."

"I *said* Susan."

"You did not," Danny came back at him, challengingly.

"Yes, I did!"

Now Danny's tone took on that of a stubborn five-year-old, "*DID NOT!*" His shout was accompanied by a sickening wave of whiskey breath.

"FUCK YOU!" Jules shouted back resolutely.

There was another short pause, and Danny added, smiling, "Only if you buy me dinner first, Big Boy!"

With this they both laughed, and Danny broke free of Jules' grip. He wound his way down the short hallway to the Dressing Room door.

Jules said, "It's a little early for a dinner break, but there will be a lot of crazy last day stuff happening later on, and I don't want to miss any of it. Everybody goes a little wild during the last couple hours."

"Just what I need, more excitement in my life," Danny added as he pushed open the Dressing Room Door.

Jules finally caught up with him, "What?"

"Skip it," Danny said quietly as he walked past his friend to the long mirror over the makeup table. He reached for one of the many boxes of tissues and the big jar of Albolene, dipping two fingers in the goocy cream and lifting them toward his face. He stopped short as he caught his own reflection in the glass.

The face staring back at him truly was frightening, and

he had the sinking feeling that the scariest qualities could not be wiped away with a tissue. It was the desperate look in his eyes that scared him most. The look of a helpless, frightened child. Or that of a raving lunatic. He moved forlornly toward the Dressing Room's tiny bathroom and slammed the door closed behind him.

The cold water from the tap felt good on his aching face. Danny watched as the various colors that had been his makeup trickled in rainbow streaks into the open drain. It was oddly reminiscent to him of the shower scene in *Psycho*. This was something he would normally have found funny but couldn't now. He rinsed his face again, and this time the water and the makeup mixed with something new. Danny's tears.

# 23

The Buccaneer Restaurant was a typical seashore sandwich shop: nautical decor, nothing fancy. The place was always filled in the summer months with hungry beachgoers, tourists, and locals who appreciated the Buccaneer's cheesesteak sandwiches. "The Best Cheesesteaks East of Philly."

Danny and his little entourage were seated at a table beside a big open window. Their dinner plates were stacked neatly on one corner of the table, awaiting retrieval by the waitress. The Castle loomed outside the window, like a massive school mistress watching over her untrustworthy class. The bizarre thought crossed

Danny's mind that the building itself was watching him. Little did he know that the Castle's wayward child had not missed a single move that Danny had made that day.

Sandy's voice pulled Danny away from his weird thoughts and toward her perfect, smiling face, impeccable with just a touch of street makeup, "Certain people are notorious for pulling ridiculous last day pranks, she was saying, "Jules, Rollie and Barry are probably the worst offenders. And I wouldn't be surprised if Little Mack suddenly showed up to join in."

At the mention of Little Mack's name, Danny bristled. He fought the urge to speak, as Sandy went on. "Every year you guys do something incredibly dangerous and destructive." She directed this last bit at Jules. Turning back to the others, she added, "Then Richard gets pissed off and tells them that they'll never work here again."

"…And next year he'll hire us anyway," Jules reported through his shining smile.

Susan looked at Sandy, her face showing genuine concern, "What do you mean by *dangerous and destructive?*"

"Oh, stuff like hanging off the top of the building, or dropping stuffed animals…"

"Which we stole from one of the arcade games…" Jules interjected.

"Right." Sandy met his eyes gleefully, "…dropping them off the top of the building at unsuspecting people on the pier below." Everyone laughed at this, fueling her storytelling, "Or having a battle with fire extinguishers in the Plaza."

Jules stopped her in mid-sentence now, "Yeah. Harry was not too happy with that one." Still smiling, he sat forward with his arms folded on the table, "The best part of it is when the monsters all follow the last group of customers through the Castle, harassing them all the way."

"Harassing?" Sandy asked in a surprised tone, "More like *abusing* them all the way!"

In truth, the abuse had been taking place since the middle of July. That was around the time when mere scares had lost their excitement for the bored cast members. That was when the fetal position contests and the notion of the "ultimate scare" were first conceived. Someone had aptly crossed out the letter M on the big sign out in front of the pier and scrawled their own message. The sign now read THE HAUNTED CASTLE AND *ABUSEMENT* PIER.

Jules continued, his obvious mirth undaunted, "Then, when they leave the building, we chase the most willing ones down to the end of the pier..." His voice trailed off into a pregnant silence, waiting for someone to ask the obvious question.

"...And then?" Susan asked anxiously.

"Then they find whoever was playing Dracula during the last shift, and they throw him into the ocean." Sandy replied dryly before Jules had the chance to glamorize this dangerous practice. It was obvious from her tone that she disapproved of this segment of the Castle ritual. It was, indeed, extremely dangerous. The sporadic tides below the pier had a way of turning such antics from foolhardy to fatal. Luckily for them, nothing more serious than a sprained ankle had ever been the result of the ridiculous tradition. The fact was that despite the large number of vampires who had taken the plunge, very few injuries had actually occurred.

Now Jules added, "That's why that asshole Bobby wimped out and disappeared right before Closing Day. He knew that we've all been *dying* to toss him in the water all summer."

"It makes no difference who's playing Dracula anymore. By the time it's all over just about everyone ends up in the ocean anyway," Sandy said.

"That sounds dangerous," Susan remarked as the color drained from her face. The prospect of either herself or Gordon being pushed off the pier and plunging forty feet into the ocean filled her with dread.

Sandy and Jules looked at each other, smiling at Sue's words. They replied together, as if on cue, "Dangerous and destructive."

"Now you're catching on, "Sandy added for good measure. Danny had been conspicuously silent throughout all of this. His thoughts were elsewhere, in a dark corner of that building, where anything could be happening to a poor unsuspecting victim at that very moment. The soothing effects of the alcohol had worn off now, leaving him with an uneasy feeling and an unrelenting migraine. The familiar panic was back now, fully piercing his consciousness as it had before.

"Hey, Danny! Are you with us, or what?" It was Sandy, calling him back to reality.

He touched her arm softly and closed his eyes, "Ssshhh. My head hurts." He said this in little more than a whisper.

Jules' voice assaulted him from across the table in a louder- than-ever tone, "Did you take some aspirin?"

"Several hundred," Danny replied stiffly as he held his aching head. Now Susan touched Danny's wrist tenderly, as she would that of a lifelong friend, "Can we get you anything?"

Danny looked up into her concerned eyes, "Yes. A gun."

"C'mon," she replied, "It *can't* be bad enough to want to kill yourself!"

"It's not," Danny said, "I want the gun so I can kill the four of you for being so goddamned *cheerful*!"

They all laughed, with Danny giving in to it sparingly.

"Dan the Man, snap out of it!" Gordon said. "Enjoy yourself. Have some fun tonight!"

"Get wild!" Sandy added, flinging her arms up in a bad portrayal of abandon. She realized how silly this sounded immediately.

Danny just sat and looked blankly from face to friend's face. It was as if they were all aliens to him. Finally, he stretched his legs forward, sending his chair back from the table with a loud screech. He observed the others from this new distance for a few seconds, then said, "Well, if you party animals don't mind, I think I'll skip the excitement this evening."

An unforgiving frown crawled across Gordon's face, "We should've known," he nodded to Jules knowingly.

The disappointment that plainly registered on their faces made no difference to Danny. He had decided that he wasn't going to put his weary brain through another shift. He had had enough. He conceded defeat to his massive gray opponent, eyeing the building through the window. The Castle had won, he thought, hands down. No technicalities, no rematch.

He looked back at his companions, still staring at him from their seats. Suddenly a boyish grin shattered the pensiveness, "Hey, I wouldn't want to disappoint anyone by actually having *fun*!"

They all faked a laugh (poorly), and Sandy pushed her chair back hurriedly and stood, "Oh, shit! We're late, and you guys have to get back and punch in again!"

Gordon stood quickly, then realized what Sandy had just said, "What do you mean, *us* guys? Aren't you working tonight?"

"Nope," Sandy said as she gathered up her huge satchel of a purse. "I'll do all your makeup, then I'm just going to walk my dog on the beach and catch the madness at the end of the night."

"And hit the Sand Bar," Gordon added smiling, as though she had forgotten the most important part.

Sandy smiled back at him, "Big time."

Now the waitress arrived at their table and laid the check gently amid the clutter of napkins and empty cups. She smiled at the group and walked away. As if taking her cue, Jules pushed his chair back quickly and rose beside the others, "Okay, I guess we're outta here." Dropping some cash on the table, he headed toward the exit.

Outside the restaurant, splinters of the magnificent sunset that was taking place on the bay side of the island kissed the edges of the Castle and illuminated the dentil tops of the Parapet like a golden crown. Turning his back on its hulking form, Danny began to walk in the opposite direction. Sandy's voice came from behind him, and he turned to face her.

"What are you going to do with the rest of the night?"

Danny smiled at her, "I just need to go home and clear my head. The past couple of days have really gotten to me. Not to mention the bottle of JD I polished off this afternoon."

"You can't just go home without finishing your shift… Besides, you didn't pick up your paycheck. It'll be a bitch getting money out of Harry after the pier is closed."

She had a point there. As much as he would have liked to just keep walking and never set foot in the damn place again, Danny had to make at least one more trip to the Castle. He considered going home, taking a quick nap to wash away the last bit of inebriation he was feeling, then returning later. Or he could simply go there now and get it over with. Sandy's look was enough to convince him.

"Just finish up the night. It'll take them a while to

get the checks cut, so you might as well be there when they say they're ready. You don't have to stay for their stupid games. Just get changed, grab your check, and leave while the others are tossing each other off the end of the pier."

There was a pause as Sandy stared longingly into Danny's eyes. *She* wanted him to stay. He could see that in her face. She had used the only weapon in her arsenal that had any chance at all of convincing him. Herself. He smiled weakly, and she knew immediately that he would go back.

"I'll do your makeup for you super quick, then I *have* to walk Ceto." He looked up at her, as though he had been deceived. Sandy immediately sensed his nervousness, "Don't worry, I'll be back right after that!"

She took hold of his hand before another moment could pass, during which he might very well change his mind, and they walked toward the Castle together.

# 24

Standing at the railing of the Actors' Area, the Watcher could see Danny and Sandy walking along the street toward the pier. A spark of genuine hatred ignited the fuse in his brain, and the rhythm of his heartbeat grew faster. The game was nearly over. It was time for his playmate to die.

He looked up fearfully at the towering form of his mother, standing imposingly above him. He turned back to see the approaching couple, now walking arm-in-arm. The sunset was bright on the purple horizon of the bay, and its brightness was multiplied by an explosion of brainstars. The Watcher shielded his eyes as the stars moved rapidly toward him, pelting his face and chest like wayward fireworks. Fireworks that existed only in one warped and diseased mind. He opened his arms wide to accept the sparks with his entire being. He could feel them sear his clothing and ultimately burn deep into his flesh. He wanted the pain. He needed it. It fed him. The pain. The fire.

# 25

It was a great relief to Jarrett to find that he would be roving the Castle for the rest of the evening. It meant that he wouldn't be stuck in a scene with any other actors, and he could take as much of his precious medication as he needed. He was beginning to feel as though he might need to take a lot of medication tonight. In addition to his usual measure of pain, Jarrett was feeling an extreme amount of anxiety. Without warning, his heart would pound, and his breath would grow short. The fear that had permeated his dreams had spilled over into his reality now. Jarrett pictured the shrouded man in his mind's eye constantly. He was tired. More tired than he had ever been before in his life. Even during his brief career in the military Jarrett had never felt exhaustion like this. He was feeling consumed by it, and if sleep ever *should* come to him again, he might never wake up.

He had been eating the multi-colored capsules by the fistful, walking through the halls of the Castle like a real-life zombie. He found a safe, secluded spot behind the huge stuffed figure of a white horse, just past the Ripper Scene. It was here that Jarrett laid down to rest "just for a minute". It was here that sleep finally found him.

# 26

All that was left of the sun was a tiny orange sliver, clinging to the smooth edge of the horizon. The gray line of the bay that met with the setting sun seemed to sizzle with its contact.

The bustle inside the Dressing Room was a direct counterpoint to the peacefulness of the evening just outside its door. The purples and pinks on the floorboards of the pier outside were replaced on the inside with the artificial glow of fluorescent tube lights. The invigorating ocean air was exchanged for the smell of greasepaint.

Gordon stood before the side mirror, trying on various silly hats to go with the bizarre costume he had selected for the evening. He was dressed in a sporty mini dress, complete with handbag and pearl necklace. Sandy had spied him from across the room as he primped and posed in the mirror. She walked toward him with her hands on hips, not trying to hide her amusement.

"Would it be silly for me to ask what position you're playing, dressed that way?"

"First Cage," Gordon answered directly. His eyes never left his own reflection in the mirror as he adjusted the hem of his dress.

"First Cage," Sandy repeated, without emotion. She bit her bottom lip and turned to look at Danny, who sat on one of the stools across the room.

Turning back to Gordon, she added, "I *thought* it might be silly of me to ask."

This prompted a round of laughter from everyone in the room. The laughter was abruptly cut short by Richard's voice, shouting in the Actors' Area. He was clearly visible in the doorway as he stood holding his clipboard, chewing out an unfortunate actor wearing a shroud.

At one point he slammed his clipboard and the big hoop keyring from his belt loop onto one of the picnic tables for emphasis. He was now screaming wildly at the actor.

"...I don't give a fuck *what* you had to go do! If you're responsible for a scene, I expect you to stay in that scene until you're told to leave! You don't go talk to somebody down the hall, you don't go smoke a joint on the Parapet, you don't go take a piss out the window, *you stay there*!"

The actor started to move one hand as if he might interrupt Richard's words, but Richard was much too fast and too mad for him.

"No. Don't say anything. Shut up a minute! What the hell do you think this is, anyway? 'It's the last day. Richard can't fire me'. Well, you're wrong, I CAN! I want you out of here. Now! Get changed. I want you the fuck off this pier! You're gone!"

During this tirade, Sandy watched nervously as she saw Richard grasp the lump in his jacket pocket repeatedly. She wasn't used to this sort of outburst from Richard. Sure, he usually had things to complain about, but he always approached problem situations calmly, rationally. Sandy knew that there was nothing calm or rational about the man standing outside the door right now. She felt a strange feeling. She was frightened of him. He was a stranger with a gun to her now, nothing more.

The actor who had been the target of Richard's anger had shed his shroud on the spot and headed down the pier ramp. He was wearing jeans and a wife beater. He didn't even bother to return to the Dressing Room for his tee shirt.

When Richard was out of sight again, and safely out of earshot, Jules made the first of the inevitable observations, "Wow. Richard's really on a roll tonight."

"That seemed like a bit much for just leaving his position." Gordon's serious look was made comical by his attire. No one was laughing now, though. They were all still mildly stunned.

Sandy jumped to Richard's defense. Not so much out of loyalty to Richard, but more as a precautionary tactic to prevent any of her friends from ending up the next one to cross him. After all, she thought, she was the only one who knew what that heavy bulge in Richard's jacket pocket really was.

"He's having a bad day," she said, "Nobody's cooperating today, and he's still mad about the Butcher Shop window being smashed. I think he might have fired Greg, too. I haven't seen him since it happened."

Danny sat up straight on the stool, a look of concern replacing the smile on his face, "Hold on, did you say that the Butcher Shop window was broken? When? Was it when Detective Hartnett was inside?"

Sandy looked over at him, "Detective *Who*?"

"Detective Hartnett. He went inside with one of the groups to check on something I had seen in the Butcher Shop…". Danny considered telling her exactly what he had seen there, but there were too many eyes and ears trained on him now. Besides, if Hartnett hadn't reported seeing anything, Danny thought, it was very possible that Juanita's corpse had been nothing more than another frightening figment of his rampant imaginings.

"I assumed that Hartnett hadn't found anything unusual when he went through, so he left."

Gordon turned his gaze from the mirror to look at Danny. "Wait. Back up. You didn't think it was strange that he didn't let you know anything before he left? I know that if you had sent *me* through this place on a wild goose chase and I found nothing, I'd be back to bust your balls about it!"

"No, I guess I didn't really think about it. The guy kind of thought I wasn't all there to begin with. He only went through the place to shut me up." He paused, then added,

"As a matter of fact, I think he really just went in to piss Richard off."

"Richard…" Sandy said, under her breath but audible enough to draw a curious look from the others. Sandy could only think about one thing. The gun in Richard's pocket. Could Hartnett's quick disappearance have had something to do with Richard and their obvious argument in the Actors' Area? Did Richard threaten him with the gun? This wasn't a joke anymore. Hartnett was a police officer, and no one to fool around with. The air in the Dressing Room had grown heavy. Suddenly the silence was broken. It was Danny who was laughing out loud now. Gordon looked at his friend sternly, "What the hell is so funny?"

The smile on Danny's face was obscenely inappropriate to their conversation, "Now all of you are making up murder mysteries in your heads. I'm getting the feeling that insanity is contagious around here."

A moment later, Richard walked through the door from the Actors' Area. He was obviously still extremely agitated. He stopped and stood motionless in the middle of the room, oblivious to the anxious eyes that were watching him. In another moment he had exited into the Castle. The half dozen or so faces had turned away by then and were busying themselves unobtrusively.

Sandy quickly put a few finishing touches on Danny's Dracula makeup and coaxed him off the stool, "There you go. You're ready. Now get outta here before Richard comes back and finds something to scream at you about." She turned to the others, prompting them into instant motion. "All of you! Get to work!"

Jules inspected Danny's costume with an impish grin, "Dan, I hope you're prepared to get wet. Dracula inevitably gets dunked at the end of the day."

Sandy's face appeared between Jules and Danny as she walked by, "Not if he gets out of the Castle before everybody else is done."

Jules forlornly picked up two stray audio cassettes from a nearby table and headed for the Castle door. Pulling the door open with one hand, he let in a whirlwind of screams and soundtrack moans. Then he turned back to his friends, "You guys are no fun anymore." And he was gone.

Danny and Gordon moved up the Belltower stairs to their positions. As they reached the gate to the Butler Area, Gordon held it open for his friend to pass through. Danny just shook his head.

"I think I'll take a quick rove through the place before I get into the Portrait. I want to see if anybody noticed Hartnett when he went through. I'll catch up with you later." He continued making his way up the stairs, and Gordon called quietly up to him, "Hey, Dan."

Danny stopped and looked back at him, "Yeah?"

There was a thick moment of silence, then Gordon simply replied, "Be careful." Danny turned back to the spiral of stairs still ahead of him and continued to climb without another word.

# 27

Out in the Castle's Lobby, a group of elderly ladies stood gazing at the strange oval mirror that bore a painted scroll above it which read THE ORACLE OF THE SEA in a poor attempt at Olde English calligraphy. One of the ladies dug into her purse and produced the necessary quarter to activate the machine. With a rattle and a click it all came to life. The mirror transformed instantly into a window, revealing the figure of an old, wizened man in gypsy garb, who stared into an oversized crystal ball. The sound of crashing thunder that normally accompanied the appearance of the Oracle was conspicuously absent. In its place, a loud burst of music came through the machine's speakers. The mechanical movements of the old gypsy inside seemed to oddly sync up with the song's lyrics, as it voiced robotically, *"When a problem comes along, you must whip it. Before the cream sits out too long, you must whip it...".*

Sandy's trained ears could pick out even the slightest deviation in any of the Castle's soundtracks from her post at the makeup table. It hadn't taken more than a second for her to realize that the Oracle of the Sea was not himself tonight. She smiled as the loud New Wave music emanated from the Oracle's speaker, shaking her head knowingly. It was evident that Jules had been up to his usual Closing Day tricks. She opened one of the makeup table's drawers and fumbled through the little pile of cassette tapes inside, finally retrieving the one labeled "Oracle".

She moved toward the rack of black shrouds beside her table and parted the shrouds at the center to reveal a little door in the wall, hidden behind them. As she opened the door the sound of the *Devo* song intensifed inside the Dressing Room, drawing several curious stares from others standing in the room. Working as quickly as possible, Sandy replaced the blaring cassette with the proper tape. Instantly the inappropriate gales of *Whip It* were replaced with the crash of thunder and the trill of the old gypsy's voice.

Turning toward the table, Sandy's shoe caught on something inside the little niche below the rack of shrouds. Ceto's cache of booty spilled out onto the floor at her feet, and Sandy stared down at it in astonishment. The muddle of hairpins and coins slid forth from under the hems of the shrouds, but only one thing in the little pile truly caught her eye. She stooped immediately to pick it up. It was a small object with rounded edges, that glinted in the meager evening light of the Dressing Room. She held it low against her body to scrutinize it. Confirming what she already knew, she quickly tucked the bullet into the wide front pocket of her smock. Acutely aware of any eyes that might be following her, Sandy took hold of the tie- dye collar around Ceto's neck and walked out into the Actors' Area with him, then down the ramp to the beach. She needed to think now.

# 28

The Hangman Scene was just another dark alcove along the Swamp's path, like so many others scattered throughout the Castle. It contained poorly constructed gallows on a short platform, and was manned by a lone actor, who played the part of the Hangman. When groups of customers assembled at the scene, he pulled the lever that dropped a trap door beneath the weighted dummy that hung by its neck in the noose. Like the First Cage, this was one of the most dreaded positions in the Castle, where the actor worked alone and would begin to go stir crazy after an entire shift spent in the tiny area.

As Danny approached the Hangman Scene he could hear faint whisperings. He moved closer, keeping just enough distance to remain unnoticed. It was then that he realized that he was hearing not one, but *two* voices. One was the nervous but unmistakable voice of Eric, today's Hangman. But it was not Eric's voice that froze Danny's blood in his veins. It was the other voice. The low, raspy cackle of the Watcher, goading the frightened boy on.

"You *do* want to play by the rules, don't you, Eric?"

Danny rounded the corner for a better view. He ducked behind some bushes and peered silently at the two figures in the scene. Eric was nervously staring at the Watcher, whose shrouded back remained toward Danny. The tall blonde boy's voice cracked and trembled as he replied, "Y-Yes, I do. I want to, uh, play…"

The Watcher exhaled loudly, interrupting him. The sound came out hard and brittle. Danny was forced to move closer to hear their conversation clearly.

"Then take the dummy out of the noose, Eric. Hurry up. I'm becoming impatient, and that's not good, is it?"

The blazing eyes of the Watcher were riveted on him as his fingers worked at the tightly wound rope. Eric finally managed to pull the dummy's head through the noose successfully, letting the heavy stuffed man drop to the floor with a thud. The Watcher reached into his shroud. In another instant, he held aloft a short black billy club. The kind of nightstick used by policemen. The dull thud of the club against the back of his head sent Eric sprawling against the dummy on the floor, where he began to slip into unconsciousness. Deep confusion mingled with the pain and the mist in his head as he let out a single short gasp and pushed his forehead deeper into the back of the stuffed dummy.

A scant twenty feet away Danny lurched impulsively, unable to hold himself back. He leapt forward into the dim light of the Hangman Scene. Words were jumping from his lips, "Wait! Eric!"

The Watcher spun to face Danny, his shroud billowing in a single ballet-like motion. His face was concealed inside the shroud's hood by an intricately detailed latex mask. It was the wrinkled face of a very old man. It was one of those masks that had become a favorite at Halloween, not terribly frightening in and of itself, yet in the sharp pin spot of the Hangman Scene it held an unparalleled horror. The searing eyes of the Watcher within the slits of the mask imbued it with an even more sinister quality. The nightstick was still poised in one of his hands. From within the mask came the hollow sound of the all-too-familiar laugh.

"Danny!" The Watcher exclaimed with genuine surprise, "How nice of you to join us!"

He took two steps toward Danny, then stopped short. He turned his head back, listening over one shoulder. The movement had the staccato jerkiness of a bird. He tilted his head to better hear the approaching group as Danny stood frozen and baffled. He barely had enough time to turn around when the first customers were already upon them.

The group, growing steadily in number, all began to pass by now, engulfing both Danny and the Watcher. Danny craned his neck repeatedly as the crowd surrounded him, trying to maintain sight of his foe, but try as he might to spot the Watcher's dark shroud in the melee, the sight of him was lost in the swell of the crowd. The group grew to immense proportions, bumping into Danny freely, coming close to knocking him off his feet. He struggled against for what seemed like a very long time.

Finally, Danny was able to leave the place where he had stood captive. He inched toward the spot where the Watcher had stood, but he was clearly gone. He scoured the crowd for any sign of the shrouded figure, searching frantically for him amid the wash of unfamiliar faces. Suddenly, he stood frozen, unable to completely comprehend the grisly sight that now met his eyes.

The limp body, swinging in time to a slow methodic creaking sound sent a stab of pain through Danny's scalp and down into his spine. As his body swung back and forth lazily, Eric's face was tranquil, as if he might only be asleep. But Danny knew better. The boy was not asleep.

The boy was dead.

# 29

Danny ran through the Swamp and Sick Room, bumping blindly into those he met, actors and customers alike. His vision swayed in and out of focus and reality was fast becoming a memory to him. He didn't stop running until he had reached the Portrait Room, where he crumpled heavily to the floor at the foot of the mantel, breathless. His heart felt like a great volcano, ready to erupt with every beat. It wouldn't have surprised Danny to have seen it burst through his chest. It was only after several minutes that he felt it begin to slow, and a catatonic wave of relief began to crawl over him. He would form a plan. He would go for help. He would get someone from the outside to look at what he had just seen. The calm in him began to spread now. He sat in his self-induced trance until he felt as though he was breathing normally again.

From outside the tunnel of his mind, he heard a voice speaking to him. The silhouetted head of the actor that Danny was to replace hovered high above him, like the face of God.

"Great. It's about time you got here! We've been absolutely *mobbed*! And I'm starving!"

The other Dracula was perched above Danny's head on the mantel. He swung his legs up and scooted through the Portrait frame to the ladder awaiting him against the side wall. In another moment he was standing beside Danny, watching him for a few seconds before he headed toward the door. He turned back one more time, making sure that Danny had heard what he had said.

"Okay." A pause. "Have fun! Take it easy Dan."

Danny sat immersed in his catatonia, the trance unbroken by his words.

"Danny?"

No answer. The other Dracula simply shrugged now and continued through the big double doors to the Butler Area. The group standing at the rope let out a universal scream at the sight of him. He shook his head at them and simply replied, "Aaah. Grow up."

"Where are you going?" It was Mary T, who had been playing the part of the Vampiress Butler all evening. She looked at him, confused. He pushed one of the doors open slightly, revealing Danny to her. He was seated on the floor beside the mantel. Taking in the sight, Mary T leaned close to him and whispered, "What's his problem?"

At this, Dracula just shrugged. In another moment he was gone, and it was her problem to deal with. She shook her head and entered the room, carefully closing the doors behind her. As she drew closer, Mary T became more aware of Danny's hypnotic gaze, riveted on her now as she approached.

She spoke to him as she would a mental patient, "Hi Danny. Better hurry up and get into the Portrait; we've got a group out there waiting." Danny's eyes remained fixed on her, unseeing. She moved closer and laid a gentle hand on his shoulder.

"Yo, Dan, are you okay?"

Danny silently mouthed the word "yes" and began the laborious task of standing, his legs an uncooperative mass of Jell-o. He tried to stave off the heavy feeling that seemed to be surrounding him now. It held him like a protective cocoon. Within its solid depths he thought to himself that this must be how it felt to be in shock. That was it. He was in shock. Danny could see Mary T extending her hand toward him. He reached out for it in slow motion, the gap between taking a painfully long time to shorten. Finally, his fingers touched hers and time suddenly sped up. The struggle inside the cocoon began to ease as he made it to his feet, and the haze that had obscured his vision was clearing. The first wonderful thing his eyes met was Mary T's smiling, though somewhat puzzled, face.

"Yeah, I'm okay. I'm good." Danny laughed at his own words. It was the laugh of a madman. The laugh of someone who was far from good. "My mind is just playing tricks on me again." Even Danny himself could not comprehend the truth in his own words.

"Okay…" Mary T replied, not too sure of what he meant by 'again'. Her laughter came out strained. She watched him take a couple of pills from his pocket and dry swallow them. Mary T recognized the pills. They were part of Jarrett's vast collection. She herself had ingested this type of pill more than once and had regretted doing so the next day.

"Give me a couple of minutes to get into position, then send 'em in," Danny heard himself tell her, though he couldn't fathom why he was saying it. He was not even slightly ready to face a group of onlookers. His nerves were an electric tangle, sending random surges to his already-overloaded brain. At this point he had managed to entirely block the horrid events of the Hangman Scene from his mind. It all seemed like nothing more than a distant memory of a nightmare he once had. A sudden laugh came out in a crazy and detached way. Mary T stared at him, awaiting his next move. Finally, she slowly moved toward the doors.

With one of the doors slightly ajar, she watched Danny climb into the Portrait frame. When the tiny spotlight hit his sallow features it sent a chill down her spine. The exhaustion and the fear shown through Danny's makeup and there was a wetness around his red-rimmed eyes that gave the Portrait a particularly hungry look.

She spoke to him from across the room, cautiously, "Okay, now. Take your time."

She was careful to be quiet as she exited, closing the double doors behind her. Danny could hear her voice through the doors, and the fog in his brain further dissipated with the thought of being by himself now. He could hear Mary T improvising with the group, adding dialogue to her already-too-long speech to afford Danny a little more time to compose himself.

Inside the Portrait, Danny shifted his weight from side

to side to make himself more comfortable. He looked down at his trembling hands, then quickly grasped the sides of the stool beneath him in a sudden bout with vertigo. He would power through this, he thought. He looked up at the inner wall of the portrait, and suddenly all his fears returned in full force.

There, attached to Bobby's cork dartboard on the inner wall facing him, hung a strange collage of papers. Upon closer inspection, Danny could see that these were all objects that had made up the contents of Detective Hartnett's wallet. He leaned forward and leafed quickly through the collection: Hartnett's Driver's License, police badge, Social Security card. Finally, his hand rested on a leaf of paper which had been torn from Hartnett's appointment book. On the line that read 2:00, written in Hartnett's sloppy police detective scrawl were the words DANIEL NEUMANN. HAUNTED CASTLE PIER. And below that, in a thick red smear, was another message: BAD IDEA. He recognized the writing as the same one he had seen on all the timecards. It was the hand of The Watcher.

Danny's stomach leapt. He looked away from the wall, frozen. The pin spot hit his face, catching the expression of stunned realization perfectly as Mary T let the group of customers into the room.


# 30

The Watcher had noticed the bright silver object behind one of the large Styrofoam rocks just beyond the Hangman Scene. It glinted and shone in the dim red lights that illuminated the pathway. It had been hidden haphazardly by someone in their haste. The Watcher was familiar with every inch of the building; he was intimate with its every curve and alcove. He could spot something out of its proper place in an instant. Any object that was foreign, new. This shiny silver piece was just such an object. He moved toward it slowly, with great interest. This was Castle treasure. Precious booty left behind in the darkness. As the Watcher drew closer, he was able to make out its shape. It was a silver flask. The kind that had commonly been carried in times of Prohibition. The kind that old tee-totaling ladies supposedly concealed beneath their petticoats to sneak a drink in secret. It was the flask that Danny had drained, and Jules had discarded earlier. The one that brought him temporary relief from the torments of the man who now held it in his hand.

He peeled off the thick rubber mask, and inspected the flask more closely, turning it in the red dimness. He slipped the flask into his pocket as a sinister smile crossed his face. He would have a use for the little silver bottle later. A very special use.

# 31

Although the air still hung hot and damp over Pete's Beach, the beach sand had grown considerably cooler. Sandy sampled its refreshing feel between her toes. The beach was all but empty, with the moon hanging above like a great apple waiting to be picked.

She hung back lazily for a moment, allowing the excitement of watching her throw the big piece of driftwood out into the waves to build. Ceto watched hungrily as she lobbed the stick a little further each time. He paused briefly, then bounded into the waves, retrieving it obediently. Vaulting the foam caps two and three at a time, he brought the stick back to her, anticipating the ultimate reward: a brisk scratching behind the ears, and that wonderful timbre in her voice. His mistress was pleased.

Ceto's eyes clung to her as Sandy hung back before tossing the stick, like a seasoned javelin thrower. His eyes never left the piece of wood in her hand. It was all that mattered in his world right now. In a strange small way, Sandy shared Ceto's feelings. For the moment, this was all there was. The cool sand, and the sound of the waves crashing against the shore. The feelings of fear and worry she had felt earlier were just visions from another time or place. Some other world.

This time she hurled the wood toward the pilings beneath the pier. It came to rest on the wet sand at the waves' edge. Ceto obediently followed the stick, and Sandy walked lazily toward him as he retrieved it. The noises from the pier above were hollow, and they blended into a single roar. Melodies from the video game machines floated down to her, along with the whoops and hollers of the Labor Day tourists. From her place beneath, Sandy could feel the last strands of summer slipping away. A few more hours and it would all be over.

Once again, Ceto brought the piece of driftwood back to Sandy with the same excited look in his eyes. She bent down to him, smiling, and rubbed his ears.

From her crouched position on the sand, the sounds from above were now challenged by something new. It was a different sound. She heard a distinct dripping amid the many other noises. It was a constant ticking sound, and most notably it was coming from very close by. She suddenly felt a cold wetness dripping onto the side of her cheek. Her fingers flew up to her face, and she brought them down quickly to see what could have splashed her. The droplets on her fingers were thick, deep and rusty. Sandy slowly looked upward, and her eyes were now met with a sight that far surpassed any horrible scene concocted within the Castle above her. Her throat tightened, and her body shuddered. She felt herself begin to gag.

High above Sandy's head, suspended beneath the boards of the pier, were row after row of cocoon-like bubbles. They were fashioned from tar and what appeared to be burlap. Sandy's eyes scanned them now. They looked like great parasites feeding on the underbelly of the boardwalk.

At first their sight was a curiosity, causing a little smile to rise instinctively to Sandy's lips. The smile faded quickly, however, when her eyes came to rest on a gaping hole in one of the cocoons. It was the one just above her head. The one from which the steady drip emanated. Sandy squinted to make sure that she was not being deceived by the frailty of her state of mind or by the dimness of the light.

From within the jagged hole above her head, Mia's dead face stared blankly down at her. The ravages of decomposition had already made their way across her once-beautiful features, twisting them into a chilling wide-eyed grin. Sandy gasped. Her hand rose to her mouth. She wanted to run, but all she could manage was a slow turn, and in doing so she was stopped by a deep raspy voice coming from the dark silence beneath the Castle itself, some thirty feet away.

"Where are you going, Saaannndy?"

She turned toward the voice. Her breath came in short halting bits, as though her lungs wanted no part of the filthy air. She could not answer, could not speak. The words were caught somewhere in her shrinking throat along with the scream that surely should have come by now.

"Shut up. Don't say anything. You asked for it. They all asked for it."

Sandy was fully turned to face the shadows that covered the voice. She peered into the blackness as the rasp came out toward her again, this time louder and more menacingly.

"I see that you've discovered my gallery. Say hello to my other playmates."

At this, Sandy felt compelled to look up at the rows of cocoons again. The horror of their sheer number finally began to sink into her confused brain. They were all neat round bubbles, formed meticulously by the Watcher's hand. These, Sandy thought, were all people. People that she had known.

The piece of driftwood that she held dropped onto the sand with the subtlest of sounds. A distant voice in her head called to her to pick the stick up again. For protection. To defend herself from whoever, or whatever possessed that disembodied rasp. She bent to pick it up, but the voice stopped her.

"Leave it. It won't do you any good anyway. We outnumber you, two to one."

Sandy looked around quickly, nervously, in every direction. She saw no one. Ceto looked up at her anxiously, certain that her movements were all part of another game she was playing with him. "Two?" She repeated as she straightened again, obediently leaving the driftwood on the ground beside her.

There was a pause. The Watcher took a deep grating breath and exhaled slowly. "Yes. Mother and I." Now his cackle trickled slowly out of the blackness at her. He laughed at his own words for what felt like a long time.

A scraping sound and puff of sulphur stopped the laugh, as the Watcher lit a wooden match at his dark post beneath the pier. He held it just long enough for Sandy to take in the sight of him. He was seated regally in the depths of the darkness, wearing that familiar shroud that Danny had spoken of at such great length. The flicker of the flame hung in the thick air for just a moment, then was gone. In that moment Sandy was able to make out another form in the darkness. The waning sunlight raced with her vision to catch another glimpse, but Sandy was certain of what she had just seen. It was the huddled form of Jules, lying in a fetal position on the swath of sand between herself and where the Watcher sat.

Even as the match's tiny flame disappeared, Sandy could still see the gray form of her friend on the ground, recognizing the mass of curly brown hair atop his head and one of his familiar Adidas, untied and lying on the sand beside him. She drew closer, carefully, timidly. Now she was able to hear the low sound of his groans as he lay there on the sand. He was still alive. Her feet made tentative moves toward him, ever aware of the watchful eye of the shrouded figure seated in the darkness just beyond.

# 32

Seated inside the Portrait, shuffling the few horrifying artifacts left by the Watcher, Danny was lost in frantic thought. He needed time to think. To formulate some sort of plan. The evening was now coming to its welcome end, and his nervousness and fear had graduated to a thick numbness that now permeated his entire being as he looked down at the badge in his hand. The badge that had once belonged to Detective Hartnett. It seemed now that his worst fears were confirmed. Hartnett had indeed seen the same terrible things that Danny had warned him about. And more.

There was no doubt in Danny's mind that the

Watcher intended to do away with him just as he had surely done away with Hartnett. He was playing a cruel game of cat and mouse with Danny that would undoubtedly come to an end soon. It was just a matter of time now.

He didn't notice the shadowy figure that had come quietly through the room from the open double doors and now stood watching from below. Danny was jolted from his daydream by this interloper's voice.

"Hey Dan, are you okay? The Butler said you were acting weird."

It suddenly became clear to Danny who the owner of the voice was as Gordon stared up at him, "C'mon, lighten up. The day's nearly over and we're all still alive. See, it *was* all just a bad joke."

"No, you're wrong. It's not just a joke. I've been through some real scary shit since I saw you."

"What? Are you saying you talked to this guy again?"

"No, I *saw* him again. And this time he got that kid Eric who was playing the Hangman."

Gordon stood back from the mantel, holding himself at arm's length as he looked up at Danny.

"What do you mean…'got'?"

Danny pointed toward the side of the mantel where the ladder up to the portrait was concealed, "Come up here and look at this…"

He motioned for Gordon to look inside, where the cork board on the wall still held the contents of Hartnett's wallet, save one key piece. In Danny's right hand rested the badge in its plastic case, completing the odd collection.

"Jesus, you've got a real art gallery in there. Where did you find this stuff?"

"Right here. A while ago. The other Drac must have thought it was some kind of joke meant for me and left it up here for me to find. Real funny, huh?"

"How did this whacko know you'd be playing Dracula?"

"I don't know. He seems to know everything. I can't make a single move without him knowing where I am!" He stopped short, then added, "Though I *did* catch him by surprise in the Hangman Scene. With Eric."

As an afterthought he added, more softly and pensively, "Maybe Eric had known about him all along too. Like me."

Gordon watched the change in his friend's expression as a wave of cold fear passed over Danny's already-haggard features. Finally, Danny snapped back into the moment and looked down at him.

"Do you believe me now?"

Gordon just stared at his friend. His tone grew somber; this was no joke. It was a serious side of Gordon that Danny had rarely seen. One that he wasn't sure he liked seeing now.

"I don't know. I don't want to believe any of it."

"Mia, Bobby, Little Mack, Eric, and now Hartnett," Danny called off the list the way a teacher would do roll call.

Gordon added, "Don't forget Juanita."

Danny exhaled a nervous laugh, "How could I forget

Juanita? I'll probably have nightmares starring Juanita for the rest of my life!"

"Wait," Gordon said slowly, "you said Little Mack. What makes you think *he's* dead?"

Danny reached down to the floor beside the stool. He pulled out the stack of timecards he had hidden there and handed them to Gordon.

"I forgot to show you *these*. I found them in the little closet in the Human Sacrifice Room. All of them are victims. I'm certain of it." He paused, adding, "Except me, of course." Another pause. "So far."

Gordon shuffled through the pile, then looked up at Danny again, "I don't understand. What do timecards have to do with murders?"

"Well, when Mr. Basketcase kills somebody, he takes their timecard off the rack in the Dressing Room. So it looks like they suddenly quit or got fired and took their card up to Harry's office to get their pay. That explains why I couldn't find Mia's card the other day."

Gordon rifled through the cards one more time, noting the messages smeared across each one.

"Did you show these cards to Hartnett?"

Danny laughed nervously, "What difference would it have made if I did? Hartnett got his own timecard punched for him by the look of things!"

"And the killer left these here for anyone to find...?" Gordon asked.

Danny's brow wrinkled, "No. I'm convinced that he meant for *me* to find them. That's why he purposely added the card with my name. He seems to be playing some sort of twisted game with me; leaving clues and hoping I'll play along." A wave of tired desperation washed over Danny's drawn features, "He acts like he knows me. He knows where I am, when I sleep, when I eat. He's made me his prey."

Gordon avoided acknowledging any truth in what Danny was saying, but his friend's fear and exhaustion were undeniable. Whether Danny's shrouded nemesis was real or imagined, his presence was taking its toll. No matter what the stakes were, the Watcher was winning his sick game.

As the double doors opened slightly, Danny hurriedly hid the cards in his pants pocket, and Gordon scrambled down the ladder to the floor. Mary T slipped silently around the open door and stood just inside. She looked from Danny to Gordon, then back again.

"Get ready. This is it…the last group. Richard just called and told me to let them in. Then we can follow them through the Castle and out onto the pier!"

Gordon ducked behind one of the plaster gargoyles that flanked the mantel.

He popped his head out from behind it quickly, before the group entered, "Are you chasing the group through with the rest of us? C'mon, this nut bag can't do anything to you with the rest of us watching."

"No, I'm gonna slip out and get changed. I wouldn't be much fun, anyway." He was amazed at the great calm with which he had said this. The words that were fighting to leave his lips were, "We're leaving this place together,

Gordon, right away, you and me. There's something horrible happening here and we're not staying a moment longer than we have to." But these words did not come out.

Danny heard Gordon's reply as if through a long tunnel. He was unable to say anything at all.

"Okay, man, I'll see you at home."

Then the double doors swung open, and the group entered. They walked silently and obediently to the front of the room as Mary T had instructed them to do. She closed the doors with a flourish, and after a few moments of heavy silence, Danny made his noisy appearance from the Portrait frame, slamming his foot on the mantel as he had seen the others do. Flapping his huge satin cape, and startling everyone in the room. Including the already-apprehensive ghoul behind the gargoyle.

# 33

Laying the girl gently across one of the worktables that lined the little room, the Watcher reached for a damp sponge from a nearby cup. Everything had been laid out beforehand, leaving no omission to chance. It had all been carefully planned.

This one was special. He had not killed her right away. He had other plans for Sandy.

The Watcher began to gently wipe the makeup from Sandy's face. The makeup that he himself had applied so hurriedly while they were beneath the pier. The hunched form of the man that still lay hidden behind the pilings would have to wait until later to be disposed of. For now, he concentrated on the girl. There wasn't the slightest trace of anger in the Watcher's being now as he went about his task. His movements were mechanical; he had laid out his plan to the letter and carried it out with the strictest attention to detail. Now victory would be his. Soon the game would be over. Sandy would be his trump card; she would watch her lover die.

The makeup came off easily. Even in her unconscious state, Sandy's look was serene. She wore a strange little smile, and the sight of it sent a single brainstar out from the maniac's eyes, falling onto the girl's lips and dissipating there.

The Watcher grabbed a long length of rope. He began to wind this expertly around Sandy's wrists, then down to her waist, tying it off in an intricate series of knots. He had practiced these knots in the darkness of the closet inside the Sacrifice Room for hours, completely unnoticed by the unwitting actors just outside the little door. He had worked at each one, practicing until he was able to tie them in the complete darkness of the closet.

As his fingers quickly worked at securing the gag behind her head, a quiet moan escaped her. The Watcher knew that he must hurry now.

As he stood upright, his finger accidentally caught on one of the big front pockets of Sandy's smock. He yanked it free, uncaring of the gentle ripping sound that came from the pocket's seam. A small gold-colored object popped lithely out of its hiding place inside the pocket and jumped to the floor. It rolled along the floorboards toward his foot. The Watcher bent down and took the object between two fingers, holding it up to inspect it. It was a .45 caliber bullet. Suddenly things had grown more interesting in his game.

Sandy's eyelids began to flutter now. He watched her draw progressively closer to consciousness, then stopped the fluttering with one single crashing blow from the back of his hand. Her eyelids calmed, and Sandy's head hung heavily to one side. The Watcher leaned down to her face, the red welts just beginning to appear from his blow, and ever-so-gently kissed her cheek.

# 34

As Danny entered the Dressing Room, he was surprised by its utter emptiness. No Sandy, no Jules, no Richard. The only sign of life in any form was Ceto, who sat on the floor beneath the makeup table, panting dutifully.

"What are you doing here?" He asked the dog innocently, "Where's your mom? Huh?" He scratched Ceto behind one ear, and the dog leaned into the scratch, appreciatively.

The huge full moon had so illuminated the sky that the light spilling through the Dressing Room's open door resembled more day than night. Danny walked out the door and scanned the Actors' Area for any sign of the others. Nothing.

They were all inside, following that last ill-fated group of customers through the building.

Danny hurriedly removed the white greasepaint from his face with a wad of tissues. He removed the Dracula cape and sash and began to unzip the dress pants he was wearing. Stopping short, he thought for a moment and zipped them up again, muttering to himself, "What's the difference? Nobody's gonna miss one damn pair of pants."

He grabbed his backpack from a hook underneath the table, with Ceto's forlorn gaze noting his every move. Finally, he checked the rack of timecards, where each card had a neat white envelope attached to it, bearing the cast's final paychecks. Danny's own timecard was not among them. Of course it wasn't. His card was still nestled amid the others he had hidden in his pocket. He shook his head at this last bit of bad luck, and then he headed out the door. This time for good.

From an outcropping above the Actors' Area, the Watcher saw Danny's quick and quiet exit. He watched him walk briskly down the ramp and across the wide street. His eyes remained fixed hungrily on him as he moved down the block and into the front door of one of the little beach houses along the boulevard.

He could feel the fire growing inside his head. But this time it was different. The fire had not been brought on by anger, but by the Watcher's own anxiousness and anticipation of the game's end. His pulsing desire to see it all finally played out. The fire would soon spread, and the pounding of his heart would become explosive in his chest. He would revel in the killing and in his triumph, and his mother would let him rest again until next year.

Entering the apartment, Danny walked to the window, stealing a quick look at the Castle. Its facade was illuminated from below with big ice blue spotlights, and its silhouette against the night sky appeared to possess an unexplained glow from behind. There was a great deal of noise still coming from that direction: the actors were screaming and chanting, and some were even jumping or pushing others off the end of the pier into the ocean. The thick summer air amplified the sounds that assaulted Danny's ears, and he could find little relief in his having left the place.

He turned and spied Jules' bottle of whiskey on the table. He took two long swigs from the bottle and reached down to replace it on the already-indelible mark etched into the wood of the tabletop. Thinking better of it, he grabbed the bottle again and took another long drink.

He plopped into a nearby chair and turned on the tall floor lamp that stood beside him. Jules' tape deck was positioned on the side table nearest to him, so after a few silent minutes and a few more gulps from the bottle he reached toward it and switched it on. Bach's Toccata and Fugue in D Minor played softly. A familiar sound. The backdrop of the last few horrible days in his life. It should have inspired fear, nervousness in him now. It should have been a mocking reminder of the terror that was all too real inside the Castle. Instead, it seemed to have the opposite effect on Danny this time. It was a reminder that it was all behind him. His nightmare was officially over. He smiled and held the bottle up in a toast, "Here's to good ole' Johann Sebastian Bach! May I never hear your damn fugue again as long as I live!"

He took another gulp, then set the bottle down. He sat back in the chair, enjoying the warmth of the liquor as it made its way down toward his stomach.

Laying his head back, and before he could realize that it had happened, he was asleep. Not dozing lightly, waiting for something to frighten him into consciousness, but truly fast asleep. The sleep of a beaten and exhausted man. Dreamless sleep.

# 35

The Dressing Room was considerably more animated than it had been in the past few weeks. There was a definite buzz about the room that mingled with the actors' energetic laughter. They were glad to be finished with their season's work. Several of the more sea-soaked members of the cast were stripping down and happily changing into drier clothes.

With Little Mack and Sandy both conspicuously missing, the Dressing Room was left in a particularly disastrous state as the actors began to trickle out the door.

For them the best part of this day was just beginning: the traditional end-of-the-year party at the Sand Bar.

The Watcher sat at one of the picnic tables and wordlessly waved to his coworkers as they passed by him. He nodded dutifully when asked if he would be joining them at the Sand Bar. He was lying. He would *not* be joining them because he still had work to do. The very thought of the work that lay ahead sent a warm wave of pleasure over him.

He looked up at the monstrous moon overhead and smiled wide. Special effects by God himself, he thought. The perfect setting for his little melodrama. It was all set: the hero, the heroine, the villain. He looked up at the Castle, standing majestically over him. The sea breeze touched his cheek like a caress. He unwittingly began to hum a bizarre little tune, over and over. It was one of the strange bits of melody from the Plaza. A snippet of Bernard Hermann's theme from *Psycho*. As he hummed it, he tossed something small and round and metallic into the air and caught it nimbly. Up and down the .45-caliber shell went, and the Watcher's smile broadened.

Why, he wondered to himself, would Sandy be carrying such a thing in the front pocket of her smock? No one could have been more surprised than he had been. Or more pleased. It showed a different side of Sandy. She wanted to play the game too.

The last of the actors had passed by him, and the Dressing Room was still and silent now. The Watcher stood and walked slowly into the room, making sure that he was alone. The room was a shambles, strewn here and there with tissues and worn costumes, wigs and prop weapons.

He stood before the makeup mirror and stared at his own reflection. All traces of vigor had vanished. His face looked haggard and drawn. The metamorphosis from living being to the death mask seemed to be taking place before him. He reached up and felt the skin around his eyes. It was milky white and cold to the touch.

# 36

One by one the soundtracks in the scenes had been turned off, leaving in their place the hot silence that was endlessly more frightening. Finally, the whole Castle was quiet and more imposing than it had ever been. It was like a great tomb, its dead inhabitants reposing beneath its belly in their painstakingly crafted bubbles.

Sandy listened as the music disappeared gradually from the building, room by room. She heard the Mortuary's organ drone stop short, then the odd guitar riff from the Baronial Hall faded until only its rhythm track played, then that stopped as well. She looked around the room frantically for something to remove the rope that bound her wrists, but everything was far from her reach. Everything had been laid clear. She shivered at the thought of what might now lay in store for her.

The sudden dead silence was enough, too, to wake

Jarrett from his first real rest in weeks. He sat up in his hiding place behind the big stuffed horse and listened. He was groggy and disoriented, and wondered for a brief time whether this was one of his horrible dreams. The setting was right, the place.

He stood with some difficulty. His feet were shaky in the tall platform boots. He felt his face, the top of his head. He wondered why he was still wearing the Frankenstein appliances and costume. He stood frozen, confused for a few detached moments, then the memory of having fallen asleep during work hours suddenly came rushing back to him. He laughed at his own stupidity.

Jarrett slowly began to lumber into the Swamp. Its stillness and complete silence were explanation enough to him that the Castle was already closed. Thank goodness the lights were still on. This meant that there was still someone left in the building besides himself, and he wouldn't be locked in.

He made his way through the Swamp as quickly as he could while still maintaining his precarious balance, then the Sick Room, bumping clumsily into walls and fixtures at every turn. Jarrett realized he must get downstairs as soon as he could. Every moment was precious. The doors would soon be locked.

Downstairs in the Dressing Room, with the silence of the Castle's passageways swallowing up the final strains of the soundtracks, Jarrett's footfalls seemed monstrous, the plywood planks creaking and groaning in a symphony of complaints under his feet.

Richard looked up at the ceiling, wondering if his mind was playing tricks on him after his late night of drinking and long day of work. He looked around himself in disgust at the condition in which the room had been left by the cast. He would make no effort to clean up the mess. Not tonight, anyway.

Jarrett's movements in the rooms above drew Richard's attention upward again. He wondered who would be so foolish as to venture through the empty Castle. From the sound of the footsteps to Richard's experienced ears, they were moving into the Sick Room from the direction of the Swamp. His fingers moved to the gun, still hidden safely in his pocket.

He reached in for the first time that day and took it out. He looked down at it affectionately, turning it over in his hands several times. Then, ever so carefully, he opened it and inspected its empty chambers. Empty. That was the key word here. He would not need the bullets now. The sight of the gun itself would be enough to scare whoever was playing games upstairs.

Richard looked around the room, searching for a suitable costume to wear for this, the game he had been waiting to play. Dreamed of playing. He needed to wear something that would scare the Bejesus out of that idiot upstairs. He found what he was looking for, grabbed it off the rack, and stored the revolver safely in its heavy folds. Then he quietly switched off the fluorescent tube lights above the makeup table, plunging the Dressing Room into total darkness.

In another moment he was through the doorway that led to the Castle's heart.

# 37

One by one the actors trickled through the Sand Bar's open front door. Some came directly from their shift at the Castle, their faces still gleaming with cold cream. Others had stopped off at their homes to smoke a quick joint or to properly wash off the traces of the day's makeup.

Gordon and Susan entered the bar, both grinning widely and obviously ready for the fun of the special day to continue. The rowdiness of Closing Day had proved to be all that they had heard it could be. Gordon had ended up in the water, flung there mercilessly by several compatriots. He went in thrashing and fighting, and not without several unwilling victims joining him in the plunge.

Susan had managed to stay far enough away from the end of the pier to avoid being thrown, however she had been thoroughly soaked by a water balloon tossed by the hands of Rollie from one of the lower parapets of the Castle.

They looked around the bar and waved pleasantly to their coworkers, who returned both greetings and cheers. The cast peopled the little space entirely, filling up the booths and barstools. Their lively chatter created a happy hum. It was their night, after all. The Sand Bar was theirs.

Gordon's eyes scanned the room for the faces of Danny, Jules and Sandy. None were there. Also, conspicuously absent was Richard, who never missed a chance to celebrate.

A screaming group of monsterettes were waving at

Susan and were quite obviously clearing spaces for her and Gordon to sit. The couple made their way to the table reluctantly and sat down. Gordon mumbled his greetings to these girls he barely knew. Once they'd ordered their drinks the conversation turned predictably to the day's events. Gordon did his best to appear interested, but all the while his eyes raced around the crowded room for the first sight of his friends.

His first beer went down easily, and then his second. By the time his third mug arrived, Gordon was actually beginning to listen to the girls' inane chatter.

**"Your father was Frankenstein...But your mother was the lightning!"**

- Bela Lugosi, as *Ygor* —
THE GHOST OF FRANKENSTEIN, 1942

# 38

The difficult latch on the gate in the Butler's Area was proving to be a real challenge for the shaking hands of the Frankenstein Monster. The threat of possibly being locked inside the horrible place overnight had given way to panic. Jarrett's fingers fought with the little clasp on the latch. After several fevered seconds, the bolt finally lifted, and he slipped through into the Belltower. He pulled the gate toward himself, and the latch miraculously clicked into the locked position on its own.

He turned around and breathed a sigh at the sight of the narrow winding stairs that he must now maneuver down to the Dressing Room.

Before his foot could make its first move, an awful sound pierced the silence. It was a sound that Jarrett had never heard before, and yet it was all too familiar to him. It was the laugh of the Watcher, Jarrett's very own Satan in his nightly hell.

Now the scraping voice was accompanied by another sound. It was the rhythmic sound of shoes on the Belltower stairs. Feet approaching him from below, slowly, slowly.

"Jarrett? Atwill Jarrett? Is that you?" The evil rasp was floating up to him in strains that were almost melodic. "You've been a very naughty boy, Atwill Jarrett." The slow clop of the footsteps continued, "You've been sleeping on the job, Atwill Jarrett."

The words themselves were frightening enough to Jarrett, but perhaps more frightening still was hearing his full name repeated over and over. Atwill Jarrett. *Atwill Jarrett.* No one had used his full name that way since he was a child, feeling big and stupid and inferior in every way. The sound of it turned him into a weak schoolboy again.

His feet were frozen in their place; the weight of the platform shoes was growing unbearable. Jarrett began to twist and pull at the insane latch of the gate to escape back through it to the Butler's Area, but it would not budge. He gave the gate a resounding blow with the side of his fist that filled the Belltower with an appropriate ringing, which set the Watcher's laughter off in raspy peals. Jarrett moved further up the Belltower, away from the gate, and toward the open door of the Mortuary. His heart pounded louder and louder in his ears as he did his best to manage the steep stairs. He could hear his assailant following him, though the tight curve of the stairs' spiral prevented him from coming into view.

Occasionally a fleck of his black shroud found its way around the curve before the Watcher's actual form could, sending Jarrett's heart into faster palpitations.

Jarrett glanced down repeatedly as he worked hard at scaling the treacherous staircase. It was all just as it had been in his dreams. The dim silence, the shrouded assailant, the voice, the fear. Jarrett knew in his heart the thing that was yet to come. The fire. He forced his weakening legs to blunder on, up to the top, away from his menacing tormenter.

In his right hand the Watcher carried a heavy lance. It was the lance that had graced the suit of armor in the Throne Room. The same lance that had taken away Little Mack's life. A trail of deep red gore still shown on its point, to boast of its accomplishments.

The shrouded man moved nimbly up the stairs behind Jarrett, always keeping enough distance between himself and his prey to elicit a grimly false sense of security. Jarrett was nearing the top now. Suddenly, the footfalls below quickened, and with a roar the Watcher leapt over the short gap that separated them. He thrust forward with an agility that seemed beyond human, as Jarrett stood watching, silent, stricken. Now they were close, their faces nearly touching. As the Watcher's laughter rang out, his hot breath accosted Jarrett's face from deep inside the blackness of his hood. Jarrett's eyes remained riveted on the point of that terrible lance, now not ten scant inches away from his heaving chest.

In a flash of silver, and with a loud clatter as the lance dropped to the floor, the Watcher pulled the little flask from his back pocket. It was the fortunate discovery he had made behind the rock in the Swamp. A gift, thought the Watcher.

Suddenly Jarrett felt the rain of amber liquid splashing onto his face and neck. The raspy voice was the thunder to accompany the storm that was now pelting him.

"Here, Atwill Jarrett, have something to wash down those pills. It'll make you feel *real* good…"

Emptied of its contents, the little silver flask went flying from the Watcher's hand and tumbled end-over-end down several of the stairs below. It finally came to rest at an odd angle against the side wall of the Belltower. It was just then that Jarrett could finally make out what the little silver object was. But the fumes that pierced his nostrils were not what they should be. It was not whiskey that had come from the flask, but gasoline. And Jarrett now wore this heavily across his skin and clothing.

Just as it had in his dreams, it all seemed to happen in slow motion, with Jarrett unable to think. But there was no need to think now. The Watcher had done all the thinking that would be necessary. And just as it had been in his dreams, the next sound was clear and distinct. It was the long, slow scraping sound of a match being struck.

Dazed, Jarrett saw the man in the shroud tossing the flickering matches at him. Miraculously he was able to dodge one, then another, moving all the while up the staircase. With each successive match the Watcher drew closer, and finally Jarrett stepped backward, through the doorway into the Mortuary. This would be the end. The fire.

He continued to back up, his eyes riveted on the paths of the oncoming matches. Another and another. He deflected each one, incredibly, until finally he was inside the heart of the Mortuary, his back against the massive stained-glass window with its flashing electrical effects.

Jarrett stood in silhouette against the window's ghastly illuminated reds and blues. The synthetic lightning bolts behind the pane of glass created a magnificent tableau for the eyes of the Watcher. Only for a second. For in another second Jarrett's legs had caught the low wrought iron railing a scant foot away from the window and he was reeling backward, crashing through the stained glass itself.

Now it was here. The pain and the burning in his limbs, his head, his chest. It was all here. The raspy laughter, and the mute helplessness of a man caught up in fate. All of his dreaded dream was here, and more. There were bright electrical flashes as the electricity and the gasoline from the little silver flask created a terrible brand of fireworks. Patches of Jarrett's clothing caught fire and burned themselves out as the gasoline fed on the window's sparks, electrocuting him slowly. The acrid smell of ozone hung in a canopy above the doomed man. Mercifully, death came quickly. Now it was over.

The hulking form of the gentle man in the monster suit lay in a tangled heap against the smoking ruin of the window. Another quick popping sound could be heard, and the entire Castle was plunged into darkness. The Watcher laughed again. He laughed longer and louder than before, his voice was stronger than it had ever been, seeming to shake the very walls around him.

Reaching beneath his shroud, he grabbed the heavy object that hung behind the huge round keyring. In another instant, there was light as he switched on the big flashlight that had been dubbed *The Peacemaker*. He shined its beam at Jarrett's body as he moved toward him. Pushing aside some of the broken shards from the window, he sat down close beside the man with the light trained on his grizzled features.

Suddenly, in a movement that could only have been born of pure reflex, Jarrett's hand shot up and pulled back the shroud's hood, revealing the Watcher's astonished face.

Jarrett's lifeless eyes seemed to rekindle just long enough to look at the face and study it for a moment. A glimmer of recognition was sparked, briefly. In the next moment he was gone, his tight grip still clenching the hood, and his dead eyes fixed on the Watcher's.

It had all been as Jarrett had dreamed it would be. The Watcher in his shroud, the searing fire consuming his body, the final discovery of the Watcher's identity. It had all happened, except for one very important detail: Jarrett had not taken the shrouded man down into the burning depths with him. The Watcher had survived.

# 39

Sandy had heard the scuffle of feet on the stairs. She knew the sounds of the Castle well enough to make out the number of footfalls and from which direction they had come. She had heard the heavy feet in the Swamp, then the Portrait Room, and finally in the Belltower. She had noticed, too, the quicker, lighter tread moving to meet him, and finally she had heard their horrible confrontation. She sat still on the floor of the Prop Closet, bound hand and foot, and listened to the chilling voice of the Watcher as he tormented his helpless victim. She had heard as they proceeded up toward the Mortuary. Their voices had grown muffled, smaller as they made their way upward. Straining to listen, she could not make out their words. They were simply too far away. Who was the monster talking to up there?

Finally, there came the frightening moment when the lights had begun to flicker, and the crackling electric sounds had filtered down through the Castle. It grew still and quiet after  that as everything went black.

She sat in the dark silence, breathing shallowly and listening. At last, there came a sound more horrible than any sound Sandy could recall. The powerful laughter of the Watcher, up above, victorious. She knew in this same dreadful moment that whoever had been up there with him was no more. And somewhere deep inside her was a prayer that that someone wasn't Danny.

After a short time, there were footsteps again, this time scurrying back and forth busily. The scurrying seemed to go on for a very long time, and Sandy slumped wearily in her bonds, where she fainted into a restless sleep.

When she awakened a short time later, the lights had been restored to the Castle. She sat up and looked around. But it hadn't been the lights that had roused her. It had been a noise. A strange loud noise that she couldn't seem to remember fully in her wakefulness. She listened closely for telltale sounds outside the Prop Closet, which was now her prison cell, but heard nothing for a long while. Her head swam, and the yellow lights of the closet gave Sandy's consciousness a jarring dose of the surreal.

Suddenly the door opened with a loud bang, and there stood the Watcher, smiling. He was carrying a heavy load, and as he set it down before her, Sandy suddenly knew what the sound that had awakened her had been.

**"A clown is a funny thing in a circus ring but what would be the normal reaction to opening a door at midnight and finding the same clown standing there in the moonlight?"**

**- Lon Chaney—**

# 40

Danny's sleep was abruptly interrupted by the slapping sound of the reel-to-reel tape, spinning on its spool. He sat up and rubbed his tired eyes, then looked at the clock on the table. It read two-thirty. Danny shook the sleep away as he stood. He stretched and walked to the front window of the apartment.

Outside, poised somberly below a moon of ungodly size, stood the Castle. All was still now; it was a silent shadow of the former madness. There was no more screaming or chanting, no more rowdy catcalling to friends across the pier. The Castle was now just a dark, brooding form, made strangely diminutive in appearance by the glowing orb that hung overhead.

Danny reached for the bottle on the table and took a quick drink. As if the very sight of the place caused him pain, he pulled the woven window shade down to hide the view. Suddenly a horrible voice came from outside the open window.

"You know, you shouldn't drink so much, my friend. It

might impair your ability to make quick decisions."

The voice pierced his brain, like a slowly driven nail. He turned cautiously to the open window behind him, as the nighttime breeze stirred the shade gently. Danny reached toward it. Then, quicker than he would have thought he could, he snapped the shade up with a loud bang.

There, outside in the moonlight, not ten feet away from Danny stood the Watcher in bright clown makeup, complete with an eerie painted on smile. It was the face of the familiar pier clown who sold balloons. But now something was terribly different. He was a crazed madman masquerading as a clown.

The Watcher reached down to the grass behind him, his eyes never leaving Danny. He pulled the huddled form that was lying there up beside him, holding it tight against one side of his body. The form squealed at the Watcher's touch, and Danny forced himself to take a step closer to the window to better see. His eyes grew wide, and words withered on his tongue at the sight of Sandy. Her hands were tied tightly behind her back, and her mouth was gagged. Her eyes lacked their usual sparkle, and in its place was a hollow look of fear.

The Watcher held her close, pressing a long sharp knife against her ribs. It was clearly not one of the prop knives used in the Castle. This was the real thing.

As he began to speak, his voice seemed to lose a bit of its rasping quality, and its intensity seemed to diminish somewhat as well. This was to be the final trick for the

Master Magician of Horror. His grand finale. He fairly spat the words at Danny.

"Here's your chance, Dan. Show her what a man you are!" The Watcher let out a short cackle and then turned and ran, half-pulling, half-dragging Sandy along beside him like a reluctant partner in a three-legged race. Danny watched in disbelief from the window, frozen. When he saw that the clown was headed for the pier, he ran for the apartment's front door. He was out the door in a shot, running toward the Castle.

He kept a safe distance behind the Watcher, fearing that at any moment the monster could use the knife in his hand on Sandy. With each long stride Danny took, his fear mounted. This time, though, his determination mounted as well.

As the Watcher dragged her mercilessly up the pier ramp, the ties around Sandy's wrists cut unrelenting gashes in her soft flesh. She could feel the warm blood running down into the palms of her hands and pooling in the folds. What she did not realize was that her face was streaked as well. Streaked with sweat and with grime. Most of all streaked with the tracks of her tears. Sandy didn't even know that she had been crying. It had already been hours that the tears had been streaming down both her cheeks, cutting light paths through the dark grit.

Finally, they arrived at the Dressing Room door, which he had been careful to leave unlocked. The door opened, and Sandy could feel herself being shoved inside. Not, however, before she was able to steal a quick glance out at the figure of the young man running toward the Castle to save her.

Danny's breath came in erratic gasps, making the final leg of his run the most difficult. At last, he reached the Dressing Room door, winded and holding his side against the stabbing pain that had found its home there.

He peered into the room cautiously, fearing whatever was waiting there for him. He tried not to think about what he planned to do once inside. The whole scene was a bit too incredible for him to grasp. The room was deserted, and he entered quietly, the pain in his side gradually beginning to melt away.

As Danny continued into the Castle, passing the Missing Link Scene and heading up the Belltower stairs, he realized that he was moving on pure unthinking disconnected energy, the store of which he had no knowledge. He approached the gate that led into the Butler Area. The bolt flipped up easily and Danny passed through. He looked from side to side for any signs of movement. There was no one.

Each of his careful footsteps seemed to arouse a new and different complaint from the floorboards below him as Danny moved slowly from the Portrait Room to the Throne Room, then into the red lights of the Sick Room. The lights in every scene were now ablaze, as they would be during the Castle's working hours. The Watcher had illuminated his way through the building in anticipation of their terrible game.

He was just about to enter the Swamp when suddenly Richard's voice rang out through the general P.A. system that ran through the entire building.

"You stay there! No, don't say anything. Shut up a minute!" Danny stopped short and looked around himself, thinking.

The sound system originated from the Prop Closet that was located adjacent to the Butler Area, so he wasted no time in heading back in that direction. Richard's voice continued, as Danny broke into a jog, and finally he was running.

"What the hell do you think this is, anyway? 'It's the *last day*. Richard can't fire me.' Well, you're wrong, I can!"

At last Danny reached the door to the closet, which he pushed open easily. There was no lock there. Not even a real latch. In fact, the door itself was nothing more than a single sheet of half-inch plywood.

Once inside the room, Danny spotted the tape deck against the far wall, playing loudly into the microphone of the P.A. system on its little stand beside it. Richard's voice had been nothing more than a recording from earlier that day. As Danny stared at the turning reels, the cloud of confusion that enveloped his brain began to lift. He took two measured steps toward the tape deck as Richard's voice continued to blast forth.

"I want you out of here. Now. Get changed. I want you the *fuck* off this pier! You're gone!"

This was the confrontation that Richard had had with that poor actor on the pier. The self-same tirade that had brought all conversation in the Dressing Room to an abrupt halt. Now Danny realized that he had been lured here, and the Watcher himself was still out there, somewhere inside the Castle.

The Sound Room door swung closed with a loud bang, and before Danny had time to turn around his eyes caught Richard's snarling reflection in the big mirror above the tape deck. He cried out at the ghostly apparition, and his heart skipped more than one beat. The angry reflection in the mirror tottered from side to side, and Richard's eyes were blank and unfocused. The sight sent a paralyzing shock through Danny's body, and he fought with himself feverishly, forcing himself to turn around.

Finally, he was facing his assailant, and he could now see that Richard's swinging body was not moving of its own accord; it hung from its impalement on the long lance from the armor in the Throne Room. Like a trophy hanging on the wall of the Watcher's private gallery. His face was frozen in the outcry that had no doubt accompanied his death. The death that had come to him not from the lance, but from his own .45- caliber bullet, which was now lodged neatly in his brain. It had been the loud bang from Richard's gun that had awakened Sandy earlier. The "ultimate scare" now belonged to Richard after all.

Finally able to tear his eyes away from the horrific sight Danny froze as he saw the young man, standing in a shadowy corner of the room. The shadows nearly hid him, but he was quite visible to Danny. He simply stood there in silence, grinning. It was Jules, dressed in the

Butcher's apron, and still wearing the painted clown face, sans the wig. He was holding the knife that he had held against Sandy's ribs as he stood in the moonlight outside their apartment window. His smile was jubilant, triumphant. A different kind of smile than usually graced Jules' cherubic face. This smile frightened Danny far more than even the death scream that was etched wildly across Richard's features.

The raspy laugh that had borne no face until now suddenly spilled forth from Jules. The sight and sound would not connect in Danny's brain, leaving him with the sickest of feelings. His eyes remained riveted on the white pancake makeup covering his friend's normally innocuous features. And then the terrible voice of the Watcher began to fall from Jules' lips.

"Hello, Danny, did you come to play with me?"

Danny shot a quick glance downward. There, on the floor just behind Jules, was Sandy. She was crying, struggling to breathe through the gag over her mouth. Jules let out a sound that was nothing less than a quick hiss.

"Sandy came to play too." With this he began to laugh, starting out in the rasp, then gradually transforming the inhuman cackle into what they all knew as Jules' normal laugh, complete with his unique croupy "cough" at the end. He was suddenly speaking to Danny in his normal voice.

"You were right, Buddy. There *were* a lot of weird things going on in the Castle. Too bad nobody believed you…not even little Sandy here." He kicked gently at Sandy's leg with the toe of his unlaced Adidas. A long silence followed, with the two roommates staring baldly at one another. The tape deck, too, had gone silent. As Jules was about to speak again a sudden blast of Bach's Toccata and Fugue ripped through the speakers, jolting all of them properly.

All but the Watcher. He laughed again, this time in Jules' own laugh. "Nice effect, don't you think?"

He looked down at the girl on the floor. She looked up with bulging, fear-filled eyes. Jules' boyish smile shone through his already-smiling clown makeup.

"Do you believe our friend now, Sandy?" Do you believe his weird tales of murder, and all his ridiculous suspicions about this place? Huh?" He paused, "Do you think now that maybe there *was* a real monster in the Haunted Castle?" He rolled his eyes mockingly and made a hokey "wooooo" sound, like the sound of a cartoon ghost. He laughed again, but the genuine sentiment of amusement washed out of this one quickly.

Danny pretended to hang on every word of Jules' twisted rant, all the while eyeing the makeup cart that stood beside him. The cart contained various pieces of the costumes and makeup that had made up the Watcher's many murderous disguises. Skeleton mask, Executioner's hood, bloody prop knives, and the trademark black shroud of the Watcher. They were all here, piled unevenly and at random atop the little cart.

Jules was completely rapt in his own words. This

was a speech he had rehearsed in his head a million times, sometimes mumbling parts of it low under his breath as his Thinking Self went about the task of undoing the traces of his killing.

"Nobody could understand what you were talking about, Dan. They all thought it was a joke. A game. Just like all my games. The most fetal positions." The laughter came again, this time ending with a lilting bit of the Watcher's rasp. He switched randomly from the gravelly voice to his own voice, then back again. It was as if he himself was unravelling, the layers peeling away from his twisted psyche.

"…The ULTIMATE SCARE! Everyone always told me that I got a little *too involved* with the Castle (he held the word 'involved' on his tongue for a few seconds, enjoying its feel)". Once more, the schizophrenic half-laugh, half-cackle escaped. His eyes drifted slightly to one side, then they clicked back onto Danny's face. Sharper, keener. He was still in control.

"You know, I always wished I could get other people *involved* in my nightmares. Quite a concept, eh? You see, I was so alone there. So, I brought my nightmares *here*." He paused as he looked around the little space, crammed with Castle artifacts of every kind. "My nightmares fit in quite nicely here, don't you think?" He smiled at his own insight now, leaving a silent gap in his words.

The silence hung there just long enough for Danny and Sandy's eyes to meet briefly, pleadingly. Jules' smile melted away and was replaced with a scowl, deadly serious.

"Only I didn't count on *you*." His anger was boiling up to the surface as he spoke now. "You just *had* to join in my game. I didn't want you to play, but you saw Mia's clothes and you started snooping around. You even brought that goddamned detective here! You played the game anyway! You made your moves, and I made mine. Well, here's the last move. Check-fucking-MATE!"

Jules' voice was booming suddenly, then it dropped off as if stifled. His eyes drifted slowly upward. He was a little boy looking hopefully at his mother.

Then his eyes dropped back down and locked on Danny's. The anger had vanished, and Danny could see a glint of tears welling up in them, surrounding the steel blue. Drowning its intensity. Jules' voice had lost all traces of the rasp, and despite his closeness, Danny strained to hear the whisper.

"You're my friend, Dan. I love you. But you know I can't let you go. Not now." With this, he lunged toward him, both his feet leaving the floor at once. Danny stepped back quickly, upending the makeup cart toward Jules, throwing him off balance and knocking him against the side wall with a loud bang. This might have been Danny's only opportunity to draw this ranting insane version of his friend from the confines of the little room. He seized that opportunity.

Pushing Richard's ghastly swinging body aside, he grabbed the door handle. The door opened easily, knocking the precariously held corpse to the floor as Danny was able to exit. He could hear his own heart thumping as he ran. And he heard Jules' crashing footfalls not far behind his own.

# 41

It wouldn't be long before last call at the Sand Bar, and the voices of the Castle actors had grown even louder and more boisterous than usual. Some of the hardier of the group talked about moving on to one of Pete's Beach's all-night bars, but most of them were well beyond the capability of continuing.

Gordon's head was swimming from the noise and the smoke of the room, although he hadn't really had that much to drink. Now he stood at the bar and glanced over at Sue, still seated at the table with her giggling friends. She felt his stare and looked up at him as he winked at her knowingly and raised his bottle of beer in a silent toast. She replied in kind.

Looking absently at his watch, Gordon moved toward the table and sat down heavily beside her. "Hey," he said to the girls at the table, "Looks like we've pretty much burnt this place out. You gotta hand to us monsters, we know how to party!" He looked around the room at the rambunctious group still crowding the bar. The party was far from over.

One of the girls shouted back to him, trying to overpower the sound of the blaring jukebox and the drunken buzzing in her own ears, "Yeah, but Gordon, where's your roomie? We were kinda hoping to have a drink with him tonight."

The girl with the curly hair across the table pointed to her friend, "Donna's got the hots for him."

Gordon smiled, "Who? Danny?"

"Yeah," the same girl replied, "I'm kinda partial to Jules, myself. He's gone AWOL tonight too. What are they having their own party, and we weren't invited?"

Gordon shook his head, "I don't know. You mean you haven't seen Jules here at all?" He scanned the room again as he sipped his beer.

"No," the girl said, "It's not like him to miss the Last Day party!"

"I asked him what he was doing tonight," Donna added, "And he gave me some lame excuse about Danny and Sandy forgetting to punch out their timecards."

Timecards. The word hit Gordon like ice water, sobering whatever little part of him might have been starting to feel the effects of the alcohol. He stammered weakly, the smile vanishing from his face, "Timecards? Are you sure he said *timecards*?"

Donna looked at him oddly, "Yeah. I thought it was kinda strange too, since it's the last day and all. I mean, what does it matter if they forgot to punch out…?"

But Gordon didn't hear the rest of her comment. He was already out the door, leaving Susan and her little group of friends in the bar, looking at one another, dumbfounded.

He ran frantically to his car, fumbling with the keys for a few distracted moments, cursing his badly trembling hands. Hours had passed since he had last seen his roommates. Hours during which almost anything could have happened to them. What if he was already too late?"

Finally, the lock clicked open, and he hopped into the front seat. In another moment the motor was running and Gordon gunned it, taking out a couple of the Sand Bar's trash cans while exiting the parking lot.

The car's tires squealed around the corner. It took all of Gordon's ability to concentrate just to stay on the road as the alcohol mixed with the confusion in his head. A police car that was parked at the corner turned on its flashing lights and followed the speeding vehicle, which was headed now at breakneck speed toward the north end of the island. When Gordon rushed through a red traffic light in the middle of town, the chase acquired yet another police cruiser.

# 42

The voices inside the Watcher's head laughed at him, taunted him, goaded him on. Loudest among them was that of his Murderous Self. He knew that there was only one relief. He must kill Danny and put his anger to bed. He must kill his playmate, and then he must kill the girl. He ran on, blindly following the sound of Danny's footfalls.

He had his prize. Sandy had fallen into his trap nicely. Perhaps even a bit too easily for his liking. Less of a challenge than he had hoped for. The shrouded wax figure of Harry had done its job, nestled eerily between the pilings below the pier, while Jules himself had feigned injury in his fetal position on the ground. Jules' book on pyrotechnics had helped him immeasurably in tricking her. Giving the illusion that the inanimate shrouded figure had struck a match. It had all worked so well. It had all been so *well thought out*.

Now that clever part of him was taking his bow. His proud mother looked on as he transformed into the insatiable fiend who found his only relief in murder.

**"He and I seemed to be the only living things between the huge arch of the sky and the desert beneath it. The barren scene, the sense of loneliness, and the mystery and urgency of my task all struck a chill into my heart."**

**- Arthur Conan Doyle -**
**THE HOUND OF THE BASKERVILLES**

# 43

Keeping his footsteps as silent as he possibly could, Danny hurried through the Swamp, negotiating the curves in the path. He couldn't hear Jules running close behind him as he had before. Just moments earlier he had noticed that Jules was gasping for air, stopping now and again to breathe. Maybe he had finally collapsed somewhere. Hopefully, he was dead. But Danny wasn't about to check on that. He must press on, drawing Jules further and further away from the Prop Closet. Danny knew that he had to get Sandy out of there somehow.

He stepped lightly over the Plexiglas-covered opening in the floor that he had crossed so many times before. It was in this space that a woman's scantily clad body normally appeared to float in a "pond" filled with seaweed. But as Danny passed over it now, he could make out only one thing: the severed and rapidly decomposing head of Juanita, placed delicately between bits of foam rubber and the familiar plastic seaweed. It floated in a mire of thick reddish water and stared unabashedly up at him. A bolt of terror coursed through him. He wanted to stop, to get out of this horrible place, but he knew he must push forward. He proceeded past the Ripper Scene, and up the stairs toward the Plaza.

The Watcher paused, silently shivering as he reached the coolness of the Swamp. He heard the quick footsteps in the Plaza Area above. A smile erupted beneath his smeared clown makeup and his eyes rolled upward, as if he could see through the ceiling, following each of Danny's tentative movements. He walked back toward the Sick Room, retracing the steps he had taken just moments before. The brainstars' sizzling burn could be felt down his throat and into his lungs.

He moved quickly through the Portrait Room, the

Butler Area, and into the Belltower, the tricky latch on the gate seeming to open by itself for its cruel master to pass through. Once inside the Belltower, he took the stairs upward quickly, his crackling laughter escaping him ever so quietly, and his strength feeding back into him with every step he took.

Making his way up past the Human Sacrifice Room, Danny could hear the blood pounding rhythmically in his ears. The sight of the room was made infinitely more frightening by the cold silence. As he passed by, Danny couldn't help but glance uneasily at the little doorway at the back of the room. He had found the bloody timecards there. He wouldn't dare look inside now, for fear of what else he might find. This was a wise and fortunate decision, because the stilled body of Hartnett sat slumped therein. Waiting to be discovered.

# 44

By the time Gordon was halfway down the island he had side-swiped several cars, run through two traffic lights and numerous stop signs, and had acquired a neat parade of four police cars in hot pursuit. Residents of the quiet beach community had come out to their front porches to watch the police chase that would no doubt go down in the Pete's Beach annals of folklore. What they did not know was that the greater tale was being played out in the Castle at the north end of the island.

# 45

The cool sea breeze on the Parapet was a relief. The perspiration seemed to dry instantly inside Danny's shirt as he stepped out into the night. The air was full of the sound of breaking waves and police sirens in the distance. Fearing that the sounds of the night might mask Jules' footsteps behind him, Danny hurried toward the door that led into the Rat Room. Miraculously when he grabbed the doorknob, he found that the door had not been locked. He pulled it open and peered inside.

The darkness of the Rat Room would not seem so complete on any other night, but with the huge full moon illuminating the sky so boastfully, it appeared quite ominous. Danny had traveled a scant ten feet when the door slammed closed loudly on its spring mechanism. He was plunged into that blackness that most of the customers remembered best about their trip through the Castle. He stopped in his tracks, listening. Hearing nothing, he pressed on. The rubber hoses that were attached to either side of the walls crashed into his unyielding legs, and more than once he tripped on a bulge in the floor.

Suddenly the silence was shattered by the low sound of a raspy laugh. It seemed to come out of the darkness behind him, and yet Danny was certain that the door to the Parapet had not opened since he had entered. This could only mean that the Watcher had been waiting for him in the Rat Room, and Danny had unwittingly passed by him, probably touching him without realizing. Before he could move the Watcher's hand shot out and grabbed his ankle. That was it. He must have been lying on the floor. Danny had assumed that the objects touching his legs were rubber hoses. In fact, they had been the Watcher's fingertips.

He tried frantically to shake off the Watcher's grip, kicking out at the darkness in the hope of connecting with a head, a chest, a throat. He landed several bad kicks before the ultimate one that caught the Watcher directly in the face. The talons of iron around Danny's ankle loosened, then fell away with the faint sound of cracking bone. In his frenzy, Danny had managed to break the monster's nose. Blinded and in pain, the Watcher sat on the floor of the Rat Room, rocking back and forth in a heightened state of disorientation. He would not see how profusely his nose was bleeding until he reached the light of the Belltower, later.

The instant that Danny felt the Watcher's grip leave his ankle, he continued down the passageway toward the Tilted Room. As he hurried through the room he caught only a glimpse of a strange figure, seated in one low tilted corner. It was the body of Eric, the noose from the Hangman Scene still tightly wrapped around his blue and bloated throat.

Danny glided down the stairway to the Mortuary. Not Jules, he thought, not Jules. He couldn't equate his friend of so many years with the horrible creature that was pursuing him now. He suddenly heard footsteps in the Tilted Room, but Danny hoped that at this pace he could still outrun the Watcher and get through the Castle.

He would have to try to pull Sandy to her feet, to start her running alongside him. It was all reminiscent of the way the clown had pulled her along, back to the Castle, earlier that evening. Danny's brain swam in a soup of fear and uncertainty as he rounded the last corner into the Mortuary.

Then, like an unexpected blow, the sight of Jarrett's burnt and crumpled body stopped Danny where he stood. The giant lay still and dead in the pathway, and Danny's feet came close to tripping over him. A glittering pool of broken glass spilled over and around the body, giving it an ethereal quality, beautiful and horrific in its detail. Though Danny knew that he must wind his way quickly and carefully past the enormous dead body to maintain his distance from Jules, he could not help but stare at Jarrett's lifeless hulking form.

A strange look still graced the man's features beneath the weathered Frankenstein makeup. It was a look that had never gone with the slow-witted man's face in life. Now, in death, he actually appeared…intelligent.

On his way down the Belltower, Danny could hear Jules closing in on him, overtaking him. His own feet seemed to be moving at a much slower pace than they normally would. The way that one's feet can never seem to move quickly enough when they are being chased in a dream.

Miraculously, when Danny arrived at the gate to the Butler Area, he could see that it had been left open. He glanced back up at the top of the stairs, and there stood Jules. He was smiling sardonically; a fresh wash of blood from his broken nose covered the lower half of his face, giving the clown white makeup a pink glow. He said nothing. He simply stood watching his prey, disconnected from reality. Then he slowly set one foot down on the step just below him.

Danny didn't need more of a cue. He pulled the gate toward himself, fastened the latch, and headed directly for the Portrait Room. He scrambled his way past the mantel and open Portrait frame, catching his foot painfully on one of the gargoyles seated there. In another second he had disappeared, limping, into the Throne Room.

Jules took several stairs in a single vault, landing noisily at the gate.

He ran into the Portrait Room, looking frantically among the various vampire artifacts for any traces of his quarry. The soundtrack tape that had been playing over the P.A. system ran short, and the frigid silence made the pursuit infinitely more exciting for him. He walked soundlessly into the Throne Room. The suit of armor that he had worn on the beach when he had murdered Little Mack stood regally against one wall. Jules walked up to it, a keen smile growing on his face. Perhaps Danny would be the one to don the suit now. He reached one foot out and gave the suit a loud kick, filling the room with a hollow ringing sound.

Suddenly, from behind Jules, a new noise joined the ringing. He turned to see the huge nine-foot-tall plaster column in the opposite corner of the room as it began to sway. In another instant it was leaning forward and falling toward him. Jules dodged it with ease, stepping to one side as lightly and gracefully as a dancer. He looked up from the shattered column, smiling his wicked bloody grin at Danny, who stood where the fallen giant had once been. He was now exposed and vulnerable, dismally unarmed in the face of his foe.

Danny grabbed for the closest object he could from the collection of medieval weaponry that hung on the wall beside him. The big cat-o-nine-tails was unwieldy in his hands, and he had no luck in controlling its unbalanced spin. Twisting back on itself, Danny felt it slip from his grip and then it was on the floor. Jules had his foot across the weapon before Danny could make another move, and he managed to land a heavy hand against the side of Danny's head as he bent down to yank the handle free.

Danny staggered forward, struggling to stay on his feet, when he suddenly felt something very strange. It was not another crashing blow from Jules' hand, as he had expected, but the entire weight of Jules' limp body falling over Danny's bent- over back. His knees buckled under him, and Danny could see the floor rising rapidly toward his face. With a great thud, his head and neck were pinned against the floor, yet there was no struggle as he wrenched free.

There was no fight forthcoming, no more rasping bitter words from the lips of the Watcher. Danny looked down at Jules' still, lifeless form on the floor. Relief and confusion mixed in his head wildly for a moment. Then he spotted the thin stream of blood that ran like a tiny rivulet from Jules' back, precisely behind his now-stilled heart. He saw the place wherein the metal prop arrow was firmly planted, stealing what would be the last heartbeats of the Watcher's life.

Danny pulled his astonished eyes away from the sight with the greatest difficulty, to see Gordon standing in the doorway between the Portrait Room and the Throne Room. He was holding in both hands the immense crossbow that was the centerpiece of the Throne Room's Weapons Wall, staring wide- eyed at Danny. He gritted his teeth as he held the crossbow up.

"What kind of dangerous fuckin' thing is *this* to have in a funhouse!?" He was saying, "Somebody could get seriously hurt." Not funny.

It took a moment for Danny to feel relief. To feel anything. He started to laugh nervously, because if he didn't laugh, he might scream.

The policemen who had followed in pursuit of Gordon began to pour into the room, surrounding them and the dead body of their once-friend. Gordon nodded at the officers, who stood with their guns at the ready. He and Danny slowly raised their hands toward the ceiling in unison as he said, "Yeah, right, just in time, guys."

As several officers rushed to place handcuffs on both men, pulling their wrists roughly behind their backs, Gordon shouted to Danny, "Are you alright?"

Danny was disoriented, as if he had been awakened abruptly, "Yeah, I think so. I'm not so sure I *would* be if you hadn't come when you did."

Gordon looked into his friend's tired eyes, "Hey, where would you be without Tonto, Kimosabe?"

Danny managed a weak smile as they were led out of the room. They could see another group of policemen  milling through the Prop Closet. From out of Their midst burst Sandy, with her arms outstretched. She ran to Danny and held him close to her. It was only another second before he was pulled roughly from her embrace by the police officer beside him.

**"The town has its secrets, and keeps them well. The people don't know them all."**

\- Stephen King—
SALEM'S LOT

# 46

The events of the next week were a tangle of facts that needed to be unraveled by the mesmerized small town police department. Higher authorities had been brought in, and the flutter of activity at the north end of Pete's Beach was like nothing the residents had ever witnessed before. It was finally slowing to a dull simmer when Sandy, Danny, and Gordon were able to catch up with one another.

They had decided to meet on the beach across from Danny and Gordon's apartment. There they sat on the cool beach sand, watching the bustle of activity beneath the pier. Sandy's wrists were still neatly bandaged where the ropes had left their marks. It had taken days for the pain to subside enough for her to be able to even move her fingers.

Gordon pulled absently at the strands of beach grass that grew up from the sand of the little dune where they sat. He looked over at Sandy, "I must say, you were right about the last day here. It *does* get pretty wild." He started to laugh, but both Danny and Sandy looked at him blankly. Danny showed no sign of amusement, answering softly, "I don't think Sandy said that. I think it was Jules."

"Oh. Sorry," Gordon said, looking down at his feet, which were buried ankle-deep in the sand. He thought for a moment, then said in a more serious tone, "I don't know how you can know a person *that* well, I mean, *live with them*...and still not know what they're capable of doing."

Sandy looked out at the ocean. Her words were distant, "He was a good actor, I guess."

"I don't think it was acting," Danny said soberly, even a little too offhandedly. Both of his friends looked up at him. "I don't even think it was *Jules*. Maybe it was that place."

The Castle, which loomed a short distance away, became another entity engaging them on that beach. It took the place of their missing friend, listening to their every word.

"It seems to make everyone a little bit crazy," he continued. "Maybe it just took Jules a step further. And then he couldn't get back."

Danny was right about that. The Castle meant everything to Jules. He had been so caught up in the excitement of it all that the reality had just slipped away.

Susan approached them now from further down the beach. She navigated the deep sand, reaching the dunes as Gordon stood up. They hugged for a long while.

"Thank God you're all okay," she said to her friends.

They watched the beach for some time, allowing the sea breeze to play with their hair and tee shirts. It was a different sort of wind. It was the kind that heralded the change of season that would soon come.

The police work at the Castle was far from over. Official vehicles buzzed in and out of the parking lot, and the work of exhuming the bodies from beneath the pier was shielded from sight by huge white tarps. One by one the cocoons had been dismantled, and bodies or parts of bodies had been taken away in bags. The grisly discoveries that began on that fateful night a week before were just the beginning and would live in the minds of the three friends for the rest of their lives.

But one memory would always hold the greatest sadness for Danny. The sordid sight of the covered body being wheeled down the pier's ramp on a metal gurney. Jules' familiar unlaced Adidas protruded rudely from the bottom of the sheet as if the *real* Jules was saying goodbye.

Gordon and Susan started to move down toward the water, leaving Danny and Sandy behind at the dunes. Gordon turned back to look at them over his shoulder and called out softly, "Excuse us. We have to discuss, umm…"

"…Astrophysics and the meaning of life?" Sandy completed the tagline for him, smiling. She was back. She was still there. Still Sandy. Her smile continued as she watched them move down the beach.

Danny put his arm around her shoulders as the wind tousled Sandy's hair.

"You're shaking," he said.

"I'll probably be shaking for a few months," she said. She leancd into him.

"I never got to thank you for that night. You were really great in there, Danny."

He pulled her closer, tighter, and she turned to face him. The haunted and tortured look had all but dissolved completely from Danny's eyes. But it had been replaced with a distinct sadness. They moved closer wordlessly and kissed. The kiss was filled with an emotion that words could not express. It was filled with love.

The sun was setting against the backdrop of the bay. The heat had not been so oppressive that day. It was as if someone had informed Mother Nature herself that she should no longer bring the heat of summer, now that Labor Day had come and gone.

The summer was over. The horrible events of that long

season were only a disturbing memory now. The stillness of the couple sitting on the beach created a weird contrast to the macabre scene of exhumation taking place just a few short blocks away from them. They suddenly became nothing more than tiny microorganisms, embracing serenely on the vastest of shorelines. Their voices were just minute sounds washed away by the din of the ocean winds and pounding surf. The four friends on the beach and the horrid Castle itself were just so many tiny specks on the immense canvas of the world.

# Epilogue

## 1990

The madness of the Castle murders had washed over Pete's Beach like a wave, swallowing up the town in its fervor. It foamed and churned and swept over everyone and everything, then retreated out to the sea. Leaving the beach dotted with driftwood and seaweed…and some new bits of folklore.

It was ten years later and thousands of miles away when Danny sat in his swivel chair and read the small article about the amusement pier burning down. This was not front-page news by any means. Well, maybe it *was* front-page news back in Pete's Beach or even Atlantic City, but the Seattle newspapers couldn't care less about a silly amusement park in some godforsaken burg on the East Coast.

Danny flipped the pages of the newspaper in the hope that there might be more to the scant article than just two paragraphs of copy and one very poor photo.

There it was. Danny's eyes remained riveted on the burning skeleton in the picture, and for a long while the flesh on his arms and back crawled. Even in her burning agony, the Castle looked regal, unrelenting. Danny could envision the red illumination of the night sky over Pete's Beach as the flames consumed the wicked structure. The wayward cries of the souls she had taken wafting upward with each cloud of thick black smoke. The toxic nature of the Styrofoam coating that was her skin mirrored the toxicity of her essence. It had blanketed Pete's Beach in a suffocating cloud for days. No one would ever know of the few random skeletons that burned, undiscovered, along with her. They were the few most cleverly hidden bodies of the Watcher's victims. The earliest kills. The special ones that had never made it to the tar bubbles along the pier's underbelly. These bodies would never be claimed, never be identified. They would slip forever into the watery grave of the ocean and would remain just a few more missing teenagers who must have run away from their problems at home. Indeed, they had no more problems now. The Watcher had seen to that.

The newspaper dropped from Danny's hand onto the top of his cluttered desk. He sat pensively for a time, then stood and looked around the messy little room. This was his inner sanctum, where he created all the wonderful characters who peopled his novels and brought them to life. The novels that had been doing so well for him, his name splashed boldly across their covers in rich lettering, with interesting dust jackets. Many of these characters bore strange similarities to the members of the cast of the Castle, some of them now dead.

The walls of Danny's office were covered with photographs of the many celebrities he had come to meet and know through his own successes as both a journalist and author. His world was a much different place than the one he had been living in when he took that job at the Castle those many years ago.

He looked to the far wall of his office, which was crammed with photos of his many rock star acquaintances. Smiling between two notable others in a group photo stood Gordon. Danny stared long and hard at his friend's impish grin as he posed with some music greats. Some of the others were as successful as Gordon was, but few were better composers or musicians. Gordon had indeed gone on to fulfill the dream that Danny had started for them, and in a crazy way Danny was still jealous of his friend. After all, he had been the one who "got the girl". Gordon and Susan had been married for several years now, and since those horrible days after the furor at Pete's Beach, there had been very few bad times for them. They were like two figures plucked from a fairy tale.

The girl. "Getting the girl". Danny found himself saying it aloud. He mused over the thought. By all rights, the girl in the tale should have been Sandy, and Danny should have gotten her. It was his right as the hero of the story. But unfortunately, Danny could not make real life work out as pleasantly as he could the endings to his novels. He had not seen Sandy for years now, although when he had first moved out to the West Coast, she had made a few meager attempts at staying in touch. Then the communiques became shorter and blander, until finally they simply withered away. From time to time Danny still received word of her whereabouts, working as a stage makeup artist at one or the other of the Atlantic City casinos. And still, the great pang of desire struck him at the thought of her lovely face, her knowing hands, her understanding eyes. The love was still there. It was the mechanics of life that always seemed to get in the way.

He turned back to look once more at the newspaper, precariously balanced at the center of his desk. His eyes could pick out areas in the chiaroscuro of the photo that looked like weird faces staring back at him. They peeked out like so many little shrouded figures from between the leaping flames on the Castle's battlements. A chill slipped down his spine as he imagined that raspy voice crying out in final agony as he fell burning into the sea, along with his domineering and omnipotent mother. The scream of pain in death that the Watcher had never actually uttered...but should have. He had died silently that night in the Throne Room. He had never even been aware that death was coming. He went with no struggle.

He thought of the horrible creature who had succeeded so well in torturing him, wearing him down, those few detached days long ago. The Watcher. He had never been able to associate the thought of the monster that lurked within the Castle with his boyish friend Jules. Not even now, ten years after the fact. And yet they had been one and the same. Danny shook his head and looked down at his hands. The palms were shining with sweat, and he realized that he had begun an unconscious nervous wringing. His fingers were red. He shook his head again as Jules' dimpled smiling face popped intrusively into his mind.

Even the tiny chirping sound of the telephone on his desk was enough to shock Danny back into reality, catching him off guard and sending his heart into a little dance of nervousness. He picked up the receiver, and the cheerful familiar voice blasted through the line before he had the chance to utter a hello.

Danny leaned back in the chair as the muscles in his neck began to slowly relax. As the voice continued, he held the newspaper up for closer inspection, and a wave of release passed over him. He knew that he was finally free. The grainy little photograph staring back at him told him so. Free of the exhausting hold that the very existence of the Castle had had on him for these last years. Free of the sorrow he had felt for the poor tortured friend who had been possessed by this dark thing that had still stood so tall and imposing over Pete's Beach these last ten years. Free from the recurring dream that Danny had been having since those frightful times. Always the same fire, burning, burning. Until finally the whole pier, along with Danny and the frightening shrouded figure, crashed into the ocean. A thousand hidden corpses began to rise from their watery graves in unison. The billowing cloud of steam went on for what felt like forever until Danny would find himself awake and bathed in sweat.

The dawn of his freedom was upon him, all over

him. He dropped the newspaper back onto its nest of clutter and finally answered the jovial fellow at the other end of the telephone line.

"Gordon. I was just about to call you."

## THE END

# About the Author

Marisa Moffa has been a lifelong resident of Southern New Jersey. She attended a local college and spent summers working at an amusement pier at the Jersey Shore. These summers became the inspiration for her novel. She began her first draft in the 1980s but was forced to set aside writing as she pursued various careers and raised her family. Finally, during her retirement she decided to revisit the Castle novel, and completed its writing, fleshing out the characters that were based on people she had known in her youth. This book is the product of her labors. She currently still resides in the same small Southern New Jersey town where she grew up, with her husband Ray. It was with his support and the support of her daughters Jessi and Cady that Marisa was able to pursue her true love of writing for a second time.